CASCADE

NOWHERE TO TURN
BOOK 5

STACEY UPTON
MIKE KRAUS

MUONIC
PRESS

CASCADE
Nowhere to Turn
Book 5

By
Stacey Upton
Mike Kraus

MUONIC
PRESS

www.muonic.com

---

www.eatwriteplay.com

---

www.MikeKrausBooks.com
hello@mikeKrausBooks.com
www.facebook.com/MikeKrausBooks

CONTENTS

WANT MORE AWESOME BOOKS?

Find more fantastic tales right here, at books.to/readmorepa.

If you're new to reading Mike Kraus, consider visiting his website at MikeKrausBooks.com and signing up for his free newsletter. You'll receive several free books and a sample of his audiobooks, too, just for signing up, you can unsubscribe at any time and you will receive absolutely *no* spam.

You can also stay updated on Stacey Upton's books by visiting her website at eatwriteplay.com or on her instagram at instagram.com/staceyuptonbracey.

SPECIAL THANKS

Special thanks to my awesome beta team, without whom this book wouldn't be nearly as great.

Thank you!

READ THE NEXT BOOK IN THE SERIES

Nowhere to Turn Book 6

Available Here
books.to/Omnzk

CHAPTER ONE

New Madrid Seismic Zone
Days Twenty and Twenty-one
"This ranch is mine."

The business end of the shotgun centered on Kevin's midsection backed up Dale Thompson's bold claim, as did those of his two companions, their faces bright with glee as their trap was sprung in the narrow confines of the wooden bunkhouse. Lying flat on the bed next to them with his hands and feet no longer bound, Vinny snickered.

Kevin pushed Deb further behind him as the trio with the guns inched closer. His frame quivered with barely contained rage. Deb could feel the tension that thrummed through his back muscles from her position behind the lean man, but the hand holding a pistol on the intruders was rock solid. The holster holding his second weapon pressed into her belly and she slowly moved her left hand so she could grab it from its holster and get off a shot.

"Easy, sister." The low growl of Thompson's voice and the flick of his eyes let her know he'd seen the tiny movement. "Hand back down."

"You've got no claim on my ranch, Thompson." Kevin's voice pitched loudly in the face of three shotguns leveled at them, their muzzles shining cold in the flickering light of the kerosene lamp Deb carried. The shake of her hand made the scene dance, the reflected light of the lantern alternating what was in light and what was in shadow, picking out the gleam of an eye, or the shadow of a finger ready to pull a trigger.

Vinny snickered again from his prone position on the cot against the wall of the wooden bunkhouse, his leer growing even wider as he mocked Deb. "I'm going to be tying you up next, Nurse Deb. See how you like it."

The two young men who stood flanking Dale, Wexel and Creighton, laughed along with Vince, but Thompson wasn't distracted by the aside, nor did he join in the laughter. He gestured minutely with the barrel of his shotgun. "Put your weapon on the ground. I'd hate to accidentally kill both you and your lady friend." The eager glitter in his eyes was unmistakable, even in the dim light.

"You want to do it on purpose instead?" Kevin sneered the words, stating what had flashed into Deb's mind, that the man in front of them would kill them the instant the threat of being injured himself was removed. "That's just the kind of weasel move I'd expect from you, Thompson. I warned Jenny not to marry you, but you conned her into thinking you actually cared about her."

"Sweet girl, soft heart for all sorts of animals." Dale Thompson's gaze shifted slightly to the left as he locked into the memory of his wife, Kevin's little sister.

Deb took her chance the instant his break in concentration came. In a single fast motion, she hurled the kerosene lantern into the wooden bunkhouse at the foot of Vince's bed where it smashed against the bedpost and burst into flame. It licked eagerly at the cotton bedding and blanket draped there, the hot accelerant catching the material instantly, turning it into sheets of fire.

Vince screamed in terror, the high pitch of it echoing through the narrow space as he tried to back away from the flames that raced up the bedframe and engulfed his arms and face, but the injuries to his legs stopped him. Still screaming, he rolled from the bed and straight into the legs of the man closest to him, the weave of the camo pants Wexel wore catching the flames in an obscene game of tag, rivulets of fire rippling along his leg. The young man screamed as well, dropping his rifle to beat at the flames with his hands. The shotguns that had been turned their way dipped and swung away as Thompson and Creighton were distracted by the two men engulfed in flames.

Kevin fired three fast shots as Deb hauled him backwards, digging her hand into his belt so they both cleared the door frame, then she slammed the wooden door shut. Deb rammed the long barrel of her rifle through the door handle, effectively locking the three men inside the burning bunkhouse.

Deb and Kevin both stumbled away from the door as shotgun blasts ripped through it, peppering it with holes, but the sturdy door and the rifle held fast against the shots and the ferocious kicks that followed it. The shouting and screaming grew more intense as the fire grew, a babble of shouts as chaos broke free inside the burning building.

"Stand back." Kevin's voice was stern, his face set as he raised his weapon. "They're going to come through the windows."

Moments later, glass shattered as a body hurtled through it, bearing wisps of flames on its torso. Thompson rolled and rose, bringing his shotgun to bear on them, his face pulled into a horrific mask of rage, his mouth contorted into a snarl. Kevin shot him with two quick blasts center mass before the man could steady himself, then whipped his gun around as two more men crashed through the broken glass. He shot them before they could stand, round after round, their bodies jerking in the dirt as he emptied the first pistol and pulled his second.

Horrible, inarticulate screams were still coming from the fully engulfed bunkhouse as the echoes of the shots died.

"Vinny," whispered Deb, surging forward.

Kevin stopped her. "Stay there!"

His demand was absolute as he strode over and yanked the rifle from the door handle, flinging it aside. He flung open the door, flinching as a roar of flames, eager for fresh air, leapt out with huge fingers of orange and red. Flinging his arm in front of his eyes, Kevin strode into the maw of the burning building before Deb could stop him. The shrieks continued for a few seconds more until a single shot rang out with a final bang.

Deb staggered backward as Kevin stumbled from the door of the bunkhouse, coughing, smoke whirling out after him, the swirls of it caught in the red and gold glow of the fire within as it spread. The back of his shirt had caught fire and she beat it out with her hands as Kevin wheezed with his hands on his knees, then vomited where he stood. Wiping the back of his mouth with his hand, he gestured feebly to the water pump.

"Gotta get it out before it spreads," he managed. "Buckets in barn." He cut short his sentence on another heave of his guts.

The terrified whinnies of the horses in the nearby barn as they smelled the smoke sparked Deb into action and she ran for the barn, pulled out the stacked buckets, then hauled them to the outdoor pump. Mechanically she filled one bucket, then two, then a third and a fourth before she hauled two of them to the burning blaze and tossed their contents onto the fire, white steam hissing and rising from the wood as water met flame, her body operating on automatic as her mind grappled with the violence she'd just witnessed.

Kevin passed her, his limp pronounced as he grabbed the two full buckets she'd left at the pump, swinging back with them as she emptied the last drops of hers onto the planks of the bunkhouse, then returned to the pump to repeat the process. Back and forth they went, filling and dumping until the shell of the bunkhouse no longer shone red and gold but instead stood black and dead, the seared remains of Vince Bozeman curled into a ball in the middle of it next to the twisted skeletons of the metal bunks. Outside the bunkhouse, the soaked and soot-covered dead bodies of Dale, Creighton, and Wexel lay where they'd fallen, limp limbs sprawled akimbo, guns still clasped in their dead fingers.

Deb dropped her final buckets and crumpled to the ground in exhaustion, her hands over her face, but tears didn't come. In their place was emptiness, a vast howl of horror at what she'd started with the toss of her lantern and the shove of her rifle to block the men's exit. She could taste the burnt flesh on her tongue, mixed with the nearly pleasant scent of a firepit, the weird juxtaposition of roasting hotdogs around a happy campfire and the fact that a man had burned to death at her hand inescapable.

She startled at the heavy hand on her shoulder, flinched away as hands reached under her armpits to help her stand. Her body was wracked with cold shudders as she stared at the bodies of the three men who'd come to take Kevin's place. "Don't touch me," she managed to say as Kevin reached for her again. Deb snapped a warning hand up as a secondary defense. "I need... I need to see to Renny."

Her legs wobbled as she made her way to the back door of the ranch house, where she paused to shuck her sodden, smoke-filled clothes and boots at the doorway, walking inside in only her underwear so the scent of fire smoke and the dead didn't permeate the space.

Renny had propped herself up on the sofa, clutching the orange and yellow cat to her. "Deb! What happened? I heard gunshots and smelled smoke, but I couldn't get myself up to see—"

Deb shook her head at the torrent of words, the movement mechanical as were the words that came out of her mouth. "I'm okay, and so is Kevin. Three men tried to take the ranch by force. They're all dead, and so is Vince."

"What?!"

"They were waiting for us in the bunkhouse with shotguns. Vince probably told them I'd be coming to give him his painkiller, and that Kevin always comes with me." The words dripped from her mouth, each one tasting like poison. "Or they've just been watching what we do."

"You got the best of three men with shotguns after they set a trap?"

"We did." Deb was overcome with a weariness which was beyond anything she'd experienced, rising like a dark blanket to smother her where she stood. "Lie yourself back down, I have to—"

She couldn't complete the sentence. Instead, Deb blindly shuffled to the bedroom Kevin had given her, using her hands to find the doorframe, then the bed where she curled into a tight ball and pulled the covers over her head. She desperately wished she could cry and release some of the horror she carried, her throat aching with the pressure of suppressed grief, but nothing came, and she tumbled into a restless abyss that was half sleep and half nightmare.

Sometime in the night, Kevin climbed into the bed next to her, curling the long length of his body behind hers, holding her. Deb wanted to push him away, but she didn't have the strength left for the effort, and because part of her cried out for the comfort of human contact. The warmth of his body seeped into hers, soothing the muscles of her back, his arm draped around her in a protective cocoon lulling her into somnolence and she drifted back to sleep.

He was gone from her side in the morning, but the slightly warm depression in the bed let Deb know he'd been there not long before. Her eyes stung as if she hadn't slept at all, and the ache in her chest was a weight that made Deb want to stay prone, perhaps never to rise again. But the smell of coffee floated through the air, and the throb of her head demanded she take some painkillers quickly before the migraine set in with a vengeance. Forced into action, Deb shoved aside the blanket and set her bare feet on the floor.

They were streaked with dried soot and ash, as were the sheets of the bed. The memory of the night before rose with a burst of residual terror. Suddenly desperately needing to wash herself clean, Deb padded across the room, still in her underwear from the night before. Pausing only to grab clean clothes from the closet and medicine and a towel from the bathroom, Deb passed through the kitchen without acknowledging Kevin, although he watched her passage, leaning on the counter, a mug in his hand.

Deb went straight to the pump, squinting a bit at the light of the forlorn grey morning. She used the freezing cold water to down the pills in her hand then rubbed the cascade of cold water over her skin and hair, removing the dirt, sweat, and ash, her skin rising in goosebumps as she worked the remains of the terrible night from her body, sluicing water straight into her mouth and swishing it as she tried to get the taste of burnt bodies from her gums and tongue.

Shaking with cold, uncaring of who was watching, her need to be clean outweighing all modesty, Deb stripped off her underwear and dried off, wrapping her wet hair in the towel as she yanked on clean clothes. Then she rinsed her underthings methodically until the black was gone from them as well.

She turned and faced the house and froze in place, the dread of talking to Kevin so powerful that the emptiness which had pervaded her was pushed out. Deb swallowed hard against the unreasonable fear of the man she hadn't had the willpower to push from her bed last night, the man who'd killed four men in front of her only hours ago, trying to will the terror away.

"It's just Kevin," she murmured to herself, her hands forming into fists at her side.

Gathering herself, Deb walked stiffly through the kitchen and straight into the bathroom, avoiding his gaze as he watched her. Renny called out to her, but she pretended not to hear her. Deb shut and locked the bathroom door with a sigh of relief, then took her time hanging her wet things, draping the towel on the rack, brushing her wet hair into a ponytail.

She caught her reflection in the cracked mirror and immediately shied away from it. Deb was no stranger to violence and death. Her years in the ER, as well as the past weeks on the road from Memphis had shown her plenty of horrible things, but nothing had prepared her for taking part in burning a man alive, a man she'd not liked but had doctored, forging an intimacy with him whether she'd wanted it or not from that process.

With a growl of frustration, Deb forced herself to meet her own gaze, staring into the depths of her bloodshot light brown eyes, noting in passing the dark circles beneath them, the gaunt paleness of her cheeks where her bones stood out like blades, creating more dark hollows beneath them.

"You did what you had to do," she said, a tremor in her voice. "They would have killed you and everyone else if you hadn't acted."

As if in answer, the building agonized screams of Vinny as the fire caught hold of his body overrode her affirmation. Deb shut her eyes and clamped her hands over her ears in a futile attempt to stop the sounds, but they were an irrevocable part of her, as were the final involuntary grunts of the men lying on the ground by the bunkhouse as Kevin emptied bullet after bullet into their bodies.

"He was doing what he needed to do, too." Her words were louder for Kevin than they'd been for herself. Deb looked herself in the face once more, the distortion created by the cracked mirror breaking her reflection into two uneven slices. She let out a long breath, gripping the cool porcelain sink, seeking some sort of center.

"It is what it is." Her uncle's old stock phrase rose in her memory, and as she spoke it aloud, the terse way he held his thin lips when he spoke accompanied it. Deb emitted a short, guttural laugh that was closer to a sob. She'd always loathed the saying, loathed the disappointed look on Willard Varden's face the times he'd said it, whenever something was ruined or damaged beyond repair, but it was the only thing that fit the situation.

"All right, then." Deb let out a final breath and pushed away from the mirror. "It is what it is."

She emerged from the bathroom ready to talk to Kevin, but he was nowhere to be seen. A coffee mug with a saucer covering it to keep it warm and a plate of food covered by a second plate waited on the dining room table for her. Her stomach gave a grumble as she took the top plate off to reveal a pile of salted, fried potatoes that had been topped with goat cheese and grilled onions, then sprinkled with fresh herbs, along with a few leftover pieces of yesterday's seared rabbit.

Suddenly ravenous as the scent of the food hit her, Deb brought her plate to one of the big chairs in the living room where she could look out of the remaining two windows while she ate. The view of the slope of the hill was a favorite of hers, the way it curved to meet the sky, the sparkle of the stream with its cottonwood trees at the base of it. Renny dozed on the couch, the slight bloom of color on her cheeks a welcome sight. Georgie ribboned around Deb's feet as she sat, then jumped onto the arm of the chair, curling her tail with its white tip neatly around her toes as she perched and emitted a little mew of curiosity, her nose and whiskers trembling as she looked at the plate of food.

"This is my breakfast. You've probably had yours already," Deb told the creature.

Georgie continued to wait, looking at her intently until Deb relented and gave it a chunk of rabbit meat. The cat nipped it from her fingers with sharp white teeth and jumped down to eat her snack. Deb savored the rest of her meal in peace, letting the view, the silence of the house, the purring of the cat, and the even breathing of Renny soothe her just as the delicious food did. Deb took in the living space slowly, letting the details of it settle into her memory. The big fireplace, the comfortable seating, the faded but warm hues of reds and browns and deep blues that pervaded the color scheme, the western paintings on the walls which reminded her of Remington and Russell's works, the scuffed wooden floor with its generous rugs.

Once she was done with her meal, she took her empty dishes outside to the pump to wash. The unmistakable sound of a spade hitting dirt came from the far side of the house in a steady rhythm, from the area where Kevin had chosen to bury his sister. After tilting her dishes so they could dry, Deb went to the barn, got work gloves and a second shovel, and walked to join Kevin in his labors.

Kevin had already dug two graves through the thick soil, and was starting on the third. He was covered in sweat, and used an arm to wipe his forehead as he eyed her approach. Deb gave him a brief nod, moved a few feet over, and started the fourth hole.

"I'm only going about three feet deep," he commented after she'd dug for a few minutes. "Beyond that, it's all red clay, and we'd need a backhoe to get through it."

"All right."

The steady, strenuous work was exactly what she needed, as was the silent company. Once they were done digging the four graves, they worked together to carry the dead men to their final resting places, and put them in, one by one. Kevin had already wrapped each of them in a horse blanket, and Deb was grateful she didn't have to look at any of the bodies again, particularly Vince's.

They covered them with the earth, tamping it down as they went, and Deb gathered a few flowers to sprinkle on top of the raw soil of their graves while Kevin cleaned the shovels and put them away. He rejoined her at the site where she stood, her hands tucked into the back pockets of her jeans, a warm breeze blowing some of her ponytail loose, the strands flowing in front of her as she regarded the four churned patches of dirt.

"Want to say anything?" Kevin asked her, pulling his baseball cap from his head and pushing back the dark wavy hair that was soaked in sweat.

"What a waste," was all Deb could come up with after a long pause.

"It is. May they rest in peace."

They stood in contemplation for a beat longer, then turned as a unit as they went to the pump to wash. Kevin finally met her eyes over the gush of the cold water. "You still leaving today?"

Deb nodded, a huge lump in her throat. "I can't stay."

He looked to the horizon, his face frustrated, his words coming out gruffly. "You mean you can't stay because you want to go to your sister's place, or because of what happened last night with Thompson and his men?"

Over his shoulder, Deb caught sight of the burnt-out remains of the bunkhouse and sighed. "Both."

"You know they would have killed us." His flat statement had anger and outrage mixed into it. "They brought it on themselves."

"I absolutely know that." The last of the water dribbled to a stop from the pump as she searched for a way to put her feelings into words. "I'm a healer," she finally said. "It's my nature to want to fix things." She paused and chuckled ruefully. "My sister Mara said it was my Achilles heel, and she's not wrong. That desire to make things whole again has given me a wonderful career, but it's also led me to put my trust—put my love—in the wrong places, too. It's brought me a lot of heartache."

"I'm not one of those wrong places," Kevin said forcefully. "I'm not."

Deb made herself look him full in the face. "I would have agreed with you before last night, but that's not true for me anymore and nothing you say is going to change my mind or my feelings. Maybe they will change with time. I can tell you with all honesty, I hope they do."

"I was defending my ranch, and our lives, Renny's too, for that matter. How was that not right?" He crossed his arms and scowled at her, all of his normal easiness evaporated by the heat of his frustration.

She sighed in exasperation. "Kevin." Her head pounded from the stress of trying to get the stubborn man to understand her need for space and time to process the ready violence she'd witnessed and participated in. "I just need to go. Can you let me go?"

Kevin's face turned red with anger and annoyance. "Sure," he ground out. "Of course. I'll get the horse ready for you." He stalked to the barn, his long legs eating the ground, sending up puffs of dirt as his boots landed hard with each step.

It didn't take long for Deb to pack her gear into her backpack. She fingered the patches she'd added as memories of the people she'd run across on her journey as she did the job. The pink and purple cross standing for Maritza, a brown one for the nameless father and son who'd blessed her journey, the words "Cooked Outside" for the Juniors, the British flag for Giles, two lumberjacks for the two Toms from St. Jude's, and the medic symbol for Spencer. They'd all played important roles in her journey so far.

"I'll have to find another fabric shop," she murmured as she rolled an extra pair of socks and added them to her bag. "I'll need ones for Renny and Kevin, too." Her lips lifted in a partial smile when she hit on what she'd like to find to represent both of them. "A cat and a horse."

"Here."

Kevin interrupted her reverie as he tossed a puffy jacket and a warm knit hat onto the bed as she was doing so. "You'll need these the further north you get, especially up in the Blue Ridge Mountains," he said shortly. "You'll be taking work gloves, too, and one of the rifles and extra ammo, and I don't want you to fuss about that. I've already done the panniers for the horse with food for you and her, some cooking gear, and attached a couple of blankets and a ground cloth onto the back of the saddle. So, Daisy's ready to go." He stared at her backpack for a beat, then turned to leave.

"Kevin, wait."

He leaned against the door with his arms crossed protectively over his chest and raised an eyebrow as Deb stopped her packing and moved closer to him. She stopped a few inches away, finding herself tongue tied. "I'm sorry," she finally got out. "I wish things were different."

He let out a long sigh, casting his eyes heavenward as he reached out with a long, sinewy arm and pulled her to him. "It's my fate to fall for difficult women," he said as he held her. "What was it you called it? My Achilles heel."

"I'm not difficult, I just have high personal standards," she said into his chest. The rumble of his laugh vibrated against her cheek as she pressed it close so she could hear the steady beat of his heart. Deb pulled away, a smile tugging at her own mouth. "I won't ever forget you," she said.

"I hope you come back," Kevin replied, pressing his lips against her forehead. "Meanwhile, I'll do my best to tend to Renny."

"And yourself," she added for him. "Take care of yourself, so I have someone to come back to, if I can." She took both hands and tucked them into his brown curls, pulling his face to hers, and gave him a full kiss on the lips. "No promises, just hope."

"I can live with that." He brushed her cheeks gently with his work-calloused thumbs before he pulled away from her and smiled. "I'll let you say the tough goodbye on your own. I'll be out by the barn with Daisy."

Deb packed the rest of her backpack with her clothes and toiletries, strapped Honey onto her waist, pulled on her green John Deere cap and the oversize jean jacket which had belonged to Kevin's sister and made her way to the living room.

Renny was awake, but she had her face turned to the back of the sofa as Deb set down her backpack and pulled up a chair to sit next to her and waited for the young woman to face her.

"I hate you," came the muffled, petulant voice at last.

"With the strength of a thousand suns, I know."

There was a pause, and then Renny replied. "Maybe only a hundred suns, but still."

Deb reached out and pulled a long strand of the girl's honey-blond hair away from her cheek, and Renny turned to face her with the movement, her big blue eyes brimming with tears. Deb's filled in response as she reached for Renny's hand and gripped it.

"You get yourself better," Deb finally managed. "No doing dumb things."

"No promises," Renny responded wryly. "You keep yourself safe."

"I'll do my best."

The little cat jumped up and bumped her head under their joined hands and meowed, causing them both to chuckle as they petted her in unison.

"You should go while there's still some light," Renny said finally. "I made Kevin pack you the last of the coffee we got at that diner. You're a horrible grump without it."

Deb could only smile and nod as her throat closed up once more. "Thanks, Renny."

"You owe me one," the girl said in blunt response. "I'll collect one day."

"I'm counting on it." With a final squeeze of her hand, Deb picked up her backpack and walked out of the living room, leaving a piece of her heart behind her.

The heat of the day had built to its zenith as she walked past the burnt out bunkhouse to the corral where Daisy stood packed and saddled. Kevin turned as she approached.

"Thanks for getting her ready for me."

He handed her a burlap bag. "That's carrots for Daisy."

"Thanks."

He pulled a second, smaller bag from his shirt pocket. "That's for you."

Deb fingered the bag as he placed it in her palm, the shifting weight of it a mystery. He smiled at her quizzical look. "It's seed corn from my crop. You have all the patches on your backpack to remind you of folk, I figured it would be something you could remember me by that had some use to it, too. I want you to plant them when you find your home."

Deb clutched the bag tightly and nodded, her words failing her once again as she studied his face, wanting to memorize every plane and angle of it before she left. "That's pretty corny of you," she said at last, laughing through her tears as she said the terrible pun, sliding the precious gift into her backpack along with the carrots.

"I see what you did there," he said, and helped her on with the backpack and buckling it firmly in place. "Bad puns only make me like you more."

"Okay, then." Deb got her foot in the stirrup and swung her leg over the horse. Kevin unwrapped the reins from the corral post and handed them to her, resting his hand on her knee as she collected them and herself. Deb smiled down at him. "I'll see you when I see you," she said.

"See you when I see you." He patted her leg gently and stepped back.

Deb clucked to the horse and gave Daisy a little kick in her flanks, and they started forward, past the blasted ATVs, across the little stream and up the far hill from the ranch. Deb turned as she crested the hill for a final look back at the Anderson ranch. The long, lean figure with one foot up on the corral post lifted a hand in final farewell, and she did the same before turning Daisy's head toward the east and the next steps of her journey.

CHAPTER TWO

The Blacksburg/Pembroke Fault
Day Twenty and Twenty-one
"Run."

The single rasped word was etched in terror as it hissed out of Eva's broken jaw, causing Mara's heart to hammer in response as the screen door slammed and booted feet descended heavily down the porch steps of her old home. Mara looked around frantically. There was a darker patch of shadows to her left, but chances were high if she moved, she'd be seen, even though she was dressed all in black. She touched her holster, but stopped herself from pulling her SIG Sauer as she considered what would happen when the sound of the blast echoed through the night. Instead, Mara curled into a small ball tensing her muscles to spring at the man once she was discovered.

With a guttural growl, Eva flung herself at the wire mesh at the far corner of the pen, the chain that wrapped around her ankles clanking loudly. She tilted her head in the opposite direction as she locked eyes with Mara.

"Cut that out, woman!" Jimmy Crowe's exasperated voice came

out of the dark as Eva did the same noisy movement, giving Mara a brief space while the woman held his attention to roll into the deeper shadows to the left of the coop. Mara stretched flat on the ground while Eva beat herself against the side of her makeshift prison, throwing her chain so that metal clangs echoed through the night air.

"What the—" Jimmy lifted the unattached lock as he reached the door of the chicken coop and shook his head. "That Emily doesn't have the sense of a flea, I swear."

He laughed as Eva staggered across the width of the pen and snarled in his face. Jimmy played with the lock as he stood in the entrance, keeping himself just out of her reach. He shook his head at Eva's continued efforts to get hold of him. "I thought me and Dale gave you a good enough beating to take the snap outta you." He lifted a long wooden object from the back of his jeans and waggled it. "Guess it's gonna take a little more."

Mara lay frozen in place as Jimmy lifted the object higher, and she recognized it as a sturdy wooden rolling pin.

"We're going to play a little game," Jimmy said, taking a furtive look over his shoulder. "I'm going to hit you as hard as I can, and if you make a sound, I'm going to do it again." He shook a finger at her. "You're making me do this, I want you to understand that. If'n you'd just behaved like a wife should—" he lifted his shoulders in an exaggerated shrug. "You brought it on yourself."

Eva scrambled as best she could to the back of the pen, her chain rattling, fear replacing her defiance, and shook her head. "I don't want you to hit me, Jimmy." The words came out slurred and barely discernable.

"Don't shake your head at me and mumble. And don't think either of those wives is gonna come to your rescue, neither. They're busy doing their nightly duties with my brothers. This is between you and me, Eva Crowe."

He stepped fully into the cage, slapping the wooden pin on his palm. A tiny whimper escaped from Eva's shattered jaw as he lifted it to strike her.

In a single rush of motion, Mara swept the knife she'd strapped to her leg free and scrambled behind Jimmy. He turned his head at the sudden movement with a startled exclamation, bringing the rolling pin around in a fast blow that landed painfully on her arm as her slash went wide. Mara stumbled to her knees but managed to cut open the back of his calves with the blade, ripping through cloth and skin.

Jimmy let out a pained howl that was sure to bring attention if he got out another one. Mara launched herself forward, knocking him down. She swarmed onto his back, slamming his face into the filth and dirt of the coop, smothering the sound of his angry shouts.

His strong, agile body was already twisting beneath her, heaving her off as he scrambled to get onto his feet, but Mara was faster. She sprang back at him, slashing with her knife across his arm as he reared it back to hit her again with the heavy wood.

The blow landed harder than the first, cracking her across her forearm, making Mara drop the knife as her fingers went completely numb.

"You b—"

Jimmy's slur was cut short as Eva brought her cuffed hands around his throat, and yanked backwards, pulling him with her full body weight, her knees in his back as she choked him. Jimmy shoved backwards, so they both collided with the back of the pen with a crunching sound, but Eva kept pulling, her face distorted in a silent scream as he kicked and fought the chain around his neck.

Jimmy elbowed Eva in her ribs, and the woman huffed out her breath, the chain around his neck relaxing enough that he was able to roll away from it. He punched her in the side of the head as he rose, knocking Eva to the ground, then faced Mara, his chest heaving, his burned face and lethal expression turning him into a monster. Jimmy flexed his fingers and sprang at her, but Mara dodged him, grabbed the rolling pin with her left hand and brought it against the side of his head with all her might, the strike dislodging the pin from her weakened grasp to disappear somewhere into the dark.

Jimmy went down heavily, and Mara scrambled on hands and knees to find the pin or her knife, crawling across the ground as inarticulate sobs rose in her throat, desperate to find either weapon before the strong young man got to his feet once again.

A gargling sound made her look up from her frantic search. Eva had spun the long chain that locked her ankles to a metal pole driven into the center of her prison around Jimmy's neck, and was grimly holding on as he thrashed and tried to spin away. Mara heaved herself on top of his bucking body to hold him still as Eva continued to strain backwards with all of her strength.

Jimmy's feet drummed on the dust as his torso writhed, but Mara kept him pinned and fought his flailing arms as he scrabbled, flinging dirt everywhere, straining to escape their grip. Eva inexorably choked the life out of the man, the effort seeming to take forever, but slowly Jimmy's desperate fight slowed, then stopped all together.

Eva was still pulling on the chain with all her might after he passed, and it took Mara several tries to get the woman to emerge from the feral dark where she'd submerged herself and stop fighting.

"It's done," she kept telling Eva until the single blue eye that worked finally focused on her and she let her grip on the chain loosen. Her hands were raw and bleeding, and she panted for breath, her whole body shaking.

"We're going." Mara said, "I just need to find my knife and I'll dig you loose from the post as fast as I can."

Eva chuckled weakly and pointed to his belt. "Keys," she whispered. "Easier." A ghost of a smile wisped across her broken mouth, and she collapsed onto the ground, senseless.

Mara's hands shook as she pulled the keys off of Jimmy's belt. She followed the chains to Eva's feet, found the key for it, and unlocked the padlock, then sorted through the jumble of keys to find one for her handcuffs, but there wasn't one she could find. Conscious of the time ticking away, Mara shoved the keys into her backpack and poured water onto Eva's face to rouse her.

Sputtering slightly, the woman swung a fist at Mara as she woke, thudding into her side. Mara caught the weakened arm as it came around again. "It's me, it's Mara," she told the confused woman. "We're going now."

Eva blinked and then nodded, gesturing to the water. She took a long drink, then Mara helped her to her feet and out of the filthy pen that had held her. Mara kept them easing along in the shadows of the trees which ringed the bottom part of the property, following the same U-shaped path with the broken woman she'd taken an hour earlier. Lantern light from the room that used to be Mara's bedroom shone out of the window, letting her know someone was still awake. She tried to hasten their steps as fast as she could, supporting Eva's weight with her good arm, the other one still numbed and aching from Jimmy's blow.

At last they reached the edge of the wood, and the light of the lantern retreated behind them as Mara favored speed over stealth, taking them on the most direct route to where she had the bike stashed. The two-mile journey through the woods was difficult, but to Eva's credit, she kept going despite the many falls they had, each time getting to her feet with Mara's help, doggedly pushing herself forward with sheer willpower.

They each took another long drink of water when they reached the bike, and Mara ate a power bar to help her flagging energy. Mara pushed the road bike from the trees and guided Eva over to it.

"You sit on the seat and hold on to my waist," she told Eva. I'm going to stand on the pedals and get us home."

"Like when we was kids," Eva muttered, her head lolling on her shoulders. "Two people, just one bike."

"Exactly. I need you to hold on, Eva." Clumsily the woman mounted, and Mara put one foot on the right pedal as Eva grasped her waist with surprisingly strong hands. Mara took the handlebars, and pushed with her left foot to get some momentum before hiking it onto the other pedal and straining with all her strength, got through one rotation, then two, eventually getting them moving on the county road, the bike wobbling precariously for the first few minutes.

Mara pushed herself to keep going beyond the pain and mental fatigue of trying to discern obstacles in the dark in time to maneuver around them. Even doing her best, they were forced to get off of the bike multiple times to get around or over fallen trees and piles of debris. Eva was barely functioning, and Mara suspected it was pure grit that was keeping her going. The woman's tenacity fueled her own determination, but she was eventually defeated by the steep hill that was the final ascent to the school from the river.

"Eva, I can't pedal us uphill, it's too steep. You'll have to walk, it's about a half mile." She steadied the woman as she groaned and nearly fell off of the bike, tilting sideways. Mara placed the woman's grip on the inside of the handlebars, as far apart as the spread of the chain between her cuffed hands would allow. "Lean on the bike. I'll push on the seat from behind. Let it steady you."

"Yeah," Eva muttered.

They didn't bother speaking again, both women focused on putting one foot in front of the other and not collapsing from sheer exhaustion. Finally, the dim outline of the school came into view. A figure was seated next to the door they used for their main entrance, huddled against the chill of the mountain night air. The clanking of Eva and Mara's feet on the downed chain-link fence as they wearily made their way across the yard startled the lookout, and Mara was glad to see the gleam of a rifle barrel as they swung toward the sound of their unsteady progress.

"It's me," she called softly. "And Eva."

The figure put the rifle down and ran over, Caroline's anxious features becoming clear as she got closer.

"You've got her, you got her." The words were spoken in a shocked whisper, then Caroline flung herself at Mara, nearly knocking her over with her enthusiastic embrace. Then she let her go and dashed to the other side of the bike.

"It's Caroline, Eva, let me help you."

"Hey, girlie."

The words slurred out, and Caroline's head jerked at the awful sound. To her credit, she simply put an arm around Eva and supported her, letting Mara take control of the bike. As Mara pushed it along, her eyes kept sliding to the closeness between her step-daughter and Eva. It hurt her to see it at a fundamental level, a cold dart that insinuated itself into her relief at being at home.

"Put her in my room, I think she just needs to sleep," Mara said as they stepped inside.

"I'm putting her in my bed," Caroline countermanded her. "You must be exhausted, too," she added a few beats later as an afterthought.

"We killed Jimmy." Eva said as they hobbled to Caroline's room, her words barely intelligible through her broken jaw and split lips. "Me and your stepmomma killed him."

Caroline startled, her eyes huge as she looked to Mara for affirmation. It wasn't the way Mara would have told a kid the news, but the cat was out of the bag. She nodded wearily. "He was going to hurt Eva some more, and I couldn't—" she broke off as the awful fight flared again in her mind's eye.

"I get it," Caroline said simply, although there was a bit of shake to her voice. She changed gears as they eased Eva onto Caroline's mattress. "I'm still on watch for another hour, then Ethan's up. We'll take care of things, Mara, and I'll let the boys know what happened."

"She's still got the handcuffs on," Caroline said as Eva fell asleep as soon as she stretched onto the mattress. "Should we—"

"Yes, the key may be on this bunch, I couldn't find it before." Mara fished the keys she'd taken from Jimmy's body from her backpack. Caroline found the small key that fit the woman's binding and gently removed them while she slept.

Mara reached out to cup the girl's chin in her hand. "I should've listened to you sooner about checking on her. I'm as sorry as I can be that I was too stubborn to listen to you."

Caroline gulped, then pulled Mara in for another hug. "I forgive you," she said into her ear. "You went, that's what really matters."

This is what really matters, thought Mara to herself as she let the warmth of the wholehearted embrace seep through every part of her being, and hugged Caroline back, the cold of her earlier stab of jealousy eradicated.

Mara barely remembered getting to her own bed after leaving Eva to rest, or removing her filthy dirt and sweat-permeated clothes. She woke in a clean T-shirt which had once belonged to Logan, and leggings, her muscles throbbing from her exertions so that even a simple stretch made them protest. The scent of food and coffee and the hushed sounds of her children nattering about something in their family area made her push forward and roll out of bed, gasping as the arm that Jimmy had clubbed with the rolling pin took some of her weight. A huge black bruise spread across the middle of her forearm, the skin tender to the touch. A cup of water with some orange Vitamin C packets and painkillers were sitting on a napkin next to her mattress and she downed them all gratefully after she got to her feet.

A small pot of water, some liquid bath soap, a washcloth, and towel were also laid out and Mara gave herself a quick sponge bath, glad to get the chicken coop smell off of her body. She changed into cargo pants, a pink t-shirt, and sneakers and pulled her hair back in a ponytail before grabbing her dirty dishes and making her way to the dining room area of the family space.

The table was bare, with multiple breakfast dishes in the bin waiting to be washed, but the brew in the French Press was still slightly warm, so Mara got herself a cup of coffee and gulped the lukewarm beverage gratefully. She grabbed a dry granola bar from their stash to stop her stomach growls as well.

"I miss toast," Mara said wistfully. "Toast with butter and honey."

The wish got her to thinking about the art rooms, and the pottery kiln she'd eyed to be a potential place to bake bread. That part of the school had fallen in the last quake, but the kiln itself was a sturdy construct. Maybe it was still there, and she just needed to clear away the rubble. Once that was done, they could get some firewood, and she could try her hand at baking some loaves. They had plenty of flour and yeast for the moment, and her sourdough starter was still bubbling away in its pot.

"First things first," Mara told herself sternly to stop herself from moving directly to the place the art wing had stood at the school. "You need to check on Eva, do the laundry, and get these dishes cleaned up."

Eva was still passed out on Caroline's mattress, the same thoughtful cup of water, painkillers, and something to wash with at her side. Sleep would be the best thing for Eva at the moment, so Mara gathered the dirty clothes basket from Caroline's room then quietly closed the door to the classroom, stopping in her own room to gather her dirty clothes and stripping the mattress of the sheets so she could start the laundry. The basket in Ethan and Will's room was overflowing, and carried the weirdly pungent aroma that was just pure boy.

Hefting their biggest pot, Mara hauled it outside and filled it halfway full of water from the jugs that sat on the unpurified side of the cookfire. There was no need to boil and strain water to do the laundry, and she'd recycle the leftover wash water to use in her garden, where the residual soap from the rinse bucket acted like a mild fertilizer and bug repellant.

Separating the laundry into two piles, one that contained what had once been whites, but had morphed into a dull beige, and the colors and darks, she started with the whites, allowing the water to heat around them before plopping them into a second pot which had a small amount of laundry soap, scrubbing and swishing them there before putting them back in the warm water to rinse and squeeze clean. She carefully avoided banging her bruised forearm as she worked, but it ached all the same.

"Washboard and wringer," she said aloud to herself as her hands reddened with the work. "Can't keep putting off finding those at an antique store."

Placing the cleaned clothes in a basket, she repeated the process with slightly cooled water for the colors and the darker clothes. When she was finished, she took the washed clothes and bed sheets to a clothesline they'd rigged between two trees. As Mara pegged the clothes to the line, she recalled when their first efforts at doing the wash had her hanging them in their basement to avoid the dirt and ash that filled the air from the continuous earthquakes. It had led to long drying times and a slightly moldy scent to everything. The better solution was to let them hang outside and beat them thoroughly to release the dust before taking them back inside.

"Thus we wear beige instead of white," she said as she pegged up the last one with a slight grimace and a roll of her aching shoulders. At least they didn't stink anymore, and there was certainly no one around she needed to impress with her laundry skills. Mara chuckled ruefully at the thought of things which had meant something once, but had been rendered utterly meaningless, like ultra-clean clothes, dream homes, credit scores, and money.

She transferred the wash water over to a basin she kept near the destroyed greenhouse and checked on the lettuce, spinach, and radish sprouts that bravely pushed their way up through the soil despite the lack of any direct sun. She'd positioned five of the remaining glass panes so at least the dim light was amplified for them and also protected them from the nights which were getting chilly far earlier than they should have been.

She waved at Caroline and Will, who were just coming back from getting the day's water, then wandered to the area where Ethan was pounding together two by fours to construct a lean-to for the animals to use in the winter.

"Hey mom." He swung easily to his feet to give her a hug without needing to use his crutches. "I hear you're a big hero."

"I didn't plan on it, but things took a turn." Mara broke off, not ready to expand on her part in killing Jimmy. He nodded, noting the giant bruise on her arm, but didn't press.

"Caroline and Will are just back with the water. You want one of them to come help you?"

"Will spotted some stray chickens he's wanting to go after," Ethan told her. "And Caroline was planning on scouting some more houses. I'm good."

She ruffled her son's hair affectionately. "Only another three weeks and you can get that cast off," she told him, pointing to the leg which had been broken on the very first day of the earthquakes. "Half-way there."

"Cannot get here fast enough," he commented before settling back to creating the walls for the new stable. Mara took a beat to watch him work, observing the way his hair flopped over his forehead with every swing of the hammer and the exacting way he placed the nails into the support boards, just as Logan had taught him to build things, the sight giving her a small bump of happiness.

The day passed quickly with the normal chores of cleaning and cooking. Mara tended to Eva as well, rousing her to drink water and take more painkillers as she washed her and cleaned and bandaged her wounds as best she could.

"I wish my sister were here," she remarked to Eva as she spread antibiotic gel on the jagged cut above her eyebrow after she'd cleaned it. "She's an ER nurse and would know what to do about your jaw."

"Nothing to do," Eva said stoically. "Seen plenty of broke jaws. Just gotta bind it."

Although Mara doubted it was the best cure for the woman's injury, there wasn't much else she could do except wrap a bandage around it, so it didn't hang heavily. She also carefully applied a pad to the woman's inflamed right eye and wrapped it as well.

"I'm throwing your clothes in the midden pile," she told Eva after she got her into a pair of sweats and a t-shirt from her own stash. "There's no saving them."

Eva acknowledged the comment with a grunt and a wave of her hand. "I could do with something to eat."

"Come on to our kitchen. I can make you scrambled eggs or some oatmeal."

Eva shuffled along with Mara, stopping in the doorway to look at the space they'd created from the old biology lab room. "Huh," was her only remark.

"Coffee?"

There was a spark of happiness in Eva's working eye as she nodded. "Don't suppose you got a shot of heat to go in it?"

Mara shook her head. "We don't."

"Them wives broke all my shine." Eva said, slurring through the sentence. "Not a jar left. Said I was brewing the devil's work."

She became sullen and silent after the observation, and returned to Caroline's room to sleep again after her meal. She paused before she laid her head down on the pillow. "I got things to say to you later."

"All right." Mara's curiosity was piqued, but Eva just turned away with a little moan, so she closed the door to let her rest.

Mara's craving for fresh bread had her diligently hunting for the kiln in a daunting pile of rubble. Even though Mara had been a librarian at the school for several years and knew the layout of it well, it took her nearly two hours to unearth the pottery kiln, hauling aside bricks, fallen masonry, lockers, tables, and chairs to reach the place where she had a firm memory of it standing.

The sturdy square kiln was intact when she finally reached it, eliciting a whoop of joy. She cleared a wide radius around it, then traced the gas line which snaked from the back to see where she needed to cap it. It had broken off near the ground several yards away. She sniffed the pipe to see if she could detect any leaking gas, but the air was clear. It would be an easy fix to cap both broken ends with an airtight seal to be on the safe side. Mara sent up a quick thanks to her uncle for showing her how to do the simple repair years ago.

"Tomorrow, I'll try to make bread," she said, once she'd capped the gas line and hauled some chunks of wood and kindling to lay next to the kiln. Her mouth watered at the thought of more delicious, fresh bread to eat along with their meals. Mara looked at her watch and switched her activities to collecting dandelions to chop and add to their meal of macaroni noodles with canned tomato sauce and the addition of a couple of tins of canned chicken for protein. It made for a slightly bland, but filling meal.

While using the canned goods was a welcome change from the egg-heavy diet they'd been eating for the past week, they'd raced through the food she and Caroline had gotten from the first two homes they'd gone into. They'd have to go on some more house hunts, and someone would need to go deer hunting as well. Mara wrinkled her nose at the thought of hunting and the work of dressing the deer, but they needed the protein and with the regular quakes passing through their valley, being squeamish wasn't an option.

Eva tottered in to join them at the evening meal, easing herself onto a stool. The family conversation was odd and stilted at first with her sitting with them, but soon it began to flow as Will chattered about the rooster and two chickens he'd found wandering by the river and had cleverly brought home by using the pet carrier they'd used to transport their two cats, Bacon and Molly, to the school.

"I just put some feed in the carrier, and they went right in!" He said proudly. "They must've been really hungry. I built a new cage for them, too and put it next to our flock, so they can get used to the other chickens before I put them together."

"So, how many chickens do we have?" Caroline wanted to know.

"Well, five that never came back after that last big quake, but we have ten from the old flock, plus these three. Lucky thirteen and a rooster to make more!" He turned to Mara. "I need a book on roosters and chickens and baby chicks. Do we have one?"

"We do. I'll pull it for you after dinner."

Mara finished her meal and took a minute to look around the table, lit by the soft glow of the Coleman lantern in the middle of it, and a thump of pride squeezed her heart. Caroline had seated herself next to Eva, while the two boys sat opposite, each pair chatting with each other. They were all banged and bruised, but the world-wide catastrophe of the earthquakes hadn't pulled them apart, and they'd been able to help someone else as well. It gave her a warm, centered feeling which only had one thing tugging out a bit of sadness, that Logan wasn't seated at the head of the table with them.

"Let's have our family meeting," she said.

"I've got the yellow pad!" Will pushed his plate aside and plopped his list on the table.

"I spotted two more houses a few blocks from here," Caroline said. "I watched them for about two hours, no one in or out. I thought I'd go check again tonight when it's dark, see if there's any lights."

"Take Will with you when you go," Mara said, then plowed ahead. "We have to supplement our food, so that means more houses, but more importantly, hunting a deer or two for fresh meat. I'll go, but I need someone to go with me to dress and carry what we take until we can get one or two of the horses used to the smell of a fresh kill." It bothered her to even say the words, but Mara schooled her expression. It was just what they had to do to survive.

Will wrinkled his nose while Ethan frowned and flipped his fork around his fingers. Caroline glanced at them and then nodded. "I'll come with you, Mara."

"Thanks, Caroline. If we turn on the generator for a short time, I can put up some of the deer meat as well, so nothing's wasted," Mara added. "I looked in the canning book, and you really do need to use a pressure cooker for meat."

Ethan sighed loudly as he dropped his fork from its spin. Mara looked over at the uncharacteristic display of annoyance. "We can't risk eating contaminated food," she explained. "I know you don't like running the generator, but there are things we need to do that require it."

Ethan shook his head. "It's not that, it's my stupid leg. I can't wait to get my cast off," he said, then added more, frustration lacing the words. "It should be me doing the hunting, not you and Caroline."

Mara looked at him with compassion. "I know it's hard on you not being able to be active."

"Don't take much to sit in a deer hide," Eva muttered through her bandaged jaw. "You could do it once the women find a good spot."

Ethan perked up at the idea that he could contribute. Mara cleared her throat, not at all comfortable with the idea of her injured son sitting in the woods alone, but then clamped her lips together, telling herself it was a battle for another day.

"Earlier, you told me you had something to tell us, Eva," Mara changed the subject somewhat abruptly. "I've been curious ever since."

Eva pursed her lips and stared at the table as silence settled over the group. Caroline put a hand on her arm gently. "You don't have to talk if you don't want to, Eva."

Mara internalized the aggravation that rose as her stepdaughter let the woman off the hook. If Eva had information about the brothers and their plans, they needed to know right away. She was about to say exactly that when Eva mumbled something low, more to herself than to the family.

"Don't owe 'em nothin'."

They all leaned in as Eva curled her hands into fists and muttered the sentence a second time. Eva raised her chin, an echo of the once bold and proud woman she'd been showing. "Them brothers took everything from me. My house, my shine, my Lloyd." Her voice broke on the last word. Silently, Caroline grasped one of the woman's hands where it was clenched atop the table, just as Mara reached for the other one.

"They're using that ham radio," she finally went on. "Lloyd's radio to reach out to their kin." Eva looked around the little table, the family ringed together in the light of the single lantern, her eye glinting with ferocity. "There's a passel of Crowes all through these mountains, and they've called them who's left to gather at the homestead. They got a plan to take over all the land 'round these parts, and to hunt you all down while they're at it."

CHAPTER THREE

The Douglas Fault
Day Twenty-one

A heavy, warm pressure against his chest accompanied by the sound of water flowing nearby were the first things to penetrate Logan's consciousness as he blinked his eyes open. Raising his right arm to clear his vision, he brushed by a fuzzy softness. He tilted his chin to look and recognized the tousled dirty blond hair of Braden, who clutched Whuff under one arm. The little boy was sprawled halfway across his torso, sound asleep.

Logan sighed with relief the toddler was safe, and took a moment to savor the happiness the knowledge brought him before he began to assess where they were and what actions he needed to take next. The sweet weight of the little boy, his limbs completely relaxed, was a balm to Logan's battered and bruised body, although his ribs weren't particularly happy about the extra mass on top of them and throbbed with every beat of his heart.

He was curled around Braden, partially laying on his right side and his backpack was still firmly attached. Logan winced as he tried to move his left arm, which had been grazed by Pamela's wild gunshot as the Pentenwell dam broke, the damaged flesh protesting the move with a sear of heat. He'd have to tend to it and get some water and food into them before they did anything else. Carefully rolling his body, he gently slid Braden and Whuff to his uninjured side and pushed up to survey the situation while clasping the sleeping child to himself. Braden stirred briefly, his lips puffing out in protest, but then he settled again in his new position.

They were on an egg-shaped island, the high watermark just a yard away from where he'd collapsed. The torrent pouring from the dammed river had retreated about twenty-five yards from that point, but they were still surrounded by lapping water which contained flotsam and jetsam ranging from clusters of twigs to entire trees which had been uprooted to parts of smashed houses, cars, and boats. The lighter objects still moved in eddies on the water's surface while the heavier ones bobbed along partially submerged, which told him the torrent which had created the flood was still pouring from the upper Wisconsin river.

He could just see the upper broken edges of the dam. They stood like disfigured sentinels in the newly formed landscape, the pillars of concrete that had supported the interlaced bow of the dam mishappen and missing sections, but in the main still holding, their underground pilings gripping fast to bedrock. Water cascaded over the remains of the dam, but the roar of it was less deafening than it had been at the peak of the release.

Logan swept his gaze in a circle as he got his bearings from his high point. The water had pooled into a lake that stretched for about a mile on either side of the dam, then it gradually narrowed back toward its original channel, losing its spread roughly two miles downriver, where it could perhaps be navigable. He looked at his analog watch, which read 7:00. He'd had his confrontation with Jasper in the late afternoon, so he must have been out for an entire night on the tiny patch of browned grass which had remained above the waterline.

His body chilled as he understood how close he and Braden had come to drowning, how lucky he'd been to reach the little summit before his will and his body simply gave out. He experienced a surge of gratitude, one that matched the peak waves of joy he'd had when meeting his children at their birth, or the moments when both his first wife and Mara agreed to marry him that he'd somehow been saved from so many disasters over the past weeks, and that he'd been given the gift of the responsibility of bringing Braden safely home to his father, and to see Gayle and her two boys to their home in Wichita as well.

"Thank you," he whispered into the gentle breeze and grey skies. "Thank you."

His stomach growled mightily, bringing him back to the present, and he unclipped his backpack to dig out two MREs and some water. He also took his pain medication, mentally clocking the time, so he'd stay on track with it. After checking the bullet graze, which appeared to go quite deep, he opted to let the medication kick in before he attempted to clean it.

"Chicken noodle stew with vegetables sounds pretty good to me," he commented to the sleeping Braden as he filled the flameless heater with water from one of his bottles to the fill line on each. Twelve minutes later, he had two hot meals ready to go. Setting them carefully aside, he woke Braden.

"Hey, Braden. Time to start our day." Logan sing-songed the words softly, gently rubbing the boy's back.

The little boy stirred, and then blinked at him as he got unsteadily to his knees. "Logan," he finally said, contentment filling his voice.

"Yep, I'm here with you. You and me and Whuff all together."

Braden pulled Whuff tightly to him and kissed the stuffed animal on the nose. "Whuff lost."

"Yeah, he was by the river. Your friend Demarius found him for you. You remember Darien and Demarius?"

"Yus."

"Well, once we have some breakfast, we're going to go find them and their mom."

The little boy looked around them at the water, which spread in all directions, and crinkled his face. Then it bloomed into a smile. "Swim?"

"I think not. I think we'll figure out a boat."

"Okay. Hafta go."

It took Logan a moment to understand what the boy meant, but then he pulled out the trowel to dig a hole and went to the edge of their little island to dig a place for the boy to do what he needed to do.

"Good job, buddy!" Logan used the wipes that were in the backpack to help clean him up and then a second time on the boy's hands and face, remembering he usually opted to use his fingers instead of his fork after a few bites of any meal. Double checking the meal pouch was cool enough to handle, Logan gave him the food and the plastic fork which came with the kit. "Before you ask, we don't have any scrambled eggs, but I know you like noodles, too, and this has noodles."

"Then the candy juice?"

Logan was confused by the question, as they didn't usually have candy after their breakfast. "I don't know what that is, Braden."

"Issa drink." Braden seemed a bit put out he had to explain it. "Is red," he added, dropping the fork, and picking up a fat noodle with his fingers and stuffing it into his mouth. "Mmm." Braden dropped his attempt to clue Logan in and focused on his food.

Logan had finished half his meal before he realized what Braden had been trying to explain to him. It was the medicine Jasper's group had been dosing him with to keep him quiet and complacent. The realization made his anger over it ignite all over again. They'd been giving him some sort of narcotic every day and telling him it was "candy juice." He rubbed his forehead as an additional worry crept in. If Braden had been kept on a steady dosage for several days, would he suffer withdrawal symptoms without it?

Finishing the last bites of his meal, he sorted through the small first aid kit Chip Garcia had supplied. He found a few blister packs of Benadryl tablets that were normally used to stave off allergies. Wracking his brain, Logan was relatively sure the liquid form was red, as Caroline had needed to take it when she'd toddled into a patch of poison ivy when she was young. Her doctor had told them she'd need to wean off of the medication after a few days to stop side effects like vomiting or headaches.

Logan waffled a bit about giving Braden more medication, but after a moment, he snapped one of the pink pills in half and handed it to Braden. "I want you to swallow this, okay, buddy? Just put it in with one of your bites."

The little boy popped the small bit of pill into his mouth and chewed it up with some chicken, his open face completely trusting.

A fraction of his worry abated, Logan took off his shirt and set to work fixing his arm. Braden watched him intently as he cleaned the gunshot divot using antiseptic wipes as best he could and then bandaged it with a square bandage and adhesive tape.

Braden pointed to a bit of stuffing coming out of a rip on Whuff's belly, who was looking rather battered. "Whuff fix too."

Logan smiled. "You want to do it?" He handed the little boy the wipe. Braden crooned to the dog as he worked. He handed Braden a strip of adhesive tape and a square bandage, allowing the little boy to manage it on his own, his tongue sticking out in concentration as he mended his toy.

"All better?" Logan asked Braden.

Braden put his ear to the dog's mouth and listened intently. "Whuff says yus," he told Logan, then turned his attention to his stuffed animal once again.

"Maybe you'll be a doctor or a vet one day," Logan said with a smile. He packed away the first aid kit and took another drink, making sure Braden had a drink as well. Then he got to his feet to survey their situation once again.

The water had receded from their perch by another ten yards as they'd eaten their breakfast, but they were still marooned on the high point by the overflow of water. Itching to get moving and rejoin Zeke, Gayle, and the boys, Logan paced back and forth as he considered the issue, his eye on the place where a crack carved through the earth only a short distance from their position. An involuntary shiver vibrated along his spine as he recalled Jasper's final look of terror as the gap swallowed him along with the water that had surged around them both.

Although the rift no longer had water pouring into it, the ominous darkness of it snaking through the mud was a stark reminder of what the earth could do, suddenly and without warning. They weren't safe on their little mound, even though it had saved them. They had to keep moving, get off their island before it turned into a trap.

He stared over the brown, filthy water. Even when receded all the way to its original riverbed, crossing the land would be slow, treacherous going, full of deep mud, tangles of branches and the debris the flow left behind. Logan would have a difficult time traversing it on his own, let alone with Braden in tow. He massaged his elbow below the gunshot wound. He couldn't carry Braden for any length of time with just one arm to use. Even once they got onto a roadway, without something like their old jogging stroller or a bike, he'd never make it the three hundred or so miles between their location and Kingston, Iowa in time to rendezvous with his friends within the ten days he'd allotted.

Logan scrubbed his face with both hands as he reluctantly came back to the single idea that made sense for them, which was to get onto the water, even though it was a treacherous way to travel, especially without a boat. As if to punctuate his doubts, a three-foot long water snake slithered by, its sidewinder motion mesmerizing. Snakes would be abundant on the water, especially as they traveled southward, as would drop-offs, the danger of a variable current, unseen snags under the water, whirlpools that could capture them, and hordes of biting insects to make the journey a misery.

He paced some more, trying to let go of the nerves which surfaced as he considered every difficult aspect of a water journey they might encounter.

"Not to mention we don't have a boat!" Logan groaned aloud.

Shaking his head at the lack of any other good options, Logan stripped off his heavy flannel shirt, gun, and belt to prepare to enter the water. He tucked the gun carefully into the pack, pushing it to the bottom where Braden couldn't easily dig it out. Opting to leave on the bandage that Sandra had wrapped around his ribs, his t-shirt, cargo pants, and boots, Logan crouched next to Braden, who'd been watching his preparations with interest. "I'm going to go get some wood to make us a raft. I want you to stay here with Whuff, okay?"

"Go?" For the first time alarm popped into the boy's face. Braden crinkled his forehead and shook his head. "No!" he said anxiously, grabbing hold of Logan's hand. "Stay!"

"I have to go into the water and find some wood. I'm going to build us a raft."

"No!" The boy crossed his arms, looking mutinous.

Logan let out his breath in a long exhale. "I'll stay where you and Whuff can see me," he promised, then unstrapped his sturdy knife from his leg before he stepped into the ugly dark brown water, feeling his way with his feet, cringing as the cold of it crept up his legs, making him shiver involuntarily. He turned to see that Braden had come to the very edge of the water. Fear spiked through Logan, and he spoke sternly to the child.

"Stop! You have to stay there. Don't follow me into the water, Braden, it's not safe."

Tears formed in the little boy's eyes, but Logan stood firm, pointing him back to higher ground. "I mean it, go on back up on top of the hill and stay there, Braden."

The bottom lip stuck out in a perfect pout, but then the little boy did as he was told. "I promise I'll be where you can see me," Logan said.

He turned his attention back to the mass of floating debris in front of him, wading until he was chest deep to reach a tree branch that was the right length and width to build the raft he had in mind. Using his knife, he sawed and hacked it away from the tangle and floated it back to the island. Braden watched him carefully as he pulled the branch up, panting with the effort of both cutting and moving through the constantly shifting soil beneath the water.

"One down, about eleven more to go," he said to Braden. "Good job staying there."

Logan repeated the process several more times, hacking broken branches away until he had enough relatively straight lengths, which were all approximately five feet long and four or five inches in diameter to build a raft. When he'd finally collected all of them, Logan waded back onto their little island and shed his wet t-shirt, setting it to the side to let it dry. His shivers were intense from his long partial submersion in the mucky water, but the day was relatively warm and the work still ahead of him building the raft would heat him. He'd also collected the driest twigs and small branches he could find as he'd worked to create a layer between themselves and the dank water.

"Braden, spread these out." He showed the toddler what he meant, so they'd dry faster. Braden set to work, but soon was simply playing with the twigs, setting them up and knocking them down. Logan chuckled to himself, relieved to see him playing. It would dry out the branches just as much and keep the boy's mind occupied.

Logan set to work with his knife, stripping the branches of small outgrowths. He took the two stoutest branches and laid them four feet apart, then placed eight across them, letting the eight extend about a foot beyond the base logs, fitting them loosely so there was a half-inch of space between them for both stability and expansion as the wood absorbed water. The final two thinnest branches were laid on top of the eight, matching the bottom two. He cut his paracord into four pieces, tied a bowline knot in each and bound the top and bottom logs together tightly with several figure eight loops so the sandwiched logs of the body of the raft would stay together. It created a small, roughly four by four foot platform which would just fit himself with Braden secured in front of him seated between his legs.

The gathering and building had gone more quickly than Logan had anticipated, although his muscles shook from the effort it had taken, and the arm with the recent wound burned. Logan put the dry twigs and branches he'd collected on top of the raft as a bit of padding and then folded the tarp on top of them, so they'd stay drier.

His delight with the finished product lasted only a few seconds before Logan groaned and shook his head. Braden looked at him quizzically when he slapped his hand to his forehead in dismay.

"Still need something to paddle with," he explained, and reluctantly waded back into the water to find a wide, flat piece of wood, eventually coming up with a broken part of someone's aluminum siding that would work if he wrapped the top of it in one of his shirts, so it didn't cut his hands. He also brought back two stout branches which had a Y notch at the bottom of each.

"This is a keep-away stick," he told Braden, showing him how to hold it so the Y folded over his shoulder and under his armpit like a crutch. He had the boy practice poking the backpack with it, so he'd get the feel of pushing things away from them.

"Let's eat some food, and then we'll launch," he told Braden. "Can't go rafting on an empty stomach." Logan sighed as he sat, his muscles aching from the effort of hauling the wood.

They shared a cheese tortellini MRE and drank the last of the clean water. Logan eased himself up and put on his flannel shirt again. "Okay buddy, it's time for us to make our move."

He'd built the raft near the edge of the water, which had descended another few feet by the time they'd packed everything. Logan turned to Braden as he finished packing. "I want to put Whuff into my backpack so he's safe on the water, okay?"

Braden gripped the toy tightly before he nodded and handed it to Logan, who buckled it into the top of the pack and then secured it to his body.

"I'm going to sit, and then you climb in and sit between my legs. You might get a little wet." Logan edged the raft fully into the water, so it was barely clinging to their mound of earth, then carefully climbed onto it, keeping his weight centered. The raft sank a bit, but held. He extended his hand to help Braden make the scramble.

The little boy bit his lip in concern as the raft wobbled when he crawled on, but he settled himself to sit cross-legged, his keep-away stick at the ready. Logan pushed off using his own keep-away stick and then slowly paddled them at an angle toward the main flow of the Wisconsin river.

Logan kept the pace as slow as possible, working them around a multitude of obstacles, not worrying if the raft momentarily eddied to one side or another or revolved in a slow circle, as long as their general direction was correct. Braden helped him push away tangles of wood, quickly learning that he couldn't lean too far one way or another, as the raft easily swamped.

"Wet!" he called out as the first slosh soaked his legs.

"Yeah, we'll have to stop early so we can get our clothes dry with a fire tonight," Logan commented as a fresh worry moved to the forefront of his thoughts. Braden didn't have any extra clothes, and the meal they'd shared brought their food supply to just four meals left, with a good eight days of travel or more once they hit the main channel of the river.

"One thing at a time," he told himself. "Just get through one thing at a time."

Using his paddle to keep them moving in the right direction, pushing away from obstacles, and maintaining their balance on the tiny raft became Logan's entire world for the next hours as they eased their way into the main flow of the river. He kept an eye out for any boats they could use instead of the raft, but only downed trees, submerged cars, destroyed homes, and drowned animals, along with several more snakes, crossed his view.

"Issa snake!" Braden pointed out as one of the things swam by. He turned and looked at Logan with a shocked expression. "Snake swim!" He didn't seem afraid at all, just surprised.

"Yes, they don't like being touched," Logan said as calmly as he could manage, threading the needle between keeping Braden safe and not giving the child things to be fearful about.

They finally reached the original banks of the flow, the pour from upriver cascading more rapidly in the center of the channel. Logan did his best to keep them in the sweet spot between the fastest water and the dangers of being too close to the banks, where they could get snagged on something beneath the surface and thrown from their precarious perch. It took continuous motion with the piece of aluminum siding, and the edges of it were wearing through his shirt, giving him numerous nicks on his hands, while Logan's shoulders and arms grew more and more tired with each passing mile.

They were making good progress; the water moving them along at a steady five-mile an hour pace. The need for the push-away sticks had evaporated, and Braden leaned against him, napping, lulled by the endless lapping of the waves and the pervasive warmth of the air. Logan gave himself a break from paddling, enjoying the rest and the feel of a light breeze across his skin.

"Like the lazy river at the water park," he murmured to himself, smiling at the memory of taking the kids to the place in the summers as they grew up, the happy grins on their faces as they all floated along in inner tubes, the cool of the water contrasting with the heat of the day to create perfection.

In his half-dozing state, the smooth curve of the water just before they hit a drop-off came as a complete surprise. Logan clamped his legs around Braden with a yell, gripping the back log of the raft with both hands as he leaned back to compensate for the sudden four-foot drop which plunged them vertically into the water, his makeshift paddle shooting off to one side as the river swallowed the raft, engulfing it completely in a black wave.

They nearly flipped completely, only his quick action of balancing the tilt of their float preventing it, but the yanking on his torso, along with the strain of locking Braden between his legs had him gasping in agony as they were tossed in the turbulent aftermath of the drop-off. Braden came out of the dunking screaming in terror, his arms locking around Logan's legs as they were tossed side to side in the turbulence beneath the drop off, spinning wildly in circles, the cold water continuing to drench onto their craft as they bobbed out of control into the faster center of the river. Without the paddle, they had no means of controlling where they were going.

"Hang on to me!" Logan shouted to Braden as his legs cramped from his tight grip around the boy.

Braden bawled out in terror but did as he'd been told, his arms clinging tightly to Logan's thighs as they continued their wild ride for several minutes. Eventually the flow slowed, and the raft steadied. Logan's heart was pounding madly with residual fear as he bent over Braden.

"You okay?"

"NO!" Braden wept. "Want off!"

Logan studied the river, the long sweep of it carrying them past mostly forested areas, with denuded sandbars sticking out of the flow. Stopping on a sandbar wasn't an option, as another earthquake could send fresh torrents flowing downstream. They'd have to get to one of the banks, but getting out of the current without a paddle wouldn't be easy. He eased his grip on Braden, forcing himself to relax so the boy could follow suit.

"That was a fun bit of the river!" Logan put as much lightheartedness into the words as he could muster.

"Not fun." Braden had stopped crying, down to a few hiccups. "Too wet."

"It was just a different kind of swim, is all," Logan said.

Braden swiveled around to look at him in disbelief, but he calmed and eventually settled as Logan wrapped his arms around him as the river bobbed them gently along in the current, which had turned more sedate as the river widened. "A few more miles, then we'll stop for the night," he told Braden.

The little boy was silent, squirming a bit as he nestled into Logan's embrace, but the fear created by the sudden drop had left him. Logan relaxed as well, letting the river float them along, but he kept his eyes downriver for the signs of another drop-off.

Starting with a few outcroppings along the bank of the river, lumpy sandstone cliffs rose higher and higher above them, topped with spindly firs still clinging stubbornly to the rocks. The river split in two, the current taking them into the channel on the right side of what Logan guessed was a large island. A giant bend to the right approached, the curve caused by one of the bluffs; the water slowing substantially as it approached the curve, then speeding up into white ripples as it made it around the outcrop. A sandy bank anchored by the same pine trees stretched in front of the bluff itself, a perfect landing place if Logan could get them there.

He quickly unlaced his boots and unbuckled his pack, stringing the laces together through one strap, working as fast as he could before the current robbed them of their opportunity. "Braden, I'm going to get in the water and kick us to shore. I want you to lie flat on the raft for me."

"Don't want to!"

"Gotta work with me, pal." Logan eased his legs from the boy's grip, and pushing him to lie down. "We're stopping for the night."

He pushed the backpack and his boots toward the center of the raft with Braden as he rolled into the water slowly, gasping as the cold of it penetrated his clothes and hit his warmed skin. "Stay flat, buddy."

The river grabbed at the square raft, threatening to rip it from his grasp before he even began his push. Grasping the rough branches, Logan beat his legs furiously, frothing the water as he held on with both hands, pushing the raft forward as if it were a giant kickboard, angling against the current. For a long minute, the water tugged him persistently downstream, and he barely made any headway, the river doing its best to carry them away from the little beach. Putting his face in the water and stiffening his arms, Logan streamlined his body to remove any extra resistance and kicked as hard as he could, only lifting his face to suck in gasps of air.

He nearly rammed his head into the back of the raft when it beached. Bending his knees, he stood on the bottom of the river and shoved the raft forward a few feet higher onto the sand. He waded from the river on shaky legs, pausing to gasp in air as best he could as his ribs flashed bright pain around his torso and his wounded arm throbbed.

"Hop off, Braden, and help me drag the raft." Logan said through chattering teeth, the late afternoon breeze adding to the coldness of his body.

Braden lit up at the idea of helping, and he dug his heels into the sand as he grasped one end of the raft and pulled. Logan did the work, but smiled wearily to see Braden do his own small part as they hauled the water-logged craft all the way onto the sand, lodging it next to a pine tree. Logan groaned as he straightened, then he put on his boots, gathered his backpack and the tarp from the bottom of the raft and offered his hand to Braden.

"Let's go find a campsite."

The sandy beach led to a wider area that had been used for picnicking before the world turned upside down. A sturdy brick grill and a picnic table still stood forty-five yards from the water's edge in the shade of the white and red pine trees, maples, and oaks. A stand of river birch shivered in the breeze nearby. The ground was dry, showing no signs of being inundated, and there was plenty of seasoned wood to burn, while the cliffs protected them from the elements to the west and south. A few crows cawed their indignation that their peaceful spot had new guests, flapping away to circle elsewhere.

"I think we'll be okay here, Braden." Logan set his backpack on the picnic table gratefully and pulled Whuff out to hand to him. "I'm going to get a fire started. Can you and Whuff help me find dry sticks?"

Once the fire was going in the grill, he gave Braden an empty jug, and carrying three more of his own, they traipsed to the river to fill them. On the way back, Braden struggled a bit, but managed to carry his half-full jug the whole way without Logan helping him.

Boiling water for them to drink was first on Logan's list of things to do. While it was heating in his cookpot, he took the time to change the bandage on his arm, cleaning it, and reapplying antibiotic gel to the wound. He filtered the first batch of water through a bit of cloth into an empty container, then started the next batch to boil as he and Braden took long drinks.

"Are you hungry, Braden?"

The little boy nodded vigorously. "Scram?" He asked hopefully.

"No, we have beef stew or chicken and rice." Logan made the two meals dance on his knees. Braden stabbed a finger at the chicken and rice, and Logan got them cooking with a bit of the water and got Braden cleaned up with wipes. Once Braden's meal was cooled a bit, he handed it to the boy, along with the other half of the Benadryl tablet, to continue the weaning off process. He took his own medicine at the same time, noting he only had a few more doses to go before he was out of the opioids.

"Use your fork with this one. It's too messy to eat with your fingers."

Braden did his best with the fork, but in the end, Logan had to help him with dishing up his bites, so he got more of the meal in him than on him.

They ate their meal in a comfortable silence, the chirr of the bugs, the calls of the birds and the tapping of a woodpecker the only sounds besides the endless chatter of the river passing them by and the sigh of the wind through the tall oak trees which clustered just past the pines.

A patter of acorns accompanied the movement of the wind in the trees. The sound of them gave Logan an idea about how to supplement their rapidly disappearing stock of food without the risk of going into a town.

Once they were done eating, he set to gathering as many acorns as he could find before they lost the light entirely. Braden joined in the game, proving to be good at finding the little brown nuts, stooping, and dropping them in the shirt Logan gave him to carry his loot.

Once they had a good quantity, Logan filled the pot with water and scooped out the acorns that floated, throwing them to the side. He went through the rest, getting rid of any that had holes. The remaining nuts he wrapped in a shirt and had a giggling Braden walk on top of it to crush the shells. He picked the meat from the shells, then set his pot of water on the stove with the acorns in it, letting it boil until the water turned brown. He dumped the brown water out and refilled the pot again, repeating the process until the water ran clear.

Night had fallen by the time he was done leeching the tannins from the acorns. Logan put them back on the grill in the pot to dry roast them over the fading coals as he prepped their sleeping space beneath the picnic table to protect them from night dew, laying the tarp down and draping their damp clothes to dry overnight on the benches of the table. He gave Braden his extra shirt to wear, the thing enormous on the little boy, making him giggle, then handed him Whuff before covering him with the metallic emergency blanket.

"Get some sleep, buddy," he said. "Night."

"Night."

The little boy was asleep in seconds. Logan stayed up another half an hour, tossing the acorns in the pan until they darkened, then he seasoned them with salt packets from the MREs. He banked the remains of the fire and set the hot pan to the side before he got his gun out of the backpack. Carrying it with him, he eased under the blanket next to Braden, curling himself around the small body, and let himself drop into oblivion.

CHAPTER FOUR

Hayward and San Andreas Faults
Day Twenty-two

Ripley touched the crusted blood on her head as she sat splayed on the dingy grey carpeted floor of what she'd come to understand was a makeshift prison cell. While she had no memory of getting to the room, the fight that had broken out on the parking lot at the National Lab was clear enough. She'd charged the ever-smiling Sam after Daniel Chang had revealed himself to them, but the fight had been short-lived. Sam and a few more of the men nearby had easily overcome her and taken her sidearm.

She'd woken in solitary confinement inside of what had once been an interior office space scratched and dirty, her head pounding from the blow that had knocked her unconscious for her transport to the space.

Ignoring the pulse of pain from her head, Ripley pushed from the floor and paced the dingy, dark space, counting her steps in the ten-by-ten square room as she went over what she knew. Her repeated demands to be set free and to see Fred and Flannery had gone unanswered. Two men stood guard at the office door, visible through a narrow strip of reinforced glass which ran the vertical length of the doorframe that was the only source of light for her prison. New pairs of guards appeared every four hours with military precision. A third guard was called when she needed to use the portapotty they'd placed in a room at the end of the hallway, which was simply a long line of interior offices, all without windows like hers. All the guards were men in their thirties, all of them had been uncommunicative.

They'd brought her rations once a day for the past two days, each time a single MRE along with a 32-ounce bottle of water. Her assumption was that either the facility was low on supplies, or Chang didn't deem her worthy of full rations of either food or water. She had a blanket to use on the office floor when she slept. No one had responded to any of her questions, and her only outlet to counteract the strain of her confinement and growing nerves was pacing. Her steps had created a worn path in the carpeting as she spun through possible escape scenarios in her head.

She'd tried three of them as they'd occurred to her to no avail, the first a thorough search of the office she'd been assigned. Aside from a standard issue metal desk, it had been empty, the walls barren. An exhaustive search of the desk had brought up nothing but dust.

"Not even a paperclip," Ripley muttered to herself, then snorted in derision. It wasn't like she was some action hero who could turn a paperclip into a successful escape. She'd pulled the drawer out to use as a club on any guard who opened the door, but the big, burly man who she'd tried it on had taken it away from her with a few expert twists, giving her a pitying look which had hurt nearly as much as her fingers had when he ripped the metal away from her grasp.

Her second attempt had been to drag the desk over to the wall, climbing atop it to examine the air vent, which was only a foot wide and eight inches tall. She'd eventually concluded that even if she could get the grating off somehow with the plastic knife she'd secreted into her jog bra from her first MRE, she'd never fit through it, and had given it up.

The third try was a brutal physical assault on the door of the office, screaming and kicking it repeatedly until the men outside had opened it and taken away her shoes and socks, then bound her hands and feet together, gagged her and left her alone for several hours. The man who'd brought her meal had untied her and spoken the only words she'd heard since her capture.

"If you try that again, you won't like the consequences."

The phrasing had been unsettling, as had the flat delivery and the unwavering stare the man had punctuated the short sentence with. Ripley had given him a single nod that she understood, and he'd left her unbound, taking the gag and ropes with him when he left.

Barefoot, she walked the path she'd made around the perimeter of the room in a continual loop. It was exactly forty-two steps around the edge of the room, the count echoing in her head whether she wanted it there or not.

The click of the door handle had her whirling, then blinking at the flood of light the open door let into her dull grey room. Sam, the smiling man who she'd first met when their helicopter landed, was wearing a slimy, ubiquitous grin as he greeted her. It made Ripley want to rip it off with her bare hands, but instead she gathered her dignity, folded her hands together and raised an eyebrow, waiting for him to speak.

He gave her an acknowledging nod. "Good afternoon, Ms. Baxter. President Chang would like to have a word."

"President Chang?" Ripley's derisive laugh was high and long as she stuffed her jangled nerves as deep as they would go to put on a brave front. "I don't meet with delusional people, Sam." She waved a hand at him dismissively.

"You can walk with me to meet him, or I'll have one of our fine guards do a fireman's carry. Your choice."

"I'm not walking anywhere without my shoes." Ripley crossed her arms and lifted her chin in defiance.

Sam rolled his eyes, bent, and plucked her boots from just outside the door. "Here. There's fresh socks, too. Yours were a little gamey." He sniffed delicately and deliberately. "Sorry there's no showers available. I know you could sure use one." The smile turned mean as he insulted her.

He held the boots out to her, forcing Ripley to walk forward to take them, something shifting in his eyes as she approached. For a moment she thought the man might snatch them away from her, use his height to make her jump for them as an extra cruelty, but he let Ripley take them without a word.

Ripley took her time doing up her laces, forcing him to wait for her before she stood and brushed her palms along the front of her army camo. "After you," she said, gesturing with her hand.

"We've got a bit of a walk," he told her as they exited, the two men who'd been her guards remaining rigidly in place as they moved past them. "I thought I'd give you a brief tour."

Ripley shrugged, hiding her eagerness to learn as much as she could about the facility as she looked along the long corridor, which was lit by dim fluorescent lights in the ceiling that hummed and flickered. Somewhere, the group had a generator and the fuel to run it.

"Where are my men?" she asked as they progressed through the long hall.

"See, if you'd been smart, you'd have refused to come with me until I answered that one," the reply came back along with his nasty little smile.

"You'd have refused, I wouldn't have my boots, and some burly meat-head would be carrying me right now," Ripley replied evenly. "My guess is your boss is keeping you in the dark, and you have no idea where Flannery and Fred are."

"You'd be wrong." The reply was lazy, but as she slanted her eyes toward Sam from beneath her eyelashes, she caught the anger that flashed across his face. Her stab in the dark about his lack of information had been correct. Sam didn't know where Fred and Flannery were being held, and it irritated him she'd pointed it out.

They walked along the long corridor of windowless rooms, two more of which had a guard next to the doors. Ripley peeked in each as Sam hustled her by, but didn't see who the occupants were. "We're bunking in this section," Sam explained. "It's been stable so far, and affords all of us some privacy." He opened the door at the end of the corridor and indicated that she walk ahead of him into the stairwell. Steps ran both up and down from the landing, the area lit by a few inset lights in the middle of each flight, shadowing the corners of the stairwell in darkness.

A bolt of pure fear went through Ripley. "We've been underground?" She fought the urge to shake her hands loose and take off running as wave after wave of nerves danced through her body, and her pace increased as she ascended the four flights of stairs until she was nearly running up them.

"Technically built into the hill, but you could say that, yes. There's four floors under the ground, we sleep on level two." He sounded amused as she ran toward the crash bar, the long rectangle of reinforced glass letting in a bit of daylight at ground level.

In ordinary circumstances, Ripley would have breathed deeply of the fresh air when she hit an open area, but one look at the ominous dark-grey overcast which had both thickened and lowered during her sojourn underground had her pinning her lips together and keeping her breath to small sips. An oddly sulfurous scent overlaid the salted sea breeze, and looking more closely at the sky, Ripley observed white puffs of steam rolling beneath the cloud layer.

Sam pointed at the white puffs that swirled without an obvious breeze to move them. "That's part of the reason the President wanted to talk to you. Our resident geologist claims he has no idea what it is, or why the air stinks like rotten eggs. This way."

He crossed the parking area where they'd touched down. Their Black Hawk helicopter was still sitting where Fred had parked it forty-eight hours ago. Ripley turned her head to get her bearings as they moved across the parking lot. The tumbled modern section that had looked like stacked shipping containers had slipped further down the mountainside, and the surface of the parking lot had new, long cracks running through it, the carefully painted H cut through the middle with a two-inch wide gap.

Ripley considered the implications of the new cracks as she and Sam strode over them, one of which was wide enough she had to hop to get across it. The surface they walked on had been solid when they'd arrived, she was sure of it. These new cracks had either happened in a series of small, non-detectable quakes, or the soil beneath the mountain was undergoing a slow liquefaction which would eventually result in everything simply slipping into the sea that lapped only a hundred yards away. She shivered with the insight of what the future held. Sam's insouciant air that all was well was a clear indication he was unaware of the danger they were in. Either in hours or days, the whole National Lab was going to succumb to the quakes and the eager sea that waited to drown it.

She swallowed hard and refocused her attention on learning all she could about her surroundings. To their right, a few buildings like the one they'd come out of still stood, just one story high at ground level, built into the side of the mountain just as the one they'd exited had been. Several men hurried toward the buildings, carrying flats of rations across the open parking lot from one of the two hangers, which were open instead of closed as they'd been when Fred had landed them. Ripley craned her neck to see what was inside the hangers.

One of the hangers was being used as storage, supplies laid out in long rows which were not stacked at all, just single crates lined end to end in precise rows. The other hangar held a Black Hawk helicopter and what looked to be two Little Bird helicopters next to it. A fuel depot stood just to the side of the hanger, and a man was just putting the equipment away from a refuel. No doubt it was the helicopter Chang had stolen, and perhaps the two smaller birds were the ones that had belonged to the facility.

Sam waved a hand in the direction the men were headed with their flats of rations. "Our team has a common room where we cook and eat, got some ping-pong tables and a bunch of books. That's where our medical facility is, too. We have a full-time doctor and two nursing staff."

Ripley nodded as if she was impressed. Perhaps her men were being held in the hospital area. She gave a bright-eyed inquisitive look at Sam. "You told us there were twenty-two people to be rescued, looks like it's more to me. You must have a large, well-run organization going." Ripley commented. "And who's your resident geologist?"

Sam cocked his head to the right as he considered her questions, puffing a bit at her compliment. "Well, we didn't really tell you the truth there." He grinned as if he was proud of lying. "We have four guests. Two girl hikers who came in on day three, and two scientists who we managed to pull out of the rubble of the cyclotron." He gestured with his thumb at the iconic round building which had collapsed on itself. "Our core group stands at fifty, and we've got more headed our way as they're able to." A note of pride colored his words. "There's a whole other branch near the White House, and more in the Blue Ridge Mountains who are organizing, plus we got word that there are clusters of militia in the Midwest, too, all of them loyal to President Chang." Once the man got started, the information tumbled from his lips as he shared what he clearly believed were impressive statistics. Ripley didn't bother to let him know that she, Thaddeus, and President Ordway had thinned out the number of men who were at the branch near the White House.

Instead, Ripley played into his expectation that she would be impressed. "Wow, I had no idea you had such a large organization." She looked once more at the hanger which held the helicopters and twisted the verbal knife as he basked in her prior compliment. "Hope you've got a good evac plan in place. Looks to me like only twenty people at most could escape if there's another bad quake."

Sam lost his smile at her comment, then scoffed. "Place has stood for three weeks, it's not going to fall down."

"That's what the folks at Mount Weather thought," quipped Ripley. "I guess your resident geologist didn't tell you about the cumulative effect from the vibrations?"

He looked at her blankly, so she continued. "You're sitting on top of both the Hayward and San Andreas faults, Sam, and really near Cascadia. Those are the ones most people have heard of. You can't be that naïve about the danger you're in, surely?"

"President Chang has everything under control," Sam retorted. "We're going to be living like kings soon. Maybe not for a few months, but we're going to be the kings." He picked up the pace, putting a hand under her elbow to hustle her along, his voice clipped with irritation. "Tour's over. I'm taking you to him. That geologist Emerson is with him. You can bore him with your warnings. I'm not interested."

Ripley was glad he'd surged ahead, nearly dragging her along so he couldn't read her face when he mentioned the name of the geologist who was advising Chang. Emerson wasn't the most common name she'd ever run into, and one of her best friends at college had been Emerson Davies. He'd landed a plumb job just outside of San Francisco, the last she'd heard.

Her excitement that one of her friends had survived the quakes was dampened by the fact that he was working for Chang. She mentally reviewed what Sam had told them about their "resident geologist," and it gave her a little pop of hope. It could be that Emerson was fighting back the only way he could against the militia, downplaying dangers and giving them poor advice. The young man had been a quiet, unassuming person at college, someone who it would be easy to dismiss if you had a colossal ego. And if anything was evident to Ripley, it was that Chang—dubbing himself as a President—had a massive ego. It was something she could play off of, and use the advantage Fred had pointed out she possessed. That people didn't see her as much of a threat.

They continued to cross the campus, hiking a series of stairs which had been hastily repaired with loose bricks jammed into the hillside in several spaces where rifts in the earth had crumbled. They ascended to the rectangular cinderblock building, which was directly beneath the tall radio tower, extending behind it by several yards. Ripley could see the tower had been fortified by more bricks, these carefully mortared into place, bracing the four legs. Even with the fortification, it had a decided lean to the right. A lone man was working with a bucket of mortar, more bricks, and a ladder, extending the repairs on that side of the edifice. Next to him, a large generator hummed with life, a multi-gallon container of gasoline standing next to it.

"Go on in," Sam waved Ripley ahead of him toward the closed door.

"Oh, so you're just the errand boy, not in on the actual important discussions. Good to know." She breezed past as the smile fell from Sam's face.

The first room inside of the radio tower building was equipped with a long table which held a variety of communication instruments and electronics. A single man monitored the channels, which hissed with static, a few words popping through at broken intervals. A second man stood in front of a closed door, hands folded behind his back in parade rest. He glanced at Ripley and held a hand up for her to wait in place, tapped on the door, and then entered.

"You can go in," he said when he re-emerged, and held the door open for her.

The second room was outfitted like a small apartment, with a sitting area that held two metal folding chairs and a loveseat. Underneath the single window at the back was a table containing a microwave and coffee pot, while shelves beneath it held supplies and a small refrigerator. A single bed stood against one wall, with a nightstand and a lamp. A pile of books was on the nightstand, their spines turned away from Ripley.

Two men were in the room. Daniel Chang lounged on the love seat, taking up the entirety of it with his arms spread over the back. He wore golf attire on his trim, fit figure, khaki pants, and a short-sleeved collared shirt in a light purple. A fancy watch decorated his wrist, and he wore a holstered gun on his hip.

The other man in the room was her friend from college, Emerson Davies. He was perched on a folding chair as he glanced from his clipboard full of notes, clearly annoyed at the interruption when she entered, but his expression changed to happiness at the sight of her, opening his mouth and standing to greet her. Ripley gave him the slightest shake of her head and a warning flash with her eyes. Emerson clapped his mouth shut and frowned, clearing his throat to cover over his joyful surprise at seeing her.

"Ah, Ms. Baxter." Daniel Chang rose from his chair to usher her inside.

She adroitly avoided his outstretched hand, simply saying, "Chang." Her abrupt acknowledgement was intentional. She maneuvered around him and extended her hand to Emerson, hoping he'd play along with her pretense of being strangers. "I'm Ripley Baxter, President Ordway's Science Advisor."

He gave her hand an extra-hard squeeze. "Emerson Davies, currently advising President Chang on the earthquakes and their potential hazards." His soft blue eyes had dark shadows under them, and he was thin and pale. A red, scraggly beard and mustache had been allowed to grow unkempt, and his black-framed glasses were taped together at one side. Emerson had lost weight as well, weight he could ill-afford to lose, making him look as if he were ill.

Ripley roused herself from her contemplation of her friend and turned to Chang, disparagement lacing her words. "President? Really? I thought Sam was joking."

"It's a new world, Ms. Baxter. We can reshape it as we choose." Her effort to get under Chang's skin didn't seem to be successful, as he waved her to the remaining folding chair. "Please have a seat. Would you like a cup of coffee?"

"Yes, please." Ripley was glad to be seated so he wouldn't see her knees trembling. "With sugar, if you have any."

He got up to make her the coffee, and when his back was turned, Ripley widened her eyes at Emerson, silently questioning his presence. He made a little motion with his hands next to his head as if it were exploding while he puffed out his cheeks, turning his gesture into a face rub as Chang came back with a Styrofoam cup of black coffee. Ripley curled her hands around the cup, enjoying the warmth of it before taking a long drink of the beverage, needing both the caffeine and the sugar in advance of the verbal jousting she had no doubt was coming.

"My scientist, Mr. Davies, is stymied by a few things. Maybe you could help him," Chang began pleasantly. "Since you're here."

"Stymied about what?"

Emerson gestured to the window. "That steam is new, but I haven't been able to determine its origin. The smell of it suggests a deep, volcanic source, but I've not been allowed to go up in a helicopter to scout for it."

"I've told you, the helicopters are for important uses only. I can't be using them for scientific expeditions to quench your curiosity." Chang was dismissive of the young man, and refocused on Ripley. He clicked his tongue in dissatisfaction as she drained her coffee cup. "I'd much rather have someone with more experience to help Emerson, but I'll use what I get. Can you help him?"

Ripley wasted no time countering his offer and tried to school her irritation as she spoke. “I might be able to. In fact, I have a good working theory, but first I want to see my men. I'm sure you understand my concern.”

Chang nodded as if he'd expected her demand. “I'd never harm a helicopter pilot, they've become a rare commodity. Supply sergeants, on the other hand, particularly ones who fight even when they're outnumbered five to one, are a different matter, I'm afraid.”

Ripley's hands went to ice, her gut clenching. “What do you mean?”

“Sadly, your Sergeant Flannery got into a fight which he lost, and he succumbed to his wounds late last night.”

“I don't believe you.”

“You don't want to believe me, but it's true.” He fished out some dog tags on their chain, leaned forward, and dropped them in Ripley's lap. “You may want to hold on to these.”

Her hand shook as she picked up the tag and read Liam Flannery's name on it before she clenched it tightly in her fist. “I still don't believe you.”

He spread his hands. “I have no reason to lie. Your helicopter pilot is in the medical wing. I believe he had either a stroke or a heart attack when he went to Sergeant Flannery's defense, but I can assure you, I have our best doctor at his side.”

The psychic blows from the information dripping from Chang's lips and the silly smile he wore as he spoke them were nearly too much for Ripley, but she curled her toes in her boots and clenched her muscles tightly to hold on to a sliver of calmness. “Your only doctor, I believe you mean.”

There was a flicker in his complacency. “Ah, Sam was chatting with you as he brought you to me?” He shook his head with a sigh. “I thought I could trust him to just do the job.”

Ripley couldn't restrain her impatience any longer, and she was desperate to focus on something else other than the chance Flannery might have died and that Fred was in the care of a doctor. “What exactly do you want from me, Chang?”

He snickered at her anger and then launched into a pompous speech. “Nothing difficult. I want you to call Ordway, and tell him to release the codes for all the FEMA bunkers in the USA so that I and my men can access them, cede all the lands west of the Rockies to me, including the safe zone you so thoughtfully identified on the Navajo and Hopi lands, and to lend you to me permanently. As a gesture of good will, I'll send back his helicopter pilot along with the Black Hawk, and give him Emerson to use as his science advisor, and he can have control of everything east of the Rockies."

It was so grandiose she nearly laughed aloud. "And why would I do any of that?"

"Because you value your life, and the life of your pilot."

"Pretty sure the USA's mandate of not negotiating with terrorists is still something President Ordway adheres to."

"As I said before, we're shaping a new world. New rules are called for, and new leadership."

"I won't be calling anyone until I see both Fred and Flannery." Ripley was firm in her demand.

Chang considered her for a long beat before he sighed. "You know, when you walked into that conference room under the White House a few weeks ago in your cheap black jacket and sensible shoes, I remember wondering what on earth Jerry Johnson had been thinking bringing such a neophyte in to brief the President. Yet you got him, all of us really, out of there in time with the courage of your convictions about the quakes. I feel I might owe you a bit of a debt for that."

"You certainly do. And an apology for leaving the President, his Secret Service men, myself, and Thaddeus behind, trapped in the rubble."

"Well, I had a lot on my mind." Chang had the temerity to chuckle. "A whole militia to activate. Good thing I did, too, or your President Ordway wouldn't have made it out." He tapped his lips with his fingers. "In retrospect, I probably should have just let him suffocate, but at the time, I thought I'd need him as a figurehead."

Emerson's head had been swinging back and forth with their conversation, frowning. He held a tentative hand up. "I'm sorry, I'm not following what you're saying to each other at all." He turned to

Ripley. "You were called in to advise the White House on the quakes?"

"Just after the first one went off in Arkansas. Everyone else from the USGS offices were at a conference in Philly," she explained. "The Chief of Staff had accessed a theoretical paper I'd written on triggered earthquakes and their P-waves, and he figured I was as close to an expert as he was going to get."

"And then you were trapped there?"

"I was, and barely got out, alongside the Director of Homeland Security."

"And then you met back up with the President?"

Ripley gave Chang a sideways glance. "In a manner of speaking."

Chang's lips had turned into a frown, and he crossed and uncrossed his legs. "Emerson, we don't have time to catch you up on everything."

"He needs to know who he's working for," Ripley interrupted, and turned back to face Emerson. "Chang is taking advantage of the disaster to usurp power from the duly elected president. He stole the supplies he has. He's a traitor, through and through."

"That's enough! Benneton!" Chang had lurched to his feet, shouting over the top of her last few sentences.

Ripley did the same, moving so she was only inches from the man. "If you want my help with what that sulfur smell is, and how long you have before this place collapses - and I can tell you it *will* collapse - you'll take me to see my men." She slapped at the guard who'd dashed into the room on Chang's command as he grabbed her shoulders. "Don't you touch me!"

Chang seemed on the verge of ordering her bodily taken from his presence, but Emerson slammed his clipboard onto the floor. "You'll not get any more information from me unless you do what she says."

"You need him!" Ripley said quickly, as consideration moved across Chang's face as he fingered his sidearm. "He can't pull scientific data without testing. If you want answers about the poisonous gases you're inhaling, you'll have to put him and me up in a helicopter. Your time is running out, Chang."

As if to punctuate her words, the ground gave a sharp snap before vibrating violently back and forth, the metal structure above their heads groaning in protest as its structure was compromised by the growing earthquake. Ripley moved to the door frame to get out of the building, but the burly soldier was in her way.

"We can't stay in here!" Ripley yelled, and pushed at him. "Get out!"

The man caught her fear and ran out of the door, with both Ripley and Emerson directly behind him. Chang followed as the shaking became stronger. Cries of fear rang out around the compound as the rattling continued, the bounce becoming so aggressive they couldn't stand, forced to hands and knees to scramble from underneath the tottering radio tower.

The shriek of the metal was long and high as the tower finally succumbed to the power of the earth beneath it. It bent, then ripped from the ground, taking the building they'd just been in and enormous clumps of earth and rock with it, the supporting struts along its length breaking with a series of pops. The generator and the gas next to it exploded as something sparked, a roaring fireball expanding sideways, the sudden heat scorching Ripley's skin as she flattened herself to the ground. The entire structure slid down the hill, taking out the buildings below with a thunderous roar, pushing them before it, creating a tremendous splash as everything entered the bay.

The heaving subsided, then stopped. Ripley stood and helped Emerson to stand as well, moving aside some bricks that had landed on his body. She averted her eyes from the nearby corpse, its back scorched deep black where they'd been caught and consumed by the fireball. Chang rose to his feet, as did the guard that Ripley had pushed outside. Below them, a few people stirred, the low brick buildings, and the hangars still miraculously intact. The Black Hawk stood erect and unharmed as well. The sight of it gave Ripley an idea. With a tug on Emerson's shirt, she ran down the hill, taking advantage of the confusion that reigned supreme in the quake's aftermath. He stumbled after her, both of them hustling as loosened soil ran before their feet in gathering trickles.

"The whole mountainside is liquifying," Ripley said as they ran. "We don't have much time."

"I know," Emerson said grimly, his face wracked with pain as he gripped his right leg.

Behind them, Chang was shouting orders. Ripley risked a glance backward. Both the guard and Chang were charging after them.

"Stop her!" Chang bellowed.

"I'm going after my men in the hospital wing," she panted to Emerson as he lagged behind her, his leg hitching. "Then the Black Hawk, if we can make it."

"I can't run anymore," Emerson gasped out. "You go on."

Ripley threw an anxious look around the compound as she hit the relative stability of the parking lot. In front of her, men gathered in a thin line, running toward her. Her mind spun as she calculated her odds of achieving her objectives.

"Tackle me. Pretend you're still with Chang," she gasped out. "We'll never make it."

He grunted his understanding, snatching at her with his long arms. Ripley shoved him, dashing awkwardly to the side, her movements purposefully slow. In moments, Emerson had tackled her, tumbling them both to the ground before Chang's men reached them.

"I got her!" Emerson shouted. "She's down!" He rolled with her, gripping both of her hands in his as she struggled against him.

He held her in a tight grip while Ripley continued to pretend to try and get away. Chang hustled next to them, the fit man barely breathing hard as the rest of the men who'd been after Ripley circled them. Suspicion etched his features as he stared at them.

"I got her Mr. President!" Emerson said triumphantly.

"Get off of me, you stupid idiot!" Ripley cried, putting everything she had into making Chang believe Emerson was still his ally. Mentally asking forgiveness, she bit the hands which held hers as hard as she could.

Genuine shock rolled across Emerson's features as he snatched his bleeding hand away with a cry of pain. "She bit me!"

Chang grunted, the suspicion fading. "Not bad for a scientist." He gestured to his men. "Put her back in confinement."

The terror of being interred under the ground for a second time seared through Ripley. With a wild cry, she twisted, slamming her shoulder against the ground as she wrenched her arm back and out. Her shoulder popped out of the socket as she purposefully dislocated it, her shriek real as she forced the injury, weeping in the aftermath with the sear of pain. She sold the move by trying to scramble away, sobbing as hands reached for her.

"She's injured," Emerson pointed out as she writhed in agony on the ground, clawing at the pavement. "That woman needs the doctor." He tried to stand, then crumpled again as his leg gave way. "I do, too."

"Take them to the hospital wing," Chang said reluctantly. "And find me another place to bunk."

CHAPTER FIVE

The Wisconsin River
Day Twenty-two and Twenty-three

Braden had become more and more whiny as the hours rolled by on the river. Logan struggled to keep the square raft afloat and away from the myriad of debris that flowed downstream with them in the Wisconsin River. They were mainly simply pushed with the current, the raft difficult to steer even using the makeshift paddle he'd crafted just before they'd left their camp at midday, whittling a piece of soft pine with his combat knife.

Logan turned his wrist to see the time, wincing when he saw that it was late afternoon. They'd gotten a late start because he'd opted to give Braden another swimming lesson, making sure the boy understood how to float on his back with his feet pointing downstream in case the worst happened and they were upended. Braden had proved to be an apt pupil, and had managed to swim several yards, his arms and legs kicking furiously as he moved from the shore to Logan's waiting arms in the safe waters of the little inlet where they'd camped.

"I swam!" the little boy had crowed as he wrapped his arms and legs around Logan and dashed a flop of wet hair from his forehead.

"You sure did, and you had your face in the water too, a lot of kids have trouble with that."

The little boy had beamed at the praise. "Not me!"

"Let's see you get a breath from being face down," Logan had suggested.

Without fear, Braden had plopped into the shallow water face down, and then twisted his body so he floated face up. He puffed in and out several times, waving his arms horizontally next to him to stay atop the water before Logan had scooped him up.

"Excellent! I think that deserves an M&M."

"Two!"

Logan had smartly saved the M&M packet out of one of the military MREs to use as unabashed bribes for the little boy. He'd done the same encouragement campaign with his two kids when they were young, luring them on longer and longer hikes by doling out the candies at intervals along the trail. He had no shame about it all, and the pure bliss that appeared on Braden's face as he sucked on the candy made his day.

Paddle made, and his worries eased slightly by the swim lesson, Logan had broken their camp in the Wisconsin Dells and pushed them back into the main current on their raft, Braden once more firmly between his knees and Whuff ensconced in the backpack.

They'd encountered two more drop offs, but he'd been ready for them. Logan had been able to take them over the silvery curl of water at a diagonal, minimizing the swamping of their little craft. Braden had done a good job clinging to his legs while Logan clamped them together, so although they'd gotten wet, they'd easily bobbed back to moving with the current.

They'd passed Portage and the late afternoon had overtaken them as they drifted into the spreading entry point that was Lake Wisconsin, their pace slowing considerably as the waters of the river poured into the lake, forcing Logan to paddle to keep them moving at all. He hugged the right shoreline, which the map had told him was the most direct route to pick the river up again on the far side. Stroking on first one side and then the other with his single makeshift oar was becoming debilitating, the repetitive motion stressing his healing ribs until he gasped with each stroke and Braden craned his neck to look back at him with concern.

"Want off!" Braden demanded.

"I hear you," Logan gasped as he repressed a moan. "I'm looking for a good place right now."

He kept his eyes ahead, his anxiety mounting when a long line of residential houses came into view along the chewed-up shoreline, but as he paddled them closer, the extent of the destruction became clear, and his tension eased. Some homes had tumbled into the water, while others had been shaken into rubble. Only a wall here and there still stood. One house had collapsed so thoroughly it had become a mound of debris wearing a roof like a hat. Braden stopped wiggling as they slid past the destruction.

"All fall down," he said at last, turning to Logan, his eyes big.

"They did, from the earthquakes."

It pained Logan to watch the boy take in the sight, especially when he recalled it was the toddler's first real look at what had happened to human construction from the natural disaster. Braden had been drugged when Jasper and his party had taken him through La Crosse and the other cities upriver, and before that, he'd been in Minnesota, which had emerged relatively unscathed from the cataclysmic events of the past weeks.

Logan looked for a good place to put in along the ravaged shore, angling further into the lake to take them away from the flocks of buzzards and crows and thick clouds of flies and gnats that swarmed the first sections of shoreline they passed. Chunks of debris left behind by the quakes made a shore landing difficult, as did the trash and dead things eddying in the shallows, which created a barrier he wasn't able to get their blunt raft past. Stymied, and to the point of utter exhaustion, Logan finally steered them toward a half-sunken pier that extended into the lake to help them exit, as the end of the pier had broken off and dropped into the water.

He paddled the raft until it bumped against the pilings and the dropped section of pier. Logan bit his lips in consternation as he studied the possible exit from the lake, their raft rhythmically bumping against it with the gentle movement of the water. Braden would have to climb out first, using the spaced wooden boards of what had been the deck of the pier as a ladder which ascended five feet upward. To Logan's eye, there was just enough room between the boards for Braden's little feet and hands to find purchase and climb to safety, but it was risky. He turned Braden so the little boy faced him, his blue eyes wide and anxious.

Logan smiled and spoke easily, trying to reassure him. "You like going down slides, right?"

"Yus."

"You can climb a ladder to get to the top of a slide, right?"

The little boy's face crinkled as he worked to understand what Logan was saying. Logan moved his hands to help illustrate what he was talking about, then pointed to the broken part of the pier that descended into the water next to their raft. "Climb."

Braden nodded uncertainly, then swung his gaze to the thick boards with the tiny handholds. "Up?"

"Yes, you climb, and then wiggle onto the flat part."

Braden's head swiveled between the boards and Logan, who gave the boy a reassuring smile as he stood him up on the wobbly raft and stretched the boy's hands to the first crack, swallowing his fears. What had looked like a short, easy climb of a couple of feet when he'd been angling toward it was, in actuality, much bigger.

"Just move one hand or one foot at a time, Braden. I'll come up after you."

Braden nodded solemnly and started his climb. Logan helped as best he could, keeping a firm hand under the boy's bottom as he climbed the first few feet, repeating his instructions as the child moved beyond his reach. "Move one foot or one hand at a time, good job."

Logan kept his eyes on Braden the whole way until the little boy's feet disappeared atop the structure. A moment later, Braden popped his head over the edge and grinned.

"Wow! Great job. Okay, go on to shore." Logan waved him on.

Braden nodded, and obediently trotted along the rickety thing until he got to the shore several yards away.

Pressing his hand against his lungs, which hadn't quite been able to get enough air while the boy was climbing, Logan lodged the raft under the piling, so they'd not lose it. He gathered their ground cloth which had lined the bottom of the raft, folded it, and slung it across his shoulders, then tossed the backpack to the flat section, the landing rocking the entirety of the structure in an alarming fashion. Taking a deep, centering breath, Logan moaned as he reached as high as he could, his ribs pinging sharp jolts of protest, and jumped to clutch the upper edge of the pier with his palms, scrambling with his feet and pulling his bodyweight up at the same time. Ungracefully, Logan pulled himself out on his belly, spreading his weight as best he could, the boards bobbing, stressed pilings threatening to snap beneath him as he dragged the backpack along behind him, crawling rather than walking to reach the shore.

Braden clapped his hands together as he reached it. "Good job!" The unbridled enthusiasm for his accomplishment made Logan laugh out loud, and he gathered Braden into a big hug as he surveyed their landing point.

The section of shore was dotted by expensive vacation homes spaced several acres apart, the closest one the owner of the pier they'd used to exit the lake. Together they walked up the sloping lawn to the multi-million dollar home which had fallen into ruins, the big picture windows that had held pride of place at the rear of the home emptied of glass, the wooden second story collapsed onto the mortared stone of the lower section, the interior dark and still. Logan chose a thick stand of bushes which stood at the side of the wrecked home for them to pause and take a long drink of water, needing the space to make a difficult decision, as he could smell the sweet scent of rot grow stronger as they approached the house.

"Braden, I'm going into the house to see if I can find us some food. I want you to stay here."

The fear, which had been mostly absent from the little boy as he'd swum and gotten dunked on the river, and had bravely climbed the pier, appeared as soon as he said the words. Braden flung himself at Logan's legs with a loud cry. "No! No go!"

"Whuff will stay with you," Logan tried to reason with him. "I won't be long."

"No!" the shriek was piercing, the sobs heartrending as the little boy clung to him as hard as his little arms could hold him.

Logan inwardly cursed Jasper and the trauma he'd put the boy through, but he carried blame for the response as well, having left Braden behind early in their time together, thinking it would be the best for the boy. Even further back than that, the child had lost his mother. Braden had good reason to be fearful of people leaving him. He sat on the ground and gathered the shaking boy into his arms and let him cry out his fears, patting his back gently to calm him.

"Let's get Whuff out."

Braden hiccupped as he raised his tear-streaked face to Logan's, his voice tiny. "'Kay."

Logan unpacked the backpack and strapped on his gun, handing the toy to Braden, the residual effects of Braden's fear evident by the way he tracked Logan's every move. A gust of wind swirled around them as he snuggled his toy.

Braden wrinkled his nose, then swiped at it with his sleeve. "Iss stinky."

He got out their wipes and rubbed the boy's face clean. "I need to go into the house, so we have enough to eat." The little face grew mutinous again, so Logan added, "you can stay here, and watch me, or if you want to come with me, I'll have to carry you and you have to close your eyes the whole time, and it's going to be even more stinky inside."

Braden's eyes were enormous as his lip drooped into a pout. "No."

"That's not one of your choices. You either wait for me with Whuff, or if you come into the stinky house, you have to hide your face the whole time."

"NO!"

"Braden." Logan let sternness creep into his tone.

"Stay," he finally said as he pouted, the tears welling again, but this time they were more frustrated than terror-induced.

"I think that's the best choice." Logan emptied the backpack, then made a show of brushing off a section of dying grass revealing the dirt below, and seated Braden beside the patch he'd cleared. "Do you remember your numbers?"

Braden blinked at the transition of subject, then rapidly counted from one to ten in a demonstration. Logan nodded with encouragement and handed him a stick. "I want you to count to ten very slowly, and each time you finish, mark a line in the dirt with the stick. I want to know how many tens you counted when I get back."

The task interested Braden, and he took the stick eagerly, sitting Whuff in his lap. He looked expectantly at Logan, waiting for him to go.

"Count slowly," he'd reiterated, before turning to the house. Behind him he heard the little boy's long, drawn-out rendition of "One."

Logan stepped through the broken glass into what had been a vast living room filled with pure white furniture which was moldering from exposure to the elements. His gun was drawn for caution's sake, but the smell was a good indication no one was going to interfere with his search for food. He shook his head grimly as he recalled it'd been the start of the summer season when the quake had hit, with schools out and people eager to recreate, so the home had likely been full of family members, which would account for the strength of the stench. It was simple to identify where the odors were coming from as he moved deeper into the home and ascended a short flight of stairs to the next level. The people who'd owned the place had died in their bedroom areas crushed beneath the fall of the upper stories of the home. Logan quickly marched past the open corridor which led to those rooms, that portion of the house a collapsed ruin, and made his way along the short corridor leading to the kitchen, partially walking on a wall as the house tilted on a precarious slant.

The kitchen area was enormous, and Logan flashed on what Mara might make of such a place with its expansive marbled counter space, and huge island, the owners going for all white in the kitchen as well. The room as a whole had remained mostly intact, although the floor was littered with dishes and glassware which had been flung out of their cabinets, and a raised crack which had toppled the double-door refrigerator onto its face, partially blocking the entry. Squeezing past it, he was able to open the door to the pantry a few inches, just enough to reach his arm inside to feel for food that might still be viable after nearly a month. Logan hesitated before sticking his hand inside, swallowing against the concern that there would be rats within who'd take an exception to his rummaging around.

Focusing on his needs rather than his fears, Logan stuck his arm inside the space with a quick movement and banged against the wood to scare anything away. His searching fingers touched the sliding kernels of a bag of popcorn that he drew out before eagerly diving back in to find unopened plastic jars of peanut butter and jelly, sleeves of saltine crackers and several cans of ready-made chili. He pulled out a round container of oatmeal, a package of cookies, a box of raisins, and several cans of soda, quickly placing them into his pack before he turned his gaze on the rest of the kitchen.

Logan crossed to the space next to the sink, his spirit buoyed by the finds he'd made so far. They'd used a Keurig for coffee, so he couldn't resupply his stash, but they had bagged tea, and a squeeze container of honey as well as packages of sugar, salt, and pepper, and individual packages of parmesan cheese and red chili flakes that had come from pizza deliveries. He took cooking oil from a cabinet, a flashlight and extra batteries from the drawer, and a box of gallon-sized baggies and aluminum foil as well as an excellent all-purpose knife that had a protective sleeve on it, and a knife sharpener.

Logan opted to take a larger pot with a lid with him as well. He wouldn't be able to fit it in his pack, but if he found a boat, he could keep it and it would be helpful to have a second container to do their cooking and boiling in, and it would be perfect for making popcorn. Logan was hyper-aware that the little boy was outside, counting, the pressure of it constantly in his mind, but he took a quick detour to the hall closet, where he hoped to find something for Braden to wear. Nothing was Braden's size, so he took two rain jackets, a small woman's winter coat, and a baseball cap to replace the one he'd lost at the first drop of the river, as well as a long woolen scarf tucked into the back. Keys to various things hung on a pegboard inside the closet, one of which was marked boat house. He grabbed it and hurried back to Braden.

"How many?"

Braden's tongue stuck out as he counted the marks he'd made with the stick. He paused when it reached more than ten, so Logan helped him. "That's eleven, twelve, and thirteen."

Braden whispered the new numbers under his breath, then louder. The thirteen came out with a bit of a lisp, but when Logan had asked him to count to thirteen again, he was able to do so on the first try.

"I'd say that deserves a chocolate chip cookie," Logan remarked casually, grinning when the boy lit up.

The day was growing short, so Logan built them a campsite in a copse of short firs which stood between houses, building a Dakota pit fire as a stout breeze blew off the lake to keep the flames both alive and hidden as they cooked their feast of canned chili and popcorn, topped off with a half a can of soda each. He boiled more water to fill their containers, and took one of his pain pills against his exertions of the day, and gave another half of a Benadryl pill to Braden, who'd been rubbing his head with a little frown and getting whiny, both signs he was having withdrawals from the massive doses of medication he'd been given.

"Story?" Braden had asked hopefully as he wiggled into the cozy coat Logan had obtained and wrapped Whuff carefully in the scarf.

"I know an excellent story about a bear named Winnie the Pooh," he'd said. "How about that one?"

They woke up refreshed the next day and feasted on oatmeal that Logan added roasted acorns, raisins, and honey to before they packed. Logan took the time to double-bag the food and medicine he didn't want to get wet in the plastic bags from the house, as well as bagging the gun and ammo. Their next order of business was to find the boat house that belonged to the key he'd found. He let Braden lead the way on the hunt, making a game of it, the little boy jumping up and down when he found a rigid prefabricated metal storage shed which was remarkably intact. Once Logan had unlocked the bolt, he wrestled his way through the door, which had been knocked out of line with its frame. The inside was filled with a massive pile of junk that had made Logan heave a sigh before he tackled it.

He found heavy work gloves after a few minutes, which he immediately put to use, as the place had not only been a boat house but also the storage for garden equipment and seasonal decorations. The tall metal shelving holding it all had collapsed, adding sharp, angular shafts to the heap. The job was daunting, but they couldn't go further in the raft without a massive effort of paddling on his part, so he kept pulling aside bits and pieces until he unearthed treasure.

"Well, will you look at that?" Logan broke into a huge grin. "Just what we needed."

Pushing away more debris, and pocketing several packages of carrot, tomato, and marigold seeds for Mara, Logan hauled his find out into the light with loud crashes and scraping of metal as he shoved and pushed. He proudly showed it to Braden. "Our new boat," he explained as he ran his hands over the pretty twelve-foot long aquamarine kayak, checking for damage beyond the scratches he'd just given its hull.

The kayak had a dry hatch as well as room fore and aft to stow bigger items, and as he picked it up to turn it over, he grinned in delight at the ease with which he could lift it. He guessed the craft weighed less than fifty pounds and it had a cushioned, adjustable seat which would support his back and plenty of room for Braden to sit in front of him if he put the footpegs in the lowest setting.

"I just need to find the paddle," he told the boy.

It took a lot of digging, but Logan finally found the double-bladed kayak paddle near the bottom of the shed. He shouted with glee as he hefted it like a spear. "We're going to have a much easier time of steering!"

He went back a third time to search for life vests, but came up empty for the safety equipment, although he did find a pair of outdoor chair cushions for Braden to sit on in the boat, which would also make their night camps more comfortable. After packing up their gear, he hauled the boat to the edge of Wisconsin Lake and placed their backpack in the rear of the enclosed space of the kayak, and the extra cookpot in the front.

The sleek craft was easily pushed into the disgusting churn coating the shore of the lake, a mix of dirty brown foam, pieces of debris and evil-smelling vegetation. Logan adroitly seated himself before placing the cushions one in front of the other, so they folded along the sides of the craft, both cushioning and insulating the front of the kayak. He swiveled to help Braden clamber in and settle in front of him, the little boy wiggling in delight at his new perch.

The kayak had good stability, but still rocked quite a bit as he got settled, so Logan draped one of the raincoats around Braden's front against splashes. With a few easy strokes of the double paddle, Logan cut through the mess of the shoreline toward their old raft. Logan paused and took a few minutes to untie the paracord he'd used to tie the raft together, coiling and stuffing the four pieces of line into the dry hatch, and then with a farewell wave to the collection of floating branches which had once been their intrepid little craft, they arrowed across the inlet to the main body of the lake.

Logan had studied his map the night before and kept to his original plan of hugging the right shoreline. They made good time, Braden trailing his fingers in the cool waters or pointing out big blue herons and massive flocks of crows. A gigantic black bear with two cubs pawed through some trash at the side of the lake as they paddled by, eliciting a round eyed gasp of delight from Braden. They passed a large number of soft shell turtles in the water as well, the animals flippering gracefully out of the way of their boat, their movements mirroring the quick flicks of the swallows in the sky.

The idyllic interlude was short-lived as the sound of thundering in the distance let Logan know they were coming to another dangerous section of the river, the place where it had been dammed at the lower end of the lake. Directly after it, the river narrowed as it passed through the heart of Prairie du Sac. Logan's chest tightened, as did his shoulder muscles. The narrows would make it easy for people to ambush them, and they were prime targets riding atop the sleek kayak.

Logan kept a lookout for a takeout for the kayak as they got closer to the big dam which had been split in several different places, the water pouring through in fast gouts of water, but there was nothing accessible still standing. He paddled backwards against the building current that rushed toward the dam, considering their options, frowning deeply as he strained against the water. Logan reluctantly came to the conclusion they only had one option, which was to let the kayak carry them over the falls created by the broken dam to reach the lower section of the river. The kayak was built for rapids, so he was confident of the integrity of their craft, but not of his guidance, nor did he know how big the drop would be. His heart raced as he bent to Braden, already needing to raise his voice over the noise made by the upcoming fall.

"Hold on to my legs and push your feet against our pot as hard as you can, okay?"

Braden didn't respond, but his little arms gripped around the bottom of Logan's knees, which he then squeezed tightly around the little boy, keeping his feet on the footpegs to maintain the stability of the boat. He stopped backpaddling, instead began whipping the paddle in and out of the water to get them moving as fast as possible with the current as he steered them to the widest of the breaks in the dam.

Muttering a short prayer as he dug in the last few strokes, he jammed the paddle securely into the boat with one hand and kept his grip on it while he curled his other arm around Braden's shoulders and leaned back to jam his shoulders tightly into their craft as the kayak tipped over the edge of the dam, hurtling twenty feet straight down. He and Braden screamed out in a mix of terror and adrenaline-induced excitement as they plunged nose-first into gut-clenching, freezing cold water that bubbled in black and white as they were forced under by the force of the water. They tumbled sideways beneath the water for two rotations before the buoyant craft bobbed to the surface, spinning in the white water below the dam, the thundering fall pushing them away and into a raging current. He immediately checked Braden, who was coughing and sputtering, his face pale.

"You did it, we're good!" Logan shook with cold and residual fear as he held the boy close, panting for air.

"Not good," the little boy protested as he coughed and spat, but he wasn't crying. "Not fun."

"No, but we're out now. I'm going to paddle really fast past the town. I want you to lie flat until I tell you to get up."

"Iss all wet." The little boy fisted a handful of water from the inside of the boat, his voice echoing with defiance and disbelief at what Logan was asking him to do.

"Everything's wet Braden, we'll get dried off later. Lay down like I told you."

Braden pulled a face, but did as he was told, and Logan used the extra room it gave him to dig deep and use his shoulders and core to paddle past the looming city of Prairie du Sac as fast as he could, grateful for the extra push the pounding water behind them gave to their speed as they passed a collection of tents perched on the banks above them. His spine itched, and he paddled even harder as they zoomed by several men standing watch with rifles, bending in half to protect himself and Braden as he anticipated bullets to come ripping after them, but the guns had remained silent.

"Moving too fast, maybe," he whispered to himself, but kept paddling rapidly until the city disappeared from view, and then added another few miles before his muscles began to cramp and he was forced to slow his pace.

"Okay, you can sit up again, buddy."

Braden wiggled himself upright and shivered. "Cold."

"I have another jacket for you, hold on."

Logan pulled the woolen coat and second rain jacket out of the dry storage and removed the first raincoat and his soaked shirt, pushing them to the front of the kayak before he wrapped the two coats around Braden to help warm him. He also pulled out a stash of cookies he'd put by in anticipation of needing a snack. They both munched on the treats and had a drink of water as they let the current continue to carry them while Logan rested and took one of his last heavy-duty pain pills.

He watched the banks slip by, counting between geographical points, and figured the river was moving at four miles an hour. With his paddling, he could bring their speed up to six or seven miles per hour. The Mississippi was about eighty miles from their current position, according to the rough calculations Logan had done the night before, so they could do a bit more than half the distance before they had to stop for the night. Then they had another two hundred miles from the confluence of the Mississippi and the Wisconsin rivers to reach the little town above Burlington, where Mara's aunt and uncle had their homestead.

"We want to get there in daylight hours," he said with a rueful chuckle. "So Willard doesn't shoot me."

His wife's uncle had a poor opinion of trespassers, and had bragged about "winging" people who'd wandered onto his property enough times that Logan took him seriously. He looked skyward as he did the math in his head and calculated once he was on the Mississippi, two long twelve-hour days of paddling with the current would hopefully put him within thirty miles of Helen and Willard's farm, so they'd be arriving around midday or a bit later.

"I can do it," he told himself. "Barring any surprises."

CHAPTER SIX

Eastern Tennessee Seismic Zone
Days Twenty-four and Twenty-five

Deb groaned as she dismounted from her horse behind a copse of trees that hid her from the road. She had to grab the stirrup to stop herself from falling to the ground as her lower back gave her a vicious stab, and her inner thighs tremored. Daisy turned her neck to look at Deb reproachfully as the movement yanked on her torso. The horse snorted and shook her head in disapproval, her tawny mane flipping from one side of her neck to the other.

"Sorry, girl." Deb stroked the sorrel's neck as she reached into the pocket of her roomy jean jacket for a carrot. "You've been doing all the work, haven't you?"

Deb flat-handed the treat to the animal, who happily lipped it from her, chomping on the treat as her back foot cocked up. Over the past two and a half days of riding, Deb had come to recognize when Daisy shifted to stand on three legs that meant the horse was ready for a rest. She turned to look back to the west, the direction they'd come from, then continued her turn to survey their entire surroundings to be sure they were alone before she pulled the map of

Tennessee Kevin had provided from the inner pocket of her jean jacket.

She fought the map's folds to open it to the correct section, chuckling to herself as she did so, remembering the road trips before cell phones when battling a paper map had been a daily occurrence. "Everything old is new again," she muttered, tracing the route she'd chosen from Kevin's ranch to her approximate location, just north of Murfreesboro. They'd made decent time, traveling roughly seventy miles over the two and a half days, and had encountered no resistance, except for necessary detours around the gigantic cracks which had continued to widen, and stopping when the ground gave a shake beneath Daisy's hooves.

She stroked the horse's white blaze. "No really big earthquakes for a few days. Maybe they're calming down. What do you think, Daisy?"

The horse just gave her a lazy blink as she settled into her resting pose. Deb turned her attention back to the map. She'd turned off the long ring road that circled Nashville to the south and had picked up Lascassas road to take her further east. The route was taking her through what had been a series of bedroom communities and upper-crust neighborhoods with the attendant mini-malls and restaurants. On the map it had appeared to be a minor road compared to the I-40 to the north, but it had turned out to be more urban than she would have liked. Twice, the sound of ATVs closing on her location had alerted her, forcing Deb to kick Daisy into a run so they could get behind some cover.

"Once we reach the end of this road, I'm taking the Nashville Highway east through Smithville to Sparta and on up to Crossville." The route had a few rivers to cross, but it avoided the bigger cities that lined the I-40. Deb tucked the map away and rubbed her thighs, wincing at their tenderness. She eyed the saddle with distaste and swiveled to gaze at their surroundings once again, her nerves still jumping from their near encounters with other humans.

A cluster of what had been large, three and four-thousand square foot homes loomed nearby, climbing a low hill to form a graceful arc around a central pond. Several of the homes still had a second story, which meant the likelihood of survivors was higher. Deb shook her head and frowned. Although it had a water source, it wasn't a safe area to stay in for any length of time.

"Technically, we're on day three," she continued conversing with the horse. "So tomorrow would be a rest day for both of us. As much as I hate to say it, Daisy, we need to go another five miles or so and get ourselves into a rural area, a place where we can stop for two full nights without worrying too much about running into people."

Deb took a long drink from her water bottle before tucking it back into the pannier, grasped the pommel of the heavy-duty western saddle, and hauled herself back on the horse. Settling her green John Deere cap more firmly on her head, she laid the reins over Daisy's neck and gave a light kick to get the mare moving again. As they continued east walking parallel to the road in the long grasses, the homes got further and further apart, becoming farmhouses instead of mansions, the fenced fields attached to them growing a variety of dying crops. The low rise of hills in front of them, which had been misty, became more distinct. A breeze blew up as afternoon turned to early evening, blowing dust and debris to scuttle across the cement road.

A plastic bag caught the wind, flipping and turning in the air as it floated ahead of them, the motion mesmerizing and balletic as it drifted, its windblown dance ending as it snagged in a bush which had been partially uprooted by a thin crack snaking across the road. Deb was half-tempted to dismount and grab it to use for waterproofing or carrying something in the future, but dismissed it, discouraged by the idea of getting off and on the horse even one more time than was necessary.

The trickle of water caught her ear, and in a few more steps, a small stream appeared from under the road and burbled to their right. Deb angled the horse to follow the steady trickle for several hundred yards into a mix of scrub and low bushes, skirting the corner of a denuded field. She only needed to clip her way through a barbed wire fence once to continue following the rivulet. They came to a dip in the land where the stream gathered itself in a shallow pool before it fell in a happy rush for two feet over ancient stones grown smooth from the water's movement. The lower part of the stream was lined with an extensive brushy area near the stream and had some clear sections of long grasses that would be good for the horse to crop. Further back, a sizeable mixed stand of beech trees, sweetgums, and black oaks interspersed with a few stunted water oaks and hazel alders rattled their leaves in a welcoming sound. Poison ivy wrapped around the base of some of the trees, but she'd be wearing gloves when she gathered wood for her fire, so she'd be safe from the plant.

Paw-paw trees with clusters of ripening fruits growing near the bigger trees made Deb smile. Seeing them was like a sign from her sister that she'd found a good place to camp. Paw-paws were Mara's favorite fruit to forage in the wild, with their creamy centers that tasted like a mix of banana and mango. Deb sniffed the air, the tropical scent of the ripening fruit clusters pungent, their color ranging from light green to yellowing with black spots over their skins, just waiting to be harvested. The scent transported her with a flash of bright memory. Her sister grinning at her when they found a patch of them at the edge of the forested lands near her homestead in Roanoke. They'd opened several of the fruits right then with Mara's foraging knife, inhaling the custardy treats, and spitting out the big seeds before gathering the rest to take home to the kids.

Deb stood in the stirrups to scan the horizon in all directions. The road was out of sight, and the closest building was a partially fallen barn, its once-proud, red-painted walls slumped to one side about a half mile away. Beyond it was a wrecked two-story farmhouse. She didn't see any movement, lights, or the flicker of a campfire in any direction, nor did she hear the roar of any machines, just the sigh of the wind through the trees and the trickle of the stream. With an extended sigh of relief, she dismounted.

"This is going to be our camp tonight and all day tomorrow, Daisy."

She stretched, her aching muscles welcoming the slow movement after so long in the saddle when she wasn't used to it. When Kevin had told her the horse would need a full rest every fourth day, she'd accepted his experience, but had inwardly chafed at the idea of extending the timeframe of her journey, though as she took the panniers off of Daisy and set to work setting up a camp by the little burbling stream, she could admit she needed the rest just as much as the horse did.

Tending to her mount was the first order of business. Deb took Daisy's tack off and laid the bit to the side to clean. She used Daisy's lead rope, which had been looped around the pommel of the saddle, to take her to the flat pool of water to drink her fill. After the requisite carrot treat for being an excellent horse, Deb gave her a thorough brushing and picked her hooves clear of the small stones and mud she'd picked up during the day's journey, the horse patiently allowing her to pick up one hoof at a time. Once she was done, Deb placed leather hobbles on her front legs and let the horse wander free to crop the long grass at the edge of the stream. She paused to dig several dandelions from the edges of the grass to add their greens to her own evening meal, as well as some broad-leafed ramps, which tasted like a mix of garlic and onion. As she collected them, she thanked her sister mentally for teaching her some of the plants that were good to forage.

Deb placed her two-night camp in an area which was flat and ringed on three sides by thick growths of winterberry and dogwood bushes to hide her presence. She chose a spot far enough away from the trees so they wouldn't fall on her during one of the big quakes. It was only a few yards from the stream, making the gathering of water an easy chore. Deb scraped an area free of grasses, digging down about ten inches with her camping spade, so the fire wouldn't be noticeable unless someone was right on top of her, and it would be contained in a quake. Moving to the trees, she gathered bundles of dry sticks and leaves, then used her hand axe to split several thicker branches to get thicker kindling. Wanting a long-burning fire which would burn for the duration of her stay, she found a downed tree in the thicket, then chopped and dragged a couple of two-foot long logs from it to her dug out space, making sure there was air flow between and beneath them by propping them up with a few stones she'd removed from the soil when clearing it.

She used the ferro rod to spark into the dried leaves and kindling she'd placed directly on top of the big branches, patiently adding fuel in building sizes until the fire had charred into the slightly damp wood of her base. Deb placed two more logs perpendicular to the fired logs and placed her metal grill and cookpot on top of them to heat her first pot of water. While it was warming, she affixed her tarp to two short poles and created a low tent that didn't stick above the brush line, pegging it in firmly on the sides. She unfolded the ground cloth to cover the inner space, then placed the saddle and tack, panniers, rifle, and her backpack along one side. She put the horse blanket down for insulation against the slightly damp ground, then unrolled her blanket roll on top of it. Deb pulled out her single change of clothes as the sun began to set, as well as the puffy jacket and hat Kevin had given her to wear during the night, when the temperatures plummeted.

The boiled water was strained into two water containers, then she set another pot to warm so she could wash herself, her hair, and her clothes by the stream. She moaned slightly as she scrubbed her fingers across her scalp, massaging her neck and shoulders. Deb used a sliver of soap to clean the thick accumulation of dust and sweat from her skin, using a hand towel to rub herself dry as night folded over the campsite.

As she thrust her legs into her spare pair of jeans, put on a fresh t-shirt and underwear, changed her socks, and pulled on a long-sleeved dark blue chambray shirt, Deb reflected that clean clothes had become a luxury, rather than a rote experience for her. Using a rock she found near the stream, she pounded out the dirt from her clothes, rinsed them with warm water, then squeezed them out and draped them on the bushes to dry.

Her belly growling, Deb pulled a can of spam from her dwindling food supply, sliced it, and put it in the pot to cook along with the last two small potatoes from Kevin's garden chopped fine, roasting in the fat from the canned meat. She tossed in minced ramps and dandelion greens at the end to give her meal extra vitamins, seasoning it from the twist of salt and pepper he'd added to her supplies. She finished her meal by eating three of the paw-paws plucked straight from the tree, tossing the seeds and rinds back in the same area so more trees could eventually flourish there.

Daisy had wandered back near Deb from her own evening meal and, with a sigh, folded her legs and lay on the grasses not far from the fire. The red of the fire danced off of the russet of her coat. Deb smiled at the animal, glad of its presence, although she ached with missing both Renny and Kevin as companions.

"Going to have to forage some food from somewhere tomorrow, but you don't have to go," she told the horse as she downed some ibuprofen and a multivitamin to close out her meal. Rinsing her pot in the stream, she pulled out another potful of water to boil before she banked the big logs for the night, the smoke from some green branches that she piled on top creating a decent bug deterrent, and the extra warmth welcome. She put on her puffy jacket and hat, pulled out her gun so it was near to hand, then Deb wrapped the bedroll around herself and fell instantly to sleep.

The following morning Deb woke early, the darkness just beginning to give way to the ubiquitous grey covering of ashy clouds which had become the norm. She ate a granola bar and allowed herself two cups of coffee before banking the fire again so it would safely smolder in her absence. Deb slung her emptied backpack over her shoulder along with the rifle, and belted Honey, the gun she'd inherited from her nurse friend in Memphis, onto her waist. She patted the horse in farewell and made her way across the field behind her camp to check out the barn and farmhouse, which were the nearest dwellings.

She took her time crossing the open space of the field, stopping often to listen for any sounds that might betray human inhabitation, but after a half hour of stealthy approach, Deb was at the side of the big barn. It was only partially tumbled but had the deserted feel empty dwellings always seemed to possess. There was something else underpinning the emptiness that had the hairs on her arms standing on end that she struggled to identify. After a long hesitation studying her surroundings, Deb peeped around the front of the structure a final time to be sure she was alone, then made her way to the small door within the larger barn doors, which were firmly sealed with a lock. Catching the sickly sweet scent of death emitting from the barn, she hesitated again before pulling her kerchief over her nose and mouth, then eased the smaller door open.

A rancid stench of decay which had festered too long in a mostly enclosed space had her slamming the door shut seconds after opening it, coughing violently, her gut heaving as she fought to keep her breakfast down. There had been many animals lodged in the barn and they'd not died well.

Several deep breaths later, Deb gave herself a little shake to compose herself as she looked toward the farmhouse, her uneasiness building. Part of the roof had caved in, and the front porch had collapsed, but the foundation had held strong, as had all four walls. It appeared that the kitchen and its pantry at the back would be intact. She could gather tinned goods without risking entering a town, but the horrible smell had rattled her to the point where her fingers were still trembling.

"Don't be a potato head," she told herself sternly, using one of Kevin's disdainful nicknames to try to steady herself. "Just go to the back door. There's no one in there, or they'd have taken care of the poor animals in that barn."

Drawing a shaky breath, Deb undid the holster strap on her Ruger and brought the rifle around her shoulder to hold at the ready. She kept her eyes moving as she crossed the yard between house and barn, noting a chicken coop whose frame had bent and twisted in an upheaval which had left half of it a good foot higher than the other half, the structure empty of birds.

Step by step, she approached the back entry. A few yards from it was an overgrown kitchen garden. Deb paused at its edge, her hands still trembling, before she gathered her courage and ascended the three concrete steps that led to the back door. The knob turned easily in her hand, the door sticking slightly, the wood swollen into the frame. It gave with a sudden burst as she pushed, so she nearly fell into the farmhouse kitchen.

She had a quick glimpse of three bodies lying in the tumbled kitchen, their bodies black with decay on a green linoleum floor. Deb flung her hand over her nose and mouth at the foul stench that rolled through the air, the taint of it more than just death. It reeked of contagion, of sweat, vomit, and oddly of burnt shoe leather. It was the same stench the barn had produced, just in less quantity, but horrific all the same. Any thought of foraging anything from the terrible place fled as she heaved the door shut again and stumbled down the three steps, falling to her hands and knees, coughing to rid her throat of the awfulness that had swirled inside the dwelling.

Not looking at the terrible place again, Deb crossed to the overgrown garden. Fighting her desire to look over her shoulder every few seconds, she rapidly picked a few overripe tomatoes, pulled onions and several handfuls of turnips, parsnips, and carrots, barely registering what her hands were doing as her mind tumbled with the implications of the contents of the house. Green beans hung thickly on vines, most past their prime, full of bug holes and rot, but she was able to garner a handful that were still edible. In the herb section, she gratefully gathered handfuls of basil and rosemary, crushing the sweet smelling, prickly herb to her nose to lessen the phantom odor that still lingered in her olfactory senses.

Stuffing her backpack as quickly as she could with the bounty of the garden, Deb wasted no more time at what she'd mentally dubbed "the contagion house," and crossed the long fields which had once been farmed by the occupants at top speed, glad of the distance between her camp and the house. Once she returned, she stripped off her clothes, built up the fire and heated more water. Shivering with cold, Deb scrubbed herself in the stream, following the wash by swiping antibiotic wipes over the skin that had been exposed. She scrubbed the clothes she'd been wearing in hot water and soap, pulling on her still-damp clothing she'd washed the night before in their stead, even though the clinging moistness was annoying.

Contagion was something she knew intimately from her years in the ER, taking care of people who'd caught bugs from others or from tainted food and waited until it was nearly too late to get their persistent cough or tummy trouble checked by a doctor. While modern medicine had done a wonderful job of eradicating a lot of formerly lethal diseases, pathogens were patient and getting stronger all the time as they grew resistant to the things used to kill them. The earthquakes had killed hundreds of thousands of people in a very short time. Most had not been buried, so it stood to reason that viruses and other organisms had taken advantage of the lapse, and were multiplying.

Boiling water had always made sense, but it would be a necessity in the coming years, until the scavengers and time took care of the problem of the dead. Deb held herself and rocked as she forced herself to face the medical facts about the aftermath of a mass extinction. Humanity would be culled again by disease, even after the quakes stopped their destructive force. Disease and the actions of people like Trent, Dale Thompson and the Bozemans, who believed the world owed them more than their fair share, whose need to feel powerful and in charge stripped them of their humanity and compassion.

She shuddered at the inevitability that she and all the survivors of the quakes faced. Breathing in deeply to steady herself as she wiped away the tears that kept falling, Deb's determination to reach her sister as soon as possible intensified. In a world where a once-easily curable illness could become fatal, her sister and family needed her nursing skills more than ever.

She was startled out of her horrible reverie when Daisy nudged her shoulder firmly, the horse nearly knocking her over. Deb stood and wrapped her arms around the mare's neck, burying her nose in the agreeable smell of horse and grass, the solid warmth of the animal soothing her wild thoughts. The horse stood the embrace patiently for a few moments, then stamped her front hoof and nudged her shoulder again.

"You smelled the carrots, didn't you?" Deb said when she'd steadied herself. "You're right, I found some fresh ones." She gave one to the mare.

Deb resolutely busied herself with washing the vegetables she'd gleaned, and made a tomato-based stew with them, adding in some of her dried noodles to give it more heft. She fed a few of the carrots to Daisy as the meal simmered, as well as a crunchy turnip. The horse seemed a bit puzzled by it at first, perhaps expecting an apple, but ate it in only a few bites all the same.

After her meal, Deb was restless, and with too much of the day left before she could bed down, she finally got to her feet again, slinging the empty backpack on once more. "I'm going to see what else I can forage," she told Daisy with a pat, then hesitated. She dug in the panniers until she found her single N95 mask she'd had since she found some at her old hospital in Memphis. She eyed the dirty front of it, and the fraying along the elastic that wrapped around her ears with disdain, but tucked it into the side pocket of her pack.

"Better to have something than nothing," she commented to Daisy, who merely flicked her ears and went back to contentedly munching grass.

Deb followed the stream back to the road, pausing to mentally mark a cluster of plantains to pick on her way back to add to the remains of her vegetable stew, as well as the location of more dandelions. Bending and stooping had helped her to stretch her sore muscles, and the steady pace of walking was a balm to her troubled thoughts. Before long, she was back at the road where they'd turned off for the night. Deb tightened her grip on the shoulder straps of the backpack. Going into any formerly inhabited region had proved to be a dangerous proposition over and over again, but she needed more tinned and dried goods for the days ahead. It was a risk she was going to have to take, and doing it in a tiny town was a better choice than a larger one. Her hands damp with perspiration, Deb pulled out Honey and held the pistol as she walked along the road to the east, passing several small farms before reaching a gas station, her senses on high alert, the knots in her shoulders building.

The gas station would have been a treasure trove for her at one point. It was the kind of service area that contained fast food, as well as a small grocery store besides dispensing gas, but it had been turned into a pile of rubble and had also suffered an explosion and consuming fire at some point over the past weeks, leaving a charred hole where the gas tanks had stood. The grocery area had been obliterated, only a few metal shelves left to speak to its former iteration. A mechanic shop stood adjacent to the place, the cars that had been in the shop charred hulks. She passed it by and continued along the road, averting her eyes from the corpses that lay where they'd fallen in both store and shop trying to escape the conflagration.

A combination hair salon and beauty supply was the next building that appeared on her route. A single story red brick, it had only partially fallen. Putting on her mask, Deb stepped carefully through the broken glass of the main window. She poked through the downed shelving and beauty stations which were closest to the front of the store, finding a pair of sharp scissors and a stack of three unused N95 masks. Deb discarded her old one, replacing it with one of the new ones immediately, and moved into the beauty supply section. As she searched through the piles of broken containers, she found several tubes of hand cream and some facial cream in a high SPF that she put into her bag, as well as a bottle of her favorite shampoo and three bars of soap.

She moved on through the store, wracking her brain for different uses for the products which were still intact and scattered on the floor in front of her. Nail polish remover could be used as a disinfectant. Vaseline and a bag of cotton balls could be added to her first aid supplies. Her search also yielded a stash of gum and bagged candy, as well as several bottles of water.

The dim confines of the place lacked the haunted feel that had emanated from the farmhouse and the gas station, and it appeared as if there were no corpses hidden among the rubble, so Deb was emboldened to squeeze past a tumbled wall and go deeper into the store to enter the area where the employees had small lockers. They lay in a toppled heap, but some were still accessible with a bit of digging. Inside one she found two cans of soda, and in another a paperback legal thriller book she'd not read by an author she liked. The little kitchenette had a few instant ramen soup cups that were still intact, as well as packaged sugar and dried creamer, and her best find, a whole can of coffee and coffee filters.

"Renny would be jumping up and down with joy," Deb murmured with a smile as she tucked the finds into her backpack, along with a hand-held can opener and several plastic utensils. The backpack was about half-full, and she considered calling it a day and hiking back to camp, but then sighed. Her discoveries had been well and good, but aside from the noodles, she'd added nothing of real food value to her supplies.

"Onward," Deb told herself firmly. "There's got to be a grocery or a convenience store beyond what the gas station offered. Or a coffee shop."

The weight of the backpack was comforting as it nestled between her shoulder blades, but her nerves had created a sheen of sweat that caught the dust rising in swirls from the destruction of the main section of town. The tail end of a red firetruck turned on its side blocked her passage, the wheels blown from hitting a rift that ran across the width of the road, heaving half of it two feet above the other side, the wide crack between them one of the hideous, dark vertical shafts which by all appearances simply dropped to the center of the earth. Deb moved along the edge of the monstrosity until she could leap over the crack with no danger of slipping into it and continued along the single block that made up the center of the town.

Earthquake damage was heavy, with most of the stores and two churches that had lined the road in tattered heaps. From what stuck out from them, Deb determined one had been an appliance shop, another the post office, and the third a diner. She paused in front of the diner, but whatever had been in it was well buried under its roof. She'd need the camping shovel to even make a beginning to rummage for canned goods, so she carried on.

A low tremor vibrating through the ground had her crouching low just before the quake hit, the slam of the ground kicking her into the air just as she did so, tumbling her to the ground, where she rolled helplessly with the quake. It was fast, hard, and violent in its motion, but mercifully the shaker passed within a few seconds, leaving a thick cloud of dust and debris swirling in its aftermath. Deb brushed herself off and walked on, determined to make the trip from camp worth her while.

She crossed the road to check on the businesses on the other side of the street. A second hand store offered no food that she could find, and the pizza place was equally as destroyed as the diner had been. The other building appeared to have been law offices and the police station, all buried beneath a pile of rubble, inaccessible without some heavy equipment or more people to help.

Beyond the block of businesses was the firehouse the truck had belonged to, and then it was back to single-family dwellings sitting far apart on wide lots, simple chain-link fences surrounding property lines. Her steps slowed as she considered looking inside any of them. After her experience at the farmhouse, Deb was reluctant to try going into anyone's home again, especially these mid-century brick homes which hadn't been built to withstand quakes, and were more likely to contain corpses inside than not.

A series of sharp barks had her whirling. To her surprise, two little Chihuahuas raced toward her, their intent to attack her clear as their tiny paws raced across the lawn of one of the fenced yards. They hurled themselves against the metal fencing one after the other like tiny time bombs, bouncing off it, gathering themselves and leaping at it again, yapping all the while, eyes bulging.

"Barty, Briar! Enough!" A slightly mussed older woman with snow-white hair partially pulled into a braid, leaning on a cane, hobbled to the front porch of her home to shout at the dogs, who continued to snarl and yip. She waved at Deb, acting as if the encounter was an everyday occurrence. "Sorry about that! They've got minds of their own."

Deb lifted her hand in response. "No problem." She hesitated, then went on. "Are you okay?"

"Right as rain, dear, thanks for asking." The woman gave her a gummy smile. "Weather's still terrible, isn't it? Don't know where the sun's gone." She squinted at Deb, her sunny disposition turning ugly in the space of a breath. "What're you wearing a diaper on your face for?"

Deb lowered her mask and approached the fence, studying the woman. "Allergies," she responded lightly as she looked skyward. "I think the clouds are here to stay for a while. I meant do you have enough food and water? Your town is in rough shape if you need resupplying," Deb went on, indicating the rubble that lay behind her.

"I've got a good bunch of what I need, and my granddaughter and her husband will be coming soon to fetch me." The woman gave a kindly if dismissive wave to Deb. "Take care."

"Excuse me," Deb called out as the woman turned slowly to limp back inside, the little two-pack of dogs leaving the fence to run after her. "How do you know they're coming?"

"Got my phone, don't I? I was just talking to them the other day, said they'd be by."

While the woman seemed sure of herself, the phones had been the first things to go just minutes after the first quakes hit. Deb's curiosity compelled her to continue the conversation. "How long ago?"

"You're a pesky sort, aren't you?" She sniffed disdainfully, then turned her eyes skyward to think. "Maybe two days ago, or three, or..." Her face went fuzzy, her whole body frozen as she got lost in the middle of her sentence.

Deb edged closer to the chain-link fence since the dogs had ceased hurling themselves at it, studying the older woman with a clinical eye. "Do they live nearby?"

"Yes, of course they do, just two towns over, dear." She waved a hand in a general easterly direction, then let it hang there a moment, forgotten. With a sharp intake of breath, she came back to herself, and looked around and appeared to be confused she was standing on the porch. "Must get inside. My tea is nearly ready. I do like my hot tea."

The casual comment put Deb on alert, as there was no electricity or gas working to make hot tea, any more than there were phones that still worked. "I'd love a cup of tea," she said. "May I join you?"

"I'm not in the habit of letting strangers into my home, young miss!"

"I understand." Deb was at a loss how to help the elderly woman, who was quite frail. Her wildly vacillating mood swings were also worrying. "Would you like a soda? I have one in my bag."

"Tea will do me fine, dear. Run along, I'm sure your mother is worried about you, it's nearly suppertime."

"Can I visit you tomorrow, please?" Deb called out as the woman shuffled to the doorframe. "School's out," she added as the woman wrinkled her nose, about to turn her down, hoping the woman's ideation that she was just a child would help.

"If you'd like, dear. I'll see you then. There might even be cookies." She paused to let the dogs inside with her, the screen slamming behind her as she disappeared.

Deb stood on the sidewalk, her heart aching for the woman who was suffering from perhaps Alzheimer's or dementia. "You can't help everyone," she reminded herself, the words bringing an even deeper pang, which made her rub her chest to rid herself of it. Even though the statement was true, it didn't salve her dismay. It wasn't as if she could bring the woman and her dogs on the road with her, not knowing what lay ahead. She was best off in the comfort of her own home, even though staying there was more than likely to end in her death.

Biting her lips in frustration, Deb turned with determination to the houses just past the elderly woman's, intent on finding some food and water to leave on her porch, even if she could do nothing else for her. Stopping only to affix her mask more firmly around her nose and mouth, Deb walked to the back of the home and knocked on the back door, stepping well back with her gun at the ready, even though she didn't expect a response. When none came, she squared her shoulders and stepped inside.

CHAPTER SEVEN

The Blacksburg/Pembroke Fault
Day Twenty-five

"They got a plan to take over all the land 'round these parts, and to hunt you all down while they're at it."

Eva's words about the extended Crowe clan descending into their valley echoed through Mara's mind as she completed the chores which needed doing for her family to survive. Mixing her sourdough starter with a combination of white and wheat flours in her latest attempt to make a good batch of loaves in the school's pottery kiln, her thoughts circled around possible solutions to what could become a terrible impending battle for their lives.

Mara frowned as she worked the dough, feeling the texture change beneath her fingers, and added a splash more water. It didn't seem fair that another serious problem loomed on the horizon. They'd been through so much already, and despite setbacks, they were at last making great strides in making the school into a working homestead which would sustain them through the winter. With Eva sitting in a chair outside as a guard while the rest of them did assorted chores, the day-to-day things had gone much more quickly, enabling them to do the extra jobs that were making a huge difference in their comfort level.

She and Caroline had successfully hunted a deer, then field dressed and butchered it on site. They'd carried the fresh meat home across their shoulders using poles they'd made from the mops in the janitor's closet, draped with multiple sturdy plastic bags. On their return, Ethan had made half of the deer meat into a huge pot of stew, supplemented by the last of the loose potatoes, onions, and carrots from their stores which had been about to go bad without a cold cellar to keep them in. Mara had fired up the generator to can the stew, as well as the unused deer meat, giving them a month of dinners. She frowned again. The meals had come at an uncertain cost, as the noise from the generator had been terrible compared to the normal deep silence of the area where they were living. Ethan had been correct in his assessment that it was a dangerous thing to run, attracting unwanted attention, but everything she'd read had told her putting meat up without a pressure cooker was a dicey proposition as well.

"Giving my family botulism wasn't an option." Her kneading grew more forceful as she reiterated the reason for her choice, the movement of her hands and arms releasing some of the worry she still carried. "Everything has consequences these days," she muttered. "Good and bad."

Yesterday held a perfect example of the vagaries of making choices. Will and she had scouted the antique stores that lay on the outskirts of town, and scored a washtub and a washboard which had a hand wringer attached to the top of it, so the laundry took half the time it had done. On the other hand, the expedition had also yielded a fishing rod, tackle, and a net from the ruins of the sporting goods store they'd passed on the way home, the end of the rod sticking out from the hunks of concrete, its red and white bobber luring Will to find it. Of course he'd been eager to try it out, the find leading him to go fishing first thing earlier in the morning.

She paused to wipe her forehead with the back of her wrist and consider the texture of her dough, prodding it with her finger and counting the seconds it took to spring back. Mara cast a worried glance at her watch as she counted. Will had taken the rod and a cooler with him to the river hours ago, eager to get them something different for dinner. She clucked her tongue impatiently at her incessant worrying. He'd also taken his gun and Gretel, so it wasn't as if he was all alone and unprotected on the river bank.

"He'll be fine," she told herself firmly, although her maternal worries over the eight-year-old still hovered. The river was a common ground for the people who'd made it through the quakes, and after their ordeals with the Crowes, Mara's once-easy trust of people had evaporated.

Her dough ball had taken too many seconds to regain its shape. As she added another dollop of sourdough starter to her bread attempt and kneaded it in, Mara's gaze shifted to the teacher closet they'd transformed into a pantry. Several of the shelves had been filled with canned goods, spices, bags of rice and pasta, boxes of cereal, and a cannister of oatmeal, thanks to the run she and Caroline had made into two more houses the day before as Ethan had stood guard. They'd also scored another bike, one with fat tires that would withstand the broken roads well. That'd been the good part of the journey; the bad had been the stench that greeted them in both homes. Mara wrinkled her nose as the memory of the terrible smell that had permeated the place, making them gag even though they'd been wearing masks.

Mara pulled the dough into a huge round, then placed it into an oiled bowl to have its first rise as she considered the corpse problem. While she wasn't versed in medical things like her sister was, she knew enough to be concerned about diseases the dead might create because they were unburied. There were just so many of them that she couldn't fathom a way to ease the problem.

"We could toss the bodies into the bigger cracks," Ethan had suggested when she'd posited the issue to him. "At least the ones nearest us," he'd added. Treating people with such disrespect made Mara's stomach turn, but logistically, it was the first solution that made even a little sense, and at the end of the day, her family's health was paramount. But there was the issue of how to extract them from the rubble of their homes to consider as well, which might expose them to more pathogens.

Adding equal parts flour and water to her sourdough starter to feed it, Mara placed it back on the shelf beneath their final intact glass window so the ambient light could warm it, then forced herself back to the positive to help her shake her worries. Will's integration program of the new hens and the rooster was going well, and he'd had time to help Ethan finish the simple lean-to shelter which stood next to the school, with just enough room for their three horses and three goats as the nights got colder and colder.

Mara smiled slightly that they had three horses instead of just two as she put away the flour and wiped the surface of the cabinet they used as a counter. One more of their original five-horse herd that had run off during the enormous earthquake had returned. They'd found it happily cropping grass next to Aragorn and Sugar Lump two mornings ago. Lacking a name, the family had offered naming rights to Eva, but she deferred it to Will, who beamed when she did so.

"Buttercup," he'd said promptly, naming the buckskin, whose coat had a slightly yellow color. They'd all chuckled at the name, as Princess Bride had been one of their favorite family movies to watch at Christmastime.

"I was thinking Arwen, to go with Aragorn," Caroline had said. "But I like Buttercup more."

"Twue Wuv," they'd all chorused together, quoting a funny bit from the movie, baffling Eva when they burst into laughter.

"I think I have the original book in our library," she'd told Eva later, not wanting the woman to be left out. "It's a fun little story with pirates and princesses in it."

Eva had turned away with a grumpy shake of her head. "Never did read much," she muttered. "Never had the knack for it. And with this —" she'd broken off and pointed to her ruined right eye, which wasn't healing very well.

"I bet Will would love to read it aloud to you," Mara had said. "He needs the practice, as I don't see any semblance of school happening for these kids for at least another year."

"I guess."

The concession had been given reluctantly, but it was a start at integrating Eva into the household. The woman was prickly and difficult, but Mara didn't blame her a bit after what she'd been through at the hands of the Crowes. It had been why she'd opted to trust her with a gun to stand guard duty, although it had been a difficult decision to do so.

Her cleaning done, Mara wiped her hands on a dishtowel they'd brought from their old homestead. She gave it an affectionate pat before setting it aside. Grabbing two bottles of water, she went outside. Eva was kicked back, her chair leaned against the warming brick with her chair tilted on two legs at the rear door, a shotgun at her side. Her good eye shifted to Mara.

"I brought you some water," Mara said. "I can take over for a while, if you want a break."

"I'm okay."

Eva let the chair tilt back to square as she accepted the water. She downed the bottle in a long series of gulps that would have put a seasoned college beer chugger to shame. Eva wiped the back of her mouth with her hand, wincing a bit as she crossed abraded flesh. "You ready to do something about those brothers?"

The question came out of nowhere, making Mara choke on her sip of water. She bent over her knees, coughing, eliciting a low chuckle from Eva.

Once she finally got her breath back and blew her streaming nose with her handkerchief, Mara shook her head. "I'd rather stay away from them if we can."

"You don't want your own home back?" The question came in the form of a demand.

"Well, yes, I loved our homestead, but—"

"No but about it. I want my home back, that's the straight of it. I want my porch, and my barn, and I want to set up my still again and pick peaches when they ripen in the summer and make me some good brandy, and get my mash going and make shine and put up that clear lightnin' in quart mason jars just like my grandpappy taught me and his taught him. I want to build a memorial for my Lloyd. And I darn well want to kill those brothers."

It was the longest string of words Mara had ever heard Eva put together. "You've been thinking about it for a long time?"

"Nothing but." The woman squared off her body to face Mara. "We need more people, and we need to act fast before more Crowe kinfolk get to our places and start thinking those homesteads belong to them."

"You need to get the radio away from them before you do anything else." Caroline appeared from around the corner of the building. She held up both hands when both Mara and Eva gave her a stern look. "I couldn't help overhearing. I was doing the laundry, and voices carry these days."

Mara sighed. Without the undercurrent of cars, mechanical things, and a hundred thousand people going about their business, the Roanoke Valley was incredibly quiet, and she hadn't been sensible enough to lower her voice to compensate for it.

"Girlie's right," Eva chimed in. "It's how Shiloh and Dale are calling out to folks. It's at the back of my house."

"I don't care if it's hanging from a balloon tied to a walnut tree." Mara's fear and temper surged as she faced Eva. "Or how much you want your home and your still back." She turned and shook her finger at Caroline before the girl could speak. "You, in particular, are not going near those brothers. You've had too many close calls."

"And you haven't?" Caroline retorted.

"That's neither here nor there, Caroline. The point is, we've got an okay, safe place that's getting better by the day, so there's no good reason for us to go to war over what's been taken from us. I won't risk your life, Caroline, or your brother's lives either. What's done is done."

It was as if all her worries had coalesced, and the words tumbled from Mara's lips in a furious rush. Both Eva and Caroline were silent for a long moment in the aftermath of her tirade.

"Well, when I'm better, I'm planning on getting what's mine back." Eva folded her arms over her chest. "And I say you can call it caution, but I know cowardice when I see it."

"Name calling isn't going to work on me, Eva." Still, the words stung a little.

"You don't know those Crowes like I do," Eva muttered. "They'll find this place and come for you sooner or later. Best to get them first, before they see you coming, is what I'm saying."

"Two women and three kids trying to fight those Crowe brothers, especially if they were calling in reinforcements is a terrible idea!"

"So's waiting for them to come take this place from you."

"We're miles away from our homesteads, and we haven't seen any of the brothers out this far," Mara said, fighting the unease that precipitated her quick rebuttal so she could speak reasonably. "We've always been careful not to leave tracks they could follow."

"Oh!" Caroline startled, and abruptly grabbed a hank of her hair and started pulling on it, a crease of worry forming between her eyebrows.

Mara put a hand over Caroline's to prevent the girl from yanking harder. "What is it, Caroline?"

"I wrote a note."

Mara gritted her teeth to stop her anger from erupting a second time. "What note?"

Her stepdaughter paced, chewing on the length of hair she still had between her fingers. "When I was worried about Eva and went over there, I left a message for her." She turned to Eva. "I put it on a shelf in the little shed by your still, because I figured only you went there."

"Usually, I am the only one. But they was all down there when the wives decided to smash all of my brew." Eva tilted her head to the side. "I didn't see no note, though. But then I was pretty busy trying to stop them. What did it say?"

Caroline swallowed hard. "I said we were at the old school, and if you needed help, to leave a message in the shed, or in back of our old pond."

Mara's hands turned to ice as she ground out her words. "You wrote out where we were?"

The girl nodded miserably. "I didn't think it through. I just wanted to help her. I'm so sorry, Mara."

A profound silence descended on the three women as they pondered the consequences of the note.

"I'd say this changes things some, don't it?" Eva laughed, short and sharp. "Call me a lop-sided bunny if it don't."

"Oh my gosh," Caroline's eyes were huge, her face pale. "I've ruined our safe place. I should never have—"

Mara's temper snapped. "Just stop. Stop right there. Invoking 'should've' or 'could've' or their cousin, 'if only' isn't going to get us closer to a solution. It'll only make you feel bad about yourself so you shut down again, and I need you at one hundred percent, Caroline." Mara gripped her hard by the shoulders. "One hundred percent, with me."

"But—"

"Enough. We don't have time for recriminations, and maybe there was no harm done." Mara's anger and fear reformed into a need to take immediate action, her mind racing for solutions. "The first thing I need to do is go see Ritchie, and see if he'll join us, because you're right, Eva, we need more people if things turn ugly. Next, we need to go to where your still is tonight and see if the note is there."

"I know exactly where it is in the woods. I'll come with you." Caroline said, her face anxious. "I have to come with you, don't say no, Mara."

One more time, a problem had arisen which didn't have a good choice, just one between two bad ones. Mara sighed and rubbed the back of her neck where her tension hummed. "Is it hard to find?"

"That was kind of the point," Eva said dryly, her dark humor rising yet again. "Keeping it hidden. It's tucked back, you'll need her to find it, because I sure as heck ain't going." Eva's gesture to herself was disgruntled.

"Okay." Mara reluctantly agreed. "Eva, we need you to stay here on guard, along with the boys and Gretel. Until we have the note in hand, we can't be too careful."

"Nothin' sayin' they didn't read it already, though." Eva mused. "Although readin' isn't their strong suit."

'You're right, but it's the best we can do."

"Since we're going to be at the back of their place anyway, maybe we can try to get the radio?" Caroline tip-toed through the proposition.

Mara scrubbed her face with her hands as all the ways things could possibly go wrong whirled through her mind. "I don't know. Let me think about it while we do some prep. Caroline, I want you to grab Ethan and get him cleaning the guns and doing a new inventory of our ammo. Will can help him when he gets back from fishing. You do the same with our first aid supplies after you finish the laundry. When I get back, I'll get the bread baking and get dinner started." She turned to Eva. "Can you continue to stand watch?"

"I can. Back from where?"

"I'm going to talk to Ritchie. He's not far away, I should've gone to check in on him, anyway."

"No 'should-ing'!" Caroline was lightning-fast with her retort. "If I'm not allowed to use it, and second guess myself, then neither can you."

Mara was shocked into silence, then nodded. "You're right. It is what it is."

"Not like you've been sitting around eating bon-bon's," Eva added. "Y'all have been working your behinds off. Anyone can see that."

The kind words, even if spoken with sarcasm, took Mara by surprise. "Thanks Eva."

The woman dismissed the thanks with one impatient flick of her wrist. "Get going, I'll keep an eye out."

Ten minutes later, Mara was on the move down the hill to get to Ritchie's house. She carried a rifle on her back, her holstered handgun, and a jar of their venison stew in her backpack, along with a mask in case things had taken a turn for the worst at Ritchie's place.

Her steps slowed as she turned onto the downward slope of the street the man lived on. The same one her friend Anita had lived on. Mara had promised Ritchie she'd come back and help him bury Anita, but she never had, as things at her old homestead had tumbled from difficulty to difficulty. It couldn't have been helped—and there was that word again, couldn't, and with it the surge of regret and self-recrimination that she literally had no time for in her changed world—but she'd brought the jar of stew all the same, as a token apology.

She eased along the silent street, listening and watching for any movement, particularly from the house next to Ritchie's, where a group of people lived who'd attacked her and taken away her ATV. Lingering behind the garage of a house which stood diagonally to Ritchie's as she assessed the dangers of crossing to his door, Mara's gaze turned to Anita's place. Its curtains were neatly drawn in the front windows, but the house had crumbled on the side that had held her bedroom, the sturdy bricks disarticulated from the frame, so the bedroom and a portion of Anita's living room stood open to the elements.

She turned away from the sad sight. At least they'd rescued Anita's cats, Bacon and Molly, and the animals were thriving on the combination of dinner scraps and the mice they hunted in the shambles of the school. Grumpy Molly had picked Mara as her person, and curled in the crook of her legs nearly every night. Bacon had done the same with Ethan, creating a bright spot in the sad situation.

Mara lifted one foot behind her at a time to stretch her thigh muscles in case she had to make a run for it. As she flexed, she considered how strong and fit she'd become in less than a month with the constant exercise and effort it took just to obtain their daily water, let alone the other lifting, carrying, and hiking she'd done. The carrying of the water from the Roanoke river was a major sore spot for her, and of all the things she missed about her homestead, it was the ease of getting fresh well water from their hand pump that stood out from all the rest.

"Almost worth getting into a fight about," she breathed aloud as she replayed Eva's taunt that she was just being a coward.

There'd been no movement anywhere in the minutes she'd stood watching. Pushing aside the thoughts to deal with later, Mara hurried across the street, and opened the gate in Ritchie's chain-link fence, closing it carefully behind her as she walked up the weedy sidewalk to his front porch. It had turned rickety in the intervening days since she'd been at the place, and she stepped carefully. Standing well to the side of the door, she banged on it with her fist, several hard knocks, then drew away in case Ritchie decided to answer his door with his old shotgun blazing.

When there was no sound, she repeated her banging, her heart sinking when no response was forthcoming, not even the barking of Trinity, his scruffy mutt of a dog. She turned the handle of the door, but it was locked. Unwilling to give up on the man and his dog, she moved to the back of the house, noticing one side of it was cracked and falling in just as Anita's had done.

"One more big shake, and it's coming down," she commented as she turned the corner to the back of the house. Mara stopped dead in her tracks as the rear of the home was revealed to have completely collapsed, a heaped pile of rubble where Ritchie's kitchen had been, the second story piled atop it in a jumble of broken furniture, walls, and roof.

She sunk to her haunches and stared at the destruction, blinking back tears. Letting out a low, long sigh of sorrow at the loss of Ritchie and his cute little dog, Mara stood to return home when a frenzied, muffled barking caught her ear. Mara turned in a circle, trying to identify where the sound was coming from, a bubble of fear forming that the dog and his master were trapped beneath the rubble of Ritchie's house. She hurried to the area, but the barking grew more distant. It was coming from further back in the yard instead of under the house.

Following the continual sound, she found a wooden door that was inset into a small rise in the back yard, so it was hidden until she was almost on top of it.

"A storm cellar!" she exclaimed.

The barking was coming from inside. Bending, Mara knocked on the wooden door and called out, "Ritchie, are you down there with Trinity? It's Mara, Anita's friend."

The door opened a few inches and the little scruffy dog scrambled out and hurled herself at her knees, jumping to lick Mara's face, tail wagging madly. Its owner peered up from the opening, his antique double-barreled shotgun in hand, his wrinkled face a pale spot in the gloom of his storm cellar. "Thought you'd gone for good," he commented.

"I'm sorry," she said as she bent down and petted the deliriously happy dog. "I'd planned to come back."

"Mmph." He made a sound which was half-accepting and half-condemning.

"I'm glad you had a cellar to shelter in. I haven't seen many around here, but in Iowa there were lots of them."

He acknowledged her comment with a nod. "You came back to check on us?"

"I did." Mara fished out the jar she'd brought. "And to bring you some venison stew." She waited for him to take the next step, remembering Ritchie marched to a different drummer than most.

He reached up and took it from her, hesitated, and then waved his gun a bit. "Want to see inside?"

"Sure."

He opened the door all the way so Mara could descend the five wooden steps into the bunker buried in the earth. It was small, no more than eight feet long and six feet wide, and Mara had to stoop a little as she moved past the opening. The walls were lined with cinderblock, the raw earth visible between the blocks, making the air damp and chilly. There was just enough room for a neatly made collapsible cot, shelving for food and water, and an unlit little wood stove whose exhaust pipe extended through the dirt above their heads. A Coleman lantern was held up by a peg driven into an earthen part of the wall, and a braided rug Mara recognized as coming from his living room lay on the dirt floor. Trinity's food and water bowls were next to the stove, and a few clothes hung on a rod that hung behind the wooden steps, as well as several shotguns and boxes of ammo.

As Ritchie carefully placed the jar of food on the shelf, Mara observed there wasn't much else to eat sitting on them. Ritchie appeared to be even thinner than he'd been the last time she'd seen him.

"It's a good shelter," she said stoutly.

"It'll do." Ritchie cleared his throat. "I buried Anita like I promised."

"Thank you, Ritchie. I'm sorry I wasn't there to help you."

He shrugged. "Needed doing." He paused again. "The knuckleheads next door disappeared. Took all their ATVs one day, and never came back." He gestured to the food on the shelves. "Some of that is theirs, figured if they left it, I could have it."

His tone was defensive, and he looked away as if he were ashamed of his actions. Mara nodded her head to agree quickly. "Caroline and I and my boys have been doing the same thing."

He frowned, then snapped his fingers. "She's the blue-haired gal who came to find you." His voice tapered off as he spoke, and Ritchie turned his head aside to cough, waving her away when she took a step toward him.

After he'd gotten his breath back, Mara continued the conversation, her concern for the man deepening. "That's right. We're living at the high school, Caroline and my two boys and our old neighbor, too. In fact, it's the main reason I came to find you. We want you to come and stay with us, Ritchie. You and Trinity, instead of being by yourselves. We've got a good store of supplies."

"No. We're doing okay." He sniffed and didn't meet her eyes.

Mara spoke gently. "For how long, though, Ritchie? I know you don't care for people much, or being outside your home, but it's just up the block, not far. We could be there in less than ten minutes."

"I don't mind people so much. I just—I don't leave the block, haven't left my block in ten years."

"I remember you saying that. But, Ritchie, the truth is we need you. I need you. There's more knuckleheads out there than the ones that were next door, and I could really use your help defending our place from them."

"I can't."

The dog looked between them as if she understood the words being said. The little terrier mix whined a little and thumped her tail.

"Oh, don't you start," he scolded the dog.

"I'm baking fresh bread," Mara said, desperate to find something that would convince Ritchie to leave his hole in the ground. "There's three loaves rising to put into the kiln at school."

"Kiln?"

"We're finding a lot of new uses for the things that were left in the school. You'd have your own room to yourself. All I ask is you help us guard the place. Please, Ritchie. I'd feel so much better if you and Trinity were with us."

He slumped onto the bed and covered his face with shaking hands. Mara perched on the stairs and waited for his response. Trinity plopped her behind down and panted, her eyes not leaving Ritchie's form.

"I don't think I can do it," he said at last, fear lacing every syllable. "But I know it's not good for Trinity down here." He coughed again.

"How about if you carry Trinity, just hold her, and I'll fold and carry your cot for you, and your rug, too, so you have things from home. We can put Trinity's dishes in my backpack. You don't have to look at anyone or anything, just your feet."

"Rather hold my gun," he mumbled.

"All right," Mara said. "You carry your gun, and I'll get the rest. I'm sure she'll stay with us, right, Trinity?"

The dog barked on hearing her name.

"What about the rest of my things?"

"I'll come back tomorrow and get them for you."

Stark terror washed over Ritchie's face, coloring it to a bright red. He stroked his snow-white hair and then pulled on his scraggly beard with a trembling hand. "Let's go before I change my mind," he said as he pushed off the cot. "I'm taking all my guns."

"That'd be good," Mara agreed. She quickly put the dog's bowls in her backpack, then rolled up his bedding, folded the cot, and carried it outside, returning for the rug, which she put with the bedding. It was a big pile to carry, but the cot was easy to sling over one shoulder, and they weren't going far. Trinity raced up the stairs behind her, followed much more slowly by Ritchie, who carried all three of his guns cradled in his arms, his pockets stuffed with ammunition.

"I'm closing your storm cellar door," Mara said. "Then we'll just go around the side of your house and take a left. Ten minutes, and we'll be at the school, and you'll be in your own room."

"Okay." His voice wheezed out as his breathing hitched and tears formed in his eyes.

"Just keep your eyes on your feet, I'll guide you. Don't look anywhere else," Mara advised, worried he was about to have a full-blown panic attack. "We're already at the street, just go left."

Trinity circled them, her tail wagging as they plodded along the sidewalk. As they stepped off of the curb onto the main street which led to the school, the guns Ritchie carried clattered together as his whole body shook and a low, terrified cry emitted from his lips that tore at Mara's soul.

"Hang in there, Ritchie, you're doing really well. Can I do anything to help?"

"Row, row, row your boat," Ritchie began to sing under his breath, his voice trembling and tears squeezing past his squinting eyes.

Mara joined in immediately and together they walked, keeping time with the old song. Mara's eyes stung as she blinked back her own tears, in awe of the courage the man was showing in the face of his deep-seated phobia. She kept singing with him until they were at the fence line. She waved to Caroline, who was at the back door with Eva to come help.

Mara laid a light hand on Ritchie's arm as Caroline ran to them. "You know Caroline, Ritchie. She's going to take your cot and rug and put them in your room while we walk together the rest of the way inside." Mara signaled silently to Caroline as she said the words, and the girl nodded, picking up that she needed to prep a room right away.

"Hi, Ritchie," she said, then took his things from Mara. "Will's back with fresh fish for dinner," she added, then paused before going on. "And he found a couple more things, too."

"Oh? More chickens?"

"People," Caroline said, as she made a face. "Kids. I think we probably have to keep them."

CHAPTER EIGHT

The Blacksburg/Pembroke Fault
Day Twenty-five

"I can't believe Mara talked him into coming to the school." Caroline muttered to Eva as she passed her, arms loaded with Ritchie's bedding, floor rug, and his folding cot.

"Your stepmomma's on a mission," Eva responded with a shrug. "Guess I should've grabbed me my own private classroom when I had the chance." Her lips twisted wryly.

"There's still two more," Caroline pointed out. "I think you just like my company."

Eva snorted at the teasing, but a crinkling around her one good eye signaled to Caroline she wasn't wrong. "Keep dreamin' girlie."

Caroline hurried to the first available of the three empty classrooms that remained in the ten-room wing and bumped the door open with her hip. She did a quick survey of the space as she entered. The place was relatively clean, its desks shoved against one wall, leaving the teacher's closet open. They'd boarded up the broken windows, leaving the two which were still intact to provide light and at this time of day, the room was fairly bright and welcoming.

She dropped the cot she was carrying along with its bedding and a once-bright braided rug. With a few deft movements, she had the cot assembled next to the shelving that had been cleared of earth science books. Caroline arranged the sheet, pillow, and patchwork quilt on it. The quilt had been lovingly handmade from old baseball t-shirts, something a parent would make for their child. Caroline placed the rug at the side of the cot, twitching it into place just as Mara pushed open the door supporting Ritchie, who was murmuring something under his breath and staring at his feet. The man's scraggly terrier mix pushed past his legs to explore the room, wagging his tail as Mara put his food bowl and water dish at the foot of the cot.

"Thanks, Caroline," Mara said with a sincere smile. "Look, Ritchie, there's your cot, and your quilt, and your rug. I'm going to grab you and Trinity something to eat and drink, and leave you to get comfortable in your room."

The elderly man looked around, confusion on his features. He clasped three old shotguns to his chest, and ammo bulged from his pockets.

"You could put your guns in the closet," Caroline offered helpfully, pointing at it.

He shook his head. "Under the bed, where I can get 'em."

Mara exchanged a glance with her, signaling she should just go along with whatever Ritchie said.

"Sounds good!" Caroline chirped, then sidled out of the door to let Mara finish dealing with the odd old man.

She'd barely made it into the corridor when Will stopped her, panic on his face. "Sis, you've gotta help me. Those kids don't want to take a bath, or change out of their clothes." He clutched her sleeve, his voice turning plaintive. "I'm scared they're going to try to leave if I make them, but they need a bath bad!"

Caroline stifled a sigh and her impulse to ask her brother what on earth he'd been thinking of when he'd brought the two kids back with him. "Where are they?"

Relief flooded his features as he tugged on her sleeve. "In their room. I mean, it's just blankets on the floor until we find them mattresses or beds, but it's better than living in the bushes by the river, right?"

"Have they said anything except their names yet?"

"No, well, yes. They said yes when I asked them if they wanted to split my granola bar down by the river, so yeah."

He pulled her along the hall to the classroom positioned across from the one she and Eva were sharing and opened the door. At first Caroline couldn't see the kids at all in the dim light, as the room had all its windows broken, so the family had boarded them with plywood from the shop class stores, and they hadn't switched on the lantern they'd put inside for them.

"Sophie? Aiden?" Will called out the sister and brother's names, looking to Caroline for support when there was no reply.

"Who wants to go pet the horses?" she called out.

Movement in the far corner coalesced into two shapes, one taller than the other, holding hands. The brother and sister were both rail thin and filthy. The sister scratched her head, giving Caroline a shiver along her spine as she imagined how many bugs must be living in her matted hair. Will was right. They couldn't walk around the school smelling like they did, the whole place would pick it up. The first order of business was to get them out of the living space.

"Follow me." Caroline turned around and walked out of the room, with the expectation they'd follow her, ignoring the quizzical look her brother gave her. Turning right instead of left, she pushed past the plastic sheeting they'd put up at the far end of the hall, holding it aside so the siblings could emerge, followed by Will.

"I told Mara you brought home strays, by the way," she whispered to her brother as he passed her.

He blanched. "Was she mad?"

"I don't think so. She brought home one of her own, so I don't think she can say much." Caroline shrugged as she turned to the pair who huddled together, their eyes too big in their starved faces.

"Sugar Lump's the nicest horse, so we'll start with him," she told the pair, then turned on her heel to march over to the old practice field where the horses and goats were grazing, using her same trick of expecting them to follow her like little ducklings.

"Will, bring out the lead rope and a couple of carrots, please?"

He nodded and took off to the lean to he'd built with Ethan. While he was gone, Caroline continued to walk just in front of the brother and sister. She tossed her comments over her shoulder to the sister, who was the older of the pair.

"I'm his older sister, and I boss him around a lot. Do you do that with your brother?"

The girl, who Caroline guessed to be around nine or so, shook her head after giving it another vigorous scratch. Her little brother, who might be a year or two younger than Will, gave her a disbelieving look.

"Do too," he said abruptly.

The boy's sister gave him a death stare, which nearly made Caroline laugh out loud, but Aiden didn't back down from his statement, his little treble voice resonating with resentment as he went on in a torrent of words.

"At home, she used to make me do her chores sometimes. Like drying the dishes, and feeding our dog, and even taking out the trash, and sometimes she'd say I did something bad when it was her that did it, and then dad would yell at me!"

Caroline got a punch of affinity for Aiden's sister when she responded with the same exaggerated huff of annoyance she'd used a million times with her own brother. "We're not supposed to talk to strangers!" Sophie paused and added, "Especially not personal stuff."

Caroline smiled inwardly that the reason for their silence had been revealed. "Oh, that rule doesn't really count anymore," she said breezily as they got closer to the horses, and she made a kissing sound to call them over. She waved a hand around to take in the world in general. "I mean, so much has changed, right?"

Sophie wrinkled her nose as she considered the argument, but then got distracted as Aragorn and the other two horses approached. "They're so big!" She cowered a step back, pushing her brother behind her.

"They're like big dogs. They won't try to hurt you. You said you had a dog, right?"

"Yeah." Aiden looked sad. "She was in the house with mom and dad when it fell over though."

"Well, we have our dog, Gretel. You met her already, she likes kids, and then our new person, his name is Ritchie, he has a dog too, named Trinity. We have two cats as well as the horses and goats and chickens." Caroline spoke rapidly to distract him from sad memories as Will ran up with the lead rope.

"Here you go, sis."

"Thanks." She put the rope over Sugar Lump's head. "I'm going to let you pet Sugar Lump and Will is going to show you how to feed him a carrot, but—" she paused dramatically. "You have to promise you'll wash your bodies with warm water and soap, and change out of your clothes so we can wash them right after we're done." Caroline gave them her best copy of her dad's stern look, which meant a bit of a frown which creased the line between her eyes and crossing her arms.

"Okay," Aiden said meekly, caving after only a few short seconds of looking between Caroline and Sugar Lump.

Sophie shook her head, true fear gleaming from her face. "I'm not taking my clothes off in front of any boys!"

"Nope, you can have your own space, no problem, but I'll help wash your hair for you if you want me to."

The girl gave her a doubtful look, but Caroline waited her out, letting silence work its magic. "Okay. Yes. I promise."

Caroline showed them how to pet the horse and then stepped back. Will looked at her with rounded eyes and something like hero worship on his face. "You're a genius," he whispered.

"I know," she whispered back.

The hours of the afternoon flew by as Caroline filled them with chores, including helping Sophie wash her hair in a basin by their firepit. A quick conversation with Mara about getting rid of the lice infestation that she'd discovered had her washing Aiden's hair for him as well, following up with a rinse made of chamomile tea and vinegar to combat any remaining bugs and to soothe the itching. Caroline sucked up her revulsion and combed through their tangles gently with a fine-tooth comb, hundreds of the nasty creatures and their eggs succumbing to the grooming. Will had taken Aiden in hand to get him some fresh clothes, and she'd taken Sophie to the room she shared with Eva to pick something out. While the girl was thinner and shorter than Caroline, they'd rolled a pair of her old jeans at the waist and ankles.

"You wear a lot of black," the girl said as she looked through Caroline's stack of t-shirts.

Seeing her wardrobe through Sophie's eyes, Caroline had to agree with her, there wasn't much in the way of color. It hadn't always been that way. Her favorite colors had been pink and purple when she was growing up and her mom was still alive. Her heart gave a little twist as Sophie reluctantly pulled one of her Mordor t-shirts over her head.

"We'll go on a clothes hunt soon," she promised Sophie. As she said the words, she found herself looking forward to it. "I'm glad you're here," she said impulsively. "With two brothers, I need all the gal pals I can get."

"Thanks." Sophie looked at her from under her lashes, and Caroline got a flash of what a pretty girl she'd been before weeks of exposure and privation had made her into a living skeleton. "Maybe we can get some more hair dye, too. I want blue hair like yours."

"We'll start a trend."

The happy feeling created by the conversation hadn't lasted long, as Mara set the two kids to work washing their filthy clothes with the new washtub and mangle while Caroline tended to the horses. The job was usually a peaceful one for her, but once she was alone with the animals with no distractions, she started grinding about the stupid note she'd been so stupid to leave at Eva's still.

If only she'd just instructed the woman to leave a note herself, instead of writing out exactly where they were, it wouldn't be an issue, but she hadn't thought it through. The implications of her mistake rocketed around in her head as she brushed the horse's coats and curried their manes and tails before getting them and the goats inside their lean-to for the night. Not only had she put her own family in danger, but all the other people who were living with them at the school were going to be impacted as well.

She heaved a sigh as she leaned against Aragorn's strong warmth, eliciting a gentle snort from the mammoth horse. "I messed up," she confessed to the animal. "And even if Mara didn't say so, it's bad."

Her footsteps dragged as she went back inside, her insides a turmoil. Caroline was starving, otherwise she would have begged off dinner. She toed off her boots at the entrance to their living area and stopped as she took in the magical transformation Mara had created. Her stepmother had hauled in another lab table to make a dining area which would fit eight people, and more high stools from their storage room, but she hadn't stopped there. She'd used a sheet to drape over them, overtopping it with their old, blue checked tablecloth in a diamond shape, and then decorated it with candles in holders flickering down the middle, giving the area a soft, diffused light which created an inviting space. Kitchenware from the old cafeteria was set at each place, and their old cloth napkins in a variety of colors had been set in decorative twists atop the plates. Water in glasses had each been mixed with a vitamin C packet, which added pops of color to each place as well.

Pots of homemade blackberry jam and the soft herbed goat cheese she'd been perfecting sat alongside a bowl holding wild field greens tossed in a bit of olive oil, ready to be devoured. Mara proudly placed two of the giant loaves she'd pulled from the kiln only a few minutes ago onto the table as well, then stood back and smoothed her hair, a happy smile on her face.

"I think it looks good, don't you?"

Caroline's gaze moved to the sideboard where portions of pan-seared fish waited to be put on the table, and in addition, a big pot of venison stew, the aromatic contents sending wisps of steam to scent the air.

"That's a lot of food," she commented, mostly to stop herself from going to Mara and giving her a big hug of appreciation. She winced as she heard how snippy and judgmental the words sounded. "I mean, you went to a lot of trouble."

"I want everyone to feel welcome," Mara responded simply, then her tone changed. "This is why we're fighting," she added with a direct look at Caroline. "I did it as much for me as anyone else. I need to be reminded of what's important, why we're going back to 'that stupid Crowe place,' as you like to call it later tonight."

"I'm really sorry," Caroline whispered with tears fighting to come leaking out.

Mara shook her head briskly. "Don't do that to yourself, Caroline. You had a wonderful instinct to help someone. We'll go fix it, it'll be done in a couple of hours, then we can come back and continue to grow this home we're carving out, and have more good meals with new friends and family."

Mara waved her hands at the table, just as the two siblings came in, following their noses. The kids' eyes were huge as Mara bustled over and sat them down before turning to dip generous portions of stew. As the two kids took the aromatic bowls that contained chunks of meat, potatoes, onions and carrots, Caroline thought they might start crying.

Will bounded in next, followed as always by Gretel. "Yum!" He cried and then pointed at the fish. "Hey, my fish look amaze-balls!"

Ritchie entered with his little dog on his heels. He seemed lost and overwhelmed in the new space, and Mara moved to seat him, bringing his bowl, and whispering something in his ear which calmed the older man. Mara did the same for Eva, settling her down with a few quick words, and bringing the food to her. Watching her stepmother care so easily and graciously for the people under her roof struck Caroline to the core, and she saw her stepmother in an entirely new light as memories of their early days with Mara sprang up.

Mara had treated both her and Will with the same care when she became their stepmother, and even before that, when she was just dating her dad, but Caroline had been too angry to see what she was doing, too full of pain to accept anything that resembled love or care from her. She'd only seen an interloper, someone she was forced to share her dad with, someone who had reminded Caroline daily that she was motherless. To Caroline, Mara had been the evil stepmother from the fairytale books, the one who was on a mission to secretly drive a wedge between herself and her father, and as the child in the situation, she had no resources to make it stop other than to make Mara feel as unwelcome as possible.

Yet her stepmother had loved her through all of it, nurtured her, fed her, made sure she had clean clothes. She'd encouraged her riding, standing up to her dad when he'd wanted to say no to the expensive hobby, helped her with her English homework, and had tried to include her on a nightly basis in conversations around dinner tables which had been as carefully set and pretty as the one in front of her. Caroline had been sure all of it was a fake, tricks which would be abandoned as soon as she'd snared her father. Every effort Mara had made was another reason to reject her and anything the woman touched. But it had all been real, all of it. Mara had never stopped trying to love her, had never stopped trying to show her she was valued.

Caroline let out a shaky breath as the realizations floated one after the other like autumn leaves falling from high trees to settle into a new, softer landscape. Ethan came in on his crutches and Mara moved from her serving spot to help him into his seat and tend to him, just as she'd been taking care of everyone else, an equal amount of love and care for the strangers as she gave her own son.

Before she quite realized what she was doing, Caroline stepped in and brushed Mara lightly on the arm. "I've got Ethan, why don't you sit and slice some of the bread you baked for us, it looks amazing, Mom."

If she'd had to push out the final word in the sentence, and it had been weird saying it, her effort was one-hundred percent worth it as the candlelight caught the unshed tears that glittered in Mara's eyes. "Thanks," was all she said in return, but it was tinged with wonder and delight, making Caroline smile as something which had been biting the edges of her soul for years found rest. She served bowls of stew for Ethan, Mara, and herself with a profound sense of contentment, her stomach growling at the smell of the freshly caught fish.

A visibly happy Mara and the ever-upbeat Will kept the conversation going as the kids and Ritchie ate their fill, smoothing the awkwardness of their first meal together as a group. Ethan ate hungrily as well, as did Will, who blushed when they all gave him a round of applause for adding the fish to the feast.

Candlelight surrounded all who sat at the table with a soft, even glow, the dark beyond held at bay. At their feet, Gretel and Trinity found places under the table, and gradually a peacefulness stole over everyone as the newly formed family group shared the hearty meal.

"I thought we'd go foraging tomorrow," Mara said as spoons scraped the bottom of bowls. "For mushrooms and nuts in the woods across the river. Caroline and I saw some good bunches of shrimp of the woods, wood oysters, and lion's mane."

"What?" Sophie broke her long silence, looking utterly perplexed. "There aren't shrimp in the woods. Or lions."

"They're mushrooms," Eva offered the explanation with her slurred speech. She pointed her fork at the girl, then twitched it sideways at Aiden as well, her tone firm. "You'll go with Ms. Mara and start learning. I might go too," she added with a stretch. "Now we've got us another gun-toting man." She gave Ritchie a light tap on the arm. "Be good to get off my rear."

"Ritchie, are you up for some guard duty tomorrow?" Mara asked. "Just outside the door?"

He startled and twisted his mouth a few times like he needed help getting it moving, but then Ritchie nodded, stroking his beard. "I could sit guard, long as I have Trinity with me. Right by the door, I could do it."

Ethan grinned. "I'd love some mushroom barley soup, mom. You make the best. Or we could make mushroom gravy to go over some venison, too."

"You good to guard me while I search a couple more houses, brother?" Caroline asked, addressing Ethan.

He raised an eyebrow at her use of the term brother, then broke into a sweet smile which echoed the one Mara was wearing. "Yep, I could."

"If I take Gretel, can I go get more fish in the morning?" Will wanted to know. "There were a lot of them in this one place, right where I found Sophie and Aiden." He turned to them. "I mean, technically, you found me because you came out. I'd never have seen you in those bushes otherwise."

"We saw you before," Aiden offered. "Sophie said you were handsome and that you might be nice."

Mara fumbled her fork at the comment, dropping it with a clatter onto the floor, but waved aside Caroline's questioning look as both Sophie and Will blushed furiously at the comment.

"Shut it!" Sophie whispered to her brother.

"What? You said it like twice."

"My brother is very nice," Caroline jumped in to save her brother from further torture. "Most of the time."

"Well, now that we have tomorrow sorted, I have a surprise for everyone," Mara said, getting up from the table and bringing back a plate from the pantry. "Oatmeal raisin cookies for dessert. The oven was the right temperature, and I had all the stuff, so—"

She put the platter onto the table, revealing giant, soft cookies. Multiple hands reached for the treats as Mara grinned and snatched one for herself. Caroline looked around the table at the odd assortment of people and shook her head in amazement at how different her world had become from a month ago. The only home she'd known was gone, her father was gone, her world literally upended, but somehow they were making it work, and were slowly turning the weird mix of people into a family and her old high school into a home.

After supper, Ethan took over the dish washing with the two new kids helping while Ritchie disappeared into the library with a lantern, and Will went outside to get the chickens settled for the night. Eva sat where she'd been for the entire dinner, nibbling on her cookie and removing the raisins as she did so.

"Too hard for you to eat?" Mara had asked sympathetically as she bussed the dishes off of the table to the lab sink.

"Don't like 'em," was the succinct answer, but then the woman had sighed. "The cookie part's good, though."

To Caroline's surprise, instead of taking offense, Mara had laughed and scooped the raisins off of Eva's plate and popped them in her mouth. "Good, more for me, then."

That had made Eva bark out one of her rare laughs as well. It died in her throat a moment later, a spark of heat flaring as she looked between Caroline and Mara.

"Wish I could go with you and whack a few Crowes," Eva said, then added forcefully, "you should grab Lloyd's radio."

"Caroline and I will be okay, but we're not—I repeat, not—whacking anyone tonight," Mara said.

Eva made a little face. "All right, then. You be careful, the brothers started doing their call-outs maybe a week ago, so new folks might be there already." Eva turned to address Caroline. "You're clear where the set-up is?"

"Back corner of the house. Go in through the three-season porch, turn left at the doorway into the main house." Caroline responded.

"Lloyd and me never locked it, but them wives made the brothers lock it like buncha scaredy hens. Key's in the coffee can next to the screen door." The single bright blue eye burned with intention. "You go take that radio away from them."

Once the younger kids were in bed, Caroline and Mara got into dark clothes and smeared mud on their faces. Eva and Ethan walked with them as they wheeled the bikes to the fence line and handed them their go-bags.

"I don't think we'll be more than two hours," Mara stated as she strapped hers on.

"I dunno, Mom, every time you do an estimate, you end up being way late." Ethan's brow crinkled with concern.

Mara sighed. "Dealing with you kids is like handling a water balloon, I swear."

Everyone turned to her as she hunched her shoulders in frustration. "Just when I get a good grip on one relationship so it's working right, the next one bloops out and goes wonky."

"I think she's calling you wonky and bloopy," Caroline said to Ethan, unable to avoid the dig at her stepbrother.

"You wouldn't be teasing me if I wasn't on crutches," he replied grumpily. "Cause I'd give you the worst knuckle noogies of your whole life."

"Have to catch me first," she sassed back as she buckled on her backpack. "Never happen."

Ethan arched an eyebrow and nodded his head. "I'll bide my time, but once my cast is off—" he ended with a pretend sad look. "Your bragging days will come to a small, sorry end."

Cheered by the exchange, Caroline mounted her bike and took the lead as she and Mara rolled around the edge of the town. They didn't use lights, allowing their eyes to become accustomed to the darkness, weaving through new obstacles along the way, things that had fallen as the consequence of the continual quakes, although there hadn't been a large one in several days. Caroline stopped peddling a good half mile from their destination.

"We should go in on foot from here," she said in low tones to Mara.

Together they crept through the woods on the downslope from the Crowe homestead, moving tree to tree, both listening intently for any crackling leaves which would betray a stalker.

After nearly an hour of careful movement, they crossed the little stream that burbled directly below Eva's still, but when they reached the place where the big iron pot and fire ring and the shed had been, it was empty. The only reason Caroline was sure she was in the right place was because she spotted the cauldron, which had been rolled on its side to rest against a tree trunk.

The fire where Eva's still had been centered had been scattered, charred logs thrown in all directions. Broken glass shone in the undergrowth from the remains of her quart jars, and a faint aroma of moonshine permeated the ground where the contents had been spilled. The little shed Eva had used to store her goods and where Caroline had hidden the note was utterly gone. It had been ripped apart into disparate boards, the vindictiveness of the Crowe brother wives evident in the thoroughness of the destruction they'd wrought on the place where Eva had once cooked up her "devil's brew." Even the burlap bags which had held the simple grains Eva used in her mash had been ripped apart, their contents scattered to blow away, the good grain wasted in the wake of the rage the wives and the Crowe brothers had inflicted on the place.

Caroline wanted to howl in frustration that they couldn't know if the note had been found and read due to the completeness of the destruction. Mara must have read her mind, as she touched her arm lightly and pulled her ear close.

"It's done. Let's get closer and see if we can get Lloyd's radio."

A tiny bit of glee worked its way into Caroline as she nodded. At least something good might come out of their mission.

They ascended the steep hill slowly, the overcast sky and the surrounding forest rendering them nearly invisible. Caroline only knew where Mara was when she moved, the soft rustle of leaves unavoidable. The house was directly above them as they edged closer, angling to the side of the house where the doorway to the three-season room was located. It was the smell of a cigarette that warned them just before they made their final approach through the cleared back yard. The two women stopped as a single unit as the acrid scent wafted across their path. Crouching low at the edge of the trees, they both watched the porch, and sure enough, a moment later the bright end of a burning cigarette flared, quick as a lightening bug, then vanished.

They melted back into the trees. Mara gestured with her hand to go around toward the front of the house and Caroline nodded her understanding. They moved back several more yards into the wood, then continued their slow, cautious movement around the homestead. Both stopped in dismay when they got to where they could see the front of the house. A line of six ATVs stood in a neat row beside the outdoor fire, which had a huge haunch of venison roasting over it. A man neither of them knew turned the spit while two more men with shotguns casually draped over their arms sat on kitchen chairs nearby, facing away from the fire as they kept watch.

Caroline shared a horrified glance with Mara as she grasped what they were seeing. The extended Crowe clan wasn't just on the way. They'd already arrived.

CHAPTER NINE

The Hayward and San Andreas Faults
Day Twenty-six

Chang's men had configured their makeshift hospital area in much the same way as the army had done with its base outside of Durango, putting Ripley and other people who had lesser injuries in a single room that held six cots. An armed man sat by the door, and used a walkie talkie to fetch the doctor if an emergency arose. The doctor had created his office and exam room in the next office cubicle and the one after it was where the emergency cases were tended to and kept for close observation.

Ripley had been perp walked past the first two rooms on the way to her ward when she'd been brought in for the dislocated shoulder she'd given herself. It had been worth the pain for multiple reasons. Most importantly, she wouldn't be placed back underground in her original holding cubicle, which had defeated every attempt Ripley had made to get out of it. The infirmary rooms might have more options for escape, and were on ground level. Finally, Ripley had bet that the infirmary was the best chance she had of regrouping with the men on her team and from there, they could plot a course to get them all away from Chang's takeover of the National Lab before it succumbed to the sea.

Daniel Chang had claimed Liam Flannery had been killed days ago and had handed Ripley his dog tags as proof. He was an unreliable source of information, however, fully capable of lying to put her into a weakened psychological state or just to see her squirm. He'd also claimed that Fred, her helicopter pilot, and a man she'd come to rely on as both a mentor and a teacher had suffered a heart attack or a stroke when he'd gone to Flannery's aid.

Chang hadn't been lying about Fred. He'd had a heart attack and occupied the cot two down from hers, laying listless and still for most of the hours of the day, although his face had brightened when she'd been brought in. Ripley had been able to gather from watching what the doctor did on his periodic visits that Fred was being given narcotics as the only treatment available other than simple rest and supplemental oxygen. She'd had a pistol drawn on her by the guard when she got out of bed to ask the doctor if more could be done for him, but the physician had barely looked at her before shaking his head and walking out, waving his hands to the guard to retake his position on the door.

Two of the other beds were taken by the scientists who'd been on site when the first quakes rolled through, destroying much of the National Lab in the first few hours of the cascading disaster. They'd been on the tarmac when Ripley and her team had been taken, their injuries disguised by the clothing they'd been wearing, forced to be a part of Chang's ruse, both prisoners just as she was.

"We were in the cafeteria when that first quake hit," the nuclear physicist in the bed next to her had explained in a hasty whisper during a change of guards as the two men chatted just outside of their door. "Dr. Zhang and I were sent to get coffee by our team." He smiled sadly. "We had been pulling an all-nighter, waiting on our latest batch of radionuclides." He'd shaken his head sadly. "The team was working with the cyclotron. None of them survived, and Dr. Zhang got caught under the vending machine when it fell." He'd looked over at his compatriot, whose torso, right shoulder, and arm were bandaged and had been heavily sedated. "Then there was an explosion, and everything was on fire."

"You pulled him out?" Ripley asked.

The man held up his bandaged hands and forearms. "I did. We were both on fire, but I didn't let go."

"You're a brave man, Dr. Liu," Ripley said with respect.

He'd shrugged modestly. "I'm glad he's alive, but I fear none of us will live through many more quakes." His intelligent eyes swept over her face. "I am sure I'm right."

Ripley had been forced to nod silently in agreement as the new guard settled into place. Although none of the quakes in the past three days had been bigger than the one that had knocked down the radio tower, they'd continued with regularity. There was a crack in the wall by her bed, which lengthened every time one swept through.

She moved her shoulder surreptitiously so the guard wouldn't notice she had full range of motion back again. It was still sore, but Ripley was well aware that the doctor was no fool. The next time he checked her, he could very easily dismiss her from the hospital ward, and she'd be taken back to her underground cell. Her friend Emerson Davies had already been removed after only spending a day under the care of the doctor, who'd pulled a length of metal that had punched into his leg, swabbed out the hole, given him painkillers and sent him away with a single crutch to aid his movements.

Emerson had given her a quick look as he passed her cot as he exited, but they hadn't been able to converse. At least the non-contact had furthered the illusion that the pair didn't know each other, which was one of the few advantages Ripley had at her disposal.

Ripley lay back on the cot that smelled vaguely of mold and went through what she could use to effect an escape in the next few hours besides having a secret friend in Emerson. She had her knowledge of what was creating the steam clouds which wafted through the encampment, emitting a truly noxious smell of rotten eggs. She could fly a helicopter in a pinch, as long as someone else landed it, and they hadn't taken away her watch so timing the quakes was still possible.

Beneath her cot were her boots, and she still wore her own clothing, but there was nothing in them that could be considered a weapon. Fred was just two cots down, but he was in and out of consciousness. Dr. Liu, to her left, might be an asset, as he had no connection to the men who were under Chang's delusional command. Ripley blew out a frustrated breath. While all those things were positives, nothing added up to a way to defeat Chang and escape the National Lab before it succumbed to the forces of nature that were pounding on it with regularity. The only things Ripley could really count on was her intelligence and her wits.

President Ordway had said he was depending on her using them when he'd sent her and her men out on the rescue mission. The words he'd spoken when they were in the meeting room on the base outside of Durango were seared into her brain. "This well could be a mission that leaves you and your team stranded without the fuel to get back to base if those FEMA trailers are underwater, but of all the people I have on my team, I think you're the most resourceful, Ms. Baxter. If things go sideways, I'm counting on your brain working on the solutions to get you, your team, and any survivors you find back here in one piece."

Ripley closed her eyes and blew out another long, centering breath. President Ordway was a positive thinker, but he was also an astute judge of character. While Ripley often had doubts about her abilities, both Ordway and Thaddeus before him had been stout in their assurances she could be trusted to get the job done, so that was what she was going to have to do.

A second guard entered and pointed in her direction as he spoke to the man on duty before he left again. Ripley closed her eyes to feign sleep, hoping she'd get longer to think up plans for an escape, but it didn't matter. The man shook her roughly enough that her cry of pain was genuine. The man startled backwards at her screech. "Put on your boots. President Chang wants to see you."

"Not my president," she muttered to herself as she bent over to tie her laces, careful to not let the guard hear her. It was a small and futile thing, but saying the words fortified her sense of resistance.

She needed to get her brain thinking several moves ahead, and messing with the guard's equanimity was the easiest place to start.

"I want my pain medication before I go anywhere," she said as she stood. She added a heavy dose of whine as the man frowned. "My arm really hurts, it hurts so bad."

The guard shifted uncomfortably. "He said right away."

"I can't focus without it. I'm in pain." She shifted tactics again as he reached for her, snapping into petty high school mode and yelling. "I'll tell him you refused me—" Ripley paused and looked at him as if he was a piece of dirt. "What's your name, anyway?"

"Franelli. Come on."

She evaded his grasp, peering at the muscular man. "You look familiar, Franelli. Were you at Durango with the real President?"

The man looked discomfited and wet his lips. "He's not the only President anymore."

"So you were there. You make poor choices, is what you're actually telling me," Ripley goaded him.

"No, I don't." The aggravated man reached to grab her by the arm, and Ripley screamed as if she was in agony before he could even touch her, shrinking away from him.

"You leave her alone!" Dr. Liu sat up and gestured with his bandaged hands.

"I didn't freaking touch her!"

"You should just go get her what she wants," Dr Liu said forcibly. "Or call the doctor in if you are incapable."

Franelli pinched the bridge of his nose and pointed to Ripley's cot. "Sit there. I'll be right back. I'm locking the door behind me, so no funny business."

The moment he was out of the door, Ripley scrambled to Fred. "Fred, can you hear me?"

The grizzled old man swung his head in her direction. "Ripley."

"I'm going to get us all out of here. Be ready." She got a partial smile from him before he faded again. She gave him a light shake. "Fred?"

"Flannery's down," he rasped.

Gut punched, Ripley's energy flagged. "Are you sure?"

Fred nodded. "He fought, but there were too many of them."

Ripley swallowed hard, but then considered Fred's lack of sorrow over the loss of the red-headed Flannery. "Fred, when you say he's down—he's not dead?"

The older man shook his head nearly imperceptibly back and forth, his dry lips bleeding as he formed the words. "Hurt bad. Holding him."

Ripley flashed to the guards, who had been on duty outside two other classrooms in the long hall where she'd been detained. "I think I know where he might be. Fred, stop taking your meds, palm them, or something, you understand?"

The clicking of the door's lock had her dashing back to sit on her cot before Ripley could tell if the man had understood what she'd asked him to do.

Franelli shoved a water bottle and pills at her. "Here."

Ripley pretended to take the pills, but drank the water. "Thanks, Franelli."

"Yeah, whatever, come on." As he turned away, she slipped the pills into her pocket.

Ripley's muscles were stiff from the lack of exercise, and she had to focus on her steps as Franelli walked her along the short corridor. They passed the doctor's office, which was vacant, and then the single-bed emergency room. Ripley's quick peek through the reinforced glass confirmed Flannery wasn't inside, and heaved an inner sigh of relief.

Franelli took her to the outer door of the repurposed building and passed her on to a second guard. "Don't touch her arm if you want to keep your hearing," he muttered to the second guard, giving Ripley a nasty look before trotting back to his post.

"Come on," the new man said, moving ahead of her. "This way."

The stench of rotten eggs was much stronger outside of the walls, causing Ripley to cough and hack. The noxious fumes created by the crack in the earth that lay eastward from their position had increased a hundredfold during her stay at the infirmary. "We should be wearing masks," she commented to her escort.

He gave her a worried glance as he led her across the parking lot which had crumbled badly over the past few days of her confinement, pushing the concern she had over the air quality to a backseat. They might only have hours before the liquefaction was complete and the entire mountainside they were on collapsed.

The only good news was that the Black Hawk was still on the tarmac, although it had bounced off of the painted H where Fred had so expertly put it down, and stood at an angle, one set of wheels higher than the other as a crack ran between them, angling the blades out of true so they'd scrape the pavement when first started.

Ripley frowned as she contemplated how you could take off from an angle on an unstable platform, going over what she'd been taught by Fred. You'd have to adjust your rudders, and there'd be sparks and a danger of snapping a blade, but once you'd lifted the collective, and applied the throttle it should level out in moments. Pleased with her potential solution, Ripley was internally smiling as she was escorted to the hanger which held the rest of the helicopters and other equipment.

They passed through the open double doors of the metal building, entering the gloom within, only a small transition from the deeply overcast skies. A temporary room had been built from bolted wood framing and drywall into the front corner of the space. The man escorting her rapped once on the door, and it was opened immediately by Sam, the man with the greasiest smile on the planet.

"There she is," he said, gleefully rubbing his hands together. "The President is waiting for you."

Ripley sailed by his tall form, not bothering to acknowledge his presence, stopping after only two steps as Chang swung around in the small room, a frown on his face. "You can go, Sam," the man snapped. "See we're not interrupted and get those choppers and personnel ready."

"Yes, sir!"

Chang waved her to the sitting area that comprised the front section of the temporary room. It was much the same as his old room had been, half sitting space with two chairs, a coffee table, and a cot in the corner, but it was much more spartan.

"Love what you've done with the place," she quipped. "Too bad it's all going to be subsumed in the next quake. Why haven't you evacuated everyone?"

Chang looked at her, his face drawn, his buoyant energy at a low ebb. "I don't need another person doom and glooming me, Ms. Baxter. I've been convinced by Mr. Davies that I can't ignore these sulfurous gases covering the base. He claims they are full of noxious chemicals. I'm sending him up in a helicopter to gather more information so we can guard against them."

"Okay."

"You're going with him."

While her heart leaped for joy, Ripley forced fake alarm onto her features, clutching her hands at her chest as if terrified. "I'm sure your scientist is perfectly capable of doing the work on his own. I can't go. I hate flying. I just vomit the whole time."

"I don't care."

"You should pack everyone in those copters and leave instead," Ripley told him earnestly, the truth of the situation giving her cadence an urgent edge. "The gases are secondary to the Hayward fault, if you want my honest opinion."

He wagged a finger at her as if she were twelve. "You won't get out of flying that easily, Ms. Baxter."

Seizing on his ego, Ripley kept leaning on her pretense of frailty and fear. "Dr. Liu would know more about those gases. Send him and Dr. Zhang with your scientist instead of me."

"Who?"

"The scientists you have in the infirmary. They're quantitative specialists on amorphous poly gaseous expenditures and incendiary quantum flumes." Ripley threw in as many scientific sounding words as she could as she lied about Liu's qualifications, pleased to see a crease of puzzlement snake down the center of Chang's forehead and his lips puckering as he struggled to follow. "It was what they were working on when the first quake hit."

"You're just trying to throw me off," Chang said angrily, pacing in the tiny room. "You're going in the air, and that's final. And that pilot of yours is going to fly it. I don't care how sick he is. My pilot has better things to do with his time."

"It's the scientist in me. Sorry if I used too many big words," Ripley said sweetly, her eyes downcast in mock contrition. "But the two doctors are here, so why not put them to good use?"

Her mind ticked along at a furious pace as the man paced back and forth. Chang was practically serving up their escape on a silver platter, and if she could continue to wind him up and nudge him in the right direction, she might be able to save the two Asian men as well as herself and Fred. That just left finding Flannery and somehow getting him aboard as well.

"Don't think you can outwit me and somehow escape," Chang said, as if he'd gained the ability to read her mind, the words sending a cold spike through her. "I'm sending along men to escort you on your Black Hawk with orders to shoot you at the first sign of insurrection."

Ripley decided to double down on reverse psychology, and added in pleading to appeal to his ego. "You don't have to do that. Just keep me and Fred on the ground, and send the two doctors and—what was his name again? Your scientist?"

"Emerson Davies," Chang replied, then smiled nastily. "I'm surprised you don't know each other; you have the same alma mater."

Ripley hesitated for an instant too long as he studied her, her lie sounding awkward to her own ears. "I wasn't very social, if that's true."

"He said the same thing. Do you take me for an idiot?"

"Not in the slightest."

"Don't try to play me, you'll only embarrass yourself. I've waited too long for my time. I'm not going to let it slip away."

"I really don't know Mr. Davies," Ripley started, but he cut her off with an emphatic swipe of the hand.

"Your boy Flannery also gave up the location of the FEMA cache at Nike, and I'm sending a group of men there today to get what we need."

Hope flared through Ripley. "I thought you said he was dead?"

"He is." He stumbled over the words before puffing his cheeks and going on. "I never said we didn't make him cough up information before that happened. He also told us the master list for all the other caches is there and the codes remain unchanged since my tenure in Ordway's cabinet, so my primary need to capture you is, as they say, status mission accomplished."

He preened as Ripley did her best to look utterly miserable, forcing tears into her eyes by digging her knuckles into her eye sockets until they hurt. Chang had been a good liar for a long time, but she was sure he was lying about Flannery. "Those caches are for all Americans," she started, not bothering to add that President Ordway's instructions were to leave the caches open to all, even for Chang and his men, which rendered Chang's 'victory' to be a hollow one.

He pointed at his chest emphatically. "I'm the real America. The new America, and those supplies are going to my people. I have my men here, another contingent at the White House, and branches in both Oklahoma and in the Blue Ridge are forming that are quite powerful. There will be more who will rally to my cause, especially when I control all of those FEMA trailers full of water, food, and medicine, not to mention weapons. Once the groups who are loyal to me are in place, with the aid of the contents of those caches, I'm going to blow Ordway and the Indians he's cozied up with to kingdom come. I was willing to give him half of the USA and live in peace, but I don't have to. You picked the wrong side, Ms. Baxter."

His arrogance grated on her as she struggled to get through to him. A minor tremble jarred the chairs they were sitting in, causing her to clutch the armrests until it passed. Ripley pointed at the floor. "That's what should be worrying you. You're focusing on the wrong things. If you want to be the President of anything, evacuate everyone ASAP!"

He paused as if considering her words, then a cruel little smile crossed his face. "Did you know you were the ninth choice on a list of nine to brief Ordway?"

The jab stung, as he'd intended it to. "I'm fully aware that most of my colleagues were at a conference when I was called to brief him," she said, gathering her dignity. "I showed up, though."

"I'll have a t-shirt made for you. 'I showed up.'" He spread his hands as if holding a banner, then laughed derisively. "I'm making do with who I have to help me, and that is, unfortunately, you. That's all, Ms. Baxter. Your helicopter is leaving within the hour, and I expect results and a solution to the foul air."

He brushed his hand in her direction to dismiss her. Ripley made a final desperate attempt to get Flannery on board the same helicopter she and Fred would be on. "Please, I have a request, Mr. President."

His dark eyes glittered dangerously. "Sucking up already?"

"It might be too much to ask. I just want to bury Flannery if you haven't already?"

"We don't have time for burials. Don't waste my time."

"Please, President Chang? It would mean so much."

"No, and don't ask me again. Sam!"

The obsequious man was inside in half a moment, and Ripley would have bet money he'd been listening to their conversation through the door.

"Take Ms. Baxter, get her some food, and tell the doctor that I need the helicopter pilot—" he broke off and paused for a long moment before continuing. "And the two scientists in his care ready to go in an hour."

"Yes, sir!"

Ripley stopped in the doorframe, and tried one more tactic to jar Chang from the lie that Flannery was dead, and get him out of his cell so she could move forward with some sort of rescue attempt. "I know you don't think much of me," she wheedled. "But I'm a solid geologist, and you'll remember I was right about the quakes from the beginning. You're a smart man, so I have to believe you'll listen to me."

Daniel Chang partially turned back toward her with a huff of air, and she clenched her hands into fists to stop herself from being too aggressive in her push to get him to listen to her.

"I feel that I have to tell you this, Mr. President, so you don't waste our precious resources—Flannery was lying about the codes not being changed. I guess we'll never be able to access them, since you killed him." She poured bitterness into her voice, which was only partially feigned. "We all need those supplies. That cloud cover isn't going away for at least a year, you'll have nothing to feed your people with, nor will you have the fuel or weapons to defeat Ordway, as you intend to do because you killed him. Blake Ordway has plenty of resources and the loyalty of most of the army. By killing Flannery, you destroyed your one chance to give yourself a fighting chance."

Chang's face colored in anger, but he controlled himself with an effort, his words spitting through gritted teeth. "Thank you for telling me the information, Ms. Baxter." He waved them away.

Sam shook his head as he escorted her from the hanger, which buzzed with activity as the helicopters inside of its protection were swarmed with men prepping them to leave. "Like he doesn't have enough to worry about," he snapped at her.

"This base isn't safe to live on. You should try to talk him into evacuating it," Ripley responded, gesturing to the cracks in the ground. Her attention was diverted by the sight of a group of men straining to get her Black Hawk leveled by shoving two by four boards under the wheels, which were lower than the other pair. She'd counted only twenty men total between the hospital wing and the men working in the hangers.

"Looks like it's all hands on deck," she remarked to Sam casually.

He stopped and gave her an abrupt shake that snapped her teeth together, his face pink with anger. "Stop trying to get information out of me, like how many men are on base," he said. "President Chang is going to be the power in this country moving forward, and any moves you make against him aren't going to come to anything." He spoke with the fervent passion of a true believer, his former slick smile gone.

"You have half an hour to eat, and do what else you have to do," Sam continued as he passed her off to the guard at the front of the hospital unit who had walked her over originally. "Tanner, get those two scientists and the helicopter pilot dressed to deploy in thirty minutes after you get this one some chow, ask Franelli to help you."

With a final frown that Ripley took to mean she was supposed to behave, Sam strode toward the wing where she'd been kept prisoner. Keeping her fingers metaphorically crossed that she was getting Flannery out of his cell with her blatant lies about the FEMA trailer codes, she turned to the guard who had escorted her across the tarmac.

"Tanner, that's your name?" He nodded. "Before I eat, it'd be best if I explain to Drs. Liu and Zhang what President Chang expects of them," she told him. "It'll just make your job easier, I think."

Tanner was a somewhat reasonable man and nodded. "Two minutes," he told her.

Ripley wasted no time dashing to the infirmary, brushing past Franelli. "Dr. Liu, a word, and then you can tell your compatriot the news," she said.

"Yes?"

"I explained to President Chang your expertise in geological phenomena in terms of aeration and the gaseous parameters of basaltic-geophysical formations as they relate to heavy matter," she rattled off in an excited, girlish tone, hoping he'd understand she was speaking in nonsense words and that he was to play along.

The Asian man looked utterly blank before he nodded. "Yes, Dr. Zhang's and my specialty as physicists of geology," he said back slowly. "And gaseous ephemera."

"Exactly! Yes! We're getting on a helicopter in half an hour to study the phenomena to the east," she said, keeping her eyes locked on his. "We need to be ready for anything." Ripley emphasized the final words.

"Got it."

She smiled and turned with a happy little hop and clap of her hands to Tanner. "I just need to tell our pilot too, and then let's go eat, I'm starving!" Her voice was so high pitched she sounded like a squeaky toy, but the man shrugged agreeably.

Fred was awake and able to focus on Ripley as she pressed gently on his upper arm. "You're going to be flying me and some others to that crack in a few minutes," she said. "You remember the one I mean?"

"You sitting in the co-pilot seat?" he whispered.

Ripley smiled and leaned down, as if giving him a kiss on the cheek. "I told Chang I hate flying and get sick," she whispered.

"Heh, okay." He grunted as he tried to push up.

"No, stay there, and let the nice guard help you," Ripley said more loudly as she backed away.

Ripley ate a hearty meal at the cafeteria, and stashed two power bars in the pocket of her filthy army-issue cargo pants while Tanner's attention was attracted by the cook bobbling a heavy tray, and he rose to help the man.

"Am I going to get a backpack or equipment of any kind?" She asked Tanner when he got back.

He gave a shrug and spread his hands. "Dunno. I'm just duty bound to make sure you don't run off."

"We're on an island. Where would I run to?"

He chuckled slightly. "Just following what I've been told, sorry."

The young man had been civil to her, which was more than Ripley could say for the other men who'd been in charge of her. She plucked at his sleeve. "Ask to come with us," she said. "It'll be safer in the air than it will be sitting here on the convergence of the San Andreas and Hayward fault lines."

Tanner shook his head with a lopsided smile. "I'm not on that duty."

Even though he'd chosen to side with Chang, the young man seemed decent, and Ripley gripped his hand tightly. "Change with someone."

He gave her an odd look. "You're serious, aren't you?"

"I really am, Tanner. And I'm more comfortable with you holding a gun on me than someone else." Ripley spoke as honestly as she could, hoping he'd listen.

He considered for a moment, then nodded. "I bet I could get someone to switch with me. I don't get airsick and some of these men do."

"I can wait for you here," she said.

"Can't do that, but if I can switch, I'll see you in ten. Let's get you to your bird." He gave her a gentle hand under her elbow to help her up and they moved outside to the Black Hawk.

Chang was on the tarmac, going through a clipboard of papers, his expression frustrated and angry. Sam stood next to him, as well as the doctor and Fred, who wheeled a cannister of oxygen on a dolly, the clear plastic hose of it leading to his facemask that clouded with each breath he took. Fred's eyes were steady when he locked onto hers, giving Ripley a boost of confidence that she was getting him off of the base. Emerson was standing with them as well, equipped with two backpacks full of what Ripley presumed was science equipment, his leg bandaged and leaning on his crutch. A moment later they were joined by Zhang and Liu, and two armed guards.

The doctor was trying to talk to Chang. "I must repeat, sending a man who's had a recent heart attack—"

"Where's the third guard?" Chang interrupted the doctor querulously, looking away from him to Sam. "I don't trust these people at all."

Sam frowned and looked around, then pointed. "There, sir."

Tanner huffed over, outfitted with a rifle and guns. "Franelli wasn't feeling well sir, so I'm filling in." He gave Ripley a wink when Chang turned his back.

Beyond Chang, the second Black Hawk emerged from the hanger, rolling forward. Behind it, men were loading the two smaller Little Birds onto dollies so they could be pulled outside as well. Ripley could see the form of the pilot in the Black Hawk moving through the initial checklist. He was alone in the copter, but then a heavily armed man who was gripping the upper arms of two bedraggled women emerged from the prisoner's wing and hustled to meet the bird. They were followed by two more armed guards who were half-carrying, half-dragging a tall figure with red hair toward the helicopter, the man's legs not able to hold him for more than three steps in a row.

Ripley whipped around quickly to hide her elation that Flannery was still alive, and being escorted to the second Black Hawk, and to prevent Chang from realizing his lies about his death had been revealed. Liu and Zhang had already been loaded into the helicopter, along with their guards. Only she, Emerson, and Tanner remained on the tarmac with Sam and Chang.

Ripley shook her head vehemently as she backed herself into Tanner. "I can't go on that thing, I'll get sick!"

Fred played his part well. Frowning, he weakly gestured to her from the cockpit. "That one hurls. Hope you've got a big supply of airsick bags."

Sam slanted an exasperated look in her direction. "You're wasting time. Get in."

Emerson extended his hand. "Don't feel bad, I get airsick too. I need your expertise," he said simply, evidently buying her distress, so she took it with a squeeze and wedged herself inside.

Chang addressed his men. "If any of them tries anything funny, you have my permission to shoot them, or throw them out of the copter. Tanner, you ride up front with the pilot and his oxygen. Deprive him of it if anyone acts up. I expect you all back within an hour with answers about the stink." Chang slapped the side of the helicopter and backed away as Fred started the sequence that would get them aloft.

The other Black Hawk had already ascended and a moment later Fred had them in the air. Ripley buried her face in her hands so no one would see the pure joy which had surged the moment the wheels left the asphalt, and they became airborne. A man's hand stroked her back, and she looked sideways at Emerson, who was gazing at her with concern, although his own face had taken on a distinctly green color. She gave him a partial smile before burying her face in her hands again, leaving just enough room between her fingers so she could watch the National Lab float away from them as they angled east.

The place soon disappeared behind the rise of the mountains, the sound of the blades precluding any conversation. Ripley sat up and continued her pretense of feeling nauseous for the sake of the guards, who stoically kept their rifles at the ready. Her gaze swept past Liu and Zhang, who didn't seem particularly clear on why they were in a helicopter as his eyes darted to and fro, and focused front where Flannery's helicopter spun a few hundred yards ahead of them.

She'd gotten herself and her men into the air and away from the base, which might collapse at any moment, along with some innocent civilians and Emerson, which filled her with relief. It immediately dried up again as Ripley considered the armed guards and their mandate to shoot at the first sign of trouble. Added to that was the impossibility of communicating anything above the din of the helicopter in flight, and the fact that Flannery was on a completely different helicopter than her own.

Ripley moaned and buried her head in her hands once again, but unlike the first time, her distress was real, as she had no idea what to do next.

CHAPTER TEN

The Mississippi River
Day Twenty-six

Logan smiled as Braden filled another bucket with damp sand and dumped it over, adding to his castle structure on the narrow shore of the Mississippi River, humming a little ditty to himself over and over again. Occasionally he would consult with Whuff, who'd been ensconced on a piece of driftwood nearby, agreeing or disagreeing with what his imagination provided, then got back to work building, making long pathways for water to curl around his sandcastle and decorating it with found pieces of wood, stone, and bird feathers.

The tranquil scene was a balm for Logan as he stretched out nearby during their final lunch break from the river, his head propped on his backpack, a bottle of water in his hand, his shoulders losing some of the tension they'd been holding for days on end. That Braden had even a single hour which was close to normal was a precious gift after all they'd been through on the river over the past four days of hard, wet, dangerous travel on both the Wisconsin and the Mississippi rivers.

He ran his fingers through the cool, damp sand as he rolled his cramping shoulders. He raised his hand to gaze at the deep-set wrinkles ridged with white which had been caused by long exposure to the dirty, wet, and cold Mississippi river. The journey had taken a heavy toll on his body and strength of will, but it was nearly over. Only a few more hours, and they'd be at the Kingston Landing, or if it had been washed out by the backflow of the river, they could always exit at the sturdy Burlington pier, only a few miles to the south, and hike back to the farm.

Logan let out a weary breath. He could at least be glad they'd be arriving in daylight, no matter what. Facing down Mara's stern Uncle Willard at any point after it turned dark was something to be avoided. Willard was a shoot first, ask questions later type of man, and Logan in no way wanted to be on the receiving end of that combination. He sighed gustily as he admitted to himself that Willard and his wife Helen weren't the nicest of people, and if he could have avoided making their homestead a destination, he would have done so.

"Logan!"

Braden's voice snapped him out of his contemplation of the hours to come, and he brought his attention back to the toddler, who was proudly showing him his creation of sand. It was quite expansive, and Logan took his time examining all of it, letting Braden point out various things in an excited babble. He wished he could take a picture of the castle and its creator, but his cell phone was long gone, lost at some point in his journeys through the upper Midwest.

"It's a most excellent castle, Braden." Logan sighed as he stood and stretched. He was reluctant to move from the comfortable little beach where they'd stopped on the Mississippi for their lunch, but they only had about three or four hours of paddling left before reaching their destination.

He moved to turn the kayak back over from the driftwood pile where he'd left it to drain. The moment he flipped it over, Braden plopped into the sand and had a full-on meltdown.

"Don't wanna go! No more boat!"

His cries echoed loudly as he broke into sobs, Braden's fists striking the castle he'd just built, destroying it in angry bursts of temper, his feet kicking up sand as he rolled and screamed. Logan sighed, rubbing his temples where the throb of a headache was coming on, his temper fraying at the edges. He picked Braden up and held him tightly, absorbing the kicks and punches. The boy's forehead burrowed into his chest, hot and wet as the tantrum began to slow to sobs instead of angry screams. He rocked back and forth until the sobs eased and he was able to get the little boy to take a drink of water.

"It's time to go, buddy, so we can get to our friends, Ms. Gayle, and Demarius and Damien, and Mr. Zeke."

Despairing tears flowed down the boy's face as he shook his head hopelessly, shoving against Logan to be released, so Logan let him go. Braden's legs churned as he dashed for the woods on a path directly away from the river and the dreaded boat. For a moment, Logan sat still, fighting his anger and frustration until he regained a smidgeon of patience, then Logan pushed up with a heartfelt sigh to chase after his charge. He shoved past the bushes where Braden had disappeared and came into a clearing which was filled with fallen leaves and overturned trees, and then stopped short as he gasped in fear.

A long brown and black timber rattlesnake had curled into itself and was shaking its rattle at the boy, who had paused uncertainly a few feet away from the dangerous creature, his shoulders hitching with sobs. "Braden, don't move." Logan fought to keep his voice level and himself from dashing in to grab the child, which would just make the snake more likely to strike. "Just stay where you are."

"'Kay." The quaver in his voice was heartbreaking.

The snake remained alert and ready to strike, the rattle buzzing, its tongue zipping out and tasting the air. Logan eased his gun from his holster as the thing remained in a threatening position, but his angle was poor, with Braden between himself and the snake. Moving to get a good shot might startle the creature into a strike, so he let the idea go.

"Doing great buddy. Keep still."

After a long minute, the creature finally stopped rattling, uncoiled, and slithered into some nearby leaves, disappearing within seconds. With a deep exhalation, Logan swooped Braden into his arms and crushed him to his chest, and carried him back to the beach.

"He didn't bite you, did he?" Logan held the child away from him, looking at his legs and arms carefully once they'd reached the safety of the open sand.

"No." Braden's lip quivered. "Scary."

"Yeah. Yeah, that was super scary."

Braden swallowed hard and then collapsed into Logan's arms, shaking. "Time to go," he whispered.

"Yes, okay, get Whuff."

They were packed and back on the water in record time. Logan wrapped Braden in the roomy rain jacket, which the boy found comforting, nestling into it with a little sigh. As Logan expected, the child fell asleep soon after they got on the water, exhausted by his tantrum and the snake episode. Logan tugged the rain jacket over his face and let his heavy body sink back against him, keeping his paddling to just his arms in an easy flow.

Logan focused on the river as he paddled to rid himself of the horrible guilt that flowed in the aftermath of the encounter. It could've so easily gone horribly wrong. He'd let the little boy out of his sight, then had been slow to go after Braden, selfishly taking the moment for himself. Logan shook his head at the images of what could have happened if the snake had struck. Getting someone to the hospital to get antivenom treatment belonged to the old world, even in Iowa, where the quakes hadn't impacted the population as badly as everywhere else.

He'd been compartmentalizing so many things. Logan took a hard look at his past activities as he dipped his paddle in an easy rhythm, neatly avoiding an eddy of black water which wanted to suck them in by angling directly across it, then flipping their direction to avoid a huge log that drifted into their path. While he and Braden had gotten through a lot of dangers, there was still a long way to go, first to Wichita with his group, a journey of five hundred miles, then the road onward to Addison, Texas would be an additional three hundred and fifty miles, across terrain that was subject to ongoing earthquakes. Three hundred and fifty miles where anything could happen as he traveled alone with a toddler, and after leaving the boy with his father, it left him with nearly a thousand miles to traverse to reach his home, a month and a half of travel on foot. The tug to simply take Braden home with him wormed and twisted into his mind like a noxious weed, chipping away at his will. The sweet whisper added that if he cut directly east from Iowa, he could be back at his homestead and his family in Virginia in less than three weeks.

As always, his best defense was to put himself in the other father's shoes. How would he feel if someone had his son Will safe and sound, but didn't bother to bring him home? In a flash, the nasty, wiggling notion of abdicating his responsibility vanished.

Even once that one was conquered, more dark thoughts hounded him as he paddled the vast river with the sleeping child breathing softly nestled against his chest. He'd managed to avoid people for the most part by traveling via the river, the speed of their kayak whisking them through the places which were inhabited. He'd camped in riverside parks, as far from cities as he could get, not willing to risk a second round of the disdainful looks and intolerance toward refugees like they'd encountered in Minnesota.

Logan swallowed hard as tears welled, and he was attacked by self-doubt and fear, shaking his head against the onslaught. "Can't think of it in big chunks," he told himself firmly. "Just need to get to Helen and Willard's. You can manage that. Just keep going, one mile at a time."

Chanting a mantra of "one mile at a time" under his breath, Logan dipped the paddle into the muddy flow of the water and took the next stroke.

As they closed on the landing that led to the tiny town of Kingston, population forty-nine last he'd checked, there were more and more craft on the river, from simple Jon boats whose fishermen raised a hand as he paddled by to other kayakers. There'd even been a cabin cruiser loaded with teenagers partying as if nothing out of the ordinary had happened to the world. He'd moved aside twice, shoring the kayak as barges moved by, loaded with massive containers of military supplies as well as Jeeps and trucks anchored onto the wide, flat barges being pushed upriver by the mighty tugboats.

Braden had been fascinated by the sight, even trying to stand in the kayak in the first thrill of seeing the gigantic behemoths of the river being pushed steadily upstream. Logan had gently reached around the boy and helped him sit back down as displacement waves lapped against the place he'd stopped.

"It's something else, isn't it, Braden?"

"Uh-huh." The excited grin was infectious, and Logan pulled the little boy into a hug, which was returned easily and naturally. Braden gave him a kiss on the cheek as well.

"Okay, only a little longer and we'll be at the farm where Mr. Zeke, Darien, Demarius and their mom are," Logan said as he pushed off from the weedy shore once the wake of the massive barge had subsided. "The last time I was there, I saw horses and goats and even pigs."

Braden sat erect as Logan moved them downriver, his head on a swivel, looking for his friends. Logan did the same, not wanting to overshoot the little dock if it still stood. He rounded a bend in the river, feathering the oars easily over the top of the water. A small figure wearing a baseball cap sat cross-legged on the wooden pier, bouncing a yellow tennis ball.

As the turquoise kayak got closer, the person peered at them, then leaped to their feet with a holler of joy, hands raised high overhead, jumping up and down.

"Mr. Logan! Mr. Logan! Braden!"

Logan nearly burst into tears with happiness, a tremendous weight falling from his shoulders as he paddled the last few yards to the dock. "It's Darien, Braden. We made it."

Braden's eyes widened at the sight of the boy and gave a wave back as Logan arrowed to shore. Darien helped pull the boat in and then reached his arms towards Braden.

"I've got you, Braden. Hey!" The little boy clambered onto the wooden dock with Darien's help.

"It's so good to see you," Logan said as he held the kayak steady next to the wooden pier. "Is everyone okay?"

"Yep, it was kind of an awful trip, but we all made it!"

"Are Helen and Willard treating you okay?"

There was a slight pause before the boy's response, but he nodded. "Yeah, they are. We made homemade peach ice cream with a hand crank last night. It took forever, but man, was it good!" Darien jumped up and down with excitement. "Come on!"

Logan clambered up and pulled the kayak onto the dock, and wrapped the boy in a big hug. Pulling out his backpack, he gestured to the carrying toggle on the front of the boat. "Think you can manage to help me carry this to the house?"

"For sure! Come on Braden, walk next to me, little buddy."

"Whuff?"

Logan gave the boy his stuffed dog from the backpack, and then strapped it on, pushed the paddle into the kayak, and clasped the rear toggle.

"Lead on, Darien."

"One of us has been watching out for you all the time for the past three days," Darien told him as they walked at Braden's pace along the single lane road that led from the river to the town. "Mr. Willard has us doing chores otherwise." He wrinkled his nose. "There sure are a lot of chores, but Ms. Helen makes real good food for us, and we have beds and hot water, and she's teaching Mama how to can fruits and vegetables."

"Yep, living on a homestead means there's always something else that needs to get done," Logan affirmed.

The path led them through fields of corn that were withering, their tassels turning black months early. The acreage would need quick harvesting unless Willard planned to let it all go to seed.

As they topped the rise, the spire of the Methodist church that Willard had helped build over fifty years ago came into view first, followed by the rest of the four-square, solid place where Logan and Mara had been married. It stood proudly on the left of the road, the white clapboard standing out in the midst of the yellowing green of the fields, backdropped by a low roll of wooded hills that stretched for miles just to the west of the farmstead. There were patches of russets and yellows amid the deep green of the forested bank, a reminder that although Iowa had escaped the quakes, they were dealing with the three-month early onset of fall due to the continued overcast sky.

Helen and Willard's simple two-story house stood just across the road from the church, the bottom half of it faced with red brick, the top with white siding. Willard had built that structure too, from the foundations and cellar all the way through the attic. He'd put in the sizeable garden Helen kept for her vegetable canning, and planted the rows of apple, pear, and peach trees which formed a windbreak to the north of the house. In the back was his woodworking shop, the single bay garage for their truck, and the crowning glory of the farmstead, the barn. It overtopped everything with its sturdy, red-painted planks of oak that stood two and a half stories high with a sizable hayloft that kept the animals in food through the deep, dark winters of Iowa. Willard had gotten help raising the barn, but the design of it was his.

Darien hastened their pace the last hundred yards, dropping his end of the kayak as they entered the front yard and dashing inside. "I'm going to go tell mom!"

Logan pushed the kayak against the side of the house as Braden moved closer to him and wrapped a single arm around his leg. He reached down and picked him up. "We'll stay here tonight, buddy, maybe another day, too." He walked him over to the pen that held a few hogs, pointed out their bulk to Braden. "Those are pigs, Braden." He turned in a circle so the boy could get a perspective on the fertile spread. "This whole place is a real, live farm. What do you think?"

Braden's eyes were solemn as he took in the place. "Ee I Ee I Oh," he whispered, making Logan laugh.

The back door from the kitchen slammed open, and Demarius tore outside with his brother right behind him. "Logan! Braden!"

Demarius hugged them both, then waggled Whuff's ear. "I'm glad you got Whuff back, Braden. I found him next to the river."

"Well, aren't you both a sight for sore eyes?" Gayle stood on the back porch steps, closing the screen gently behind her, hand on her heart. "Hey little man!" She brushed at the sides of her face as her tears rolled. "Logan Padgett, I'm that glad to see your annoying self still in one piece, that's for sure. Let me give that boy of yours a squeeze."

Logan's throat grew tight with emotion at the happy sight of the beaming woman as she plopped onto the stairs, extended her arms, and beckoned with all ten of her fingers at Braden.

Braden wiggled to get down and the little boy dashed over to Gayle, who enveloped him in her arms. "I've sure missed those hugs." She met Logan's eyes over Braden's head. "Good job, Logan."

"Thanks, you too. Where's Zeke?"

"Out hunting. I gotta say, soldier boy's been a wonder, been bringing in fresh meat nearly every day."

A dry voice interrupted the happy reunion as a white-haired, tall, lean man came from the barn, wiping his hands on a rag, three bluetick hounds swarming around his legs as he walked over. "You made it."

"Willard, it's good to see you again."

"Likewise." The older man had a bit of a stoop to his shoulders, and his weathered face was a mass of time-worn wrinkles, but the hand that clasped Logan's for a moment was hard and firm. He looked at Braden, still wrapped in Gayle's arms.

"You must be young Braden."

He stooped so he was at Braden's height, his easy agility impressing Logan. "Glad you're here, young man."

Braden pointed behind him. "Issa pig?"

"It is, we call them hogs, but yep, that's right. We've got horses and cows and goats, too. Maybe one of these boys can take and show you." He straightened as he spoke, and both Darien and Demarius nodded.

"We can take him," they chorused, both extending their hands to him.

"I'll hold Whuff for you," Gayle said, plucking the toy from him.

"'Kay."

Willard clapped Logan on the back twice, which was one more than he'd given him when Logan had married Mara. "Good man." He was spare with his words, as he'd always been, but the bright gleam of approval in his eyes was something Logan had rarely seen.

"Thank you, sir."

"You made it," Helen said, echoing her husband of fifty years as she stepped onto the side porch from the kitchen. The years had left their mark on Helen, but her hair was still a copper color, and coiffed in a perfect chin-length helmet, not a strand out of place. Mara told him her aunt used nearly a half can of hairspray every day to make sure it stayed put.

"Hello, Helen." He took a couple of strides toward her, intending to shake her hand, but she held him off with a sniff.

"Looks like you had a long, hard journey and brought half the dirt with you. Shuck those clothes before you come inside my house. I'll start you a hot bath, and I'll have a meal for you when you're done." She turned to Gayle. "That toy needs to be washed, too. We've got to get those jars out of the canner, see that the seals are tight." She turned and walked back into the house.

Gayle rolled her eyes at Logan, but got up and followed Helen. "See you on the other side," she remarked, putting Whuff on the stairs with a pat.

"Good to see not much changes around here," Logan remarked dryly to Willard, whose eyes crinkled slightly in the corners in acknowledgement.

"There's a pile of fresh clothes waiting for you that she gathered," he commented. "And for the tyke." He stuck his hands in the pockets of his worn overalls and cleared his throat. "You heard anything from Mara or Deb?"

Logan shook his head. "I got a message to Lloyd, one of our neighbors, letting Mara know not to expect me until next month or the month after. He said the homestead came through those early quakes all right."

"We've been getting news about the world in general. Maybe, after you clean up and eat, you'd like to take a walk with me around the fence line, we'll have a jaw about it?"

"Certainly, Willard."

"You're fixing to take the boy back to his father in Texas is what Gayle tells us, is that right?" When Willard got a nod of affirmation from Logan, he shook his head. "Seems a long way."

"It's the right thing to do."

The crinkles came back around Willard's eyes, and he clapped Logan on the shoulder a third time. "That's right. I'll be in the shop when you're ready."

The hot bathwater turned black as Logan bathed himself and washed Whuff in Helen and Willards pink bathtub. Wiping away the steam on the mirror with his forearm, he examined his wounds in the mirror. The beating Traeger and Chertoff had given him had paled to yellowish bruising, and he could touch his ribs with his finger without getting a twinge of pain. The bullet wound Pamela had given him had carved a serious divot out of his arm, but it was also healing over, the scar long and narrow, the skin pink.

The long days in the boat had helped his legs recover from the miles of walking and running he'd done, healing the shin splints which had begun to form, and he'd developed muscles he'd never had before, even with all of his Ironman training. He was thin, and his beard had grown bushy with streaks of grey and white that hadn't been there before. His hair was a curling wild mass as well, the chestnut of it peppered with streaks of grey that he fingered in astonishment.

Logan trimmed the beard closely, then shaved, the sharp blades of his cheekbones standing out even more prominently than they had when he had the beard, the hollows showing as well as new lines around his lips and dark-shadowed eyes. He ran his hands over the bones of his ribs as he looked in the mirror, reminded of a character in a movie he'd seen years ago, where a man had become a plane wreck survivor on an island. After brushing his teeth three times, Logan slipped on new underwear and socks, a fresh dark blue t-shirt, and a pair of soft, worn jeans and put on a belt that he had to slide to the final hole. He stepped back into his worn boots and pulled one of Willard's old flannel shirts checked in shades of black and blue and followed his nose to the kitchen carrying a damp Whuff.

"I'll just put him out on the line," he said as he passed through the kitchen which was mostly taken up with canning supplies, the air steamy as the two women and Darien worked to put up the vegetables from Helen's immense garden.

"I threw your old clothes out," Helen remarked. "Feed yourself and the boy before you do anything else. You're as thin as a shadow. And tell Demarius we could use his help in here."

Logan wiggled his eyebrows at Darien, who'd given him a deeply understanding look as Helen gave her orders. "Yes, ma'am."

He found Braden happily poking bits of straw into the pig pen next to Demarius. As Logan stepped next to them, Demarius ran inside the house without being told. Braden was dressed in new clothes, his blonde hair still wet from being washed with the rest of him.

"You're all clean," Logan remarked. "Did Ms. Gayle give you a bath?"

"Yus," Braden said. "In the sink." He looked into the distance with a wistful smile, as if remembering the love of his life. "With bubbles."

"I washed Whuff for you, we just need to let him dry." Together they went to the lines that stood behind the house and pinned up the toy by the ears and tail then went inside hand in hand.

They ate their late lunch at the dining table that took up part of the main living area, the beautiful china cabinet Willard had built of local oak standing next to it, the old dishes Mara had told him belonged to her great-grandmother holding pride of place. A long piece of intricate tatting decorated the center of the table, done by Helen. Her crochet work was visible in the living room in the form of arm protectors on the arms of both chairs and the sofa. On the long, low coffee table, another length of tatting stretched and gracing it was the same bowl of pink, yellow, and green candies that had been there the last time Logan had visited.

He and Braden devoured sandwiches made with fresh baked bread, slathered with sweet cream butter, and loaded with cured ham. Slices of sweet, crisp red apple sat on the side of their plates. Logan added grainy mustard to his sandwich, and let Braden taste it. The boy had waved his hand in front of his stuck out tongue.

"Too hot!"

"It's an acquired taste," Logan agreed as they drank fresh milk and finished their meals off with huge oatmeal-raisin cookies still warm from the oven.

"Mara uses your recipe for those cookies," he told Helen as he brought the dishes inside. "It can't be beat, what a delicious meal."

The comment brought a brief smile to Helen's lips, then she touched his forearm. "Willard says you got word to her," she said, then her lips pinched together tightly as the strong vertical line between her eyes deepened. "We've not heard anything from either of the girls."

"You raised them to be strong, resourceful women," Logan assured her. "My money is on both Deb and Mara coming through any trials that they get served."

Helen cleared her throat, and nodded, brushing her nose clear with an embroidered handkerchief. "Leave those dishes, I know Willard wanted to speak with you." She turned to Braden, who'd followed Logan to the kitchen. "Have you dried dishes before, young man?"

Braden shook his head no, so she put a dishtowel into his hands. "I'm going to show you how, and when we're done, I have a whole box of toys you can play with." She shooed Logan out the door. "We'll be fine, you go on."

Bemused by the way Helen had effortlessly corralled Braden into learning how to do chores, Logan strode across the yard, his muscles relaxed, the good food, clean clothes, and company combining to make him feel healthier than he had in weeks, and entered Willard's woodworking shed.

"Still want to walk the fences?"

Willard put down the wood he was sanding. It looked to be the final front panel for a beautiful double chest of drawers; the furniture made with the same care and love he'd lavished on the china cabinet in the living area. Logan ran an appreciative hand over the satiny surface of the piece, letting his finger curve along with the curls of ivy which twined along the sides, carved with precision and delicacy. "Beautiful work, Willard."

"It's meant for you and Mara. For your one-year anniversary."

Willard put away his tools neatly. "I was nearly done with it when all this nonsense started, wanted to get it finished."

Logan was stunned. "I don't know what to say."

"Thank you is customary." The crinkles at the corners of his eyes were back again. It seemed to Logan that he and Willard had turned an invisible corner in their relationship, as the man was much easier to talk to and deal with than he'd been at the wedding. Willard tucked wire cutters into his overall pocket and picked up a spool of wire as he handed Logan a pair of work gloves. "Come on, let's walk and fix things."

Helen and Willard's property was roughly twenty acres, so walking the perimeter took about an hour, but they paused to repair the triple strung wire fencing as it was needed, righting a couple of metal poles that had gone out of true in spots. They walked and worked mostly in easy silence, Logan content to wait for whatever it was Willard wanted to say to him.

"You're sure you want to move on with Braden?" He asked at last.

"One hundred percent."

Willard sniffed and stared at the horizon. "My thought is things are going to get worse, not better. We're hearing there's organized, militant factions wanting to take control from Blake Ordway, that they're preparing to fight. I didn't vote for him, but I admire what he's doing in this disaster, I can tell you that. Last thing we need is more bloodshed and loss because some so-and-so's have a wishbone up their collective hoo-haws."

Logan stifled a grin at Willard's colorful language. "Ordway stepped up and took care of us refugees in Minnesota," Logan agreed. "It was bleak before he did that."

"He's opening the FEMA caches, too, according to the Browns." Willard waved a hand to the north. "That's our neighbors. They've got a working ham radio, keep us posted on things. Guess there's a good chance the skies won't clear for another year or two, or longer if the quakes keep rolling, which is why Helen's putting up her vegetables like a madwoman. US Government's moved to Indian land, out in Arizona, where it's safe like it is here, we hear tell." He stopped moving, and Logan stopped with him.

Willard crossed his arms over his chest and stared at his boots for a long spell before nodding. "Guess what I'm trying to say is you and Mara and the kids would be welcome here if you need a safe place. Yours might not be safe, if what we're hearing is true, that those militants are gathering right there in the Roanoke area of the Blue Ridge. Wouldn't be hard to build you something on our property if you'd want it."

Logan was taken aback even as bubbles of fear wormed their way into his gut about his family being in harm's way. "That's generous of you, Willard."

"We take care of our own. You're family, and your kids are, too."

They'd come back in sight of the Mississippi river as they walked the eastern section. "The river rose clear to the top of the bank," Willard pointed to the muddy line which had stopped just short of flooding the corn field. "Never seen the like, flowing backward a couple of times, too. Almost made a praying man out of me." Willard said seriously.

"I'll remember your offer once I get back to them and see how things are," Logan promised. "It means the world that you extended it."

They continued walking in silence, turning up the dirt road that Logan had walked earlier in the day, just the trudge of their work boots and the late trills of meadowlarks and the harsh calls of the blue jays swooping to their nests, breaking the silence until Willard cleared his throat.

"Helen wants to ask Gayle and her kids and Zeke to stay on with us. We're old, could use the help, and from what I've gathered, they might not have homes left where they're headed. Think they'll go for it?"

Logan stopped, stunned by the pronouncement. Willard sighed when he took in Logan's expression and started walking again. "I know. Helen and me don't seem like the type to take in strangers for more than a meal and a place to lay their heads before sending them on their way. Truth be told, I never thought we'd be wanting more bodies in our space, but Helen says Gayle is all right, and so are her kids. I think Zeke is too." He paused, then chuckled. "I nearly blew his head off when they came traipsing down the road, but he shouted he was your friend, so I gave him a chance."

"I was worried something like that might happen. To answer your question, I think Zeke is set on getting back to his family outside of Elizabethton in Tennessee," Logan replied slowly, thinking it over. "Gayle was firm about getting back to Wichita, too. But it wouldn't hurt to ask them."

"That's what Helen said." Willard nodded as they paced side by side. "Guess we'll ask. When did you plan on moving on?"

"Tomorrow, or the next day at the latest." Logan gestured to the black tassels of the corn. "If you need help getting your corn in, I'm happy to stay an extra day."

"We could use the help; I'll take you up on that. Helen has put by supplies for everyone, and clean changes of clothes, too. I'll drive you to the border in the truck to help you make up some time, and to make sure you get across. They're saying the only safe crossing is way out in Nebraska, but Helen says that'll work for you to drop straight to Texas." He cleared his throat a second time, and Logan suspected the man had already spoken more words in the past half hour than he had in a month.

Logan was awash in gratitude, the warmth of it spreading through his body. He stepped in front of Willard as they crested the rise, the long twilight throwing everything into shades of soft greys and dusky blacks to stop his movement. "Thank you doesn't seem to be enough for all that generosity, Willard. Can I give you a hug?"

Willard peered around Logan, then gave him a nod. "Just don't let Helen see, she'll think I've gone soft."

The hug was brief, but heartfelt, and as they walked toward the lamp-lit home that Helen and Willard had shaped by dint of hard work and dedication, the soft glow from inside showing through the windows as the darkness swarmed past the hills and over the fields, Logan's tension melted away again.

"You've made a good home for yourselves," Logan remarked, scenting what might be apple pie floating over the air, alongside grilling meat and frying onions. "I can only hope I can get my place looking as good one day."

Willard grunted. "I've got faith in you, Logan Padgett."

CHAPTER ELEVEN

The Hayward and San Andreas Faults
Day Twenty-six

Fred flew their Black Hawk on a northerly trajectory a few hundred yards behind the second helicopter which carried Flannery and more soldiers, along with the two women. Both of the birds flew at a low altitude, the pilots wisely choosing to stay below the ever thickening blanket of debris and ash which completely blocked the sun.

Ripley stole a look at her watch as she stayed bent over, clasping her belly, pretending to be fighting motion sickness. The helicopters had lifted off from the broken asphalt at the National Lab only a few minutes before Ripley expected the next earthquakes to hit, and she'd managed to get the people she cared about on board. She'd done her best to get all the people who were living on the crumbling bit of rock that still rose above the Pacific ocean evacuated as well, but her pleas had fallen on deaf ears. Chang, their ostensible leader, had been too immersed in his plans to take over what was left of the United States to see the danger that was literally at his feet.

Emerson bent low next to her, talking in her ear so she could hear him above the noise of the helicopter, since none of the passengers had been given sound-muffling helmets with an intercom system which would allow them to speak to each other easily. Only Fred and Tanner, who sat in the co-pilot seat, had them.

"You're not really sick, are you?"

Ripley shook her head surreptitiously, then tapped her watch. He gave her a pat on the back to let her know he'd gotten the message just as one of their guards nudged him with the end of his rifle and shouted at him to lean back and not talk. Emerson raised his hands in the air and settled back into his seat.

Ripley bent completely over, her head between her knees as she counted the minutes until the next quake. If it were a small one, all of her work to get them in the air would be for nothing, as Chang's orders were for them to be back in an hour. Once they were ensconced back at the base, Ripley was sure he wouldn't let them have access to the helicopter again. They were valuable assets and cost a lot in terms of fuel to operate.

An N95 mask dangled in front of Ripley's face. She looked at the kindly visage of Emerson, who pointed outside as he urged it into her hands. Emerson passed masks to everyone, using his long arm to reach the front of the helicopter with a mask for Tanner, who slipped it on under his helmet. Fred waved his off, pointing at the oxygen tank he was using. Ripley coughed as she placed the rudimentary protection over her nose and mouth. The closer they got to the enormous rift in the earth and the toxic gases it belched, the worse the stench of the air had become, the telltale tickling of her nose and the burning sensation on her skin evidence that the amount of sulfur dioxide and hydrogen sulfide in the air had increased significantly over the four days they'd been imprisoned by Chang. The President would need to know about the dangers of the gaseous volcanic emissions, especially if the prevailing winds continued to blow from west to east.

The groan she let out for the sake of maintaining her illusion of being in a weakened state wasn't altogether fake as her frustration mounted over their impossible situation. Ripley and her team had been thoroughly bamboozled by Chang's ruse of needing a rescue. Ripley clenched her hands into fists as she fought to seek positives and keep herself from falling into an ineffectual depression. They'd learned more about Chang's plans to take over the USA, and that he had militia groups who believed his lies that they'd all have wealth and power if they sided with him. There were groups loyal to Chang in Washington, DC, and in the Blue Ridge Mountains, and perhaps other places as well. They'd discovered the rift filling with ocean water, which might become a solution for stopping the ongoing earthquakes, and she could warn Ordway about the gases the thing was creating which could spread across the country so preventative measures could be taken. All of it was extremely valuable information. She just had to get it to the President, along with the survivors Ripley and her team had found nestled in the protection of a basalt outcropping on Mammoth Mountain.

Ripley peered out of the big double windows, which allowed light into the belly of the helicopter. The round curves of the Berkeley Hills were to her left, but on the right was only the flatness of the water that had poured into the areas where Walnut Creek and other cities had once been. She could see one crumbling mountain standing to the east beyond the flat grey of the water, which had to be Mount Diablo. Ripley swallowed hard as the epic proportions of the seismic activity hit her yet again.

"Ninety percent of the population wiped out," she muttered to herself, shaking her head.

How Chang could justify adding a fight for power on top of the natural disaster defied any logic. Ripley had a sudden, violent surge of glee that he and his oily right-hand man Sam had been left behind at the National Lab. If he was killed by the disaster, maybe his movement would fizzle, and President Ordway could make headway in helping the people who were left in the USA to regroup and find a new way of living on an utterly changed planet.

Their helicopter marked a wide circle, distracting her from her vengeful thoughts, and she looked out the windows once again. The other helicopter was landing at the Nike site, the wheels touching down on the concrete launching platforms, their rotor slowing. Beyond them stood the shipping containers, which held medicine, food, and water as well as other survival supplies. Ripley gripped her seat with both hands as her agitation grew. In a few moments, Flannery would be dragged from the helicopter and forced to open the containers. After that happened, his usefulness to Chang would end, and Ripley had no illusions that Chang had any grace or forgiveness for people he considered to be part of the enemy camp. One of the guards below hopped out and motioned with his gun at the people inside of the helicopter.

Tension filled her body, making Ripley sit bolt upright, unable to take her eyes from the scene below as Fred circled. In the cockpit, Tanner pointed his gun at Fred, clearly telling him to move on toward their objective. Tears threatened to burst from Ripley that she couldn't do anything to help either of her men.

Just then, the mountain below them rippled, then expanded, as if it were the outer skin of a balloon being filled with a giant breath of air, heaving outward in all directions at once, then diminishing in a series of shudders to its former shape. Ripley stared as the hill held together for a split second longer, then screamed as it crumbled inward, startling the people aboard her craft. Ripley unbuckled her harness and bolted from her chair to the window to see more, her eyes huge as the entire chain of the Berkeley Hills pancaked, their once solid structure eradicated as they succumbed to liquefaction and fell into the water surrounding them.

The blades of the helicopter that had landed jerked into high gear as the pilot thrust it to full power even as the helicopter dropped with the evaporating mountain. The Black Hawk was already half-submerged in the churning dirt and mud as the surface collapsed beneath it. The soldier who'd gotten out threw his weapon down and leapt for the open doors, other men inside reaching for him, but it was too late. His footing was gone, and he was sucked beneath the whorl of earth in seconds.

Slowly and painfully, the helicopter rose, fighting against the dirt and debris tumbling around it, the people inside struggling to close their open bay doors. Ripley pressed her hands against the glass as the Black Hawk finally heaved into the air, escaping its trap, then wheeled and flew back in the direction of the National Lab.

Fred, prompted by Tanner, did the same, both helicopters flying higher than before, racing back to the base as the hills beneath them gave way to the tremors below them. As the hills fell, a vast ocean wave roared up, cresting nearly twenty feet high, the seething black water carrying massive amounts of debris from the homes and structures which had been drowned, all of it picked up and carried by a quake-induced tsunami that thundered across miles upon miles of terrain, the spray reaching high enough to leave droplets on their windows.

Everyone in the helicopter stared outward in horror, the guard's guns hanging loosely as the final part of what had been the San Francisco Bay Area was completely engulfed beneath the ocean. When the two birds reached the base they'd lifted off from ten minutes prior, nothing was there but floating debris dancing in massive waves which were flung high into the air then ebbed back, creating a maelstrom of eddies and whirlpools.

"It's gone." Emerson turned to her, his face white. "Everyone's gone."

Ripley swallowed as she nodded, then turned to the stunned soldiers who had been set to guard them as Fred circled the area. Shouting so she could be heard, Ripley said, "I have a safe place we can go to. Can I tell my pilot to take us?"

The three soldiers looked at each other, their tough exteriors stripped away, then nodded half-heartedly. Ripley stuck her head between the two men up front and asked the same thing of Tanner.

"I guess," he said in a shaky voice. "If you hadn't said something to me down there—"

She squeezed his arm, so he'd know he didn't have to go on, then turned to Fred. "Take us back to the Reno site, please, Fred."

The grizzled man smiled at her, his normally ruddy face pale, purpling shadows rimming his tired eyes. "Yes, ma'am," he said. "Glad to."

A tap on her shoulder had her turning around to see Emerson holding a mechanical device. "I want to see what was making the sulfur dioxide and hydrogen sulfide, and get exact pH measurements, we need that info," he shouted above the noise of the helicopter as it made its turn to the east. "I want to take measurements of the air, and see what the concentration of the hydrogen halides is as well."

"You'll be able to do that," she reassured him. "We have to fly over the volcanic rift that's causing it." She turned back to Fred. "Can you talk to the other pilot, tell him to follow you?"

"Sure can."

Fred circled their helicopter around the other one as he spoke to the other pilot, then smoothly tracked to the east, the second bird following. Only a few minutes later, they were above the long crack that the sea poured into in a mesmerizingly smooth cascade of water which was sometimes interrupted as a house, or a car toppled over the edge. The falls were always followed by an immense puff of water vapor.

Zhang and Liu started talking in Chinese as they looked out of the helicopter, while Emerson opened his backpack as Fred expertly circled. Once he was ready, Emerson gestured to the soldiers to open the doors so he could use his testing equipment. The whole compartment was blasted by the odorous steam rising from the crack when they complied. Even with her mask on, Ripley was coughing and hacking in moments, as was everyone else, her skin itching madly from the presence of the sulfur dioxide, her eyes tearing in response to its toxicity.

"Do you have what you need?" She gasped the question out a minute later, barely able to get enough oxygen in the foul air.

Emerson nodded, his face grim, and waved to the soldiers to shut the doors again. Coughing, Ripley stuck her head up front to tell Fred to head further east.

Just as Ripley pushed her body between the front seats, Fred clutched his chest, then slammed the helicopter down and to the right, tossing her forward into Tanner's lap as a fast banging sound echoed along the side of their helicopter. Additionally, a blinding, mile-long sheet of blue and white fire seared next to them along the line of the rift, the brilliant flames shooting upward at tremendously fast speeds.

Ripley scrambled to her feet just as a blur of motion in front of their helicopter alerted Ripley that something was flying at them fast. Fred jerked them into another evasive maneuver. Ripley disentangled herself from Tanner as more bangs echoed off of the other side of their helicopter. Fred pushed the bird upward at a steep angle, punching through the thick dirt and ash cloud, everything outside their windows going utterly black out for a good ten seconds as they traveled through it.

There was a pelting, grinding sound as they emerged, and the rotor took on a terrible high-pitched whine as they broke free into hot sunshine and a blessed blue sky.

Ripley tore the mask from her face and gripped the pilot's arm. "Fred, what's happening?"

Fred pulled the oxygen mask from his face, which was deathly pale, and his lips were blue. He pointed skyward, his voice strained. "That's ash or debris in the rotor, and there's a pair of Little Birds that came out of nowhere. They're shooting at both Black Hawks, trying to take us down!" He looked anxiously upward as a metallic burning smell filled the cabin. "I can't safely stay at his altitude with a wonky rotor; we have to go back down."

"You know best, Fred."

"Roger. Hang on, descending."

Tanner grabbed Ripley as she wrapped her arm around his harness as Fred flew them back through the clouds. "What's going on?"

"You tell me, those two Little Birds from the National Lab were firing at us."

They were enveloped in the black of the clouds, and then they zoomed out in a steep dive as Fred fought the controls to level them out. The Little Birds lofted next to them in seconds, then flew directly at them. She blinked as bright flashes erupted from the front of the small helicopters.

"Guns at twelve o'clock!" she screamed.

Fred expertly turned and dropped the helicopter, but some of the bombardment struck the fuselage.

Shouts echoed from behind her, the bay doors banged open, and returning gunfire filled the air from their helicopter. Suddenly, Tanner grabbed her head and pushed her down, covering her torso with his body. All Ripley could see was the floor and the co-pilot rudders moving as Fred flew in a series of evasive maneuvers that had her head spinning.

Fred angled them sharply upward once again and only Tanner's grip on her body kept Ripley from tumbling into the back, her legs flying loose behind her during the steep incline. She scrambled to get purchase and brace herself, so she could see what was happening as the helicopter vibrated, and the whine of the engines sputtered as more bullets pierced the body of their craft. Behind her, someone screamed in pain as more rifle fire blasted, and the helicopter jolted as the load shifted in the back.

"Man down!" came the horrified cry.

The load shift became a serious falloff to the right, the helicopter looping sideways, and then plummeting from the top of a lazy loop. Ripley wrenched herself out of Tanner's grasp and looked at Fred. His head had lolled to one side and his hands had fallen loose from the controls.

"Move!" she shouted at Tanner, tugging at his arm with all her might to get him out of the copilot seat as the helicopter lost altitude, starting a crazy spin. She hauled him out of the seat, her fear lending her strength and speed.

Tanner fell between the seats into the cargo bay as Ripley dived forward, clambered over his legs, and grabbed hold of the collective with both hands to stop their terrifying plunge. She pulled upward as hard as she could against the helicopter's dive as the flat water below loomed closer and closer, her muscles screaming, her breath coming in short gasps as she managed to level them out. Puffing air, furiously weeping as she glanced to her left at Fred's lifeless body, she wailed in rage and made them climb again. Another strafe of gunfire had her ducking instinctively as she tried to use the rudders to steer them away from whoever was shooting at them, but they resisted her, sluggish and ungainly. Glancing to the side again, she saw Fred's inert feet were tangled in them.

"Tanner!"

She pointed at the problem, panting to catch her breath, her terror rising when more bullets struck the helicopter with loud clangs. Tanner dived forward and moved Fred's feet out of the way. He stayed where he was, head swiveling as he searched the sky, trying just as Ripley was to spot the elusive, quick helicopters that were attacking them.

Ripley got the craft leveled off and accelerated, intending to escape the area as another length of the gaseous clouds shot upward in a blanket of blue fire. She threw her hand up to block the bright flare, but was too late. Her sight seared, black dots peppering her vision. She blinked rapidly, trying to clear it, steering the helicopter in a loop to catch sight of the mountains to their east. Another tower of fire went up from the rift, and as it did so, two small dots blasted underneath the blaze as it climbed skyward, bright flashes of fire coming from the front of them before they zipped away to the side.

"The hydrogen's being ignited by their gunfire," she muttered to herself as she angled them away and upward from the area, her breath easier as she comprehended at least one of the mysteries which had confronted her so suddenly, the fast ascent of the flames making sense.

Her eyes tracked back and forth as she climbed, seeking to understand who was firing on them. She aimed to get above the cloud cover and thick vapors, out of the attacker's line of sight, but the helicopter resisted, the power declining the higher she went above sea level. Ripley checked her gages. The left tank fuel gage was completely in the red, while the right tank was at the one-third full mark. One tank empty, part of one left. Ripley continued to scan to get a visual on their attackers as she fought the controls, but the cloud cover remained out of reach of the failing engines. Shaking her head, Ripley focused on aiming them east again, sighting the mountains in the distance that bordered Nevada. She had to get them over the range while the helicopter could still make the climb and hope they had enough fuel to get back to the Reno FEMA site.

To her left, Tanner was doing CPR on Fred, who continued to be unresponsive. Behind her, another long round of gunfire rattled as the guards in her helicopter fired. Streams of white mist that had billowed from the rift and drifted east made her eyes burn from the foul air so that tears streamed from them. She dashed them away to clear her vision.

White blobs coalesced into the form of both of the Little Birds from the National Lab site flying in unison nearby. Both sent a stream of .50 Cal machine gun fire, the sparks arcing in an elegant line to strike her helicopter on the lower left, the force of the bullets shredding the bottom of her craft, blowing the tires.

"Tanner! Get to the gun!" She pointed at the fixed forward 50-cal on Fred's side of the helicopter. Tanner abandoned his CPR and reached over Fred's lifeless body to reach its controls as Ripley arced over the Little Birds to come around behind them. Behind her in the cargo hold, someone fired their rifle at the attackers, but she couldn't tell if anyone was hit.

Ripley also scanned for any sight of the other Black Hawk, but could see nothing moving in the sky.

"Coming around," she shouted.

Ripley put the helicopter on a dead-head course for the nearest of the little helicopters. It took evasive action, but she'd lined it up correctly and Tanner's bullets hit square, the line shattering the windshield and the man piloting it, his head snapping back in a burst of red. The Little Bird dived to the left in a horrible arc, and plunged into the heaving water below, splashing into the shallow of it. Black plumes of smoke and red fire smothered almost as soon as they began as it sank out of sight.

Ripley dove hard to the right as the second copter flew at them, guns blazing, the bullets pinging off of metal, peppering the fuselage and into the mechanics above her. She did the only evasive maneuver possible with the sluggish rudder and flew straight into the steaming, noxious gas clouds, holding her breath as she did so.

They blasted out the other side, but even in that short time, Ripley's skin had been burned painfully by the chemicals belching from the magma and seawater mix, the shouts and screams from the back of the helicopter confirming the deadly maneuver shouldn't be tried again with the bay doors open.

The helicopter bucked her as she tried to fly it higher, get a better view, find a place to fly through that wasn't engulfed in the poisonous clouds. On what had been the Pacific side of the vapors was nothing but ocean. She had to get back on the other side to get them to the safety of the mountains beyond Sacramento.

"Swing by them again." Tanner shouted, his face utterly focused. He pointed to a relatively clear patch where the mist was thinner and Ripley flew for it as fast as she could make the bird move, hoping to clear the rift before it billowed more fumes.

The forced speed brought a metallic burning smell to her attention as the controls shuddered in her hands. She coughed hard after they flew past the gap, her air constricted as the sulfide gases did their deadly work, the shudder calming as she straightened and downgraded their speed. Ripley kept tight control of the helicopter, focusing on the last place the second Little Bird had been.

Her course guess was right, and her swoop nearly slammed them straight into the craft, the other pilot diverting at the last minute from the impending collision. Ripley locked eyes with the shocked pilot who looked utterly terrified, and then with the passenger who'd been firing at them, his face pulled into a snarl as he wrenched his guns around for another swipe at them.

"It's Chang!"

Behind her someone fired their automatic rifle and the gunfire pinged off of the smaller craft. The pilot tried to evade, but the bullets caught the rear rudder.

"He's lost control. Give me another shot!" Tanner shouted, pointing. Ripley circled, so they were pointing straight at the Little Bird a second time. Her gut clenched as she flew straight at the smaller craft, accelerating as she did so, her knuckles turning white on the controls. Tanner blasted the helicopter with his gun as Ripley kept them steady.

The Little Bird tried to climb out of the way, but Tanner's aim was deadly. The engine burst into flame, and the helicopter nosedived into the water below, and then sank beneath the waves.

Panting for air, Ripley circled once to see if she could see any survivors in the water, but the wave action created by her downdraft made it impossible to see anyone. Ripley stole a look over at Fred, tears popping into her eyes at his still form. Ripley was just about to take his wrist to see if he still had a pulse when a sudden shout jolted her attention away.

"Below!"

Tanner leaned over her and gestured frantically at the water just ahead. Ripley craned to see what he was pointing at, her chest constricting as the shape of the second Black Hawk became clear to her. It had crashed into a shallower section of the inland sea. A small part of the fuselage remained above water, as well as a single broken blade pointing skyward. Instead of creating waves by going closer in, Ripley took her bird higher, scanning the water for a red-haired, lanky figure.

"There!" Cries from behind her had Ripley frantically looking. Tanner clasped her arm and gestured that she should aim for ten o'clock, making a fist for her to slow after a few moments.

"Two!" He shouted, then moved to the rear, coming back to her a moment later.

"Can you hover?"

"I don't know!" While she'd been in the heat of the fight, Ripley had instinctively flown the craft, but she'd never learned how to hover. "I'll try, but hurry!"

The door of the cargo hold slammed open, shaking her, then the helicopter wavered and dipped as the men behind her deployed to rescue the people they'd seen in the water. Ripley kept her eyes steady on the far horizon, matching the nose of the helicopter to it to help her maintain a level altitude. Ripley fell back to her old trick of counting to keep herself calm as the men did their work. She breathed in for a count of five and out for a count of five, making minute adjustments with the pedals as wind drafts caught them, or the weight in the hold moved. Her palm was sweaty and kept slipping on the collective as she fought the helicopter to keep it firmly locked in place, a slight stutter in the engine and a grinding sound letting her know the machine was failing.

Ripley tossed the worry about machine failure out of her head and focused on the task at hand. The altimeter let her know when she broke more than two feet from her position, so she split her focus between the instrument and her line of sight on the horizon, occasionally glancing at the fuel gages. One tank was empty, the second one showed she had just over a quarter of a tank left.

The craft bobbled to the right, and she hissed as she adjusted for whatever weight was being added on that side, her breathing becoming in for three and out for three as her heart rate accelerated. Beads of sweat stung her eyes, but she didn't dare blink them away as the helicopter jerked with whatever was happening behind her.

The solid clunk as the cargo doors closed was one of the best things Ripley had ever heard, and she let out a final breath in a low whistle. Tanner grabbed her shoulder a moment later and leaned in to her.

"We can go." He shouted, then rapped his helmet with his knuckles, and turned to gently remove the one on Fred's unmoving form.

Ripley teared as she accepted Fred's helmet, the inside of it still warm from her friend's scalp. Swallowing the tears that wanted to rise, she adjusted it. In the sudden quiet it provided, Ripley spoke into the com.

"Is he gone?"

"Yeah. I lost one of my men in that firefight, too." Tanner took a breath to add more, but Ripley waved him off from giving her any more news as she pushed them forward.

"I just need to focus on flying."

Ripley kept the bird low as she flew toward the mountains, passing the remains of Sacramento and angling slightly north as she recalled the journey coming from the other way. As the adrenaline spiked by the battle and its aftermath ebbed, she was left cold and exhausted, her hands trembling as she fought her nausea, the deep grief she had over Fred's death threatening to take her over.

"You're not going to cry and you're not going to throw up on yourself, Ripley Baxter. You are going to fly this helicopter and you are going to figure out how to land it," she muttered to herself.

"What was that?"

Tanner was right by her elbow, his voice coming through loud and clear on her headset.

"I was telling myself not to get sick."

"Yeah, I heard that part, and I get it. Here's some water." He handed her a water bottle and Ripley drank deeply. "I was asking about the second part, sounded like you said you don't know how to land."

"Yeah, well, I did okay with the hovering, and I never did that before, either. Grab a map, and guide me toward Lake Tahoe or Reno, will you? None of the navigation is working, and I only flew over this mountain range the one time."

Tanner rummaged around the cockpit but didn't find any maps. He held up a finger. "I'll ask if anyone knows the area."

Ripley kept the helicopter steady as she ascended the first rise of mountain, searching for the two rocky peaks which lay fairly close to each other that she'd seen on their way out to Berkeley. More of the mountain range had fallen since she'd flown over the area, obliterating any other landmarks she might have remembered. Most of the huge firs which had dotted the lower elevations had tumbled, further obscuring the landscape.

"Looks like someone spilled the toothpicks," she said aloud, then gave a strangled laugh at the completely unfunny joke she'd tried to tell herself. "Pull it together, Ripley."

She squirmed in her seat as the foreign landscape rolled in front of her with no differentiation, going back to counting her breaths. Her last fuel tank edged into the red as she was forced to climb the side of the mountain. Fred had told her once they were in the red, they had about fifteen minutes of flight time left, and five of those needed to be used to land softly. Dr. Liu pushed his way forward and made room for himself by moving Fred over slightly with a few fastidious moves. He wore Tanner's helmet and a concerned but polite expression.

"I used to hike here. I will try to help you navigate."

"I want to go just west of Pyramid Lake and north of Reno," she said, glancing at the fuel gage. "I was looking for the two mountains that are mostly rock, near each other."

"Yes, Castle Peak by Donner Pass and Mount Lola. I know them." He stared out at the devastation attentively, pointing after a moment.

"I think that is the I-80."

Once he'd pointed out the grey line, Ripley could make it out as well, and she angled to her eleven o'clock to follow it.

"And there are the peaks you wanted," he added a moment later, pointing to two nearly indiscernible white crumbles which Ripley could have easily missed.

She breathed a little easier and put the mountain tops to her right as she aimed them north, doing her best to fly steadily and do nothing that would burn up their gas.

"Okay, we should be there within fifteen minutes," she told him. "Thanks for your help."

A deep buzzer sounded as her last tank dipped completely into the red. Dr. Liu's head snapped around and he looked at her with alarm.

Icy cold filled Ripley. She spoke calmly. "Dr. Liu, if you could strap me in and then move to the back and strap yourself in, please. Tell the others to do so as well. We may have a crash landing within the next few minutes."

He gave her a single nod, and buckled her into her harness, and then moved back as she'd requested. The smell of burning had grown more pronounced the further away from the rift they'd flown, and the helicopter was getting more and more sluggish, taking longer to obey what her feet and hands wanted it to do.

"Just a little further, you can do it." Ripley kept her heading steady as the mountain fell away from her on the downslope.

A gleam of water in the landscape ahead gave her a bit of hope as the engine sputtered for a few terrifying beats before she was able to give it some more fuel by tilting the nose of the bird down. She nudged the controls a little to the left as the edges of the lake next to the FEMA depot and camp came into view, just as the blades slowed their spin.

"Mr. Liu, tell everyone to brace for impact in about fifteen seconds. I'm going to aim to land in the lake if I can get us there."

Her hands were rock steady on the controls as the ground rushed to meet them. Ripley kept the bird hovering about twenty feet off of the ground as they soared in from the southwest, bringing the nose up slightly to slow their velocity and perhaps give them a slightly softer impact as the lake rushed to meet them. Black smoke billowed from the engines, obscuring her sight, and then they quit altogether.

With a high-pitched whine, the rotor ceased its rotation, and as it did, Ripley lost the rudders, and her ability to control the craft. The pace of their drop increased with every foot as the metal bird fell from the sky. They hurtled into Honey Lake, slamming into the tranquil surface, a huge belly flop which pushed water in all directions.

Ripley's head snapped forward onto the controls in front of her with the force of the impact. The helmet saved her skull, but the sharp blow rattled all the way down her neck to her spine. Ripley instinctively drew her knees up and turned sideways in her seat as the force of the entry accordioned the nose of the helicopter, driving the instrument panel toward her chest.

Water flooded the cockpit, shockingly cold as she fumbled in the scant millimeters she had left, pinned between the back of her seat and the front of the helicopter. She found the release button for her harness, unsnapping it and wiggling herself free. She reached over to Fred, but he'd been engulfed in metal, his blood flowing from multiple wounds.

With a sob, she half-waded, half swam through the freezing water to the belly of the helicopter, which was rapidly flooding as the bird sank. She ripped off her helmet and slapped the chests of the two guards, who were still in their seats, their eyes unfocused and confused.

"Open the doors!"

They blinked as she struck them again and pointed at the doors, but then moved to comply.

Ripley helped Dr. Liu unbuckle Dr. Zhang as the compartment continued to flood, the gush of water as the two guards got the cargo hold open pushing her into the side wall. "Go with the soldiers," she said, pointing at the two young men.

Emerson wasn't moving as the water reached her chest, his arms limp as she shoved them aside, but her searching fingers found his heart beating strongly. Ripley ducked beneath the water to unbuckle his harness. She got his long arms and legs moving toward the door, where Tanner was helping two young women she'd not seen before to float out.

"Take him!"

"Yes, ma'am!"

Tanner scooped up Emerson's unconscious body and towed him out as the compartment continued to fill. Ripley dived once more beneath the water and grabbed the two backpacks Emerson had toted aboard and kicked back to the surface, her teeth chattering as she pushed against the growing current of water filling the compartment. She took a final deep breath before the water went over her head and kicked madly for the light emitting from the open doors. Her movements became frantic as her lungs tightened, doing her best to get out of the watery prison as the copter dropped deeper into the lake, taking her with it. After a long minute of fighting, her body movement slowed as the cold and the suck of the helicopter became too much to fight against, the last bit of her air leaking from her mouth in a stream of silvery bubbles as she lifted her arms toward the receding surface.

Two men dove toward her, arrowing out of a tiny blotch of light. They grabbed her arms as she extended them forward with the last of her strength. They towed her to the surface, and the trio crested through it, coughing, and inhaling huge gasps of air. The men helped her stroke to the shoreline, taking the heavy backpacks from her as they got to the shallows. Ripley collapsed on the sand, water bubbling from her lungs as she coughed. She shivered violently as a strong breeze whipped over her soaked form.

"You could stand to work on the landing," Tanner said as he heaved himself onto the shore next to her, also wheezing.

"Hey, are you on the ground in basically one piece?" Ripley managed to quip back between breaths of glorious air.

Tanner nodded and then groaned as he stood and helped her to her feet.

"Is Emerson okay?"

"The tall guy? Yes, him, and everyone else, too. Good job." He smiled.

Ripley couldn't return the smile, shaking her head as the image of

Fred sinking below the water, trapped in the helicopter and the absence of Flannery filled her mind and threatened to disable her unless she distracted herself.

"Let's get everyone into the FEMA camp. There's food and dry clothes there." Ripley managed to croak out as she moved to support a wavering Dr. Zhang, and get him walking in that direction. She focused on putting one foot in front of the other. The rest of the group followed her with little chatter, soaked and still shocked by the events of the last few minutes.

As they reached the edge of the chain link fence, a familiar burly shape hustled toward them, accompanied by a couple of the refugees they'd rescued from Big Bear, all carrying weapons pointed at Ripley's group.

"Bruce!" she called out with a wave of her hand.

"Ripley?" Bruce Larson hurried ahead of his team, a huge grin on his face which faded as he scanned the bedraggled group behind her, his eyes darting to find more familiar faces besides Ripley's.

"They're gone, Bruce. Fred and Flannery. I couldn't save them." Her chin trembled a bit and her throat was raw, but she kept her composure as he reached her.

His face was as serious as she'd ever seen it as he nodded his understanding. "You saved these people, though."

Ripley looked over at Tanner and the two soldiers who'd been with Chang and raised an eyebrow as she locked eyes with Tanner. The young man squared his shoulders and nodded his head, muttering something to the two other men, who immediately fell into parade rest as Tanner did, dropping their rifles and sidearms to the ground at their feet.

"Those three men were soldiers with Chang, and will need to be debriefed, but they worked with us to get away from him, so I want them treated with respect. These three men are scientists who were at the lab, and I don't know about the women."

Ripley gestured to the pair. They seemed to be college-age students, both wearing ripped t-shirts with a sorority logo on them, and hiking shorts. "You were at the National Lab when we got there," she said as she recognized them.

"We were prisoners since that first quake; we'd been hiking, and they found us and locked us up when we went to them for help." One of the women said, her arm looped around the other one's waist, who was limping badly, her knee a bloody mess. "Macy and Katy."

"Go on ahead to the first aid tent. I'll get all of you fixed up." Bruce waved them ahead to the fenced compound, bringing up the rear as Ripley fell into step with him. "Chang was the one signaling us with the radio?"

Ripley nodded wearily. "That's my one piece of good news. He's gone. We shot him down over the new inland sea about half an hour ago."

"You were in a gun battle in the helicopter?"

"Yeah."

"And you won?"

"Yeah."

"Not bad for a pint-sized chick," Bruce said as he wrapped his burly arm around her. The warmth and compliment heartened Ripley, and after she let herself sink into it for just a moment, she took a deep breath and picked up the pace.

"We'll get everyone fed and rested, but at first light, we're getting everyone moving so we can get to the new US Capitol as quickly as we can." Ripley said. "I have information President Ordway needs to know."

CHAPTER TWELVE

Eastern Tennessee Seismic Zone
Day Thirty

Deb roused herself from her bedroll with a gigantic sneeze, followed by three more in quick succession. With a moan, she blew her nose, then coughed as she bent forward to stretch her aching muscles. She massaged the small of her back in small circles before rubbing her bleary eyes.

It was still raining, a cold, nasty rain that had bits of sleet mixed in with the drops, adding a slight rattle to the draped tarp above her head. Long streams of water rolled down the tented covering, creating a small moat around her raised sleeping area. Deb struggled to draw a deep breath as she blew into the embers of her Dakota fire hole, relieved to see a slight pop of an ember. She added the fuel she'd tucked beneath the tarp the previous night a bit at a time as she continued to cough and sneeze. The glow of the fire was welcome, and Deb warmed her hands before she put her pot of water on to boil. Once the water was ready, she added instant coffee directly into it, stirring as the crystals frothed into a light brown foam, then added three sugar packets from the diner she'd raided the day before along with some powdered creamer.

She held the warm cup with both hands, hunched and shivering even in her puffy jacket and wool cap. The days had gotten markedly cooler the past few days as her path took her both north and to higher elevations into the Blue Ridge Mountains. The morning before, Deb had even woken to a tinge of frost on the brown grasses beyond her hidden camp.

Her reverie was interrupted by the onrush of another huge sneeze, which shook her so hard she slopped hot coffee out of her pot and onto her knees. With a sigh, she blew her nose and mopped up the mess, then pressed her hands against the sides of her neck and her cheeks, finding the swollen glands painful to the touch.

A horsey echo of her miserable snuffle sounded loud and clear from just outside of her tarp where Daisy stood with her head hung low, pressed under the stand of trees Deb had picked as a relatively safe camping spot. The horse whickered discontentedly a second time, flicking her skin as the rain continued to pour. Daisy always thought Deb should give her a morning treat before the coffee was brewed, and invariably let out a long huff of air to let Deb know she was waiting. Deb pulled out a turnip she'd been saving for the horse's morning treat from her pack and crawled part way out of her shelter to give it to her mount. Daisy nipped it out of her palm adroitly and crunched as Deb crawled back into her cramped shelter and dug out a couple of aspirins and a vitamin C packet to help her fight off her steadily worsening cold and considered what her day should look like.

It was their tenth day on the road. Technically, they still had two days to go before they took another rest day following Kevin's recommendation of taking every fourth day off, but with her heavy cold, Deb was considering bailing on riding thirty miles in rain and sleet and instead just moving forward until they found a barn or other shelter then stopping early so she could actually get warm and dry, and Daisy could be sheltered as well.

Deb shifted uncomfortably at the delay, but as another deep cough made her clutch her sides, she had to concede it would be the smart move. As much as the drive to get to her sister's homestead pulled on her at a core level, the simple cold she'd picked up the day before changed things, especially since she suspected she was running a fever as well.

"Teach me to be nice," Deb muttered. "Bet this was a goodbye present from those kids, they both had runny noses."

Deb had run across two young children playing in a field as she'd circumvented a small town. They'd told her their daddy had fallen off a ladder, and she'd gone with them to see if she could help. The man had dislocated his arm, which was a simple fix, and she'd stayed to eat lunch with him and his grateful wife. It had been nice to stop and converse with people for a couple of hours, Deb had to admit, but a tell-tale scratchy throat had started up only a few hours later.

And she was just bone tired on top of being sick. Travelling daily was more wearing than doing her nursing internship had been, and that had been no picnic. The journey itself hadn't been terrible, Deb reflected, except for the horrible day she'd had yesterday. Most of the time it had just been physically tough as she steadily rode Daisy twenty-five or thirty miles a day and then did the work of setting up her camp, making the fire, and boiling her water and caring for the horse.

Her belly growled and Deb poked half-heartedly at her nearly empty backpack, producing her last packet of instant oatmeal and a handful of dried apples for her breakfast. Foraging for food was another chore that was becoming more dangerous and time consuming. Places like the death house she'd left behind six days ago were becoming common, the decay of the people who'd been killed in their homes or at work or school boiling up all sorts of diseases. She grunted grimly as she recalled lessons from her nursing school about the viral spread of contagion via vermin and flies as nature took its course. Added to those statistics, finding only spoiled and rotting food inside homes and stores was becoming the norm, and her stash was getting low. Deb shook her head as she stirred the paltry meal, sneezing yet again as the pace of the rain picked up and thunder rolled through the valley.

The last good place she'd raided had been when she'd gotten food for both herself, and the elderly lady with the two chihuahuas, nearly a week ago. That was where she'd gotten the instant oatmeal she was having for her breakfast, along with the instant coffee, tins of soup and canned spaghetti and vegetables. She'd unearthed a can opener as well, and a bottle of whiskey, which had somehow survived unbroken. Deb had left several cans and the opener on the woman's porch, and when she stopped by the next day they were gone, but her knocking went unanswered, and there was no barking from the house, so she'd moved on.

"A mystery I'll never solve," she muttered, then sneezed violently three times in a row.

Deb shivered involuntarily at the sound of the water pouring down the sides of her shelter. It reminded her of the terrible day she and Daisy had experienced the day before. They'd forded several large streams on their journey east and Deb had gotten the knack of securing everything, then just staying atop the horse, and letting Daisy pick her way through them. Yesterday had been a different experience entirely as they were forced to cross the Little Tennessee River, which, contrary to its name, had been quite wide and it had gotten frighteningly deep much more quickly than she'd expected, the horse stepping into the quick of the river nearly immediately up to her chest. It had meant a long swim for Daisy to reach the far bank, and the pull of the current had been strong, yanking them downstream. Daisy had tired midway through, her breath wheezing so badly that Deb had slid off of her back to help her get across the final thirty yards of the poorly named river.

"I really need to learn how to swim better," she admitted as she ate her breakfast, continuing to recall the near-death experience.

She'd lost her grip on the saddle horn only moments after she'd gotten off, the fast current sweeping her downstream as she flailed wildly. Lacking any skills whatsoever in the water and weighted down with her backpack, it had only been sheer determination as she kicked and moved her arms that had allowed her to make it to the river bank, clinging to the reeds, clawing her way through the mud, coughing up what had seemed like her bodyweight in river water.

The horse had found her on the river bank, stretched out flat on the mud, shivering and shaking and had nudged her to stand. Deb had clung to the stirrup as they'd beat their way through a mass of scrub, debris, and small trees, the mud near the river sucking at her boots, making each step a momentous achievement before they'd finally made their way to higher ground. She'd rushed to set up camp before the gathering clouds dumped their promised rain. Added to her misery had been the growing scratch at the back of her throat, which historically had always been a precursor to her getting sick.

Everything had been utterly soaked from the river, even the change of clothes she'd carried inside her backpack, and it had started raining only a few minutes after she'd gotten her camp settled, so nothing she owned was dry. At least she'd collected wood and kindling before the downpour, so she'd had the fire.

"Be grateful for the little things, and get moving," she told herself, just as her Aunt Helen had said to her a million times growing up under her Iowa homestead roof.

As Deb packed her sodden gear, tucking the last of her dry wood into her nearly empty backpack, banked the fire, and saddled the grumpy horse, she spared a thought for her aunt and uncle. They'd been taskmasters and weren't the warmest of people, but they'd certainly given her life skills and a passion for healing animals and people despite their lack of hugs or affirming words beyond an occasional nod of approval, or her Uncle Willard's slight crinkle around his eyes.

"Thank you," she said aloud into the pouring rain. "For all the good things you gave me."

The sincere expression brought a tiny bit of warmth to her, as did the rueful smile as she added, "Could have used some swimming lessons, though."

"Okay, Daisy," she said, coughing as she hauled herself into the saddle, pausing to blow her nose on the sodden kerchief she'd been wearing around her neck, then pulled the tarp over her head like a cloak, moisture sheeting down the sides. "Let's find somewhere to shelter."

They plodded cross country, Deb dismounting to clip wire fences as they came across them. Daisy's head was hanging low, her steps getting slower and slower as the wild fields turned to mud. They detoured around one of the ubiquitous cracks in the ground for a good mile before it narrowed enough for Daisy to step over it. The crack gave off a horrific stench of rotten eggs that Deb could smell through her stuffy nose and her eyes burned as bits of white steam rose from the space. It made the horse shake her head and sidestep out of control and break into a gallop to get away from it, nearly unseating Deb in the process, until they were past the ooze of the stench.

Daisy's hooves clopped on asphalt, rousing Deb from her woozy state and she reined the horse in. Gazing through sheets of rain, she could see a multitude of overturned cars and trucks stretching along the highway in either direction, with no evidence that anyone had tried to move them out of the way to use the once busy road. Curious as to what road it might be, but not wanting to pull out her paper map in the rain, she guided Daisy along its surface until she found a road sign that they were on I-75 and there was an upcoming exit 60 for Sweetwater.

The name of the town rang a bell for Deb, and she urged the horse forward when the memory flooded back. She'd visited the place with Mara when Ethan had been about eight and crazy about caves. They'd gone there to tour a huge cave system which housed an underground lake called the Lost Sea Adventure. They'd gone through a bright yellow tunnel, she recalled, and gotten on glass-bottom boats to float on the expanse of water a half-mile below the earth.

While she had no desire to go into a cave while earthquakes rattled on the hour, there'd been lots of hotels and restaurants along the stretch of road leading to it, increasing her chances of finding a place with a roof and walls. Deb turned Daisy to take the exit as she unclipped her holster so she could draw her weapon easily. On high alert, Deb kept Daisy at a walk as they passed badly wrecked buildings which were barely visible in the sheeting rain, most completely flattened. Another crack forced them to detour several blocks from the main street before they could continue forward. Deb coughed painfully as they went, her hand going to her chest, which felt heavy. Her breathing was getting steadily more difficult as well, and a ping of worry mounted. If she didn't find shelter soon, her cold would develop into pneumonia, and Deb was out of antibiotics.

Finally, an L-shaped structure emerged on her left, one end crumbled but most of it still standing. Deb dismounted, wrapping the reins around a bit of exposed rebar. She drew her gun as she moved past the broken open end of the building, stifling a cough as best she could, her head swiveling as she edged deeper. The driving rain made it hard to hear, but she didn't detect any sound or movement as she walked into the intact portion of the place, which appeared to be a mom and pop restaurant from the red-checked tablecloths that remained on the tables and the sizeable kitchen, which was in shambles, but she could make out the massive stove and dishwashing section.

After checking the place and finding it blessedly empty, Deb shoved several tables into a large rectangle to form a makeshift corral, and then brought Daisy inside. She took off the horse's tack and soaked saddle blanket, and then closed her in with a final table, draping the blanket and the tarp over it to drip dry.

"I'll find you something to eat later," she told the horse as she shivered violently, her head pounding. After taking more aspirin and another vitamin C, Deb grabbed a bucket from the kitchen and set it outside to collect rainwater, then set to work breaking wooden chairs with her small hand axe so she could get her fire going, hauling in fallen bricks to build a platform for it.

Once she had the fire going, she stripped off all of her clothing down to her underwear, wrung it out as much as she could, then hung it from chairs she placed in a circle around her fire so they could dry. Shivering and sneezing, she wrapped herself in dry tablecloths, and huddled near the fire as she pulled out her last can of soup and heated it, her hands shaking so much she couldn't use a spoon, so she waited for the container to cool slightly and just drank it from the cookpot. She heated more water when she was done, and drank that as well, pushing her fluids as she had nothing else with which to fight her illness.

The warmth of the food and water and the dry wrapping of the tablecloths eased her symptoms slightly as she broke a table into larger chunks of wood to build up the fire before she went on a hunt through the place for what she could salvage, the tablecloths swathed around her.

The kitchen was a tumbled mess, and part of it was exposed to the rain, which was still pelting, the ice pellets growing larger as the day waned toward night. Deb found huge cans of apple pie filling, corn, baked beans, and green beans, as well as tinned chicken and tuna for herself. She carried the huge cans one at a time to her campfire, then returned to the kitchen. She grinned when she found a plastic container full of dried oatmeal and scooped several handfuls into one of her plastic bags before dumping several more into a large metal bowl to bring to Daisy.

"Here you go, girl." She rubbed the horse's nose fondly, giving her scratches where she liked them best, around her ears. "There's more where that came from, too. This was a good stop."

She shivered violently as a gust of wind blew into the open section of the restaurant. After thinking for a moment, she dragged several round tables to the space and laid them on their sides to create a partial wind break before going back to the fire and turning her clothes so the back section could dry before sitting back down, unreasonably exhausted from the activity she'd performed and slightly dizzy.

Deb touched her cheeks and forehead with the backs of her hands, the skin there burning like hot coals. "Yep, you've got a fever. Okay. Push the fluids, and rest." She shook her water bottle and moaned when she found it empty.

She swayed a bit as she stood, but Deb picked up her cookpot and resolutely made her way around her makeshift windbreak to haul in the plastic bucket she'd placed outside, which was already half full of water. Dipping out a potful, she placed the rest of the bucket into Daisy's enclosure so the horse could drink, then slowly shuffled back to the fire, her cough bringing up green gunk that she spat into her empty soup can.

"That's not good. I should chop up some more chairs while I still can," she muttered, thrusting off the suddenly stiflingly hot tablecloths from her body.

Half-naked, she dragged as many chairs as she could closer to her fire, and with trembling hands, chopped three of them up before collapsing, the axe coming dangerously close to landing blade-down into her foot as her vision greyed.

"Gotta stop chopping," she said, carefully putting the axe down before she fed the fire.

Deb shook with cold as she pulled on still-damp leggings, socks, a long-sleeved shirt, and her woolen hat. Scrunching the tablecloths into a nest, Deb fed the fire, then curled as close as she could to it as her body spasmed with wracking coughs.

She must have fallen asleep, as it was pitch black when Deb woke from a terrible dream in which she struggled through an icy river as men with guns shot at her. Her fire was only dim coals, so she painstakingly fed it small splinters of wood until it crackled back to life. Feeling her forehead and cheeks, which were still unnaturally hot, she coughed hard, bringing up more phlegm.

"Better out than in," she croaked and fed the fire so she could boil the rainwater. While she was waiting, she opened the apple pie filling container and spooned the sugared contents into her mouth, forcing herself to eat as much as she could, although she couldn't taste it at all, and it hurt her throat to swallow.

A whicker from Daisy reminded her that the horse needed another feeding as well. Deb staggered to her feet and got the empty mixing bowl from the horse's stall, then put the plastic bucket back outside to gather more rainwater. She squinted into the darkness to judge the velocity of the rain. It wasn't pouring any more, but the fall was still steady, and a vindictive, icy wind found every crevice in her clothing.

Deb drew in a shuddering breath as she forced her aching body to move into the kitchen to the oats bin. She put the last of the oatmeal into the mixing bowl, but it was a paltry amount for such a big horse. Rubbing her aching head, she forced herself to think of a solution. Deb went to her campfire, and spooned in a heaping portion of the apple pie mixture, then opened the canned corn and green beans, and added portions of those as well.

"It's not the most healthy of dinners," she told Daisy as she fed her. "But better than nothing." Deb supported her weight on the table next to the horse, needing to rest before she walked the five feet back to the fire.

Her water had boiled so she took it from the fire, waited for it to cool, then drank most of it. Her headache diminished slightly as she wearily added the last of her chopped up chairs to the fire and fell into an exhausted slumber.

The light was grey when she woke for the second time, her bladder bursting. Deb got unsteadily to her feet, nearly toppling over twice as she was struck with dizzy spells. She made her way to the open section of the restaurant, nearly tripping over the bucket she'd put out to capture water. It had finally stopped raining, leaving the air cold and crisp in its wake. She edged around the corner and did what she had to do, then brought the water inside.

Her cough was still deep, but the frequency of it had diminished slightly. Her fever had broken at some point in the night, but her balance was still off, and her body ached. Blowing her nose, Deb pushed herself to get through chores of building up the fire and boiling water and filling her water bottles, then made herself a stew of canned chicken, corn, and green beans, once again forcing the food past her sore throat. She finished the meal off with vitamin C and more pain medication, then lay back on her nest, wiped out from the few simple chores.

"You should rest for at least another twenty-four hours," she told herself. "Or else you'll just dance on the edge of pneumonia longer."

Already desperately tired, she hauled herself up once again to tend to her horse, slinging the shotgun over her shoulder in addition to her pistol. Deb moved away two of the round tables as well as the table holding the obedient creature in her makeshift stall and put the mare's lead rope around her neck.

Leading Daisy outside, Deb picked up the plastic bucket, and they went in search of grass to crop and a stream to drink from. The grass was easy, as they were next to what had been a residential area. Deb perched on a downed mailbox to catch her breath. She held the lead rope loosely as Daisy cropped the browning grass and still-green weeds, her thoughts drifting as she focused on forcing deep breaths to help clear her lungs of mucus.

Her head pounded to the beat of her heart, but she resolutely led the horse to a broken line of trees, and found the stream she'd expected to find at their base. Daisy ambled to the rush of it and drank for a long time, her tail swishing contentedly. Deb filled her pail partway with water and they made their way back to the restaurant, the details of the devastated town much more apparent in the daylight.

It saddened Deb to see the destruction, which had flattened nearly every structure in the town. While it didn't have the horrifying X shape of two cracks eating the town bit by bit, the place had a haunted feel to it, and when the wind blew, there was an empty howl which gave her the shudders, as well as a prickling sensation on the back of her neck as if she were being watched.

"I wish we didn't have to stay here, Daisy. But I don't think I can ride yet."

They stopped every few yards so Deb could put the bucket down and rest before moving on, the horse contentedly cropping more of the dying grass and weeds as she waited for Deb to collect herself to move again. Once they were back at the restaurant, Deb left the bucket just inside, put the horse back in her enclosure, and with the last of her strength, pulled the windbreak back together as the room spun around her, tumbling to her knees, a flush of heat through her body letting her know her fever had kicked back in again.

She crawled the few feet back to her nest of tablecloths. The fire had gone out, but Deb had nothing left in her to get it started again. She managed to take a few sips of water, and then curled into a ball and passed out.

A quick, sharp pain in her gut startled Deb awake, curling around herself instinctively. Another sharp pain in her shoulder had her crying out, and she tried to sit up. The distinctive snick-click of a bolt-action rifle being readied froze Deb in place.

"Stay put." A light tenor voice told her.

Deb couldn't help herself and let out a massive sneeze, followed by several hacking coughs. Heaving for air, she patted her hands, trying to convey she wasn't trying anything foolish.

"She's got that crud, Dad." This voice was younger, a bit scared.

Deb peered into the gloom. Three figures surrounded her and her dead fire. A man and two girls, one perhaps three years older than the other, neither of them in their teens yet.

"Could be, honey. Or she's just got a bad cold." The man studied her indifferently.

"Hey there's a whole can of apple pie filling! Can we take it?"

"Not if she's sick and been eating it."

"C'mon, if we cook it, it'll be okay."

Deb nodded at the girl who'd just spoken, her mind screaming at her to make a connection, to show she was a human being just like them. "If you cook it, you'll be okay. Take it if you want."

"That's rich. Telling me what I can take." The man who held the rifle kicked her with his booted foot, hard enough to start Deb coughing again.

"Dad, she's got a bunch of medical supplies, too."

"Grab 'em, take that whole backpack and those other cans, too. This woman won't need any of it. You girls grab the horse and tack and wait for me outside. Go down the block a bit."

"Yes, daddy," the pair chorused.

There was a scurrying as the two girls did as they were told. The man tightened his lips and settled his shoulders as he raised the rifle. "You should close your eyes," he said.

Terror filled Deb as she blurted, "I'm an ER nurse."

The gun lowered a notch. "Oh?"

"Yes. I worked at the Memphis ER for years. I'm just on my way to my sister's homestead in Roanoke, not here to cause harm. I just stopped because I was sick and had to get in out of the rain." Deb was gasping for air after the words tumbled out.

"Can you deliver babies?"

"Yes. I've done that several times."

The man's finger played with the trigger and his head cocked as he regarded her. Deb raised her chin and met his gaze, although her whole body was shaking. He abruptly swung the gun so it rested on its butt.

"Take off your gun holster and push it over here, nice and slow, then get up."

Deb did as she was told, using her hands to help her stand, wavering slightly as the room spun. She stumbled, and he caught her under the arm. He smelled of smoke and blood to Deb, and her breath hitched in fear as she instinctively recoiled from him.

The man placed her puffy jacket over her shoulders and picked up her gun and holster, slinging it over his shoulder, before gesturing she should walk in front of him. "My wife's due any day. I'll keep you alive until then. Let's get you on your horse. We've got a ways to go to get home, and you're sick as a dog."

CHAPTER THIRTEEN

The Blacksburg/Pembroke Fault
Days Thirty and Thirty-one

"There's at least twenty men living at our old homesteads when I checked two nights ago."

Mara placed another chunk of the tasty chicken of the woods mushroom in her gathering basket, adding it to the batch of oyster mushrooms and stinging nettles she'd already collected on Mill Mountain. "Could be more on the way, too. One of the men looked like he was on Lloyd's radio when I was scouting over there."

"Yep." Eva's curt reply came with a grunt as she struggled to rise from the ground where she was resting, her elbow leaning on a pail full of black walnuts. "You need more people, like I've been telling you."

"I made a list of everyone I know who lives in Roanoke," Mara said, moving to give the woman a hand up, steadying Eva as she wobbled on her bad leg. "So did my kids, not that we know all the addresses."

"Caroline told me." Eva shrugged a dismissive shoulder before going on, a wistful smile tugging on her lips. "I have a mile long list of regular customers who loved my peach brandy and 'shine, but no addresses. We'd meet 'em at that rest stop in Sam's Gap with their order in the bed of the truck, park and go inside for a while. When we came back out, the moonshine would be gone, and an envelope of cash would be in its place." Eva readjusted her eyepatch and sighed wistfully. "It was like Santy Claus for grownups."

"You sound like you think reaching out is a lost cause." Mara put down her basket and rifle and took off her backpack to get a drink of water.

Eva took the bottle when it was offered. "You're a bright little ray of sunshine," she commented after she'd drunk. "I know better."

"What's that supposed to mean?"

"Nothin' other than what I said, don't get your panties in a twist. You look on the happy side of things most of the time. It's not realistic."

"I suppose you think we should just let the Crowes and their pals just roll over us?"

"Not at all. Am I not speaking English, the same language you speak?" The woman huffed impatiently and rubbed her thigh with a hiss of pain. "I'm still getting knots in my leg if I sit too long."

"What am I missing then, Eva?" Mara forced herself to be patient. The woman was savvy, even if her meandering way of getting to the point was irksome.

"Seems to me if people survived the quakes, they're hunkered down with those who're important to them and not likely to join in a fight where they don't have a stake." She groaned as she hefted the bucket. "Gotta show 'em what their stake might be."

Mara narrowed her eyes as she tucked her water bottle away. "First of all, give me that walnut bucket and you take my basket, it's lighter."

"I can manage."

"Eva, I already know you're a tough old broad. You don't need to prove anything to me. Give me the darn bucket."

Eva let out a brief burst of laughter and shook her head. "Have it your way."

Eva enjoyed poking at her, but Mara didn't miss the look of relief that crossed her face as they traded burdens, and began the two-mile hike back to the school. "Tell me what you're thinking might work to convince people to join us," Mara prompted. "Before we get to the oak tree grove where the kids are."

Below them on the trail was a patch of oaks whose deep roots had kept them upright. Caroline, Aiden, and Sophie were busy foraging for acorns while Ethan stood guard. Mara planned to turn the bitter nuts into baking flour, as her white and wheat flours had both dwindled to less than a week's supply.

"They either need to be scared of those Crowes and the militiamen, or they need to see their lives would be better off with us than on their own, or both."

"Sounds reasonable. How do we do the second one?"

"We make our place welcoming, set it up so another dozen or so people can see they have a place, continue the fortifications so it's solid, and I get brewing some shine and peach brandy." Her single eye blazed as she turned on Mara. "And don't get on some high and mighty moral horse about my liquor. It's a commodity that is sorely missed and makes something you can trade."

"I didn't say anything," Mara protested.

"You looked like you were going to," mumbled Eva.

"You're so sensitive," Mara teased the woman gently, earning herself a nasty look.

"People need a way to forget their troubles when there's so many of 'em on a daily basis."

"I don't necessarily believe mixing grain alcohol with firearms is a good idea, I have to say."

"You would. You're not from Roanoke, are you?"

"Eva, what does that have to do with anything? Just because I grew up in Iowa doesn't mean I don't understand people."

"There you go with the bright side again. You don't understand my people, the ones who've been planted for eight, nine, ten generations, just like them Crowe brothers. Got to give 'em community, Mara."

"Well, we agree on that point."

Eva nodded firmly. "Good. It's settled. Just need to find some cracked corn, barley, and wheat then go back and get my still a piece at a time. Those wives didn't find it, I'm nigh dead on sure about that, they didn't know nothin' about making liquor, thought they destroyed it all by ruining my mash stash and cookpot. We've got a few of them big pots from the school kitchens to start the mash in." She pointed to a fast-moving stream that tumbled toward the river next to the trail they were following. "I'd set up by this stream, get me some easy clean water."

It was good to see the woman's spirit coming back, and although Mara suffered a wiggle of discomfort about getting into the hooch trade, much of what Eva had said made sense. "We've got a good load of barley we got out of the feed store, and cracked corn, too. But let's talk over bringing more people inside the school at dinnertime," she modified her agreement.

"Mara, you just need to tell 'em that's what we're doing," Eva retorted. "There's not a lot of time to waste on chatter and opinions. Those Crowe brothers and the militia they're a part of are bent on killing you and yours, and taking over. You know that just as well as I do. Stop being nice."

Mara shook her head. "Not the way it works with us. Yes, it would save time, but it would raise resentments, too. I feel the tug to get moving on a solution right away, just like you do, but I'm not going to compromise democracy for authoritarian rule. I'm no dictator."

"You've read too many books."

"Guilty as charged. Speaking of books—you ready for another one yet?"

"Don't push your luck, girlie. I think a book a month is enough for me."

Gretel barked a happy greeting as she rushed to meet them, and the three saddled horses tethered to a tree pricked up their ears. Ethan gave them a wave from his guarding position lower on the trail, where he could easily see anyone on approach from below, his rifle at the ready.

"Time to head back, kids," Mara called out as she looked at the masses of nuts that Aiden, Sophie, and Caroline had collected onto sheets spread on the ground. "Wow, good job collecting acorns, let's get them loaded onto Buttercup." She gave the pretty little horse a pat as she passed it, checking the horse's cinch which ran under her belly, as she had a tendency to blow out to loosen it.

"We saved you a step," Caroline said. "We already tossed out the cracked ones and the ones with holes in them."

"Good thinking. Aiden and Sophie, after lunch you can have the fun job of stomping on them to crack the shells, then separate the nuts out and put those into a big pot of water for me."

"That doesn't sound fun," Sophie remarked with a wrinkled nose as she gathered the corners of her sheet and handed it to Caroline, who tied the bundles onto Sugar Lump. Mara gave the young girl a head tilt. "Everyone pitches in, Sophie."

She dumped the hickory nuts and the contents of her gathering basket into Aragorn's panniers, who stamped, annoyed at the awkward weight bumping his sides. She stroked his neck fondly and then moved to help Eva clamber onto Buttercup, handing her the pail and gathering basket to carry.

"You could help me butcher a deer instead," Ethan said as he swung on his crutches to join them, gun slung behind his back. "I'm salting and drying deer meat this afternoon." He gave Mara a nod. "That book you found had great instructions, and we won't need to run the generator."

"Yuck," Sophie said succinctly. "Me and Aiden will stick with the nuts." She boosted herself onto Sugar Lump as Mara made sure her stirrups were in the right place.

Mara gave her son an approving nod and a smile about the way he'd handled Sophie as she gave him a leg up onto Aragorn, then swung Aiden to ride in front of him. She tied his crutches onto her backpack, swung her rifle around to her front, and started down the trail in front of the trio of horses, Gretel at her side, and Caroline bringing up the rear, her rifle at the ready as well.

"I'd say you've all earned yourselves peanut butter and jelly for lunch, and some chocolate cake," Mara called back to the kids, smiling when they cheered..

Ritchie's dog Trinity barked and met them at the outer chain-link fence that once more stood erect as their outer perimeter, the poles which had fallen in the last big quake back in the ground and reinforced with concrete. Ritchie rose holding his shotgun from the inner defensive wall he was constructing along with Will. The assortment of metal lockers, bricks, and concrete blocks strengthened with rebar looked odd, but it was a welcome addition all the same. When it was completed, the wall would stand four feet high and stretch in a U-shape around the narrow end of the school about fifteen yards away from their wing.

Seeing who it was, Ritchie went back to his job, precisely adding another brick to the wall. It created an inner courtyard which would be easier to defend and was also a windbreak that would be useful as the weather turned bitter.

"Hi Mom!" Will called out cheerfully, waving the trowel in his hand and spattering himself with bits of mortar. "I got the bread into the oven and then took it out like you asked while you were gone. It turned out great!" He was covered in the concrete and sand mixture, smears of it drying white on his face and hair.

"Oh my gosh," Caroline said to her brother. "You've got more on you than on the wall."

Will shrugged happily. "Yeah, but look how far we got!" He gestured proudly at the new stretch of wall they'd completed, then at a length of dug earth that was six feet long and two feet wide. "And I dug that so we can pour our concrete footing for the next section, and found more rebar for the cinderblock parts, too."

"Will's a big help," Ritchie said in his dry, cracked voice. "And he also talks non-stop."

Mara stifled a laugh at the second part of Ritchie's sentence. "Great job, both of you. Lunch will be ready in about twenty minutes if you want to take a break and get cleaned up. Will, you have no options on that one. You'd best try to get some of that off of you before you turn into a statue."

The day passed quickly, as they always did, filled with hours of labor that made their new homestead functional, their tasks discussed and divided at the start of each day. They'd constructed a watchtower from the scaffolding and lumber that had been in the theatre department and placed it at the outside corner of their living space, lofting whoever was on guard duty ten feet in the air, with a sturdy barrier of lockers footed by cinderblocks for protection on the low part of it and bricks and cooking sheets on the upper level. It gave a person standing on it a wide, three hundred and sixty degree view. They'd also constructed a solid end cap to the far end of their living hallway with bricks and the concrete mortar collected from the maintenance department at the school. It no longer stood open to the elements, and they'd completed it with a functional framed wooden door from the theatre scene shop to use as a second entry.

Ritchie had become their chief construction engineer and builder on the projects that were fortifying the homestead alongside Ethan and Will. Eva stood guard most of the time unless she was foraging with Mara or helping to do the laundry or cleanup, her wounds preventing her from more active tasks. Mara and Caroline had taken on raiding empty houses, barns, and stores for the things they needed, their finds ranging from weapons and ammunition to warmer clothing to food to three full sets of tack for the horses. Their best discoveries had been three fifty gallon plastic barrels and a small cart they hitched to Sugar Lump, making hauling wood and water much easier, although they only managed to transport one half-full container of water from the river at a time. Even using two people, it was a struggle to heft the thing on and off, but fewer trips was a godsend. They left the other two barrels at the corners of the building with guttering to catch rainfall.

Will continued to fish every few days at the river if it wasn't raining and was always on the lookout for chickens and goats to build their herd. Five goats grazed in the wide expanse of the fields surrounding the school alongside the three horses. One of the new goats was a male, so Will had high hopes for kids to appear in the spring. His chicken flock was up to eighteen birds and two roosters who guarded them ferociously in the enclosure they'd built for them. Will had a chicken nesting section carved out in a protected area so that any eggs that hatched into chicks had a better chance of surviving.

Ethan, Mara, and Caroline did most of the cooking, assisted by the two young children who'd joined them. Mara baked as much as she could, and tended her sparse garden. The older kids and the adults split the night time guard duties, keeping to a schedule of one person on for four hours, who was then relieved by a second person, so they all got at least two nights of uninterrupted sleep in a row. They'd also taken to posting a person on duty during their meals as well, a plate kept warm for them.

After tucking away a meal of boxed macaroni and cheese and a ragout of venison, foraged mushrooms, stinging nettles, dandelions, and lambs quarter, they had their evening family meeting over cups of hot rose-hip tea laced with honey to boost their immune systems. Caroline switched out guard duties with Eva, who came in and nibbled on her food. As usual, Will kept the notes and started with all the positives they'd achieved during the day.

"I'm on first watch tonight," the boy finished what he'd dubbed 'the good news report.' "Eva, you're relieving me at one, and Ethan, you're on early call at five." He spread his hands. "New projects for tomorrow?"

"Gonna finish the first section of our wall." Ethan said. "Then start on the left side." He looked over to Ritchie and got an affirming nod.

"I'm using the kiln to dry out the acorn meat, and make flour." Mara said. Eva gave her a long, penetrating stare. Mara shifted in her seat uncomfortably, but then went on. "Also, Eva and I have discussed bringing more people here. We're looking at ways we can attract them, so we can continue to make the school a stronghold that can withstand anything." Mara chose her words carefully so as to not frighten Aiden and his sister or Will.

"We could stockpile cots or sleeping bags, and as people come, we can rearrange our rooms, maybe create some partitions ahead of time that we could throw up in an hour or two," Ethan suggested.

"I'd like to keep the library and this room and the bad-weather animal room as they are," Mara added. "That leaves us with seven potential sleeping or living spaces. I bet if we're willing to lose a bit of personal space, we could house another ten or so people."

Ritchie frowned. "I don't know as I'd like that."

"Think about it," Mara said kindly. "We'd have partitions, like Ethan said. It's not happening tomorrow, so turn it over."

"You don't have a lot of time to think," Eva stated bluntly. "You can't slow walk this, Mara, or phrase things nice. Those men are coming for you, and soon, and they sure as spit aren't slow walking."

"Eva!" Mara flushed with anger and nodded her head toward Sophie and Aiden, who were listening intently.

Eva pointed to the two children. "Those two kids survived for weeks on their own. They can take what I'm saying, and so can your two boys. Stop being nice, Mara. You want my opinion, go after those men on their ground before they find you on yours."

Mara was startled, blindsided by the woman's new tactic. "I thought we were going with making our place attractive to others. That was what we discussed."

"I've had time to think about it some more. You need to go after them." Eva crossed her arms defiantly.

"How would we do that? You're lame and one-eyed, Ritchie's old, and Ethan's in a cast. Caroline and Will and I can shoot, but we're not sharpshooters. It's crazy to think we can take on twenty or thirty men." She snapped the words out, a coil of fear winding around her gut as she considered the implications.

"Which is why you need to stop doing your little baking projects and get out there and find the people you wrote on your list. You've spent long enough making this place homey. Too much time if you ask me."

"Eva—"

"She's right." Ritchie's surprising affirmation rocked Mara back in her chair, a sinking feeling in her gut. Had Eva been discussing it with everyone else during the afternoon?

Ritchie cleared his throat and went on. "Switch your priorities. A wall is good, but it's not going to hold up against a coordinated assault. I did my stint in the Marines back in the day, and yep, you need more people bunking in the school, ready for what's coming. I guess me and Trinity can share a room if we have to." His fingers twitched as he spoke, and his leg vibrated, but Ritchie met Mara's astonished gaze with determination.

"You want us to prepare for war." Mara drummed her fingers on the table, looking at her sons, and at the two little children in her care and the bile rose in her throat.

"War's coming whether you want it or not," Eva stood, and slapped her hands on the table, the tremble of them visible as she pushed down. "Surviving isn't enough anymore."

"I agree with them, mom," Ethan said steadily. "We have a good store of weapons, but we need more, and more of us to use them."

Will's face was pale, but he nodded as well. "I want our old homestead back. It's not right. They're living in our house and in Eva's house."

Eva gave her a triumphant look and gestured around the table. "You said you wanted to discuss it. Looks like it's been discussed."

Mara wanted to scream and tear her hair out at what appeared to be a coordinated attack orchestrated by Eva, her fear rolling out before she could stop it as she gazed at Will and Ethan. "I couldn't stand it if you got hurt, or—" she couldn't even finish the sentence.

"Mom—" Ethan flushed with emotion. "You can't protect us forever, and we can't hide for years on end and hope we'll slide under the radar of those militiamen and the Crowes. The world's changed too much."

"You're a mama bear about your kids," Eva was relentless. "I get that. Be a mama bear and fight. Fight with everything you've got."

For a moment, Mara wanted to flip the table over, or leap across it and punch Eva in the face, anything to stop the horrible words she was saying, or what her children were saying she should do. Her hands shook as she gripped the table, her knuckles going white.

"Don't you let your fear take you over, don't you dare. You're better than that, Mara Padgett." Eva leaned across the table. "Get your big brain working and let's get rid of those no-good Crowe boys and their pals forever." She took a deep breath. "I've got dibs on Shiloh."

Mara let out the breath she'd been holding in an effort to keep her anger and raging fear in check, then nodded, nearly laughing at the absurdity of putting dibs on a man you wanted to kill like you were calling out dibs on the front seat of the car. "You're right. We'll put our efforts into fortifications and getting more firepower and people, and we'll figure out a way to take the fight to them. In fact—" Mara's eyes landed on the remains of the mushroom-laced meal. "I have an idea about how to weaken them and buy ourselves some more time."

"Well, all right then." Eva gave her a nod of approval, as did Ritchie. "Sophie, Aiden, get rolling with those dishes for Mara so she can set a spell and settle."

"Okay," the girl said, her voice subdued, worry putting a crease along her forehead. "Am I going to have to shoot a gun?"

"You might like it," Eva told Sophie. "But if you don't there's other things you could do, so don't worry yourself none."

Will hopped out of his chair and flung his arms around Mara's neck as people began to rise from the supper table. "It'll be okay, mom, we'll find more people."

She held her stepson's warm body tightly as he gave her a big hug, then patted his back. "You go get some rest before you do your guard duty."

Ethan swung over on his crutches. "Be strong, mom. We can do this. We have to." He gestured to his leg. "I get my cast off in less than two weeks, then I can do a lot more."

"I wish—" Mara stopped, hearing the futility of what she'd been about to say, and rubbed her face with her palms with a sigh.

Ethan gave her his trademark lopsided grin. "I know, mom, you wish none of this was necessary. But we're going to grit it out. You can do that. You've been doing it ever since my dad was killed."

"You're right." Something settled in Mara at her son's accurate words. While the world had turned upside down, and she'd been forced into a lifestyle she hadn't seen coming, they'd come a long way already. "I can do grit."

The next morning, Mara was up early, getting the coffee boiling and starting the bake for the day. She put the acorns on a second boil to get rid of the tannins so she could make it into flour. Regardless of the dismissive tone Eva had used about her baking, an army needed to eat. Mara cracked several dozen eggs into the skillet and scrambled them with the last of the oyster mushrooms and the stinging nettles she'd foraged the day before adding a good pinch of salt and grinds of pepper to season the dish.

She'd seen other mushrooms out there, ones she'd not touched, the ones that had given her the idea last night. There'd been a large patch of the pretty, red capped, white-dotted mushrooms growing under a stand of birch trees. She'd always called them "fairy mushrooms" as they looked like the drawings in the old fairy tale books that the little winged creatures sat on. In reality, the fungus was called fly agaric, and was highly poisonous and a hallucinogenic. Eating a few of them caused nausea and drowsiness if they weren't cooked properly. If she looked deeper in the woods, it was also possible she'd find death's cap mushrooms as well, a single one of which could kill a grown man. It was a sneaky poison, as you vomited and had diarrhea for a while, then you'd feel better before dying from it a half a day later from liver and kidney failure.

Mara shuddered as she brought the eggs with their non-lethal fungi inside and got out the last of the bread from the day before for everyone's breakfast, setting the table as usual with blackberry jam and honey for the bread. Death's cap wasn't a particularly common mushroom, but it grew in the temperate forests of Virginia, and she could find it if she looked hard enough. A mix of the two mushrooms boiled down and poured into the well water would incapacitate and likely kill whoever drank it, even if it got massively diluted, even dogs and horses. Mara frowned at the idea of killing innocent creatures. Not the death caps then, as there was no way of telling how long the poison might linger, and her family would need the well water once they moved back to the homestead.

"Just the fly agaric in the well water." Mara told herself. "But I'll collect some of the other in case I think of a way to use it."

"Talking to yourself again?" Caroline entered the kitchen area and helped herself to the French Press.

"Just ruminating about natural poisons," Mara replied, forking up some eggs. "Eat. You and I are going to find some people to talk to about joining us, starting with my book club."

"Because your book lady friends are the most likely to know how to shoot guns at the bad guys," Caroline scoffed as she rolled her eyes.

"No, because I know where they live, Ms. Smarty Pants. I've been to their houses."

"Well, let's be sure to take hostess gifts for the ladies who use books as an excuse to get together and drink wine."

The girl was still being sarcastic, but her comment had Mara pointing at her and nodding in agreement. "Exactly my thoughts."

Half an hour later, they set off on foot. They both wore backpacks and carried rifles along with their pistols. They walked quickly in the brisk air.

"I can't believe it's August," complained Caroline. "It feels like November, and there's frost on the grass."

Mara pointed at the thick layer of yellow-brown cloud cover. "That's what happens with no sun for a month. I think it's going to be a long time until we see it again. I miss blue skies." She paused at a corner, looking around. "I'm pretty sure Jessica lives up this street."

"Well, a few of the houses are mostly standing. Let's check it out," Caroline said, but Mara held her back.

"Slowly, and not down the middle of the street," she said, memories of being attacked by Ritchie's neighbors flashing through her mind.

They reached the split-level home where one of the eighth grade teachers had lived. It had completely collapsed into a heap, nothing but splinters and broken concrete left to mark the spot where a home had once been. With a sigh, Mara pulled out a paper lunch bag that had "Jessica" written on the front of it, popping a piece of paper she pulled from her pocket inside before she placed it on the doorstep.

"What's in the bag and on the note?"

"Couple of food things. The note tells her to come meet me at the old bridge off Thirteenth street by the river at noon."

Caroline nodded slowly. "Good idea. It's pretty clear around that point, so you can see people coming from a distance. And it's a long way from the school. Do you have those hostess gifts for all the women in your book club?"

"I do. Let's go. The next one's just two blocks over, in a cul-de-sac. We're going in a big loop, maybe seven or eight miles total."

Caroline groaned. "We should have ridden the horses."

Mara shook her head. "Too obvious. Cheer up, I brought good snacks for us. Roasted, salted acorns, yum!"

"Kill me now," Caroline moaned as they walked on. "Good snacks are like, goldfish crackers, or trail mix with raisins and chocolate bits."

"You mean like this?" Mara pulled out a big bag of trail mix and laughed as Caroline grinned.

"Now you're talking," Caroline said. "Seven or eight miles is a piece of cake when you have good snacks."

"I have the acorns too," Mara said just as they reached a series of cars blocking the short street, which was an offshoot from the one they were on. She crouched and pulled her gun. The formation of vehicles looked intentional to her, and she went on high alert, looking for movement beyond the barrier.

"All yours," Caroline whispered in saccharine tones as she crouched next to Mara, pulling her pistol as well.

"It seems super quiet," Caroline said a beat later, a glint of worry creasing her face.

"I agree, let's just go on to the next house," Mara said, her unease growing. She rose from the ground to back away.

"Stay where you are!" a man's voice echoed from the roof of the nearest house. "We've got guns on both of you."

Mara shifted her eyes toward the demand. A man lay flat on the slight pitch of the roof, his scoped rifle aimed straight at them.

"I see the guy over there," Caroline said, keeping her voice low, and the grip on her handgun firm as she looked the other way. "Looks young."

"It's Mara and Caroline Padgett," Mara called out. "I was looking for SueAnne. She was in my book club."

"No one named SueAnne here," the voice said.

"Okay, we'll be on our way," Mara replied, straightening with her hands still raised. Caroline followed suit.

"Not so fast. What's in the backpacks?"

"Lunch bags with trail mix inside."

"Cut the crap!"

"No, really, she means it," Caroline piped up. "Just bags of trail mix that we're leaving at her book club's homes if they're still standing."

"Looking for friends, that's all." Mara added, taking a cautious step back. A bullet pinged off the car in front of her.

"I didn't say you could move!"

"Carl Johnson, stop wasting your bullets!" A woman's voice echoed from further back in the cul-de-sac.

"Darn it. Just stay back!" The man named Carl shouted in irritation, waving at someone beyond Mara's range of sight. "They've got rifles and handguns, and they were approaching with stealth. We can't trust 'em."

"Fine, goodness gracious, Carl, no need to be shouting at me," the unseen woman retorted. "Mara, if that's really you, what was the last book we read in book club?"

Mara drew a blank and sucked in a panicked sip of air as she fought to find the answer. Trying to remember something from before the earthquakes was like dredging up a memory from another era, and the harder she tried, the further away any recollection of what it might have been slid away.

Caroline looked at her, widening her eyes as the seconds clicked by in silence. "Mara, you're a librarian," she hissed. "Remembering books is your job."

Mara dug into her memories. She could picture the book cover, but not the title. "It was that one about the octopus in the aquarium!" she shouted at last.

"It's her. That's Mara Padgett, the librarian at the high school. Stand down and let them in. Mara, come around to your left, the right side's booby trapped."

Mara stepped carefully around the double line of cars, edging through a narrow gap, followed by Caroline.

A short woman who'd once been as round as she'd been tall showed the effects of not eating enough food in the gauntness of her face and the way her stretch pants bagged and were rolled at her waist and ankles. She trotted over to them, a forced smile on her face that had Mara's inner warning bell going off. The once jolly, verbose woman seemed to be straining to pretend everything was normal.

"Mara Padgett, as I live and breathe, it's good to see you."

"You too, SueAnne. This is my daughter, Caroline."

"Our principal's daughter, I remember when he'd bring you in on teacher work days when you were little. I worked in the front office."

Caroline studied her, then smiled, but her hands still gripped her rifle tightly. "You always had chocolate kisses in your purse."

"And I'd sneak them to you when your daddy wasn't looking." She shot her hands in the air abruptly and clutched the center of her chest. "Where are my manners? That's Carl on the left roof, and Matty Junior, Matthew and Cathy's son is on the right. Caroline, I think you're a grade or two ahead of Matty Junior."

The torrent of words flowed through Mara as she studied the fortifications that had been made in the cul-de-sac, timber and bricks stolen from the downed houses to make a second line of defense nearer the base curve of the street where three houses still stood, mostly intact. Mara was struck once again about the randomness of the quakes, of what had been left standing, and what had fallen in the month-long catastrophe. People emerged from the bottom three houses, sending her blood pressure skyrocketing once again.

"They were watching us," murmured Caroline, her stance taut.

Mara put on a smile as fake as the one SueAnne was wearing as tension hummed through the air, the people approaching with caution. All the men were armed. Mara bent her knees slightly, readying herself to react quickly if she needed to do so. Meanwhile, SueAnne babbled on.

"These are who's left of Peppercorn Circle. Me and my Mama Jo, she's eighty and on a walker, but she can see you from the window, you can give her a wave if you want. There's Matthew, Carol, and Matty, and our recent retirees, Carl and Cathy. Soo-Yung and her husband Frank and their baby girl, Lucy. Our other neighbors—" she broke off, her muddy brown eyes tearing.

"Didn't make it." Mara filled it in for her as the rest of the neighbors continued to study her. "Sounds like you were a close bunch before the quakes."

"We were, oh we were. Our cul-de-sac won the best Christmas decorations award three years running and got the Halloween one last year. We coordinate our efforts. So, why're you visiting? You're kind of far from your homestead now I think of it. Is your son okay? And Logan?"

Caroline gave her an almost imperceptible shake of her head and Mara concurred. As friendly as SueAnne was with her bright peppering of questions, both Carl and Matty Junior hadn't left their guard posts on the roofs, merely shifted their position so they were once again in their gun sights. Everyone else except for Soo-Yung and SueAnne was carrying a gun as well. They gathered in a tight cluster around herself and Caroline. Mara wanted to take a huge step back as they closed in on them as their unwashed clothes and bodies gave off a dank reek which had her fighting not to wrinkle her nose. The people were overly thin and pale as well, their skin papery and their lips cracked, all signs they weren't getting enough nutrition or hydration.

Mara put on her best professional smile and pretended she didn't notice that the group as a whole was far from thriving. "Yes, we're all fine, but we were forced out of our homestead by the Crowe clan a few weeks ago. I'm making the rounds of book club to warn you about them."

"The Crowes who make that good peach brandy?" Carol asked as she stepped forward. "We get some every year."

"No, Eva and Lloyd were actually victims as well. Lloyd's brothers Shiloh and Dale, and more of the clan, live there now, and they're bringing in more militia types. They're well-armed and have plenty of ATVs and horses to move around on. They've been raiding and killing people ever since the quakes began."

"We're fortified," Frank said, putting an arm around Soo-Yung, who carried the baby in her arms and looked terrified. He towered over the Asian woman. "I don't see anyone taking our little street from us."

"They've got at least twenty men," Caroline stepped forward, her voice clear and crisp. "Your fortification is good, but you should make it better, get supplies in to stand up to a siege."

Frank gripped his gun a little more tightly and took a step forward. "We'll be fine. We have a system."

His aggression had Mara stepping in front of Caroline, her chin tilting to keep his gaze locked on her instead of Caroline. "She's just trying to help you."

"Oh stop it, Frank," SueAnne fussed. "I'm sure glad all y'all are okay. Where are you staying?"

"By Anita's." The white lie fell easily off of her tongue. "She didn't make it," Mara added.

SueAnne's face fell. "I was thinking of going to find her, seeing as how she was a nurse and all, in case these quakes just keep going, it'd be good to have one of those on our little block."

"She had diabetes, did you know?"

"I did not. Well, that's just a plumb shame."

A quake rumbled through, making everyone bend their knees, but it was a quick one, just big enough to cause Mara to grip her gun more tightly as she rolled with the movement of the earth.

"I hate those things," SueAnne said, somewhat nonsensically after it passed, and they all straightened again.

"Me too. Well, we're going to keep making the rounds of book club ladies," Mara said, becoming uncomfortable with the scrutiny the neighborhood people were giving both herself and Caroline. She dug in her backpack and got out a paper bag with SueAnne's name on it. "Here's some trail mix I made. Just some roasted acorns, a few raisins, baked rolled oats in brown sugar, and some M&M's. Maybe I'll see you down by the river sometime, that's where we're getting our water." Mara purposefully left out the exact location.

"That river's far," SueAnne commented as she took the bag and peeped inside, smelling the contents. "Lord yes, getting water is such a pain in the rear, pardon my French. Thanks for my little snack. I'm going to share it with my mama, good seeing you both." The woman elbowed past her neighbors and trotted back to her door hastily, not offering to share the food with them. Their heads swung eerily in unison, following her movement as SueAnne went into her house, the door locking audibly behind her.

"We'll be on our way," Mara said, keeping her voice light as she turned to go, Caroline at her elbow.

"Don't come sneaking around our neighborhood again," Frank said as he escorted them back around the parked cars. "We booby trap things in rotation. I'd hate to see you get anything blown off by accident."

"Got it. Bye!" If Mara's voice was a little breathy and high pitched, Frank didn't comment, just brushed his hand in the air to wave them off.

Mara and Caroline double-timed it away from Peppercorn Circle, neither speaking until it was several blocks behind them.

"That was creepy and got creepier by the minute," Caroline said at last. "And by the way, everyone at school knew Matty Junior was a little off, and we steered clear of him."

"I know him, too. I took a pocket knife off of him in the library once when he had detention." Mara swallowed. "I think those people don't have the wherewithal to feed themselves except by raiding houses. I'm not judging, just observing."

"They smelled bad and looked hungry," Caroline agreed. "I'm glad you didn't say where we were."

"Me too. It made me wonder if trying to get more people isn't going to backfire and bring more trouble on us."

Caroline nodded. "I hear you, but I don't think we have any other options. We can't take on all those Crowes on our own, no matter if we are the good guys."

Mara nodded reluctantly. "You up to try to find another book club person?"

"Are they all going to be scary?" Caroline wanted to know after she agreed, and they began the hike up a steep street to the next house on Mara's list.

"I can't tell you that. But I was in book club, and I'm not scary."

Caroline snorted. "Keep telling yourself you're not scary."

"I'm not!"

"You're buff, clean, and well fed. You're carrying a SIG on your gun belt as well as a rifle slung into your hands like you know how to use it, and you look everyone in the eye and stand your ground, even with weirdos like that gigantic Frank guy back there. You've changed, Mara."

Mara considered Caroline's honest words as they walked side by side, then gave her hair an affectionate tug. "So have you."

Her breath caught in her throat as she recalled the long, difficult journey she and Caroline had traveled to get to where they were comfortable walking along the street together and giving each other compliments. It was a little star of happiness amid all the troubles. Mara surreptitiously wiped away a tear, and wished Logan were there so she could tell him about the amazing, trusting relationship which had grown between her stepdaughter and herself.

Caroline glanced at her as they walked a few more steps in silence before she sighed. "Ethan is so right."

"What about?"

"You get mushy anytime we say something nice to you. I saw your discrete tear brush."

Mara slung an arm around Caroline's shoulder. "It's a mom thing," she said, then sniffled when Caroline leaned her head on her shoulder as they walked.

"Oh, man," Caroline sighed. "Here we go."

CHAPTER FOURTEEN

The Humboldt Fault Zone
Days Twenty-seven to Thirty

Getting the acres of corn in, leaving four rows on two sides standing for the wildlife, and then tucked into the long row of corn cribs which lined the barn had taken most of the day. It was demanding, dirty work, but Logan had a burst of satisfaction after they'd completed the task.

"Another day or two might've been too late," he commented to Willard.

The older man had nodded, considering. "Just ahead of an ear drop, I'd wager."

"I thought harvesting tobacco was hard," Zeke added, draped over one of the horse stalls. "I'm ready for dinner."

"Boys, what about you? Could you stand some supper?" Willard nudged his chin at the twins, who were lying flat out on a couple of hay bales.

"I could eat dinner, breakfast, and then lunch too," said Darien.

"Same," Demarius groaned, holding his belly.

"Let's wash up at the pump before we go see what your mama and my wife have ready for us."

The old man had an easy way with the two boys, never raising his voice to them and talking to them as if they were grown men. Logan followed them to the yard pump, with Zeke at his elbow.

"You still leaving tomorrow?" Zeke asked him.

"Yes. As much as it's been nice to be in one spot for a couple of days, I want to get moving again."

"Same. Although I thought I maybe might hunt up one or two more deer before I do, so's there's plenty of meat for Helen and Willard." The young man wrinkled his nose. "I saw a bunch of turkeys, too."

"Have you considered my offer to take the kayak to Cairo, then head east on US 24? It's nearly a straight shot that way for you, across Kentucky and Tennessee to get to Elizabethton. It'd save you a lot of time and worn shoe leather."

Zeke looked at his boots as if the answer might be in the dirt. "Yeah, I have," he finally said reluctantly, kicking at the ground with the toe of his boot, his hands stuck deep inside his overall pockets. He shrugged one shoulder uncomfortably. "I've got an itch to go, do exactly that, I can't lie."

"I know you want to get to your family, and it makes sense."

The young man lifted his straightforward eyes to meet Logan's. "Trouble is, I'd be leaving you and Ms. Gayle and the boys in the lurch."

"I know we talked about you traveling with us to Kansas City, especially if we took the boats, but Gayle's made it clear her rafting days are done. I'm quite sure Braden feels the same way about it." He put a friendly hand on Zeke's shoulder. "You did your part by getting them here in one piece. I have the feeling I haven't heard half the stories about your trip down the Mississippi."

Zeke grunted in agreement. "Made my hair stand on end a couple times, I can tell you."

"You're saying I don't want to hear them?"

"All I'll say is those two boys are a handful, and leave it at that."

"When will you leave?"

"Tomorrow maybe, or the next day."

Logan clapped him on the back. "I'm glad you're taking the boat. It'll shorten your trip by a lot of days, and I promise it's a lot easier to maneuver than the raft was."

"An old stump with a hungry alligator on it would be easier to use than that raft was."

When Logan made his way into the house, the smells of roasted meat and vegetables hit his nose, making his stomach growl.

"Logan!" Braden ran to him, lifting his arms to be picked up. "Come see!"

"He's been building in the living room all day with some Legos," Helen told him as she wiped her hands on her apron.

"Is it another castle like you made at the beach?"

"No, iss a house. My house! Four, four, four, one Chespeek."

The Legos spread on the floor for nearly the length of the coffee table. Braden's construction had four walls, and he'd taken some time putting in rooms as well. As he babbled, talking about where he slept, and the kitchen and the room his mommy and daddy had, Logan's heart twisted with compassion for the boy. He could only hope the house was still standing, even though the knowledge that his time in Braden's life was drawing to a close cut a painful rift straight through him, leaving him hollowed out.

"Great job, buddy! We're on our way there." Logan tucked away his misery for Braden's sake.

"Okay! Soon?"

"No, still a couple of weeks to go."

"Okay." He flung his arms around Logan's neck. "Whuff too."

"Yep, Whuff too." He snuggled the boy and put him down.

"You are going to be one big mess when you get to Texas," Gayle remarked quietly as she placed a casserole dish on the table. "Might need all the king's horses and all the king's men to put you together again."

A surge of irritation exacerbated by the fact she was right had him pinching the bridge of his nose. "It's the right thing to do, Gayle."

"I know. I'm just saying you're going to be a puddle. You love that boy, it's just as plain as the giant nose on your face. Come eat. I made hush puppies. Can you believe these folks never had a hush puppy in their lives? It was a wrong which needed righting, I can tell you."

As was Helen and Willard's custom, they held hands and said grace before diving into the feast that Gayle and Helen had put on for them. Venison pot roast with onions, carrots, and potatoes, corn on the cob dripping with butter, hush puppies, and bright green peas were passed, and plates filled and refilled.

"Never thought I'd find something I like as much as Helen's rolls, but these hush puppies are fine eating," Willard remarked.

"I hope you saved room for pie," Helen told the table. "We couldn't decide what we wanted to bake more, so there's a cherry and an apple pie, too."

"Oh, boy!" Demarius exclaimed. "I want one of each!"

"I love it here," Darien said, rubbing his belly.

"I'm glad you said that." Gayle said the short phrase with a sigh of relief as she shared a significant look with Helen. "Should we tell 'em?"

"No time like the present," Helen said with a nod.

Gayle put her fork down carefully. "Helen and Willard have asked if me and the boys wanted to stay with them, at least through the winter until next spring. I've thought about it and have decided to accept. We don't know what we'll find in Wichita once we get there."

"Wait, what?" Darien's eyes grew huge. "You mean stay here, on the farm?"

"Dude, that's what stay usually means," his brother scoffed at him, but there was no hiding his grin. "I'm down with that."

Even though Willard had conferred with him about asking Gayle and the boys to stay, Logan was still surprised it had come to pass. He'd never known Mara's aunt and uncle to be the type of people to extend their hospitality for more than three days.

"Willard and I could use the help," Helen huffed as she caught his look, reading Logan like a book. "We're no spring chickens anymore."

"Speak for yourself, woman." Willard grumbled from his place at the head of the table. When his wife of fifty years gave him a long, long look, he sighed. "I have to say, having the extra hands has made life easier these past days. You boys are good workers, and that's a fact."

"Gayle's been a godsend to me in the kitchen, and I like the female company." Helen added. "Makes for a good change of pace."

Gayle turned to Logan. "I'm sorry, I know it means you have a longer journey on your own with Braden, but I had to think about my boys."

Logan nodded, glad that he'd had a bit of warning that this change of plans might come to pass. "Of course, I understand, it makes a lot of sense." He looked around the full table, at the people who he'd been through so much with, and at the elderly couple who'd become his in-laws and experienced a pang of loneliness. "I'll miss you all."

"Well, that's out of the way, let's have pie," Helen said briskly, waving to the twins. "Boys, help me clear the table."

As the boys bustled to clear and put away the leftovers along with their mom, and Willard leaned over to talk hunting with Zeke, Logan began the process of letting go of the people who'd come to mean so much to him emotionally and mentally, a skill he'd learned to use every year when another graduating class of students left his high school. It began by being grateful he'd had them in his life at all, and then gradually imagining a bubble which encased only himself and Braden, one that could easily float away on a breath of air. Then he resolutely turned his mind to the logistics of the upcoming days of travel, which had just been so thoroughly upended.

"Willard, you don't happen to have a bike around here I can use, do you? I have a lot of miles to go."

"I'm glad you asked. Once Gayle told me what you planned to do with Braden, I did a little horse-trading with our neighbors. I have a bike that comes with a toddler bike seat for Braden. Gayle and Helen have been busy dehydrating meals for you to take as well. You'll be well equipped for your journey south."

Logan's jaw dropped. "Thank you. I had no idea you'd done that."

"You're our son-in-law. You think we wouldn't take care of you?" Willard looked a little put out.

"I didn't anticipate it, but I sure do appreciate it."

"Good answer."

The following morning, they packed a sturdy touring bike with panniers and a toddler seat already attached to the back into the bed of the truck. To Logan's surprise, Gayle walked up with her own backpack. "I'm riding with you to the border," Gayle told him. "Zeke is staying with Helen and my boys until me and Willard get back."

"Shouldn't take us more than five hours to get you west to Nebraska City where the government is recommending folks cross to travel south or west. It's a straight shot south for you to get to Dallas from there," Willard agreed. "I plan on being back late tonight, or tomorrow morning at the latest."

"Here's sandwiches and chocolate milk and leftover apple pie for the road," Helen said, then laid her warm hand alongside Logan's cheek. "Stay safe. You kiss Mara for me, and your kids too, when you get home."

"I'll find a way to get word to you, Helen."

"I'll hold you to it." The stern woman's lips trembled slightly before she pinched them firmly together and stepped away.

Logan turned to Darien and Demarius, fighting a lump in his throat as they both tilted their faces to him. "You're great kids. I'm glad I got to know you both. Don't swim in that big old muddy river until you get more practice in a pond, promise?"

"Yes, Logan," they chorused.

"One hundred percent?"

"One hundred percent!"

The twins shared a glance, and Darien elbowed his brother in the ribs. "Tell him."

"Logan, try not to get into any more fights, okay?" Demarius blurted after his twin's prompting.

"Yeah, we thought you looked pretty bad after that last one," Darien added, wrinkling his nose. "I know you said the other guys looked bad, but—" he let his sentence drift off as both he and Demarius made it clear with their expressions they'd doubted those words.

Logan chuckled at their sincerity. "I'll do my best."

"Come over here and let Mr. Logan say goodbye to Mr. Zeke," Gayle called out.

"I guess this is it," Zeke said in his thick mountain accent. "Hope you find Braden's folks for him." He reached into his pocket. "I wrote down my Ma's address in Elizabethton. Well, its more like directions on how to find our place, it's tucked back some in a tidy holler by Lake Watauga."

Logan took the index card and tucked it away and handed him a piece of paper back. "I know that lake, I did a half-Ironman there a few years ago. It's a beautiful place. That's my address in Roanoke, you're welcome any time."

Zeke gripped the paper and cleared his throat. "Glad to have it. We don't live that far away, all things considered, not as the crow flies, anyway."

Logan choked up and had to stop speaking for a moment as he remembered their first meeting. He'd been at a real low point in his journey, humiliated, hurting, defeated, sitting on the curb of a strange city with Braden melting down at his side. The young soldier had been kind to both himself and Braden. Zeke had made all the difference with his simple humanity on that day, and on many subsequent days as well.

"You're one of the good ones, Zeke Mills, and I don't say it lightly," he finally got out.

Zeke blushed and grinned. "It's been a pleasure, and you best watch out for me darkening your door one of these days. Thanks for the kayak!"

"Gotta get going if we're going to get back again," Willard called out tersely, already seated in the truck.

"Shotgun!" Gayle called, hopping in the front. "I get carsick otherwise," she added.

Logan strapped Braden and Whuff into the booster car seat which Helen had borrowed from their neighbors and then climbed into the back seat next to him. Helen passed him his backpack and rifle. "You've got ten days of dehydrated meals in there, with lots of scrambled eggs for this fine young fellow." She turned and gave Braden a kiss on the cheek.

"Scram!" Braden agreed happily, giving her a big smile.

Logan turned and looked out the back window as Willard started down the dusty dirt road toward the highway. He took a final mental snapshot of the sturdy little house across the street from the spired church. The gangly twins stood on the concrete front stoop waving their arms madly in a goodbye. Zeke was next to them, his hand raised in farewell, while Helen simply watched them go, her arms crossed and her chin resolutely up.

The miles went by smoothly enough on the county roads heading west. There wasn't much traffic except for military vehicles and the occasional farmer's truck on their rural route. They stopped periodically so Braden could run around, and so they could all stretch their legs. At midday, Willard parked under some trees next to the road and they ate the delicious lunch Helen had packed for them, talking about inconsequential things for the most part, staving off the final goodbyes as long as they could.

"Here we are," Willard said as they passed the sign announcing they were leaving Iowa. "Looks like they've got a military checkpoint or blockade of sorts."

Logan's guts tensed at Willard's words as they slowed and entered the short line of cars and pedestrians waiting to cross over the Missouri River, which marked the border between Iowa and Nebraska. Just before the long concrete bridge, two military tents had been set up, their sides open. Tables filled with warm clothes, food, and water were lined up beneath one of them, while the other was marked with a red cross, and held cots and a couple of white-coated medics tending to people. Willard pulled into the small parking area nearby.

Braden woke from his nap at the change of momentum. "Need to go," he announced. "Want out."

There was a line of portable toilets behind the tents. Logan tapped Gayle on the shoulder. "Can you take him while I find out what's going on?"

"You want me to come with you, Logan?" Willard eyed the soldiers warily.

"It's probably best if you stay with the truck."

Logan approached an efficient-looking young soldier who held a clipboard. Three other soldiers stood nearby, their poses relaxed, but all of them carried rifles.

"Private," he acknowledged. "What's the procedure here?"

The soldier eyed Logan's pistol, but didn't ask him to disarm. "Just a couple of questions and a bit of paperwork, and then I have some information for you if you intend to leave the safe zone of Iowa. Is that your intention, sir?"

Logan nodded. "I'm headed for Dallas, and then from there to Roanoke, Virginia, where my homestead is located."

"Just need your name, sir, and date of birth, so the government can track where our citizens are as we reorganize. If you could include your former profession, that would be helpful, too." He poised his pen above his clipboard, ready to hand them to Logan.

"Figures paperwork is one of the first things the government would bring back," Logan quipped.

"Isn't that the truth?" The young man chuckled appreciatively.

The exchange relaxed Logan, and he complied with the few brief questions, then signed his name to the bottom. Gayle joined him with Braden in tow.

"These two folks going with you?"

"Just the boy."

The private looked Logan's paperwork over, then consulted a list. "Oh good, you're going pretty far south. Looks like there's a FEMA trailer outside of McKinney, Texas, which is on your route." He scribbled notes onto a card and handed it to Logan. "That's the location and combination to open it if no one else has done so yet. Just leave it unlocked and take whatever you need. You don't need to stop at just taking food or medicine either. If you need a jeep and the roads are decent, you're free to take it. There's gas at those locations as well. Just be sure to sign the roster on the inside of the main door, so we know who opened it."

Gayle butted in. "You mean he can just take what he wants? It's not some trick?" She eyed the young man suspiciously.

"Yes, ma'am. I mean, no ma'am, it's not a trick. President Ordway's orders are clear. We need those caches open so the people who are still alive can survive the next year or so until we get some sort of infrastructure in place. We don't have enough troops to spare to open all of them, so we're asking citizens to do so in the areas we haven't reached."

"Well, I'll be..." Gayle was stymied.

The soldier consulted his list again. "There's one by Roanoke too, in Vinton. I've got the location and code, there you go." The young man handed Logan a second card, then went on. "I need to warn you we have intelligence there are militia troops who're intent on overthrowing Ordway gathering in the Roanoke area and in Oklahoma, too. If you could get word about their status to the new US Capitol in New Mexico, we'd appreciate it."

Logan blinked in shock, trying to assimilate the information the young man was so forthrightly telling him. He exchanged a disbelieving glance with Gayle as a churn of worry for his family gained momentum.

The soldier pulled a laminated card from his pocket. "Here's the call sign for the base in the New Capitol. There'll be a ham radio unit in the Roanoke cache, and batteries to run it. You'd be reporting to Ripley Baxter, Thaddeus Moreland, or Janet Givens."

"Janet Givens was the Speaker of the House, but I don't know these other names." Logan tried to find solid ground.

"Me either, sir. What I do know is that President Ordway would appreciate your help in this matter if you're able."

"How do you know I'm not part of the militia and you've just put all these resources into their hands?"

"Are you one?"

"No, but—"

"The President has stated he's not going to let the citizens of the USA suffer because of the actions of a few, sir." Genuine pride rang in the young man's voice as he spoke, and it went a long way to settling the alarm he'd raised with his information.

"All right." Logan tucked the cards carefully into his pocket. "You can count on me."

"Very good, sir. Do you need a map of Kansas or Oklahoma? I don't think we have any of Texas."

"That'd be great."

The private pulled paper maps from an accordion binder. "When you're ready, you may proceed across the bridge. We have troops and an aid station set up in Topeka, Kansas, with a temporary bridge over the Kansas river. You just take this road straight south, but we don't have anyone past that point yet. If you need assistance, they'll help."

"Do you know anything about Wichita, Kansas?" Gayle asked.

The young man frowned. "I heard Kansas in general was hit pretty bad, ma'am. We've had a couple of folks come from that way." He called over to one of the other men standing guard. "Hey, Carlos, didn't you talk to folks who'd walked up from Kansas yesterday?"

Carlos sauntered over, nodding. "Sure did. They said there wasn't much left standing in the cities and towns. Also, some pretty massive cracks forming, and the air was bad, that there were vapor fumes made the whole place smell like rotten eggs. The guards who rotated out from Topeka said the same thing. You'll want to take masks with you, sir, for you and the boy, if you're headed that way."

"N95s are over in the first aid tent," the private who'd taken down his details told him.

"Thank you," Logan said and walked to the tent with Gayle and Braden, digesting all the information he'd just been given.

"Well, I guess I made the right choice," Gayle said as Logan picked up masks as well as a satchel of first aid supplies that the man on duty offered him. Gayle grabbed a handful of masks and accepted a satchel of first aid as well. "You taught me well, Logan. Take the supplies when you can."

"That's right."

She touched his arm lightly as they walked back to the truck. "It's not too late to change your mind, stay at the farm. I didn't like the sound of those cracks spewing toxins." She paused. "No one would think less of you if you just headed straight for your home, either. I'm sure Willard would be fine driving you to a border crossing to the east."

Logan shook his head. "I'd think less of me if I did. My mind's made up, Gayle."

"Stubborn as the day is long," she muttered.

Willard had been watching from the truck, and lifted out the bike from the bed. Gayle strapped Braden into the toddler seat, which was mounted on the back of the bike, then tucked a warm hat on his head, and buttoned his down jacket for him. She clipped Whuff into the special tether Zeke had rigged to the toddler seat so the toy wouldn't be lost as they rode.

Logan buttoned his own jacket, tucking away the codes the private had given him into an inner pocket. He fastened his backpack onto the carrier on the front of the bike and looped his rifle sling over his head and across his shoulder. Willard offered his hand. They shook, and the deeply cut wrinkles around Willard's eyes crinkled a bit. "You know, when Mara first told us about you as husband material, I wasn't too sure, but I should have trusted her. Safe travels, Logan."

Gayle scrubbed her nose with the back of her hand and shook her head as she gave Logan a final hug. "I can't believe this is it. I'm sure glad we were assigned to your tent way back when in Brainerd, Minnesota, Logan Padgett, even though you were a pill and a half some days."

"Me too." It was all he could manage as he cleared his throat, at a loss as to what to say at this last goodbye. As infuriating and exasperating as Gayle had been throughout the time they'd traveled together, he'd grown to respect her tenacity and grit, and the pure love she had for her sons.

"My boys and I will never forget you. I hope we see you again in the years to come." She turned to Braden, whose blue eyes were filled with worry.

"Go bye?" he asked mournfully, his lip trembling.

"Yes, but I'm giving Whuff a special kiss, one that goes on for infinity, kisses for every goodnight for you forever and ever, sweet boy."

Gayle kissed the dog, tucked it carefully back into the boy's arms, and then gave Braden a final hug. "Be good for Logan," she told him in a voice that was barely a whisper.

She gave Logan a final twisted smile before hurrying back to the truck. Willard had already climbed into the cab and started the engine. As soon as she was buckled in, he did a neat turn, and drove away.

Logan swallowed hard against the emptiness which thundered inside his chest. "Okay, buddy, time for us to ride across the river," he managed.

The young soldier signaled to the men on the bridge, who raised the simple gate, and he rode across the long concrete bridge to the far side and into the heartland of America.

He followed US-75 straight south, making good time on the bike, hitting a sustainable pace of fifteen miles an hour, his training as a triathlete helping him to find a rhythm. An earthquake rumbled beneath their feet a few times, the biggest one forcing Logan to brake hard, slewing sideways before the bike hit a tremendous crack which opened just in front of them. Aside from that instance, the route was smooth as the army had cleared overturned cars, poles, and wires to the sides of the road. They rode into the late afternoon, finally making camp by a small stream that was hidden from the road by the roll of the countryside.

Braden had gotten used to setting up camp with Logan, collecting dry grasses and sticks for their campfire, and helping Logan to blow on the ember he'd sparked to get it going. Logan boiled the water and then rehydrated a corn, tomato, and venison stew Helen had sent along, and opened a packet of saltines for them to share.

As night came on full, he was glad of their new-to-them down sleeping bag they could both fit into comfortably, and the foam sleeping pad that came with it. He swallowed a couple of ibuprofen before he settled to help with the inevitable soreness that came anytime he biked over fifty miles, then banked the fire.

The first part of the next day got them to the river crossing by Topeka, where he checked in with the army men stationed at the temporary bridge, who were just as accommodating as the ones in Iowa had been. The men served them a hot lunch and provided them with gloves and neck scarves as well. One of the soldiers explained the ground to the east of the city was highly unstable and contained a terribly deep crack that belched white clouds of gas when it rained.

"I'd advise you to wear your masks from this point on, sir, and be sure your skin is covered. The vapor clouds have some sort of acid in them that can really sting. Lucky for us, the prevailing winds are from the west, so we don't get blasted by it often, but if you find yourself in a rainstorm, I'd advise you take shelter behind closed doors until the vapor passes."

Logan considered the man's warning carefully as he biked around the city and continued south. The road was littered with debris the further from the city he got, and several times he was forced to dismount, put on the backpack, then carry the bike and Braden over obstacles that blocked the road one at a time. Overall, the boy seemed relatively happy riding behind him, not fussing the way he had when they'd tried putting him into the toddler seat mounted at the front of the bike. Maybe it had been too windy for him.

They'd gotten into Burlington, Kansas where Logan had planned to stop, but a toppled sign by the road told him the lake he'd found on the map and had hoped to camp next to was actually the cooling lake for a nuclear reactor, so he'd pumped on past the place at a much faster pace, hitting twenty-two miles an hour by the gage on his handlebars. He'd kept it up for nearly two hours until it was nearly too dark to see.

"Don't want to camp near a nuke, do we, buddy?"

"Nope." The boy shook his head wisely as Logan chuckled.

After their supper, which ended up being scrambled eggs and sausage with bits of green pepper that Braden carefully picked out, Logan commented, "I think we'll reach Tulsa by tomorrow, Braden, and then it's just another two hundred and fifty miles until we get to your house."

Braden nodded sleepily. "Story?"

"Hmm, we've done Peter Pan and Winnie the Pooh. We're in Kansas. How about I tell you about a girl from Kansas who found a magical land?"

"Okay."

"There's some scary witch parts in it, though," Logan warned. "And flying monkeys who aren't very nice."

Braden conferred with Whuff for a moment, then nodded. "Iss okay."

They had a slower start the next morning, Logan paying the price for his effort to put distance between themselves and the nuclear power plant. Braden woke up cranky, needing to play and run around before getting back in his seat, so it was nearly ten in the morning before they were riding again.

Braden was also tired of wearing his mask, which Logan discovered as they had to stop to allow a heavier earthquake to roll through. The toddler was wearing the protective gear around his neck instead of where it should be. Logan sighed and moved to readjust it.

"You have to wear it. The air is dirty." The smell of sulfur had waxed and waned as they rode, even if he'd not seen any of the plumes of gas the soldiers had warned him about.

"Iss not." The boy waved his arms around as if to prove the air was clean, then pulled the mask off again.

"Braden, you have to do what I say."

"No."

Tears formed in the boy's eyes, and after their slow start, the last thing Logan wanted was a full on meltdown, which would delay them even longer. "Do you want to be a masked bandit instead?" Logan demonstrated by pulling his kerchief up and looking fierce.

Braden regarded him seriously, then nodded. Logan put the cloth around the boy's nose and mouth, tying it securely, and pulling his hat around his ears to hold it in place.

"Better than nothing, and crisis averted," Logan muttered as he started pumping the pedals once again, his thighs and lower back complaining that they were being asked to work, sending burning threads all along his muscles.

Six hours later, with the light waning alongside the last dregs of his energy, Logan pulled to a stop on the outskirts of Tulsa near a playground which still had its swings standing, and a slide. There were a few stands of thick brush where they could set up camp and be relatively invisible.

"Take Whuff and go play for a couple minutes, Braden," he told the boy, who'd lit up when he saw where they were.

"Push, please!"

As tired as he was, Logan couldn't resist the tug of his little hand. "Okay, let me just put our bike away."

Logan used all his senses to scan their surroundings for any hint of sound or movement which would indicate they were being watched or threatened. They were in what had once been a nice suburban neighborhood, he concluded. The type of place where hardworking middle-class people would have lived, but it had been hard hit. None of the two and three bedroom homes near the little pocket park were still standing, and what had been tree-lined streets were just a mess of crumpled, drying trees which had been uprooted, smashing cars and the road itself in the process.

Braden had plopped belly down in the curved swing and pushed himself and extended his arms outward like he was flying while he waited. After a last scan of the deserted area, Logan wheeled their bike into a dense stand of shrubs. Out of habit, Logan grabbed the backpack and slung it on, adjusting the rifle sling to hang off one shoulder.

He pushed Braden on the swings for several minutes, and after that, stood at the bottom of the slide holding Whuff tucked under one arm as the little boy zoomed down, laughing as he caught him at the bottom.

"Climb!" Braden said proudly as he ascended the ladder of the slide for the fifth time. "Like the lake!"

"That's right, buddy. Okay, last slide, and then we'll make our camp."

Tickling Braden as he caught him a final time, laughing as the boy squealed with joy, Logan put him down and they walked hand in hand to the thicket to the place where he'd stashed their bike. Pushing aside the section where he'd left it, Logan stopped dead in his tracks.

The bike was gone.

CHAPTER FIFTEEN

New Capitol Site
Day Thirty-five

"Just one more step, Thaddeus." Carmen encouraged the one-legged Black man. Thaddeus gripped the parallel bars of physical therapy equipment, sweat pouring off his torso. Ripley looked on from a discrete distance, her hands clasped in her lap and her lips resolutely clamped shut as the diminutive physical therapist who'd once put her through an agony of recovery worked her stern magic on Thaddeus.

"Not a step, it's a hop," Thaddeus complained. "I only have the one leg."

"One more hop, then." Carmen cheerfully agreed.

"But it's not one more hop, it's at least four to the end of the bars," Thaddeus grunted out as he tensed his muscles and swung his good right leg forward and regained his balance after a slight teeter.

"We'll take it one hop at a time!"

Ripley stifled a laugh at the murderous look Thaddeus gave the therapist. She'd given plenty of similar looks to Carmen herself when the therapist was working with her. Ripley was sure Carmen didn't care about the looks or quips and that she'd continue to push Thaddeus to heal and become strong enough to be fitted with a prosthetic limb.

Thaddeus spared Ripley her own murderous look. "That's enough from the peanut gallery."

"I didn't say anything. I didn't move a muscle!" Ripley protested.

"I could mentally hear your derisive laughter," Thaddeus said pointedly as he pushed toward the last hop. "You didn't have to emit it."

"That's handy!" Carmen exclaimed. "You can have entire conversations without talking." She grinned as Thaddeus reached the end of the parallel bars. "You should get pissed off more often. You did those last three steps faster than the first three. Great job!"

Thaddeus sagged a bit on the bars. "May I sit?" He asked with all the dignity he was capable of. "And perhaps have a drink of water?"

"You bet! Then we're moving on to core work!" Carmen threw Ripley a saucy wink as she turned away from Thaddeus. Ripley gave herself extra points for keeping her composure and not cracking up.

"Ms. Baxter?" Timothy Ordway skidded into the school gym the New Capitol was using as a rehab facility and hurried over to Ripley. "My dad—I mean the President—would like to see you in the conference room."

"Thanks, Timothy. I'll be right there." Ripley stretched as she stood up from the metal folding chair and walked over to Thaddeus.

"Do not give me encouragement," he warned as she stepped closer. "Ms. Gayoso's high spirits are enough for five grown men."

Carmen chuckled. "Mr. Moreland is correct, and I'm happy to share." She gave a little butt-wiggle and danced in a circle as she passed him a water bottle.

Thaddeus took a long drink of water, and wiped his face with a hand towel Carmen tossed to him next, nipping it adroitly out of the air.

"I will refrain from any woo-hooing," Ripley said gravely, stifling her desire to do exactly that. "But I will say how happy I am that Carmen is in charge of your rehab and how well you're doing with it.

That was an observation, not a woo-hoo!" she said hastily as Thaddeus's frown deepened. "I'll let you get back to it."

Knowing Thaddeus' dislike of public displays of affection, she squeezed his shoulder, and left the gym, but just as she sailed out the door, she leaned back in and called out, "Woo-hoo way to go!" before she darted into the hall.

Ripley smiled to herself as she hurried along the corridor of the high school, which had become the temporary New Capitol headquarters near the town of Shiprock, New Mexico. It was a fairly new, sleek building with none of the grunge she associated with high school. The floors of the hallways gleamed, and the windows shone. President Chishi had been generous with his offer of the use of the building for both a meeting place and staff housing while the buildings that would house the new heart of government for the United States were constructed ten miles outside of town, near a bend in the San Juan river.

"It's best if you are all in one place," President Chishi had intoned, his face serious when he'd ceremoniously handed the keys of the school over to President Ordway. As with most of the things the Navajo elder said, you could take his statement to be pejorative or simply practical.

Ripley had been just in time for the ceremony, after a rough three-day journey across nine hundred miles of desert and mountains on Highway 50 via an army jeep. There had been six of them traveling in two jeeps from the FEMA site, her logic being that if one of the jeeps broke down, all six could still fit in one, and it left one behind in case disaster struck and the pair of jeeps didn't make it to the New Capitol.

After an extensive, and often heated discussion the night they crashed into the lake, it had been decided Bruce would remain at the FEMA site, tending to the injured while Ripley headed back to the New Capitol to report. Emerson and Liu were coming as well, to interpret the raw scientific data about the poisonous gas clouds. Ripley had declared Tanner should go in the first wave as well. It accomplished two things; the young man had valuable information about Chang's operation, and it split up the three soldiers who had been loyal to Chang. While the men had told her they no longer supported Chang's cause, she'd been through too much to take them at their word.

The final two traveling to Shiprock were the leader of the local Paiute tribe, Odukeo, and Laurie, the fourteen-year-old who was his adoptive niece, who would function as a translator. They'd seen the crash of the helicopter and had galloped to the FEMA site with several of their tribe, ready to help if they were needed, and when Odukeo had learned of their plans, he'd insisted on coming.

"The *numu* will have a say in the new USA," he'd told Ripley via Laurie in his implacable way. "We are its westward guardians."

The following morning, the six of them had left in two jeeps which carried enough fuel for the nearly one-thousand mile trek. The refugees from Mammoth hadn't been too pleased to be left behind, but had understood the logic of the two jeeps traveling as fast as possible.

A broken axle on the second day had crowded them all into one jeep, sitting on top of the remaining fuel, and they'd ended up traveling miles out of their way due to blockages of the road which had been aptly named "the loneliest highway in America," before the cataclysm, but they'd made it in just over three days, then sent back a pair of Black Hawk helicopters to retrieve the remaining people and bring them to Shiprock.

That had been six days ago, and Uncle Odukeo had politely and firmly wrestled his way into most of the President's strategy sessions alongside the other two tribal leaders, President Chishi and Councilwoman Tewanima. There had been an intense amount of flaring of nostrils and heated, quick speech between the tribal leaders at first which had Ripley keeping a low profile as Hopi, Navajo, and Paiute navigated to find a balance between their tribal differences. Once balance had been achieved, they'd proven to be thoughtful, engaged leaders as the President's council struggled to create ways of helping the remaining ten percent of the US population to survive.

Their primary concern besides getting aid to the populace, and squelching the insurgency that was turning out to have deep roots, was the new danger of the poisonous gases pluming from the giant crack in California and others in the Midwest. As Ripley strode along the hallway to the math room the President had chosen for his central meeting room, she reflected that even though her rescue mission had been only partially successful, and the loss of Fred and Flannery an ongoing heartache, the scientific information Emerson had gathered, and their first-hand experience of the plumes had proved incredibly valuable.

Two armed guards standing in front of the classroom let Ripley in without comment, swinging the door wide for her. As she entered, Blake Ordway looked up from his paperwork at the end of a collection of tables which had been pushed together to form a square and gave her a smile. He wore a button-down shirt with a wool sweater over the top of it in deference to the growing coldness of the days, and jeans and hiking boots instead of slacks and dress shoes, but he exuded power and confidence which far outstripped his everyman outfit.

Even with his hair tousled and in need of a haircut and his facial hair far past stubble, on its way to a full beard and moustache, Ordway was a handsome man, and his energy level eclipsed that of everyone around him. Ripley had come to truly admire the man over the month they'd spent together, and counted him as a reliable friend as well as her President and boss.

Ripley flashed on the first time she'd met him, just over a month ago, and how intimidated she'd been then as opposed to her serene confidence as she entered the conference room stacked with important people. She cast a glance around the room. Chief of Staff Janet Givens was at the President's right hand, her sprayed helmet hair as perfectly in place as ever. She wore a forest green turtleneck and a chartreuse silk scarf along with her ubiquitous black business suit and skirt, pantyhose, and her sensible heels. Her steely eyes met Ripley's, and she frowned a bit, just like she always did, as if she were disappointed Ripley was still around. On Blake's other side, her friend Emerson and Dr. Liu bent their heads over a hand-held calculator, completely engaged in whatever they were discussing and oblivious to the rest of the room.

The three tribal leaders were also at the table, along with Jerry Johnson, while a dozen or more secretaries and aides ringed the edges of the room, their notebooks at the ready. The President's two Secret Service bodyguards hovered several feet behind him. Teenage Laurie, translating for Odukeo, sat at the main table, next to the elderly gentleman with long salt and pepper braids who spoke English, but haltingly. The young woman looked a little cowed, but was doing her best to mask it. Ripley walked around the table to sit next to her, as President Ordway was still sorting through his agenda.

"Hi. How are you holding up?" she asked Laurie. They'd become friendly during their three-day journey to reach Shiprock, and Ripley had been impressed with the fourteen-year-old's maturity.

"I'm okay. Kind of ready to get back to my brother and our ranch, but Uncle says it may be several days yet," the pretty blond said.

"I was overwhelmed at my first few meetings, too," Ripley reassured her in an undertone. "I think it's pretty normal to feel that way. My trick is to clasp my hands together, so no one can tell they're shaking." Ripley demonstrated what she meant.

Laurie immediately did the same thing and gave Ripley a nudge with her shoulder. "Cool," she whispered as President Ordway cleared his throat.

"Thanks everyone, I know our meeting was called abruptly," he began. "We have quite a bit of news to get through, and then I have some new assignments to confer. I'd like to start with Janet."

His Chief of Staff appeared to be discomfited as she straightened her jacket with both hands. "The evacuation of Cheyenne Mountain is complete," she stated, resolutely not looking in Ripley's direction.

A hard knot of tension which Ripley had been carrying relaxed on hearing the news. Janet Givens had fought her about evacuating the massive stronghold even though it stood on the cusp of two huge faults, the Ute Pass system, and the Sangre de Cristo, but Ripley had prevailed, creating an enemy in the process.

Givens continued to rattle off her report. "All the personnel and much of the stockpile of transport vehicles, weapons, munitions, and rations have been transferred to our current facility and to depots located in Iowa and Minnesota. I want to commend my colleague, Jerry Johnson, for helping me to expedite such a massive and unprecedented relocation effort." She nodded at the man, who waved his hand in acknowledgement.

Janet Givens cleared her throat and twisted her neck in discomfort. "We completed the evacuation a full day ahead of schedule, although I was very much against moving from the mountain," she continued. "It was a terribly complex and strenuous project, but President Ordway insisted we undertake it, based entirely on the..." The woman's pause was devastating, clearly confirming her distaste. "*Informed opinion* of Ms. Baxter."

Everyone's heads swung to Ripley. Next to her, Laurie's eyes widened as she spoke in rapid Paiute to Odukeo. Ripley clenched her hands together under the table and pressed her knees together for good measure as she tried to project an attitude of quiet competence. The censorious, accusatory tone Janet Givens was using left no room for doubt what her opinion of Ripley was. The woman despised Ripley's recommendations and very definitely despised her presence. It was also clear Givens had found the evacuation to be an exercise in futility, and was letting the entire room of leaders know it with practiced ease, hiding the disdain under ordinary words designed to diminish Ripley.

The assault struck deep, but instead of burrowing into her confidence and undermining it, Ripley flared with anger, a rebuttal rising so quickly she had to clamp her lips together. While a seething takedown begged to be let loose, Ripley respected Ordway too much to allow it free. She resolutely kept her chin up and smiled pleasantly at Janet Givens, using her trick of imagining there was a duck sitting on the officious woman's head so she wouldn't succumb to her desire to take her down a notch or two.

A wash of grey tone filled Ripley's ears as she fought to maintain her control and find a pool of calm, so she only caught the end of Janet Given's next sentence. "—four hours ago the mountain fully collapsed."

"What?" Ripley blurted. "What did you say?"

Givens gave a little tsk of annoyance at having to repeat herself. "A massive quake hit last night. Cheyenne Mountain has collapsed, wiping out the town below it which was in the path of the fall."

Ripley pressed her hand to her chest to stave off a panic attack as the memories of being buried alive flooded through her psyche. "How many people did we lose?"

"None. Both the town and facility had been completely evacuated a day ahead of time, as I stated previously." Givens ejected the words from her mouth with precise formality. "Your warning saved precious equipment and hundreds of lives, including my own. Thank you, Ms. Baxter, and you too, Mr. President. You were right, and I was wrong." Her face was stiff, and she looked as if she'd eaten an entire lemon, peel and all, but she gave Ripley a polite nod, and then sat, looking at no one.

"You have my thanks as well, Ripley," the President said as Ripley sat in a state of shock. A murmur passed around the table, and the leaders sitting at it all gave her respectful nods. Emerson was flat out grinning at her.

"I'm glad it worked out," Ripley managed to say as a surge of relief poured through her that no lives had been lost. "Well done, Ms. Givens, and Mr. Johnson," she added as she wiped her palms surreptitiously on her black woolen trousers to rid them of the panicked sweat which had surged as images of being entombed flowed through her.

President Ordway continued to run the meeting smoothly. "Dr. Liu and Emerson have been studying the data that was obtained by them on a recent expedition to California, and they, too, have good news."

Dr. Liu gestured to Emerson to stand. Ripley willed herself to focus on what her friend from college had to say, wrenching herself from a morbid contemplation of pressing darkness slowly crushing her torso.

"Thank you, sir. Well, the good news is the sea water and lava are mixing to form hydrated rock, which we believe will function as a cushion against the triggering phenomenon. That will slow the earthquakes over time. It means we're looking at perhaps two or three years of ongoing quakes, instead of a decade." Emerson shared a confirming look with Dr. Liu before he continued. "We've theorized that the cushioning phenomenon is happening in a variety of places across the globe, but we don't have communications or data as of yet to study our hypothesis."

"What about the vapors? How much of a threat are they?"

"In concentration, they kill in minutes. Even in small quantities they'll damage exposed skin and scar lung tissue, leading to severe breathing issues. We're recommending everyone in their path of to wear long sleeves and slacks, to don masks, and to stay indoors if they see the gaseous clouds. In short, they're toxic, but there's not much we can do about them."

"When Chang was shooting at us, the sparks were igniting the hydrogen, burning it off," Ripley said, remembering the sheets of white and blue flames shooting skyward. "Would it help to send helicopters to do that, burn off the hydrogen so the sulfides are less toxic?"

Emerson looked at Liu, who nodded cautiously. "Perhaps," Liu said. "It might work. Methane is also present at toxic levels, and it is also highly flammable." He looked to Emerson for confirmation.

"It's worth a try," Emerson rubbed his chin as he contemplated. "I can't see a downside, except in wasted ammunition and flight time for the helicopters."

"Consider it done. Jerry, I'd like to put you on organizing it. I don't want to use the Black Hawks, but some of our smaller birds could be deployed for a few days to see if it helps on the one in what was California. If it does, we'll let the folks in Kansas know." The President turned to Emerson and Liu. "I'll send one of you along also, to run the tests on the air quality so we can assess the results."

Uncle Odukeo raised his hand, commanding the attention of the table instantly, and muttered to Laurie, who gave him an admiring look before she communicated his words. "The *numu* are most directly in the path of these gases. We would like to be in charge of hosting the helicopter brigade. Those flying them and your scientist would be most welcome in our village while they fight this unseen enemy."

President Ordway didn't hesitate. "I think that's an excellent plan. Jerry will see to it. Thank you, although you are welcome to move your tribe here if you wish."

Odukeo put a hand under Laurie's elbow as he stood formally, pulling her to stand with him. Laurie nodded as he spoke measured words to her. Laurie translated. "Our land will protect and sustain us as she always has. But we welcome your science to assist her. We are *numu* and will not forsake our mother or intrude upon the Navajo or Hopi. I have spoken and through me, my people."

President Chishi stood and put his hand over his heart and bowed. Councilwoman Tewanima followed suit. The three Indian leaders sat once more, a deep peace resonating between them, which had been absent in their intertribal dealings earlier in the week.

"Final piece of business. Our conversations with the three soldiers who were formerly aligned with Chang have been productive," Ordway said. "I've recommended they be given positions in construction at the New Capitol site, under supervision, of course, for a six-month probationary period, and then Janet will reassess their status."

Janet Givens frowned, but nodded her agreement. Ripley resolved to seek out Tanner later—she'd have to discover what his first name was—and check on his well-being and that of his men. She owed him that.

"Unfortunately, their information about the numbers and positions of the militia insurgency has been spotty. Chang kept the groups isolated from each other, and only communicated with the leaders himself. They'll have noticed his absence. I suspect they have a 'Plan B' in place, which means you may have chopped the head off of the hydra, but there are more heads growing."

"So instead of one enemy, we have multiples," Jerry Johnson mused. "There's certainly historical precedent for the use of isolated cells which regroup once the original leader has been disposed of."

"We know about the group in DC first hand," Ordway went on. "And the soldiers we spoke with were firm that other solid units were operating out of Oklahoma and southeast Virginia. Tanner thought the Virginians were associated with the DC group. Family ties, we can assume. There are likely others in play." He paused and waited for Laurie to catch Odukeo up.

Tewanima cleared her throat in the vacancy. "It would be wise for you to stop their insurgency before it grows," she said. "Our tribe has young people who are eager to participate in the formation of our new country. They would be good choices to add to your troops if you intend to seek out and engage these cells."

Chishi nodded his head. "I agree. Many of our people are agitated that we allowed you to retake even a small portion of our lands. Giving them an active part to play would go a long way to show your promises to be inclusive in the new USA are not empty ones."

Ordway's face flushed at the implication he'd go back on his word, but he kept his voice level. "Heard and understood. I'm sending out a mission tomorrow to the Midwest, Mid Atlantic, and South to assess the danger of the insurgents, open FEMA caches throughout the area, and to get a bead on the level of destruction we're facing. While they're gone, I would welcome your personnel recommendations for follow up missions. Is that agreeable to both of you?"

The President waited for both of the leaders to acknowledge his decision before he continued.

"Ripley, I'm appointing you to be point person on that new mission, and giving you a new job title. You'll be my new acting Head of Homeland Security, and as such, you'll be able to deputize people in the field if you find it necessary to do so."

"Yes, sir." Ripley's mind raced as she considered the implications of what her new job would entail. The irony that it used to be Thaddeus' position in the President's cabinet wasn't lost on her. "Who's your new science advisor?"

"I've asked Dr. Liu to take on that role, with Mr. Davies as a second." He glanced at the pair of scientists. "They've accepted those positions."

"You'll need a team of soldiers and a scientist with you," Ordway went on. "Yourself, another pilot, and then whatever you deem best suits the mission. Nine of you in total, one of which will be your new bodyguard. Janet can assign the team for you. I expect the mission will last between two weeks and a month, perhaps more, if you're able to rout out the insurgents."

Ripley's gut clenched at the idea of being put in charge of another group of people after her disastrous first expedition, but she nodded her head. "With your permission, I'd like to take Bruce Larson in case we need medical attention, Emerson for my scientist and," she broke off, not sure how her next request would be met. "Tanner, sir."

"Tanner?" Ordway seemed genuinely surprised. "I'd like to know why."

"I trust him," Ripley said simply. From the way Ordway raised his eyebrows, it wasn't enough. "He was decent to me when I was a prisoner and then was an active participant in our successful escape from Chang. He was cool and competent under pressure, and he saved me from drowning." She paused, tapping her fingers together as she considered. "He could be extremely useful as a credible source of information if we meet up with these militias. Respectfully, they'd be more inclined to believe him than anyone from your administration."

"I can't argue with any of that. Very well, Tanner will be part of your crew. Janet, I'll leave you to staff the rest."

"I serve at the pleasure of the President," the woman said calmly, examining her hands.

"Ms. Givens, may I ask you to give me a roster of possibles instead, and allow me to choose from those? I'd like to interview them before they join my team." Ripley spoke up before the President could shut the meeting down. The last thing she wanted was Givens choosing who would be on her team without having any input.

"Of course," Givens said with a smile which looked more like a baring of teeth.

"If there's nothing further?" The President stood, prompting the rest of the room to stand also as he exited the room with his detail.

Laurie put a hand on Ripley's arm before she could leave and spoke directly in her ear. "Uncle says it was well done, not allowing that woman to choose your staff."

Ripley looked around Laurie to see the middle-aged man with his bronze skin nodding at her, a twinkle in his deep brown eyes.

"*Pe-sha uh*," she said, recalling the words to thank someone in Paiute.

"*Yaa uu pesa petuhoo*" he said in return with an inclination of his head. Odukeo cleared his throat and spoke with deliberation in his soft voice. "Keep listening to your heart," he said to Ripley. "She will guide you." He patted Laurie on the arm and walked away, his long salt and pepper braids swaying behind him.

"Can I eat dinner with you?" Laurie asked as she lingered behind. "If you're not too busy, I mean."

"Sure." The relief on the young woman's face was palpable, and Ripley guessed she might be a bit lonely, which led her to an idea. "Have you met Timothy, the President's son who acts as his aide?"

The girl blushed. "Not really, no. I mean, I've seen him running around and stuff."

Ripley read through the casual shrug the girl used to pretend she didn't care one way or another. "You might enjoy his company, especially since I'm leaving tomorrow. I'll see if he can join us, too. He's good people, just like his dad."

"You don't have to set me up or anything." Laurie crossed her arms, her blush deepening. "I mean, he is cute, but—"

"It's just dinner." Ripley reassured her.

"Well, okay, yeah, that'd be okay. Just dinner. See you then." Laurie walked away with a bit of a bounce in her step.

"There's my good deed for the day done," Ripley said as she pushed in her chair to leave, but Emerson waylaid her.

"Listen, Ripley, I'm flattered you want me to come with you, but—"

Her hand flew in the air to stop any further words. "Stop. You're who I want, so you can't say no, Emerson."

Emerson crinkled his forehead. "What do you mean, I can't say no?"

"I'm the head of Homeland Security." Ripley spread her hands. "That gives me the authority to hijack you into my service. The President verbally agreed to your addition to my team just now, so... that's just how it is, buster."

"I get motion sickness," Emerson protested. "I hate flying."

Ripley put a sympathetic hand on his arm. “We’ll get extra airsick bags for you.”

“Great.” His mournful look was pitiful to behold.

“Look, I’m sure it’s going to be a rough few weeks, but you want to see for yourself what’s going on with the quakes and the water filling the cracks just like I do.” She drilled a finger into his belly. “Don’t make me remind you I saved your life.”

“I won’t.” He made a face. “I guess I’ll ask the doctor on staff for some Dramamine or whatever it is for motion sickness.”

“Good answer. See, you’re a great problem solver, too. Get your science gear ready. We’ll be leaving early tomorrow morning.”

Ripley made it a few steps along the hall when Councilwoman Tewanima stopped her and pulled her aside with a quick jerk of her head to the side of the hallway. It was becoming a comedy of sorts, the way one person after another wanted a private word. It must be a sample of what President Ordway experienced daily. Maybe having a bodyguard wasn’t such a bad idea after all.

“Pam,” Ripley acknowledged the woman by her given name.

“You were wise not to let Janet Givens choose your team for you. I think she will never like you.” As usual, the woman was blunt with her words, but they were spoken so musically they slid down like medicine served with a spoonful of honey.

“I’m pretty sure you’re right,” Ripley agreed.

“Two things.” The woman looked over her shoulder. “I have a person who should be your bodyguard, and have insisted Janet puts him on your list of interviews. His name is Makya, which means hunting eagle in our language. He is my nephew.”

Ripley could be blunt if she wanted to be. “Why are you so eager to put your nephew in harm’s way?”

“You owe him.”

“I owe him?”

“You did not save his mother.”

Ripley got a chill up her spine, and crossed her arms defensively, not liking the direction of the conversation. “I wasn’t aware his mother, which would be your sister, was under my purview, Pam,” she snapped.

"I understand that is a truth. He does not and is angry, but won't admit it. They lived in Sedona, and your report said nothing was left. Is that correct?"

Ripley shut her eyes and nodded. It had been the first place Fred had flown them to, before their ill-fated trip to Big Bear Mountain, on Pam's request, as her daughter had lived there. All that had remained of the famous spot had been swirls of red dust swirling across a barren landscape, the result of being too close to the Lake Mary and Bright Angel faults.

"I'm sorry." Ripley's pang of regret allowed her to see past the stoic front Tewanima had put up, revealing the grief that underpinned it. It was in the woman's slow movements, and the way her normal quick responses and comments had become stilled over the past days, her features set into a mask. "I'm so sorry we couldn't bring them home to you."

"It is a hole which will never be filled," Pam said. "I pray for them every night, and it brings me some peace. But Makya, he is young, and full of anger because he feels powerless. He needs a job which will restore his power. He is good with firearms, and close combat, and he will guard you as if you were his blood."

"How did he escape the quakes?"

"He's a Specialist E2 in the Space Force, and was deployed at Cheyenne Mountain when they first struck," Tewanima said.

"Space Force? Is he a pilot?"

Tewanima nodded. "He loves flying. As I know you do. You could kill two birds with one stone, as you folks say, have your bodyguard be your copilot, which would give you an extra soldier for the grunt work. We say catch two fish with one hook, but it's the same."

"All right, I respect your opinion. I'll meet him."

"You won't like him at first," Pam warned. "He's prickly. But he will do his job."

"People say I'm prickly all the time," Ripley told her.

"They're not wrong." With a nod of her head, Tewanima turned away.

"Just so long as we're clear, if I put him on my team, it would be as a favor to you?" Ripley asked before she could go.

The woman turned, her lips pursed. "You're getting pretty good at this politics stuff. I was thinking my recommending him would be perceived as you owing me a favor."

Ripley raised an eyebrow and said nothing, a trick she'd learned from Thaddeus. Whoever spoke next would lose the argument.

"Very well," Pam admitted after the silence had stretched to an uncomfortable length. "I'll owe you one. But only if you pick him and give him a fair trial."

"Done. And, for the record, I'm not prickly. I just have strong opinions."

Pam let out a genuine laugh, which echoed along the hall. "Keep telling yourself that, Ripley."

After a flurry of interviews, Ripley had her team chosen by dinner time. Janet Givens had sent over a list of ten qualified soldiers, and she'd put three of them who she deemed as being the most level-headed onto her short list. She'd also spoken to Tanner.

"I appreciate your confidence in me," he'd told her as she concluded their interview. "The last thing I wanted was to be put on a construction detail for the next six months."

"You earned that confidence," Ripley said succinctly. "I do have one burning question, though."

Tanner was speaking before she'd completed the sentence. "I'm furious I ever listened to Chang if that's what you want to know. He promised us land, power, and wealth in his quote, New America, unquote, but it was all lies. I'm sorry I didn't see through him sooner."

"I'm glad to hear it, but that wasn't my question."

"Oh?" The almost handsome face turned quizzical.

"What's your first name?"

Tanner sighed. "Ashley. Ash for short if you have to use it. It's a family name that goes back to before the Civil War, like Ashley Wilkes in Gone With the Wind," Tanner babbled. "It just never took for me. I'm just Tanner."

"Okay, just Tanner." Ripley thought about it. "Although I like Ashley."

"You wouldn't if you'd been a boy in grade school who wasn't big enough to fight back," he said dryly. "Tanner works."

Ripley hesitated before telling Tanner her final decision that she wanted him on her team. Her brain told her the man had been aligned with a traitor, which indicated he was opportunistic and lacked loyalty. Her heart told her that when the proverbial dung was hitting the fan, he'd been there for her and everyone else aboard their fated helicopter.

With a deep inhale, Ripley went with her heart. "Okay, you're on my team, Tanner. Fair warning. If you piss me off, even once, it'll be Ashley from then on."

"Heck of a way to incentivize me," he'd protested, but she caught his low chuckle as he exited. Good, he had a sense of humor.

Her final meeting was with Makya. His lack of humor was evident from the moment he'd stepped into the room, snapping his heels together and hauling his squat, muscled body into attention.

"I was told you wanted to speak with me, ma'am" His eyes focused above her head, his frame quivering with tension. The obligatory 'ma'am' had been choked out.

Ripley took her time responding. As much as she respected Tewanima, there were two other men on her short list Ripley thought she could tolerate as her bodyguard, and several pilots who she'd gotten to know over the past week as they taught her how to competently hover and land the birds who would be easy companions in the air. However, combining the two roles would give her an extra soldier in case they ran into trouble, and it made the President's requirement of having a bodyguard a bit easier to take.

"I'm going on a mission into the Midwest, South, and mid-Atlantic, for several weeks. President Ordway wants me to have a bodyguard, and I need a co-pilot for the Black Hawk. Your aunt said you'd be a good choice, and evidently Chief of Staff Givens believes you're skilled, or you wouldn't be on my list, but I'd like to hear your pitch. If I choose you, we're going to be practically in each other's laps twenty-four seven."

"Permission to speak freely, ma'am."

"Granted."

"I have a blood debt to you. Your warning cleared us out of Cheyenne Mountain, so it is you who saved me from being buried alive. I want to fulfill it."

"By saving mine, I presume. What happens after you do that?"

The dark brown eyes briefly touched her own before sliding away again. "Then I can walk away."

"So you'd walk away, even if we were in the middle of our mission?"

"No!" Makya blurted, losing his composure for a moment. "I mean my obligation to you would be lifted. I wouldn't abandon the mission."

"Not good enough." Ripley said. "Thanks for your time."

"Wait, I mean—" he huffed out a breath with a growl of frustration mixed into it. "I have more to say, ma'am."

"Call me Ripley."

"Ripley." The name grated out. "If I don't fulfill my debt to you, your spirit and mine will be forever entwined. I don't want that," he said, a bit more of his desperation cracked through. "Frankly, I couldn't stand it, so I'd do my utmost to make sure you're safe." Makya hesitated, and then added, "And I'm a heck of a good pilot, too."

"Yes, I saw that in the Chief of Staff's notes," Ripley commented as she studied him carefully. Tewanima had been right, she didn't like Makya much. But then, she hadn't liked Thaddeus either, and that had certainly changed. Tanner had been her jailor and a traitor to the President, but she'd included him. And adding Pam's nephew to her team would create a favor she could call in if she needed one down the road. Given's notes on him had included his commendations as a sharpshooter as well as being a trained combat helicopter pilot, so he was certainly technically qualified.

"We're leaving early. Have your gear ready," Ripley told him. "Your assignment is probationary in terms of you being my bodyguard, though. If we don't gel after a few days, you'll be knocked down to just my co-pilot."

His bright white teeth flashed in a quick grin at the news before he nodded, the smile transforming his blunt features. "Thank you, ma'am. I mean, Ripley."

After dinner mess was completed—and she'd been right, Timothy and Laurie had hit it off—Ripley sought out Thaddeus in his room, bringing a cup of hot mint tea for him fixed the way he liked it, with a dollop of honey. He put the book he'd been reading aside and smiled when he saw her, and scooted over on the narrow cot to make room for her. The simple gestures were like a soft, warm blanket on a chilly evening, and she slid next to him with a sigh of contentment.

"Ms. Baxter. I hear you're off again in the morning," he said, taking the proffered tea as he draped his arm around her shoulders. "Blake filled me in."

"I am. I wish you could come with me."

"I'm a long way from being on active duty again," he said, plucking at his neatly rolled and pinned sweats that betrayed the empty spot where his leg had been. "If ever again."

"Don't be gloomy. Blake Ordway needs your intelligence twice as much as he needs your tall, athletic frame. You can have the title back if you want. I don't need it."

"Ah, yes, I forgot you're now the acting Director of Homeland Security, congratulations. And you need the title if you're going to deputize people out in the hinterlands. Pesky laws being what they are."

"Tell me I haven't lost my mind—" she began.

"Too late for that," Thaddeus quipped, then kissed her on the forehead. "Just teasing. You're one of the smartest people I know, so whatever you're going to ask me, I'm nearly certain to tell you your assessment was correct."

"I put a confirmed traitor on my away team, and assigned a guy I don't like and who doesn't like me as my personal bodyguard."

"Didn't see those coming," Thaddeus said after a stunned moment. "But I'm sure you're following your inner voice, and it's proved to be a reliable one. WWRD, after all." He took her hand and stroked it gently.

Ripley leaned against the warmth of his torso and smiled at their inside joke, remembering the first time he'd shared the acronym with her, just after they'd escaped the militia in Washington, DC, against formidable odds.

"What would Ripley do." Ripley tilted her head to look at Thaddeus and snuggled closer as she saw his love for her shining in his eyes. "I guess we'll have to see."

A quick knock at the slightly open door had them both looking up. It was Timothy, looking abashed as he resolutely stared at his feet rather than the pair in the narrow bed.

"Sorry, but dad says you both need to come to the meeting room. There's been a development and you're going to need to leave for the Midwest right away."

CHAPTER SIXTEEN

Eastern Tennessee Seismic Zone
Day Forty

If she were in the frame of mind to count blessings, Deb supposed she could say Bob Larkin's unfortunate discovery of her in the abandoned restaurant may have saved her life. They'd traveled nearly a half day to get back to his homestead, or rather, the place he'd claimed as his homestead, and it had taken the last drops of her energy to get there without falling off of Daisy in a dead faint. Once they'd arrived at the doublewide trailer outside of Maryville, he'd ordered his extremely pregnant wife Deliah to care for Deb and get her healthy, which the woman did with rough efficiency.

Deliah had made up a pallet on the floor in their living room area of old couch cushions, then had wrapped Deb in layers of warm pajamas, socks, and sweaters, and had poured weak tea laced with honey down her throat hourly. She'd fed her stale toaster strudels, ancient Ho-ho's, or Slim Jims whenever Deb had said she was hungry, and given her aspirin and vitamin C from Deb's stash of medicine with clockwork regularity. She wiped her face and wrists with cool water when Deb's fever reached dangerous levels, and changed her clothes for her when the fever broke in a torrent of sweat, which had left Deb fragile and shaking.

As she was weak as a newborn as she recovered, the woman walked Deb to the outhouse her husband had dug at the far end of the old hickory wood barn which stood on a hill in back of the double-wide trailer. There was a shed out back as well, and Deliah had pointed to it on the third day Deb had been with them.

"That's going to be my birthing shed," she'd informed Deb, pressing her hand against her enormous belly as she caught her breath. "Because Bob, he don't like to hear my caterwauling when I bring children into the world. Me and the girls have been getting it ready. I got the cookfire outside of it built and ready for boiling water, and a pallet in there, and lots of sheets and towels, and the things for the baby. If it's night, Bob says we can have the lantern."

"How generous," Deb had said dryly. The woman had eagerly bobbed her head in agreement, then hurried Deb along without another word as Bob emerged from the woods behind the barn with a pair of freshly killed rabbits tied to his belt with a bit of string.

Deb thought Deliah might be in her early thirties, but was hesitant to engage her in any conversations after Bob had casually threatened to blow her head off if he caught her talking to his wife or daughters. She'd learned not to look him in the eyes when he spoke to her as well, the slap he'd given her as her 'one and only warning' leaving behind welts on her cheek.

"I know your type. You're the kind who puts ideas in people's heads," he told her. "I can just tell by looking at you. I ran my own gas station and mechanic garage for fifteen years. I'm not some dumb hick, so don't think you can pull something over on me, either. Like I said, I know your type, you'll connive until you get what you want. I guess I don't blame you, as it's your nature, but I won't tolerate it."

"I apologize," Deb had said meekly, although what she'd really wanted to do was to deck him. She'd not been physically strong enough to be sure she could overpower him, so she'd bided her time. Deb pretended to be cowed from then on, lulling his suspicions.

Bob had brought his nearest neighbor over to show Deb off to him, offering Deb's future nursing services in exchange for the use of some farming equipment and a burlap bag of seed corn in the spring. The two men had haggled a bit, then shook hands on the deal over a warm beer.

"Old Pete, he's got a sickly wife, but loves her to pieces, so could be he'll need your doctoring a few times. That's good, means more things I can trade him for." The realization had brought a broad smile to Bob's face, and he'd allowed Deliah to give Deb a hearty portion of fresh rabbit stew instead of expired packaged goods for dinner.

The idea that she and her abilities were being bartered sickened Deb almost as much as the terrible flu she'd caught, which had come perilously close to developing into pneumonia. Being treated like property was humiliating and frightening, causing her head to spin as she thought up and was forced to discard a hundred methods of escape. At night when she drowsed, her sleep interrupted by the deep hacking cough that still lingered ten days after she'd become ill, Deb fingered the little pouch of seed corn Kevin had given her when they parted whenever her thoughts edged toward hopelessness, deriving a bit of courage from it.

Deliah had found the little satchel of corn, of course, when she'd undressed Deb the first night, but she must have divined it was important to Deb, as she'd folded her hands around it, allowing her to keep the talisman.

"I'd give just about anything for Kevin to come riding in on his horse and rescue me," Deb muttered under her breath. It wouldn't happen, of course. If anyone was going to get her out of the predicament she was in, it was going to be herself. Or perhaps one of the daughters, but she'd had few interactions with them, only learning their names. Lizzie was the older, perhaps ten, and Grace was six.

Deb further learned over a series of brief exchanges that Lizzie missed going to soccer practice, and Grace mourned the loss of her cats, and that their mom had always been at home with them, and that they used to live close to the University of Tennessee, so close they could hear the crowds and the band playing at the football games. Grace was firm that she wanted a baby brother because she already had a sister.

"Daddy's business was out here though, just down the street," Lizzie had said importantly a few days later when they'd been put to work hanging out the laundry to dry together. "And when the earthquakes came, our daddy had the presence of mind to gather all the things at his garage and gas station and bring them to this old place." It had sounded like she was parroting what her father had told her verbatim.

"Did he know the people who lived in the trailer before?" Deb had ventured to ask her.

Lizzie had shrugged as she chewed gum with her mouth open and pinned up a pink pillowcase. "I guess so. He said they wouldn't be needing it anymore, and the barn would be really good for us to have."

While Deb internally questioned how it had come to pass that the people who'd owned the trailer previously didn't need it anymore, she kept her pondering to herself. The conversation had explained the never-ending supply of old candy and Slim Jims, at any rate. They were eating the contents of a gas station. As she got better, and was able to go to the outhouse on her own, Deb timed her needing to go when Bob was out hunting for food and goods so she could poke around without getting caught in an effort to find her backpack and rifle.

Deb had peeked into the barn and discovered it was stuffed with boxes of goods and locked metal containers. It also held some stalls where he kept a couple of milk cows and three horses, two of his own, and Daisy, who pricked her ears forward and nickered when she caught Deb's scent. Deb nipped inside and discovered Daisy's saddle and bridle was there as well along with her panniers, neatly put away in the tack room. Memorizing where things were in case she was able to escape, Deb stroked her horse's neck, relieved to find her still alive.

"I'll get you out of here as soon as I can," she promised the sweet mare. Having Daisy close to hand upped her chances of getting away from Bob, as did his apparent acceptance she'd been tamed. It would have to be when he was out hunting, as he rigged an alarm system on the doors of the trailer and the windows when they slept at night that she didn't think she could disable without waking him.

As the days passed, Deb monitored Deliah, who'd been experiencing Braxton-Hicks contractions. Deliah would stop and stoop over a bit and pant until they passed, waving off any need for Deb's assistance.

"Mr. Larkin, would it be all right if my medical kit was somewhere I could get to it if you're not around?" She'd asked the question humbly during their supper ten days after she'd been brought to the doublewide. "I think your wife is getting close to her time." Deb was careful never to refer to Deliah by her name to Bob, and to give him the honorific of "mister," although it grated on her every nerve.

He looked at her as he considered the question. "All right, but only your med kit, nothing else."

She smiled and nodded gratefully.

"Lizzie, go into daddy's tall lockbox in the barn," he told his oldest daughter, unclipping a carabiner of keys from his belt where they rode all the time and making a show of flipping through the bunch until he produced one that was silver with three cutouts on the rounded head. "Here's the key. Fetch me the nurse's medical kit. You know which key unlocks the barn door, right?"

"Sure thing, daddy." She triumphantly held up a black key. "It's this one."

"No touching the guns!" he called after her.

"Can I ask, Mr. Larkin, did your wife have any complications with either of the girls when they were born?"

"Nah. My Deliah's as good a brood mare as a man could ask for, isn't that right, Deliah?"

"Sure am!" She positively beamed at having his attention, just like the girls did. "Me and my mister want a whole passel of kids, we've wanted it our whole lives, ever since we met first day of middle school." Her eyes shone. "My last name used to be Lyle, so I sat right behind Bob in every class, because of being in alphabetical order. It was just love at first sight!"

The woman was clearly content with her life. Deb could see it in every exchange, and she supposed in his way, Bob was devoted to his kids and wife. He'd found a way for them to survive, and to make a life for his growing family, and they loved him for it, despite his autocratic rule.

She'd get no help from Deliah or the girls when she escaped, Deb concluded. In fact, they'd probably do their best to stop her and earn Bob's acclimation for it. He'd already marked her as his property as far as the neighbors were concerned, so they'd be no help either. And no one was charging in on a white horse wearing a white hat to save her.

"If it's going to be, it's up to me," she said. It had been another one of her aunt's sayings, and one more time it was proving itself to be true.

Lizzie returned with the whole backpack a few minutes later. "I didn't see a kit," she explained, her breath coming in big gasps from lugging it all the way from the barn. "So I just brought everything." She looked contrite. "Sorry I didn't do it better, daddy."

There was a pause in the conversation and movement in the kitchen area of the house, as Deliah and Grace stood stock still and waited to see what sort of punishment Lizzie might get for not doing her task perfectly. Bob sucked his teeth while he stroked his growing beard and moustache with a repetitive, circular movement.

"You did the best you could," he said to Lizzie at last, in a stern voice. "But I want you to go to your room and think of two other ways you could have done it better."

"Yes, okay!" The flood of relief on the girl's face was evident as she hurried off.

Bob pointed proudly at her retreating back. "That one's going to make a fine wife one of these days. Obedient and smart alongside it. It's a fine combination."

Deb's gut churned at his casual assessment of his own ten-year-old daughter, but she hid it by digging into her backpack. Her fingers brushed the hilt of Honey's stock, and for the briefest of moments, she considered drawing the pistol, but opted against it as she felt the weight of Bob's gaze on her neck.

"Don't think of trying anything, Ms. ER Nurse," he said calmly.

She put a stupefied look on her face, as if she hadn't the faintest idea what Bob was talking about, and pulled out the first aid satchel instead. "Found it!" she said brightly. "Not that I think she'll need any surgical intervention," she added, speaking only to Bob, although pitching her voice loudly enough so Deliah could hear as well. "But it's always good to be prepared."

"Daddy, can I show you my drawing I made?" Grace piped, blessedly drawing his suspicious gaze away from Deb as she inventoried her supplies. Gloves, pads, surgical scissors to cut the cord or do an episiotomy, and disinfecting wipes, and the surgical kit in case the woman needed stitches.

"Do you have a bowl you'd like to use for the placenta?" she asked in a low voice to Deliah while Bob was engaged with his youngest daughter. "And we could use a shower curtain if you have an extra one, just to keep things sanitary. Maybe a hot water bottle and a tennis ball would help during your labor, and lubricant if you have any."

"Sure, we have those things. I'll get them and take them to my birthing shed." Suddenly, the woman doubled over and emitted a long, low moan, which rose in volume as water splattered on the floor between her legs.

Deb snapped into her ER nursing mode. "Your water's broken. Mr. Larkin, could you get the fire going for us at the shed right away, please? And fill the cauldron with water after you've got it going?"

"It's time?" He seemed as stunned that Deb was giving him orders as he was that his wife was in active labor in their kitchen.

"It is."

Deliah let out another animal-like moan, which jolted the man to hustle outside. Deb pushed her med kit into her backpack and slung it onto her shoulders. As she did so, her gaze landed on the carabiner of keys which were still lying on the coffee table in the living room. "Grace, help get your mama to the shed, please. I'll grab the shower curtain, and be there in a moment."

"Okay!"

The little girl patted her mother's hand. "Come on, momma. Let's get me a baby brother to play with!"

The second their backs were turned, Deb snatched up the ring of keys and hustled into the bathroom and locked the door. She frantically looked through the twenty-odd keys on the ring until she found both the silver and the black keys and slid them off the ring and into the pocket of her jeans. She slid the shower curtain off the rod and hurried into the living area just as Lizzie came out of the room she shared with her sister.

"Are you going to help me?" Deb asked brightly, tucking the hand that held the keys under the plastic curtain, so they were hidden. "Your mom's gone to the birthing shed."

"I'll stay with daddy," she said importantly. "Where is he?"

"Getting the fire going at the shed, go on. I just need to get one more thing for your mom."

The ten-year-old sniffed suspiciously. "I'll wait for you."

"Do you have any tennis balls in the house?" Deb edged close to the coffee table as she spoke.

"Why?"

"I roll them on your mom's back to help with her labor."

"Maybe in the closet." The girl's attention was distracted just for a moment as her gaze moved to the closet, just long enough for Deb to bend her knees and place the set of keys back on top of the table. She moved to the closet Lizzie pointed to and rummaged through it. She found her own oversized jean jacket while she was there, and snagged it before shutting the door.

"Nope, nothing there. Well, let's go." Her enforced cheerfulness wasn't making much of a dent in the young girl's frown.

"What do you need your jacket for?"

"I might have to walk your mom around outside, and it's pretty cold. In fact, can you bring that throw with you, in case we need it for her and your new baby brother or sister?" She forced her smile wider, even though she felt like her cheeks might crack. Deb grabbed the canister of Slim Jims that were on the counter and shoved it inside her backpack while the girl's back was turned.

Deb put on the jean jacket, and then draped the shower curtain over the top of her big pack before they walked out of the door, keeping all her movements casual and unobtrusive.

Trusting that the night and Bob's distraction would hide the fact she had her entire backpack with her instead of just her medical kit, Deb strode up the hill with Lizzie right behind her, their breath streaming out in clouds in the frosty night air.

Bob had a good fire going, and was returning with a heavy pail of water from their well. His eyes looked a little wild as he poured the contents into the metal cauldron hanging on an iron hob and swung it over the blaze.

"She's inside," he thumbed at the door unnecessarily as a prolonged scream poured into the stillness of the night. "There's lots of wood chopped, so you should be good." He turned and nearly ran to the doublewide.

"Lizzie, I can take the throw. You go on with your daddy," Deb said, then bent and whispered, "I think he needs you."

"Yeah, okay!" She handed the soft woven blanket to Deb and hurried after her father.

With a sigh of relief, Deb went into the birthing shed. It was lit by two Coleman lanterns, which emitted enough light for her to see that, as with most mothers who'd given birth before, Deliah was progressing quickly. She panted and whined as she walked in small circles in the space, holding her lower back, her face creased with pain as a contraction took her, letting out a deep moan, and crouching a bit as the moan built to another piercing scream.

Tossing her backpack and the throw in the corner, Deb readied the plastic shower curtain. "I'll just get this down," she said, tossing aside the sheets of the pallet. With a few expert twitches, she had it pulled together again with the plastic sheeting beneath it, then turned to the petrified Grace, who was backed into a corner, her eyes huge.

"I didn't know it would be like this," she whispered. "I never want to have babies."

"Why don't you go keep your dad and sister company? You were already a big help getting your mom up here."

With a grateful nod, Grace fled, leaving Deb alone with Deliah. Deb eyed the door after the girl ran out. If she left immediately, it would give her the best chance of getting far away, but she'd taken an oath, and the woman had cared for her adroitly during her illness.

Another contraction wracked Deliah, and she reached out blindly, crying out in agony, sobbing through the pain. Deb automatically stretched out her hands to support her and made her decision.

"Its best if you keep walking as long as you can," she advised Deliah. "And let's get your clothes off, and you into your nice gown," she added as she picked up the flannel garment from the single chair in the room. The seat of the chair held swaddling clothes for the infant. Deb kept talking in a soft undertone, giving Deliah encouragement as she helped the woman strip off her soaked pants and underwear, then her sweaty top, waiting between each movement as the contractions came nearly on top of each other, simply letting Deliah grip her shoulders for support.

"I'm going to get a bowl of warm water if you're ready to lie down," she said after doing a quick check of the woman's cervix. "I think you're nearly there."

Deliah could only nod as another contraction hit. Deb eased her down as she writhed and gripped the sheets, then dashed out to the cauldron to soak a few towels. The water wasn't nearly hot enough, but it was better than nothing, and she hurried back in just as Deliah was hit by another massive contraction.

"You're crowning. Give it a ten count, and then one more big push, Deliah, you're doing great."

With a final scream from Deliah, the baby emerged into Deb's hands, who quickly cleared its nose and mouth and was gratified to get the first gasp and shocked wail of the infant, who pinked up almost immediately.

"You have a baby boy, just like Grace wanted," she told Deliah, who had collapsed back onto the bed, weeping with relief. "I'm just going to clean him for you," she added. "He looks perfect. All ten fingers and toes. Good job, mama."

"Robert Junior," Deliah whispered, her face radiant with joy. "After his daddy, that's his name."

Deb cut the cord, tied it, and cleaned the baby before she swaddled him, and placed him into Deliah's eager arms. She massaged the woman's stomach with firm, deft movements, and a few moments later, the placenta emerged. She cleaned the woman, then packed towels around her before wiping her own hands on a towel as she did a final quick visual assessment of mother and child, her heart racing.

"I'll just get you some more hot water," Deb said, as she grabbed a couple of the towels and a sheet and stuffed them into her nearly empty backpack, then picked up the throw from the corner. "And something to drink, too. I'll only be a few minutes."

Deliah nodded absently as she blissfully held her newborn to her breast, completely engrossed in her new child, hardly aware of anything else around her.

Deb eased out of the door, and with a quick glance at the silent house below, she let loose a long, guttural scream, imitating Deliah's birthing cries.

"That should hold them another few minutes," she muttered as she ran for the barn, digging out the two keys. The barn door creaked as she swung it open just wide enough to slip inside, but she was confident it was placed too far from the trailer for them to hear it.

Her eyes already adjusted to the darkness, her first stop was the tack room where she grabbed a horse blanket and Daisy's saddle, as well as two lead ropes and halters. Her panniers had been emptied of food, but she took them all the same. She raced to saddle and bridle the horse, then led her out of the stall and into the main barn. Daisy must have sensed her urgency, as the mare allowed herself to be geared up and took the bit without any of her normal shenanigans.

A quick peek out of the doors showed all was quiet. She ran down the hill a few strides and let out another imitation of Deliah in labor before ducking back into the barn to unlock the only "tall" metal locker with the silver key. Deb hit paydirt as four rifles were revealed hanging in the space, with boxes of ammunition on the shelf below, as well as a variety of combat knives. She grabbed all of the guns, including her own. Deb wrapped the soft sofa throw around her head and shoulders for warmth and a bit of padding before she slung the rifles clumsily over her shoulders and dumped boxes of ammo into her emptied panniers along with two of the combat knives.

"Consider it payment for services rendered," she said, as she slipped the halters over the other two horse's heads and led them from their stalls as well, her heart hammering, an inner voice telling her to hurry, that her time was running short.

"Bob!" Deliah's cry echoed from outside, a note of panic in it. "Bob!"

Deb flung open the barn door then tossed the panniers over the saddle before she mounted Daisy with an effort. The bulging panniers pressed her thighs awkwardly and the guns rattled, banged, and bruised her back as she tried to find her balance, the weight of them pressing her forward as she kicked the horse into action. She held onto Daisy's reins with her left hand and gripped the lead ropes of the other two horses tightly with her right as she urged the horse forward.

They emerged from the barn just as Bob and his daughters rolled out of the doublewide, heeding Deliah's frantic calls.

"Daddy!" Lizzie screamed and pointed at her as Deb urged Daisy to more speed, cutting across the back part of the property, aiming for the place where the woods began.

"Get back here!" the man demanded, and a pistol shot cracked immediately afterward.

Deb ducked instinctively, gripping Daisy with her knees as the horse burst into a run, terrible fear giving her the strength to hold onto the other two horses that nearly dragged her out of the saddle as Daisy surged deeper into the forest.

Another pistol crack sounded, but it was more distant, as were the mingled cries of the Larkin family, but she didn't slow her mount. Her intention was to put as much distance as she could from the people who'd captured and imprisoned her and to keep her freedom, no matter the cost.

With no real food, no camping gear, and no warm clothes other than what she wore on her back, Deb urged the horse forward into the black of the deep forest and the forbidding mountains beyond.

CHAPTER SEVENTEEN

The Blacksburg/Pembroke Fault
Day Forty-five

Mara had gone daily to the Thirteenth street bridge at noon, but none of the messages she'd left for her book club women had borne fruit. The only addition to their compound had come from Ethan's list, the part-time Spanish tutor he'd used to pass his language requirement. José Sánchez had approached her cautiously at the riverbank a few days after they'd finished taking the trail mix to the addresses of people they'd known and left notes for. He arrived pushing his four-year-old daughter, Carmen, in a stroller, the bottom of which was packed with food and a few of Carmen's clothes and toys. He also carried a massive hiking backpack which held more survival gear.

They'd integrated them into the community easily. Aiden had been thrilled he wasn't the youngest child at their encampment any more, and having an extra adult on the guard rotations had been a blessing. José was an excellent cook, and had brought a quantity of spices along with his stores. He'd also been willing to be taught how to use firearms, and under Ritchie's somewhat impatient tutelage, was becoming a decent shot. Little Carmen was quiet, her big brown eyes taking in everything. She seemed to enjoy being around people and had taken to climbing onto Eva's lap in the evenings after supper, sucking her thumb as the woman rocked her, a look of quiet contentment on Eva's face that Mara had never seen before.

The days had clicked by swiftly, with a few large quakes shaking them, but none had done serious damage to the high school or to their sturdy wall, which grew quickly with another man helping to slap mortar and dig footers. Eva had set up her new still in the mountains and had started her first batch of moonshine while Mara had busied herself finding the "fairy mushrooms" which could incapacitate grown men but likely wouldn't kill them. She'd chopped and distilled them into clearly marked plastic bottles she put on a high shelf in her living space. Mara went on a second hunt for the death cap mushrooms that could kill early in the morning when they'd be fruiting. She found them at a high elevation, where the pine trees were just beginning to take over from the broad-leaf oaks and elms. The large-capped mushrooms were pale, with a faint tinge of yellow, with a large skirting underneath and smelled honey-sweet if you got your nose right next to them.

She'd carefully picked them wearing disposable gloves, and once she got back to the high school, Mara put them in an old tea canister she'd found in the destroyed antique shop she'd gotten her washboard and wringer from, sealed it shut with duct tape and then gathered everyone in the household so she could explain they were not to touch it and the deadly reasons why.

"Got it!" Will said in his ever-cheerful voice.

"Huh," Ritchie stroked his beard, which had come in full and white, giving him the appearance of a grumpy Santa Claus. "Glad you're on our side."

"Are you a witch?" Aiden wanted to know, his voice a little breathy.

"No, I've just studied plants," Mara said. "Speaking of which, it's school time. Caroline, take Carmen, too, please." She looked over their heads at Caroline, who wrinkled her nose, but went down the hall to the library which they'd equipped with a small play area carrying the little girl on her hip.

Predictably, Sophie groaned, and even Will had shifted on his feet a bit. "I want to go help Ethan and Ritchie finish the wall," he protested. "We've only got a little way to go."

"And you can get to that in two hours," Mara replied affably. "Two hours a day doing reading, writing, and arithmetic isn't a long time. Off you go to the library room. Caroline's got the math workbooks ready for you and Aiden and Sophie. Then I'll come in and we'll do writing and reading."

"Ugh." Sophie said. "I hate writing."

"After that, Ritchie's going to let you and your brother practice loading the guns, and there's going to be snickerdoodles for your afternoon snacks."

The girl had brightened, grabbing her little brother's hand. "Come on Aiden, let's get it over with."

The three kids scuffed their way along the hall, looking exactly like reluctant grade-schoolers who'd rather be playing than studying should look. The little brush of normalcy gave Mara a sense of well-being and a boost of fortitude that had her humming as she gathered the unused bits of the greens she'd put into their morning meal from the kitchen then walked outside to tend to the chickens, bees, and the remnants of her winter garden. If she could string enough bits of normalcy together every day, like going to school, eating cookies, and having family dinners, they'd get through the transition from the old world to the new.

"Maybe we'll even learn how to thrive," Mara said aloud as she stepped into the yard and gave a wave to Eva who was seated in their watchtower, a pair of rifles at the ready. Gretel greeted her with a happy bark and trotted over for a pat. At the dog's shoulder, the scruffy Trinity did the same, then raced back to the space where Ritchie, José, and Ethan were finishing the final end cap to the wall.

They'd extended the combination of school lockers, bricks, and rebar-reinforced concrete blocks to go past the area where her greenhouse was, as well as the chicken's yard and the beehives. Mara envisioned eventually being able to grow vines up the walls and create vegetable and bee-friendly flower beds behind them once the threat of the Crowe brothers and their cronies had been taken care of.

"May that day come soon," Mara muttered as she threw the clipped ends of her greens into the hen's yard along with a handful of corn.

Moving on to the hives, she carefully poured a bit of honey into the shallow bowl of fresh water filled with stones that was placed in front of the hives and mixed it in with her finger. The deep-pitched drone emitting from the hives let her know the bees were still there, perhaps not thriving, but surviving, which, all things considered, was probably the best she could hope for.

Her greenhouse had only half of its frames installed, and many of those were cracked. Frequent breakage was the consequence of the ongoing shakes of the ground, and she hadn't figured out a way to prevent the damage. At least she'd found a good supply of the glass frames at a local gardening store, so she could replace the ones on the side that was unprotected by the wall.

She poked her finger in the soil to see if her winter garden of spinach, mustard greens, garlic, and parsley needed watering. The soil was still damp an inch below the surface, so they could go another couple of days. The Bok choy and the green onions were doing well enough that she would be able to harvest some for their dinner. Perhaps she'd do a big stir fry with a bag of rice from their stores and some sort of protein. Next, she lifted her cold frame boxes to check on the broccoli, carrots, and onions. They were diminutive, but Mara would put money on a bet that they'd survive.

Satisfied with the steady progress of her garden, Mara looked at her watch, and was surprised to see it was nearly eleven. If she hurried, she'd have time to ride the bike to the river at Thirteenth street and wait for a few minutes to see if any of the book club ladies showed up before heading back to do a bit of schoolwork with the kids. She grabbed her digging tool and a satchel, as the last time she was there, Mara had noticed a patch of silverweed. While the leaves weren't particularly tasty, the roots were delightful, and made a good extra starch to add to their diet. The hens would appreciate the leaves.

After letting Eva and the men know where she was going to be, and asking Caroline to extend the math lesson an extra fifteen minutes, Mara donned one of their always-ready survival backpacks and grabbed a rifle.

She wheeled out one of the four bikes they'd stashed in the animal's bad-weather room, and whistled for Gretel as she unlocked the gate and left the gated portion of their compound, locking it carefully behind her. Mara shivered slightly as a frigid wind blew over the mountains, making the remaining trees dance and sway, and sent another swirl of browning leaves to the ground. In another month it would be full-on winter, which would bring another host of problems to solve.

"We should start laying in a lot more firewood," Mara mused aloud as she pumped the pedals to get her blood flowing, Gretel running easily beside her. "Make it a daily chore. A woodpile next to the animal lean-to would help keep it better insulated, as well."

As she swept past downed trees and the cars which were beginning to rust as well as the completely demolished homes and businesses that lined the route to the river, Mara could see the chore would be easily accomplished, as there was no lack of destruction to use for their fire. They should probably find a way to better insulate the brick walls and ceiling of the school as well. The thoughts of keeping her extended family warm preoccupied her for the duration of the five-mile bike to the place on the river Mara had designated as a safe place to meet people if they found her note.

The dog ran to the water's edge at the wide sweep of the Roanoke river when they reached it and lapped at the fast flow. Mara kept a hand on her bike as she wheeled it to lean against the broken concrete pillars of the bridge that had once crossed the river at this point. She took her time taking in the surroundings, studying the area in each direction of the compass to be sure she was alone before getting out her digging tool and getting to work sustainably harvesting the aptly named silverweed with its distinctive serrated leaves and silver-green color. There were even a few bright yellow flowers lingering on some of the stems which she left alone, so they'd live to propagate another year.

Engrossed in her work, Mara startled to her feet when Gretel gave a sharp series of barks and added in a growl. Dropping her digger and satchel, she grabbed out her pistol and turned.

A bedraggled woman in multiple layers of clothing jumped back and raised both hands, as did the teen girl and boy standing just behind her. All of them looked emaciated and utterly terrified as Gretel closed in from behind them, her teeth bared and snarling ferociously.

"Mara! It's me. It's Jessica." The woman looked like she was about to cry. Her nose was red and sore, and her eyes bloodshot, her voice a hoarse croak. "I got your note this morning. We went back to our house to see if there was anything left." Her voice faltered as she whispered the last few words, and the desolation of her face made it clear their journey to their former home had been fruitless. She fisted her hand in front of her mouth as a deep cough bent her in half, racking her body.

"Jessica," Mara breathed as she dropped her pistol to her side and made a discreet motion for Gretel to sit. "I left you some trail mix and that note two weeks ago. It's rained since then." Mara kept her distance from the little group, as they all looked as if they had the same respiratory illness Jessica had.

"The mix had molded," Jessica nodded, "but we were able to make out the note. Or Brian did, anyway, my son, you remember him?"

Jessica had been the harried mother of five children, two of which had been of high school age, the rest younger. "Of course I do. You like action-adventure stories," she recalled and got a hint of a smile from the skeletal young man. Mara turned to the girl. "And you're Bethany, right? You like sweet romance books if I recall."

"She takes after me with that one," Jessica said, brushing a bit of hair from Bethany's pale face. "Most of the books we read in book club were way over my pay grade, I'm afraid. But I liked the company and the time off from the kids and from Joe." She stopped talking, and her eyes filled with tears. Both of the teenagers also teared up and put supportive hands on their mother's back.

"I'm so sorry," Mara whispered, as it was clear from the family's emotional response that they'd lost the three younger children and their father.

Jessica's lips trembled as she stifled yet another cough and nodded at Mara's sympathy. "We could sure use some company. We've been moving from place to place, but we've been so sick the past week, I said we'd go look for medicine at our old house." She faltered and shook her head. "I knew where it was in my house. I thought it'd be easy to find our bathroom medicine cabinet, but there really wasn't anything left, and we couldn't bear the idea of digging through the rubble and finding—" she broke off the sentence.

Mara's heart was breaking for the woman, but as all three were consumed in fits of violent coughing, she was glad there were several yards between them as she studied the group. "I understand." Mara desperately wanted to help them, but they weren't set up for any sort of isolation space at the school. Disease wasn't something she'd considered when inviting people to swell their ranks and she couldn't bring sick people into the close quarters safely the way they had the rooms organized. "Do you have somewhere warm and dry where I can bring you medicine and food until you get better?"

The trio looked at each other. Brian spoke up, coughing deeply before he spoke. "We've been living in a tent at the back of a car wash about a mile from here on the corner of Second and Orange. It has a roof and a couple of walls, and we got a fire going."

"Okay, go there, and in a few hours I'll bring you food and whatever medicine I can scrounge up."

"Can't we just come with you?" Bethany said, her voice shaking.

"I'm sorry, no. I don't want my family to get sick as well. Are you okay for water?"

Jessica nodded dully, clutching the raggedy coat more closely around her stick-thin frame. "Yes, and we're boiling it before we drink."

"Good, that's good. Jessica, I'm so glad you got my note. You go on back, but take these." Mara dug out power bars and two MREs from her backpack, as well as a bottle of aspirin, and laid them on the ground before stepping back from the sick family. "Take these, and I'll be there with more before dark."

The two kids and Jessica tore into the power bars, looks of bliss washing over their faces as they chewed.

"I know you're hungry, but try to space out those meals, share them in small bites," Mara advised. "Drink as much water as you can." She stepped back another pace. "I'll plan to be to you before nightfall."

"Thank you, Mara." Jessica waved a hand at her kids. "Let's get back inside."

Mara waited until they'd disappeared before remounting the bike. For safety's sake, she took a winding path back to the school, stopping several times to be sure the family wasn't following her. As she turned the final corner that led to the cul-de-sac below the school, Mara caught a sudden flurry of movement that was too big to be an animal. Whatever it was ducked behind the ruins of one of the homes, just beyond the gigantic crack which divided one half of the street from the other.

With a gasp, she braked hard and used a hand signal to stop Gretel in her tracks, and then to walk at her knee as she hopped off of the bike and stealthily wheeled it behind a half-tumbled garage. The shepherd trained her eyes on Mara and obeyed, but the dog's ears twitched, attuning themselves to the place where Mara had seen movement. Crouching low, and moving silently, Mara motioned for the dog to stay as she edged to the corner of the derelict structure, then peered around it and waited.

After a long moment, a soldier in combat gear emerged, duck-walking his way between houses, edging closer to the hill that led to the school. A second man followed him, then a third and a fourth, all of them armed with rifles, and geared to do battle.

Mara nearly threw up her breakfast as fear gripped her. They had been discovered. There was no other way to parse the scene unfolding in front of her. The intruders were below the sightlines of the watchtower, and would only become visible to Eva just before they topped the ridge, and if they went in guns blazing, they'd likely strike at least one or two of the people at the school before the alarm went up. So unless the militia men had just been lucky, not only had they been discovered, they'd been reconnoitered as well.

A rise of panic swept over her, and Mara squeezed her hand over her mouth so no sound would betray her presence and sorted through her options. She had no way of alerting the school about the men. Even if she rode around the torturous route that would bring her to the front of the building, it would take at least ten minutes, and the men's attack was imminent.

Mara looked at her watch and forced herself to think calmly even though her breath was hitching slightly as she tried to control her breathing. It was just a little after the noon hour. Caroline and the children would still be safely inside the school at their lessons, but Ritchie, José, and Ethan were outside in the yard, and Eva was exposed on the watchtower. Ritchie's dog Trinity might hear something and bark, but she was a yappy dog who sounded off about squirrels as readily as she did when the horses moved, so they were all prone to not paying attention to her alerts.

Four men were on approach from below the school. The horrifying reality made her go cold all over and her actions became mechanical as she took stock of the situation. She looked at her rifle. It was fully loaded, and Mara had a spare magazine in her backpack. Her SIG was on her hip, also fully loaded. She had no armor, but the clothes she had on were all relatively drab, so she might move unseen around the base of the hill to the big oak tree that stood just outside the chain link fence, near their midden. The trunk would give her suitable cover from gunfire.

"Gretel, stay. Guard." Mara whispered as she pointed at the bike and her faithful dog immediately obeyed her and stood next to it, both of them well protected by the remains of the wall of the garage. Mara tightened the straps of her backpack, lowered herself flat to the ground, and peeked out again to see if the men had made any progress in their approach.

The first man was at the base of the hill, the other three just below him. Mara held still as one of the men swept a look behind them. She was confident he'd not notice her, but let out an inaudible sigh of relief as he continued his sweep, then gave a go-ahead wave to his group. She held her position for a long count of thirty and was just about to crawl to the far side of the hill to start her own ascent when her heart plummeted.

Another group of four men followed the first four, similarly armed, but with less body armor, and two of them were instantly recognizable to Mara. It was the remaining two Crowe brothers, Shiloh, and Dale, both of them still bearing the marks of the fireworks she'd sent screaming at them three weeks prior when they came to take her homestead.

A spark of fury re-ignited at the sight of the brothers who'd caused so much pain to her family and to Eva, eclipsing the worries she had about the people atop the hill. Before she could think about what she was doing, Mara leapt to her feet and let a barrage of bullets from her rifle fly at the brothers and their compatriots, a scream erupting from her throat as she fired on them. She had a savage pop of glee as the second group of four men dropped to the ground, either hit or taking cover. Mara dove behind the garage as gunfire from the men higher on the hill swept the area where she'd just been standing.

"Gretel, come!" Mara dashed from behind the garage, keeping the building between herself and the men, counting on her knowledge of the neighborhood below the school to keep them safe.

The rattle of automatic gunfire rang loudly as she leapt across the crack in the middle of the street, angling for the far corner of the block. Bits of concrete stung the back of her legs as she stayed just ahead of a line of bullets before a sharp stab on her thigh caused her to stumble and fall, ripping her jeans and bloodying her knees and palms. Rolling, Mara came around and blindly fired behind her, clicking on empty as she reached the end of the magazine. She continued her roll and got back onto her feet, limping as the graze on her leg swept a line of fire along her upper thigh.

Focused on reaching the cover that would be created by the curve of the hill, she limped forward as fast as she could go as the gunfire from the enemy resumed. A sharp yip of pain from Gretel stopped her in her tracks. Mara whirled, her fury doubling when she saw the bloody crease on Gretel's rear leg and her precious friend lying tumbled to the ground, whining in pain and fear as she was unable to keep running. In a blind rage, Mara screamed and spun around with her SIG at the ready, firing repeatedly as she ran to Gretel. She scooped the sixty-pound dog into her arms, wheeled and dashed forward and left, ducking behind a stone retaining wall which had the tattered remains of a hedge growing in front of it.

The dog was panting, her eyes rolling as she looked at Mara, who pressed her hand to the wound as she dumped the backpack and scrambled for the first aid kit and her extra magazine for the rifle. Moving fast, she loaded the gun then slapped a gauze pad on the dog's wound, and wound tape tightly around it to hold it in place before doing the same thing for her own leg, gulping in air with furious gasps as she did so. The dog needed better medical attention as quickly as she could get it for her. Mara looked around for a clear path to take so she could circle to the relative safety of the school and access their supplies.

Above her on the hilltop, a hail of gunfire conjoined with angry shouts and cries of pain as the smell of cordite washed through the air. Mara dashed away tears of rage and remorse. At least her barrage had alerted Eva and the men, so they hadn't been taken by surprise, which was something, but her ill-advised, emotionally driven move had gotten her dog and herself hurt.

"Get a grip, Mara Padgett," she said to herself sternly as she stroked Gretel, who whined and lapped at her hand. "Figure out what to do next." Her hands were shaking violently, so she pulled out her water bottle and drank deeply, then cupped her hands so Gretel could drink as she raced her brains as to what she should do next.

There was a pause in the gunfire, and indistinguishable shouts from the top of the hill, a conversation of sorts going back and forth. A soft clatter of broken concrete echoed near her hiding place, the sound of it jacking another bolt of adrenaline through Mara. Setting her jaw, she wiped her damp hands on her jacket and eased her rifle around, ready to fire.

A pair of legs in camo, side pockets bulging with ammunition, came into her line of vision creeping down the cul-de-sac. The torso turned in her direction, and Mara fired a quick, concentrated burst just as the man saw her and jerked his weapon toward her. He got off a few wild shots which went wide and into the air as he tumbled backward with a cry of shock, his rifle tumbling out of a lifeless hand, the light pings of casings accompanying him as he collapsed bonelessly to the ground.

Mara scrambled to her feet and moved to crouch over Gretel, her head just below the line of the broken retaining wall as shouts from just a few yards away let her know a group of men had seen what had happened to their comrade and were closing in on her. She tensed her muscles, ready to move out and fire on them when a huge explosion, followed by a second one, rocked her backwards on her heels and she stumbled to the ground, flinging her arm protectively over her dog.

"They've got grenades!" one of the men shouted, barely audible through the ringing in her ears. "Fall back!"

"Get Ronny!" another one shouted as booted feet began to run. There was a quick flash of movement as someone picked up the man she'd shot and slung him over their shoulders in a fireman's carry, loose limbs dangling to either side of his body.

Panting, Mara stayed where she was as the running footsteps faded away down the street, the whine in her ears slowly dissipating, leaving behind a terrible headache in its place. A roar of ATVs, perhaps four or five of them starting at once, echoed profanely through the stillness a few minutes later, the sound of them striking her ears as foreign after so many days of quiet.

After they'd faded into the distance, Mara eased herself back to her hands and knees, grunting as the sting of the bullet graze fired through her thigh once more. She cautiously looked out into the street, seeing only a smear of blood where she'd hit the soldier. She scrambled into the street and snatched the rifle his companion had left behind and slung it across her back with her own. Then she went back to Gretel and cradled the dog as gently as she could into her arms, avoiding the wound on her rear upper leg as she held her close to her chest, ignoring the sear of pain in her own leg.

Mara avoided a direct route up the hill, instead sweeping wide and to the side, where she had the cover of more downed homes and a few trees before she reached the area of the school, panting from the exertion of carrying Gretel. Her arms shook as she laid the dog in the browning grass before she took the final steps to the ridge of the hill with her arms held high.

"It's Mara!" she shouted as the person in the watchtower swung in her direction, the long rifle in their hands pointing at her. The person let the rifle drop as they waved and jumped up and down enthusiastically.

"That's Will," she sighed with relief. She waved back and turned to lift Gretel, her worry increasing as she saw the makeshift bandage she'd put on the dog had become soaked in blood. The dog emitted a soft whine as Mara hefted her.

"Hold on girl, we'll get you fixed up," she promised her dog as she limped past the downed chain-link fence.

"Mom!" Ethan called out, swinging across the yard toward her, accompanied by José. "Are you all right?"

"I was grazed, and so was Gretel," Mara said, her voice hoarse as her emotion rose at seeing both of her boys were unhurt. "Is anyone hurt?"

"Yes, you need to come quick," Ethan said seriously. "Eva's working on them in the dining room."

"Them?" Mara's fears surged to the forefront, and she started running, Gretel still clutched to her chest.

"Caroline and Ritchie," José said, his face grim as he ran next to her. "They were both shot."

CHAPTER EIGHTEEN

Waurika-Muenster and Sulphur Faults, The Big D Fault
Days Forty-three to Forty-five

Logan pumped the pedals of the mountain bike, the thick tires making decent time on the broken service road next to Highway 69. His legs ached all the way down to the balls of his feet, his lower back was spasming, and his shoulders had knots on top of knots from carrying Braden in a backpack carrier, but all in all it was good to be on a bike again, especially after the week of walking he'd done with the little boy.

They'd sometimes walked at the toddler's pace, at other times, Logan had carried him in the slightly too-small toddler backpack he'd uncovered in a picked-over store on the outskirts of a small Oklahoma town. He'd balanced the weight of the boy by slinging their backpack on his front and muscled through. They'd made some progress during that time, but Logan had nearly cried with joy when his habit of carefully poking through intact garages near their route paid off with the discovery of the mountain bike.

They still had to make frequent stops, as Braden got uncomfortable quickly in the backpack when he was awake. When that happened, Logan stopped, took him out, and they walked for a while until Braden got tired enough to need a nap. It wasn't a fast or a smooth ride, but they were making nearly forty miles a day as opposed to the ten or twelve they'd been making while they'd been exclusively on foot.

The other issue they'd run into was the lack of food. Helen and Gayle had given them ten days' worth of dehydrated meals, thinking their journey via a fast bike would only be about five days long, but they'd just begun their thirteenth day. Logan had cut back on the amount he ate as soon as their bike had been stolen, but even going to bed hungry, they'd run out of their supplies after their twelfth day on the road, and were subsisting on what they could find, or Logan could catch with the fishing rod he'd unearthed in one of their garage stops.

According to his Oklahoma map, which thankfully continued a bit beyond the border to show the terrain and roads into Texas, by the end of day they'd be at the Red River. Once he figured out a way across that obstacle, the town of McKinney and the FEMA depot were only another fifty or so miles. From there it was a mere twenty-four miles to Addison, where they'd find Braden's house and, hopefully, his father.

"Want down, please!"

Braden kicked his legs a bit, biting into his ribs with his stockinged feet. Logan had learned to take Braden's boots off when he was riding in the backpack, although he still had bruises from the first day he'd not taken the precaution.

"No need to kick me, I hear you. I think I see a park." Logan was more than ready for a break and some water. Parks continued to be their best bet for safe stops, as they were slightly off the main road and had excellent sight lines. They'd avoided having to interact with people on their journey south by taking secondary roads, and Logan wanted to keep it that way, even if it meant hiding in filthy mud as they had two days ago.

His neck tingled as if he was being watched as he recalled the close call and he clutched the handlebars reflexively. The well-armed squadron of men had buzzed by them as they hid in a filthy ditch a few yards off of the road, hidden behind an outcropping of tall grasses and the ooze of stinking mud. There had been at least twenty armed men on ATVs, some riding single, others double, but all wearing body armor or leather, carrying both pistols and rifles. There had been a set to the men's bodies as they weaved around the cracks on the road, which told Logan they were on a mission, not just a bunch of survivors out to hunt or find more supplies. Logan was positive he'd just seen one of the militia groups the Private at the Iowa border had warned him about, and he'd mentally marked their location in south central Oklahoma to relay the information to someone in charge when he could do so.

He slowed the bike's roll as they crossed toward the little park, navigating it once on the encircling pavement to make sure they were alone. It was a rather desolate place and only had a set of swings still standing. The slide had toppled, as had the colorful plastic climbing structure which had surrounded it, but the swings were Braden's favorite anyway.

He glided off of the bumpy sidewalk and into the deep, yellowed grass of the park to the edge of the sandy play area. Logan swung his leg over the seat with a groan and propped up the bike with the kickstand. Kneeling on the ground, he unclasped the belt holding the toddler carrier on, and then turned to help lift Braden out of its confines. Logan let the backpack slide from his front and pulled out their water.

"Drink first," he told the impatient little boy, holding the water jug for him while he took a few sips.

Logan got Braden's boots out of the backpack and fitted them to the boy's feet, tying them in double knots, as the little boy had a tendency to kick them off.

"Okay, you're good to go, buddy."

Braden ran to the tiny play area with a whoop, waving Whuff in the air, his sturdy legs churning and kicking bits of sand behind him.

Logan took a long drink as the boy dashed toward the swings, and as always, the bright, unfettered joy of the little boy made him smile. He looked around the wide-open space that looked like it had been put in place in hopes of an expansion of the nearby town. There wasn't much in the way of a neighborhood or even buildings nearby, except for a single strip mall about a mile away and a few farmhouses surrounded by plenty of land. The park had been planted with saplings, most of which were still standing, cabled to their place with straps. It also boasted a freestanding covered picnic pavilion with a few intact tables underneath a wooden shake roof. Logan was sorely tempted to set up camp for the night in the structure, especially when his legs cramped viciously as he stood.

"Oh my gosh," he grunted as he kneaded his thighs and stretched his lower back. They had a tall can of baked beans in the backpack they could use for their dinner, and there were a few dandelions growing in the dying grass of the park he could add to the mix for extra vitamins, so they wouldn't starve if they stopped.

Logan looked at his watch and grimaced. It was only two in the afternoon. If he were able to keep going, he'd be able to knock off another twenty miles or more, depending on the state of the road, and even get them across the river and into Texas.

His gaze fell on Braden, who'd made his way to the swings and had crawled onto the curved seat, taking Whuff with him by gripping the toy's ears in his teeth. Braden stuffed the toy inside of his jacket once he was seated before he started the process of getting the swing to move. The boy had gotten adept at swinging himself over the past days, eschewing Logan's help with any sort of pushing, instead pumping his legs until he got himself going. The boy continued to amaze him with his resiliency. While Braden's stubborn streak was difficult to deal with at times, Logan admired his fierce independence.

"You're stalling," Logan admitted to himself as the determined little boy get himself moving with effort. A hollowness wrapped around his chest. If all went well, in just a couple of days he'd be leaving Braden behind in the care of his father.

"Twenty minutes," he called out to Braden in a voice that cracked slightly as he pushed back his rising emotion.

Logan let out a long breath to calm himself and continued to stretch and gingerly walk off the cramping in his arches as he sipped water and ate two mints from their dessert stash to quell the growls his stomach was making. He kept a hand on the bike at all times, not willing to let it out of his grasp for even a moment. It didn't pay to think about the loss of their first bike, but it crept into his consciousness several times a day. If it hadn't been stolen, they would've been at their destination nearly a week ago, and he'd be on his way home.

The thought was inevitably followed by more yearning for his home, for Mara and the kids, along with wondering how they might be faring on the homestead. He was reasonably confident they'd do all right, between Mara's plant and foraging knowledge, and Ethan's skills as a hunter, but there was always a worry niggling at the back of his brain, one that told him he needed to hurry and get home. He couldn't deny the feeling of urgency had been growing ever since he'd left Iowa.

Logan shook his head at the futility of worrying about something he couldn't control. Hopefully, the McKinney FEMA cache had good transportation in it, an ATV, or even a jeep. He checked the tires and chain of the mountain bike as he dreamed of something which took less physical effort to move. He'd been spoiled by modern transportation, there was no doubt about that. The journey he was facing of less than a hundred miles would have been a quick two-hour drive by car, or thirty minutes or less by plane.

A cold splash of water on the back of his neck had him looking up. With the constant cloud cover, it was always a surprise to be caught by the rain. The single drop was followed by a flurry of more of them, accompanied by a burst of chilly wind. As more drops landed, they stung, but not from their impact.

"Ow!" Braden cried out. "Hot!"

Logan dropped the bike and ran to Braden, scooping him out of the swing and dashing with him to the covered picnic area. It was less sound than it had seemed from a distance. The roof had cracks in it, and some of the rain had already started trickling through them. "Get under the big table, Braden," Logan said urgently.

The boy scrambled beneath the picnic table, scared tears rolling down his face. The red blotches on his hands and face where the raindrops had struck him were clear to see, as they were on his own exposed hands. It would wreak havoc on the moving parts of the bike.

"I'm getting the bike. Watch me, but stay under there."

The acidic rain picked up its pace, blowing in biting gusts as Logan dashed back across the sand to their bike and backpack. The sting of the chemically laced drops had been simply hot when they'd first started, but as the tempo increased, the rainfall was like barbed whip lashes as it landed on his exposed hands, neck, and face. Logan snatched up the backpack with one hand and tossed the bike onto his shoulder as the rain began coming down in sheets, the chemicals in it sizzling as they struck, accompanied by the stringent stench of rotten eggs.

"Stay under the table, buddy," Logan's voice shook as he dropped the pack under the table, wisps of white smoke emanating from it, and he shed his steaming jacket as well, draping it over the bike. The roof of the shelter groaned, and sheets of rain lashed inside the open sides.

"Logan!" Braden's voice was laced with terror.

"Almost there, hang on!"

The water pelted down, the area around the pavilion steaming and the smell of sulfur getting stronger by the moment as splashes leapt up from the hard rain and dribbled across the concrete floor of the protected area, bubbling and boiling as it settled.

Logan grabbed the other two tables in the shelter and flipped them on their sides before dragging them to nestle next to the table Braden was under, one on either side, to give them a bit of protection from both stinging wisps of smoke and the rain itself. The drumming on the asphalt-shingled roof reached a fever pitch as the storm continued to grow, the wind whipping gouts of heavy rain against his hastily erected barrier as Logan scrambled under the table with Braden.

He pulled their tarp out of the backpack and wrapped it completely around them and over their heads as he lay on his side, holding Braden to his chest as the storm howled and raged. The boy shivered and whispered something to Whuff.

"Is Whuff okay?" Logan asked.

"Scared."

"I bet. Once the rain goes away, we'll leave." Logan could only hope the dangerous compounds in the churned soil and rainwater would be less toxic once they were out of the Midwest and further to the south.

Logan and Braden waited out the storm for an hour, singing old campfire songs Logan dredged from his memory, and eating a few peppermints from their supply. Logan kept them in their protective covering until the rain had stopped and the sulfur smell diminished, the burns the rain had left on his skin itching miserably.

He blinked when he finally emerged and got a look at the park. It had been utterly devastated by the rainfall. The little trees had been stripped of their remaining leaves, leaving only scarred, denuded bark that was still peeling. The grass, which had been yellowing, was a churned mass of disintegrated, blackened gook. Even the table they'd sheltered under was pockmarked with spreading holes as the moisture dripping from the ceiling continued to eat through the wood.

Logan shuddered to think what would have happened to them if they'd been without the shelter and resolved to do whatever it took to get them as close to McKinney as he could before nighttime made it impossible.

Braden didn't put up any fuss as he loaded him into the backpack, and then remounted the bike. Logan avoided puddles in the road and kept a steady pace for a good hour and a half until he finally saw the sign he'd been waiting for, telling them they were at the Red River, the border between Oklahoma and Texas.

"One obstacle down. Let's face the next one."

Logan rubbed his eyes with his fingers. They stung from the residual chemicals lacing the air, even though they'd left the rainstorm a good fifteen miles or more behind them. The area was barren except for a couple of cars that had flipped onto their sides in the parking lot, the paint scarred, the undercarriages showing signs of rust, the tires flattened and beginning to decay from exposure to the elements. He didn't see a boat dock or anything else that might be helpful to use crossing the watery expanse he expected to see.

Letting Braden out of the backpack in the small parking lot near what had once been a bridge, they both had a long drink of water from their water bottle, then walked together up the embankment that blocked their view of the river. The train had crossed the river at this juncture also, and a long train had been derailed as the bridge fell, the big shipping containers scattered across the area. Most of the containers had been opened at some point and looted, and he cast another worried glance around in case anyone was watching the border crossing.

"Will the water be hot?" Braden asked, his face full of trepidation as he clutched Whuff to his chest.

"I don't know for sure," Logan admitted. "Let's get closer." He sniffed the air, but could only smell brackish water, tinged with salt and the sweet whiffs of mortal decay which had become part of the landscape they moved through.

As they topped the rise of the embankment and peered over, Logan let out a hearty cheer.

"It's nearly dry! I think we can just walk across, Braden!"

While it was wide, the riverbed was mostly just sand and ribbons of damp mud, with only a few low trickles of water wending their way through the swath it cut between high banks, bits of dying plants clinging to the edges. After carefully looking around, and listening for the growl of ATVs, he and Braden walked across the expanse of the river's bed wheeling the bike, only needing to hop over a few meandering streamlets along the way before climbing the far bank, their feet not even dampened.

"We're in Texas, Braden," Logan told him as they churned up the red clay and sand riverbank. "Bet we can get a few more miles before nighttime."

"Okay." The response was a bit sad, but the boy allowed himself to be put back into his carrier.

He wanted to find sturdy shelter in case the terrifying acidic rain made a reappearance. His Oklahoma map extended about five miles into Texas, and it looked as if there might be a welcome center a few miles away. His hopes buoyed by the unexpectedly simple river crossing, Logan got to work pushing the pedals of the bike, aiming for the US-75, which was the most direct route to the south and the town of McKinney where the FEMA cache was located.

Only a mile or so past the river was the lopsided sign for the Texas Welcome Center, wobbling precariously on a single post. Logan entered the sweep of the entryway that curved upward in a long arc toward the top of the rise. There were overturned cars and trucks in the parking lot, and plenty of trash as if people had once camped at the site, but he didn't see any movement as he rolled up the slight hill to reach the center itself, which was isolated on a hill.

The center had been constructed fairly recently of red brick and chrome and glass, judging by the shiny remnents. It had split down the middle, and a large crack nearly three yards across bisected the area, stretching as far as Logan could see on either side of the building. Dismounting, he let Braden back out of the carrier again as they edged around the back of the building, but he didn't see or sense anything living nearby. He picked the bike up and put it on his shoulder, swinging Braden into the safety of his arms as he stepped across a large area of broken glass to get further into the remains of the building. Once they were past the glass, he put him down again, leaning the bike against the edge of a wall. Logan pulled his flashlight from his backpack, then picked Braden back up when the boy refused to budge.

Cautiously Logan moved into the dark interior of the building. He jumped as something scurried across the floor, but it was just a large rat, so he relaxed again, inching his way forward. A rack of maps hung from one peg, the contents scattered where they'd fallen, but he was able to find a Texas map in the mess, as well as one for Arkansas.

"Iss spooky," Braden opined, his voice hushed as he clasped his arm tightly around Logan's neck.

"Spooky?" That's a new word for you, buddy." Logan genially tried to distract Braden from their surroundings, which were, indeed, a bit on the scary side.

"Not."

"Okay. How else would you talk about this place?"

"Dark."

"Yes, it is. How about empty?"

"No." Braden gave him an exasperated look and pointed at himself and Logan.

"Oh, I see, because we're here, it's not empty."

"Yus."

The conversation had done the trick, and the boy's stranglehold around his neck lessened just as Logan's light flashed on a line of vending machines that had fallen over like dominos. Two were face down and inaccessible, but the other two, one for sodas and the other holding packaged snacks had tumbled onto their sides, the fronts of them cracked loose.

"Hey! Look at those! Looks like we found some food and drinks, Braden!"

"Candy?" he asked hopefully.

"There's a lot of candy." The pair grinned at one another, and Logan made quick work of breaking into the machines and pulling out bags of chips, candy, and bottles of soda and water, his hollow belly growling. Logan stuffed as much of the bounty as the backpack could carry, and then they moved out of the dim recesses into an area which was still covered, but not pitch black.

"I think we should stop for the night, Braden," Logan told the boy. "Don't go near the glass over there, though."

The corners of the building blocked the wind, and given their point of elevation, Logan opted to not make a fire that might be seen. Instead, he laid out their tarp in an intact corner so they could fold it over themselves to sleep. They leaned against the wall and ate a meal of bagged chips and packaged cookies, soda, candy, and water. It was far from a nutritionally complete meal, but anything was better than the hunger he'd been dealing with for the past few days.

Braden grinned at him, his teeth a bright orange from the Doritos he favored. "Good!" he declared.

"I can't argue with you, Braden." Logan said, then yawned. "Let's brush our teeth and get some sleep."

He lifted the boy to cross the glass to the outer section of the building and they went a few yards away to brush their teeth with water and to do other necessary business before returning to their makeshift bed. It was a little hard on the linoleum floor, but as

Braden snuggled his head under Logan's chin and brought Whuff up for a goodnight kiss, a bloom of satisfaction washed over him, and with his full belly, and the warmth of the child curled next to him, Logan pulled the edge of the tarp over them, and fell asleep in moments.

The next day, they drank water and had granola bars and chips before Logan filled the backpack with more of the snacks and bottled waters. He studied the map of Texas and decided he'd take the left fork just a few miles away and ride along the smaller state highway. It was a bit longer, but would bring them nearly all the way to McKinney, avoided the big highway, and skirted around a couple of towns.

The roads in Texas were just as broken as the ones in Kansas and Oklahoma had been, but there were a few long stretches of concrete where he was able to get up to a decent speed for a while, and the miles zoomed by. Consulting his map, Logan determined if he pushed himself and the roads stayed relatively intact, they could do the fifty miles and be to the FEMA cache before it was time to stop for the night.

Logan showed Braden the map at their first stop and pointed with his finger at what he wanted to do. "But it means you have to be in the backpack for longer times. Can you do that?"

"Don't wanna."

"We're almost to your house, Braden. If we make this push, you'll be home tomorrow."

"Four, four, four, one Chespeek?"

"That's right."

The little boy consulted with Whuff, and then gave a reluctant nod of assent. A throb of pride in Braden filled Logan, and he gave him a big hug. "Good boy," he said, and swallowed back the tears that wanted to rise.

"Squishy," Braden's voice was muffled against his chest.

"Sorry, buddy." Logan released him and gave him a scruff on his head. "Let's get going."

The ride was sometimes bumpy, and they had to get off the bike and walk alongside the road a few times when it proved to be too smashed even for the thick tires of the mountain bike, and one time they'd been forced to deviate cross-country when one of the biggest rifts Logan had seen yawned before them. Fifty yards across, the jagged edges of it continually trembled and fell in, the monstrous thing getting bigger by the minute as the engines of the earth thousands of feet below continued to agitate. They moved far back from the edge of it and walked west for another mile until it finally narrowed enough for them to cross.

Logan had looked anxiously at the sky as they finally were able to step across the far end of the crack. If it were to start raining, and the thing gave off vapors like the ones they had escaped the day before, there wasn't much around for them to shelter under. He hurried to get Braden packed back into the backpack as soon as he could and pushed himself to get away from it.

With the detours they'd been forced to take, it was nearly five in the evening before Logan came to the intersection the private's notes said was the location of the cache. Logan looked around quizzically and scratched his head. Nothing indicated there was anything special in the mostly wide-open, vacant industrial area, although the buildings just beyond a chain-link fence on one corner had been built with more reinforcement. They were all still standing, their long low forms resembling a spread-out outdoor storage facility on a smooth concrete pad that only had a few small cracks running through it.

In the near distance, machine gun fire rattled, and was responded to by more gunfire, prompting him to move around the fence with alacrity until he found an unlocked gate. He scooted them inside, and deeper into the heart of the bizarre set of structures so they'd be out of sight, his head swiveling as he kept a lookout for both danger and something which would identify the cache, which he was imagining being in a single warehouse big enough to contain shipping containers. Suddenly, Logan slapped his forehead and laughed aloud.

"The whole place is the cache, Braden!" He swept his arms around the area they'd been wandering, and then hustled over to the nearest metal building. Sure enough, a discreet, tiny blue oval above a keypad had the word FEMA blazed on it along with the sigil of the eagle with arrows in one hand and olive branches in the other. The keypad had an expensive-looking battery underneath it as well as a solar panel attached to the top of it, so Logan held his breath and punched in the code the young man had given him.

There was a snap, and the small door next to them disengaged its locks and popped open a few inches. Logan pulled it open and stepped inside. A light switch was located on the inside of the doors, but nothing happened when he flicked it on. He dug out his flashlight and shined it forward. Pallet upon pallet of goods met his eyes. He hurried over to one and examined it.

"Medical supplies," he said excitedly. "I bet each storage unit is a different set of goods."

Braden looked at him wide-eyed as Logan laughed. "We're going to find some good food for our dinner!"

He found the food on his third try, and ham radio packs and camping equipment on his fourth, which also had detailed maps of the surrounding cities. He found Braden's street easily using their grids, alleviating a big concern Logan had carried since he didn't know the area. The best container, as far as Logan was concerned, was slightly bigger and to the rear of the compound. It contained three jeeps and ten ATVs and the parts to repair vehicles. Just outside was an underground fuel depot complete with a metal plate printed with instructions on how to pump the gas, along with the date it would be good until, which was well into the following year.

"Thank you, President Ordway!" Logan said with feeling. He took the time to restock his backpack, so it was once more full of goods, ranging from first aid supplies to a water purifier and a solid hunting knife. He changed out their beat-up grungy water bottles for new ones, as well as stocking up on MREs and granola bars. After heating water on a cookstove, they both had a thorough wash, and then changed into new clothes. Logan was impressed that the FEMA people had thought to provide all sizes of clothing from infants to giants, all of which were clearly marked in separate containers.

"You're a solid 3T, buddy," Logan told Braden after they'd tried on a few. "Do you know when your birthday is?"

"Birfday?" he scrunched his face up and then shook his head. "Cake?" he asked hopefully.

"I'm one-hundred percent sure we can find some vanilla pound cake for our dessert tonight," Logan said, familiar with the contents of MREs.

"One hundred percent!" Braden echoed happily.

They had their pound cake, after a tasty beef stroganoff dinner, and washed it down with plenty of water.

"Full." Braden held his belly and blew out his cheeks, making Logan laugh.

"Me, too."

Logan set up two sleeping bags on soft camping mats on the floor of one of the containers. Braden shook his head, and wanted to climb in with him, so Logan let him, the moment a bittersweet one, as he was pretty sure this was the last night he'd have with the little boy who'd so completely captured his heart. It took a while for Logan to fall asleep despite the physical efforts of the day, the good meal and the secure surroundings.

As Gayle had foretold, the fast-approaching reality of letting Braden go was ripping him apart, yet at the same time there was a small stir of excitement that once he'd done his duty by the boy and his mother, he'd be free to move as quickly as he wanted to get home to Mara and the kids. And thanks to the US government, he'd be able to do it on an ATV, cutting days off of his journey time. Logan decided he'd lash the mountain bike onto the back of it, just in case he needed it, or until he found a better one. With a sturdy machine and containers of gas, camping gear, a supply of food and medical supplies, the thousand miles between Dallas and Roanoke could potentially be covered in seven days or less, even with bad roads and if he were forced to keep the machine under thirty miles an hour.

Logan grinned into the dark as he imagined rolling up to their homestead, and seeing the look on Mara and the kids' faces when he arrived and hugged them. Once he was there, he could unpack that nearby FEMA trailer and provide food and medicine for his family and his neighbors, and have a way to communicate as well.

On those happy thoughts, another one piled in, even though he tried not to let it, as it was just setting him up for disappointment and extra heartbreak. Logan pictured Braden in his arms as he reunited with his family in Roanoke, the hugs and joy wrapping around the toddler as well as he became a permanent part of their family.

"Enough, Padgett, the boy belongs with his real father," he scolded himself, and then drifted off.

The following morning, they had a scrambled egg and sausage breakfast, with toaster strudel to top it off. Logan was thrilled to have coffee again and savored two piping hot cups of the brew before he went to the trailer that had the ham radio setup. He brought one of the packs back to their camp, and with the help of the useful instructions, had the twelve volt lithium battery wired up in short order. He pulled out the call signs that the private at the Iowa border had given him and used the VOX, calling out on the direct frequency indicated on his cheat sheet.

Logan got a response nearly immediately. "This is AZ7CAP, we are receiving you loud and clear, you have QSO. Over."

"My name is Logan Padgett and I'm calling from your FEMA cache in McKinney, Texas. I was told to ask for Janet Givens, Ripley Baxter, or Thaddeus Moreland if I had intel on militia."

"Stand by." There was a slight pause, and then a different, deeper voice spoke over the radio. "This is Thaddeus Moreland, come back."

Logan told the man about the group of militia he'd seen in southeast Oklahoma, as Braden continued to watch him with interest. Moreland asked him a few questions, which Logan did his best to answer, about what types of machines they were riding and how well armed they were and the direction they'd been travelling in. He also told Moreland about the toxic rain he'd experienced.

"Affirmative, we're aware and are doing our best to mitigate it. Thank you, Mr. Padgett. You're free to take anything at your site, please leave it open after you vacate. AZ7CAP out."

Logan took a few minutes to radio Lloyd Crowe, but after several tries, he didn't receive an answer back, so he packed the ham radio back into its pack. He was about to put it back with its companions, but had a change of heart and tucked it into the pile of things he planned to take with him. A direct line to the new government would be a valuable thing to have, and while it would have been cumbersome to take it while he was on a bike, with the ATV, it would hardly take up any room at all.

Satisfied with his choice, Logan turned his attention to the final part of his journey with Braden to Addison. After short consideration, he opted to ride the bike the final miles into town, as the ATV would be loud in the inner city and might attract attention from the wrong kind of people. Since he was only riding to Braden's house and back, he unpacked the backpack to essentials of water and granola bars and a first aid kit and extra ammo for his rifle and his new SIG X5 he'd gotten from the weapon stores. As he buckled on a heavy duty combat knife, Logan also decided he'd lock the trailers until he returned for his things, before leaving it unlocked when he was finally on his way home to Mara and the kids.

As Logan put the goods he'd chosen to complete his journey home into the corner of the trailer that held camping gear, he got a cold shiver up his spine, as if someone were watching him. He spun quickly and looked up and down the aisles of trailers nearby, but nothing moved besides Braden who was running around the trailer he'd put his things into. Logan took a moment to watch the sheer joy the boy took in running, a sad smile on his face and a hollow place in his heart.

After locking up, he consulted the map and opted to take side streets to get to Addison, avoiding the high five and other stacked interchanges Dallas was famous for. He'd take Greenville to Park to Preston, and then they'd turn onto Braden's street.

Three hours later, they were doing exactly that. Logan weaved slowly along the suburban roads. The destruction along the way had been haphazard, with some blocks devastated and in tiny pieces as if bombs had gone off in them, while others had remained somewhat intact. A few people were out and about as well, walking or on bikes, carrying backpacks and firearms. There'd even been a couple of people on horseback as he'd ridden by. No one had been overtly friendly, but he'd not felt threatened either. Nonetheless, Logan was glad he'd opted to stay on the somewhat derelict bike rather than risk driving the high-value ATV into the heart of the city.

"Playground!" Braden cried out and pointed to a little pocket park designed with toddlers in mind. It had a low-slung swing set and a small slide, and a mother was playing with her child, watching them as they rode by.

"Is that the one you played on?" Logan asked, a sudden rush of emotion filling him as Braden started bouncing up and down in the carrier.

"Yus! With mommy!"

"Your mommy is an angel now," Logan said. A stab of emotion made Logan breathe out hard, as he remembered the sweet blonde with the big blue eyes who'd sacrificed herself to protect her child when their plane had exploded. "He's safe, Ms. Frye," Logan whispered to the air as he turned the final corner onto Chesapeake. "I brought your boy home safe."

The block was half-destroyed rubble, but several homes were still at least partially erect, and the block had been cleared of refuse. Despite the clear path, Logan's legs felt like they were moving through thick syrup as he forced himself up the tumbled block. Braden was silent behind him, but he could hear the boy's quickening breath as they rolled toward the middle of the neighborhood.

A large tree with a toddler swing came into view on the right, and somehow, Logan was sure it was Braden's house. The front of it was still standing, but it looked as if the rear of the home had collapsed in on itself.

"There!" Braden pointed and bounced. "Home!"

Swallowing hard as his heart raced in a terrible combination of hope and despair, Logan got off and let the bike fall as the little boy squirmed eagerly behind him to get out. Tears trickled down his cheeks, but he simply wiped them away before he turned to Braden to help him out of the carrier, quickly tying his boots on the little feet that were dancing with impatience.

"Let's go together," he suggested, and offered his hand and did his best to smile.

"C'mon!" Braden grinned and dragged him forward, with Whuff firmly grasped in the other.

A furious barking came from the backyard of the house next to Braden's and a black and brown lab mix threw itself over the fence, ears flopping, hurtling straight at Logan and Braden. Logan started to pull Braden back behind him, but Braden tugged away and ran toward the dog, letting the black and brown stuffed dog he'd carried for a thousand miles fall from his grasp as he dashed to meet the bounding dog who looked remarkably like the toy.

"Whuff!" he cried happily, flinging his arms in the air. "Whuff!"

Braden wrapped his arms around the dog's neck, who wiggled and licked the toddler's face as Braden laughed with joy. "Iss my Whuff!" he shouted to Logan.

Logan nodded, and smiled as tears poured down his face in response to the joyful reunion, sinking to his knees as his legs would no longer hold him erect.

The barking and shouting brought a tall, middle-aged man wearing a Cowboys baseball cap to the door of the house where the dog had escaped from. As he stepped outside, the coffee cup he carried fell from his hands to smash on the steps, his face muddling into a mix of shock and joy as he looked at the laughing child and the ecstatic dog.

"Braden!" he shouted, as he ran to meet the child.

READ THE NEXT BOOK IN THE SERIES

Nowhere to Turn Book 6

Available Here
books.to/Omnzk

Made in United States
Troutdale, OR
09/15/2025

34547351R00166